DOROTHY

was born in 1873. The third of [...] gentleman, from the age of seven [...] living, which she did initially as [...] then in north London and fina[...] mother committed suicide, the family broke up and Dorothy Richardson began a new life in London as secretary assistant to a Harley Street dentist. During her years in London her friends were the socialist and avant garde intellectuals of the day. She became an intimate of H. G. Wells, who, among others, encouraged her to write. She began in journalism and for the rest of her life she lived as a writer, earning very little. In 1917 she married the young painter, Alan Odle, who died in 1948. For the whole of their married life they lived their winters in Cornwall and their summers in London. Dorothy Richardson's journalism includes scores of essays, reviews, stories, poems and sketches written and published between 1902 and 1949. Her journalism was her livelihood but the writing of PILGRIMAGE was her vocation; this long novel absorbed her artistic energy between 1914 and her death in 1957.

PUBLISHING HISTORY

FIRST EDITIONS:
Pointed Roofs (1915), *Backwater* (1916), *Honeycomb* (1917), *The Tunnel* (Feb 1919), *Interim* (Dec 1919), *Deadlock* (1921), *Revolving Lights* (1923), *The Trap* (1925), *Oberland* (1927), *Dawn's Left Hand* (1931) — all published by Duckworth: *Clear Horizon* (1935) — published by J. M. Dent & Cresset Press

COLLECTED EDITIONS:
Pilgrimage (including *Dimple Hill*), 4 vols, 1938 — J. M. Dent & Cresset Press, London: A. Knopf, New York

Pilgrimage (including *March Moonlight*), 4 vols, 1967 — J. M. Dent, London: A. Knopf, New York

Pilgrimage, 4 vols, 1976 — Popular Library, New York

Pilgrimage, 4 vols, 1979 — Virago, London
    Volume 1: *Pointed Roofs, Backwater, Honeycomb*
    Volume 2: *The Tunnel, Interim*
    Volume 3: *Deadlock, Revolving Lights, The Trap*
    Volume 4: *Oberland, Dawn's Left Hand, Clear Horizon, Dimple Hill, March Moonlight*

VIRAGO

is a feminist publishing company:

'It is only when women start to organize
in large numbers that we become a
political force, and begin to move towards
the possibility of a truly democratic society
in which every human being can be brave,
responsible, thinking and diligent in the struggle
to live at once freely and unselfishly'

SHEILA ROWBOTHAM
Women, Resistance and Revolution

VIRAGO
Advisory Group

DOROTHY M. RICHARDSON

PILGRIMAGE

with an introduction by Gill Hanscombe

II

The Tunnel
Interim

Virago
London

TO

WINIFRED RAY

Published by VIRAGO Limited,
5 Wardour Street, London W1V 3HE,
1979, in association with
Mrs Sheena Odle and Mark Paterson & Associates

Introduction copyright © 1979 by Gill Hanscombe

ISBN 0 86068 101 7

Reproduced Photolitho in Great Britain by
J. W. Arrowsmith Limited Bristol

CONTENTS

OF THE early twentieth-century English modernists, there is no one who has been more neglected than Dorothy Miller Richardson. There are several reasons for this. First, the style she forged in the writing of *Pointed Roofs*, the first volume of the *Pilgrimage* sequence, was new and difficult, later earning the nomination 'stream-of-consciousness'. *Pointed Roofs* was published in 1915 and was, therefore, the first example of this technique in English, predating both Joyce and Woolf, its more famous exponents. Secondly, the thoughts and feelings of its protagonist, Miriam Henderson, are explicitly feminist, not in the sense of arguing for equal rights and votes for women, but in the more radical sense of insisting on the authority of a woman's experience and world view. Thirdly, *Pointed Roofs* explores Miriam's sympathetic response to German culture and in 1915, when it was first published, this was an unpopular subject which contributed to the establishing of adverse critical reaction. Undaunted, however, by ambivalent response to her work, Richardson persisted in her task of completing the *Pilgrimage* sequence, a task which occupied her, intermittently, for the rest of her life.

Richardson regarded *Pilgrimage* as one novel and its constituent thirteen volumes as chapters. She regarded it, also, as fiction, even though the life of Miriam Henderson so closely resembles her own. The reason for this was that Richardson, after many attempts to write a more conventional novel, resolved finally that she must write about the subject she knew best, which was, she maintained, her own life. This is not to claim that every incident and every character in the novel add up to a photographic reproduction of Richardson's early life; but it is to claim that the genuine impulse of her work derives from the tension between her own life and that of Miriam, her fictional *alter ego*. The whole world of *Pilgrimage* is filtered through Miriam's mind alone; the reader sees what she sees and is never told what any of the other characters sees. Fiction usually means that the author invents or imagines his or her material. Richardson used the real material of her own life for her writing, and she used herself as her central character. The fictional process in *Pilgrimage* consists in how she shaped and organised and interpreted that material. There is, therefore, much in her life and personality to lend interest to her work.

She was born in Abingdon, Berkshire, on 17 May 1873, the third of four daughters. Her father, Charles Richardson, came from a family who had achieved financial success through a grocery business, but Charles longed to give up 'trade' and to become a gentleman. He sold the business and lived off the proceeds for some years. His wife, Mary Taylor, came from East Coker in Somerset, from a family whose name was listed among the gentry in local registers. When she was five years old, Dorothy Richardson was sent for a year to a small private school where she learned to read and spell and where nothing else interested her. When she was six, the family moved to the south coast, near Worthing, owing to her mother's ill health and her father's financial straits. Her school made no impression on her. In Dorothy's eleventh year, her father's investments improved and he moved his family up to London. Her life at this stage included croquet, tennis, boating, skating, dances and music; apart from musical evenings at home, she was introduced to the classics, to Wagner and Chopin and to Gilbert and Sullivan. She was taught by a governess, of whom she later wrote: 'if she could, [she] would have formed us to the almost outmoded pattern of female education: the minimum of knowledge and a smattering of various "accomplishments" . . . for me . . . she was torment unmitigated.' After this, she was sent to Southborough House, whose headmistress was a disciple of Ruskin, where the pupils were encouraged to think for themselves. Here Richardson studied French, German, literature, logic and psychology. At this point, her father, through disastrous speculation, lost the greater part of his resources, which forced Richardson at the age of seventeen, to seek employment as a teacher. Her first appointment, in a German school, later provided the material for *Pointed Roofs*.

After six months Richardson returned to England; two sisters were engaged to be married, the third had a position as a governess and her mother was near to a nervous collapse. In order to be near her mother, she took a post at the Misses Ayre's school in Finsbury Park, North London. Her impressions and experiences here provided the material for her second volume, *Backwater*. In 1893,

Charles Richardson was finally made a bankrupt; his house and possessions were sold and the family moved to a house in Chiswick, generously provided by John Arthur Batchelor, who became the husband of Dorothy's eldest sister Kate. By 1895, Richardson had moved from Finsbury Park to a post in the country as governess to two children, her experience of which is recorded in *Honeycomb*, her third volume. On 29 November 1895, while on holiday at Hastings with Dorothy, Mary Richardson committed suicide by cutting her throat with a kitchen knife.

After this, Richardson wanted a complete break: '. . . longing to escape from the world of women, I gladly accepted a post . . . a secretarial job, offering me the freedom I so desired.' She lived in a Bloomsbury attic on a salary of one pound per week. London became her great adventure. During these years she explored the world lying outside the enclosures of social life, which included writers, religious groups from Catholic to Unitarian and Quaker, political groups from the Conservative Primrose League to the Independent Labour Party and the Russian anarchists, and, through books and lectures, science and philosophy. At this time she found the philosophers 'more deeply exciting than the novelists'. These interests and activities provided the contextual material for her subsequent volumes. From working as a secretary, she gradually branched out into translations and freelance journalism which 'had promised release from routine work that could not engage the essential forces of my being. The small writing-table in my attic became the centre of my life'.

As a result of a series of sketches contributed to *The Saturday Review*, a reviewer urged her to try writing a novel. She later wrote that the suggestion 'both shocked and puzzled me. The material that moved me to write would not fit the framework of any novel I had experienced. I believed myself to be . . . intolerant of the romantic and the realist novel alike. Each . . . left out certain essentials and dramatized life misleadingly. Horizontally . . . Always . . . one was aware of the author and applauding, or deploring, his manipulations.' In 1917, at the age of forty-four, she married Alan Odle, an artist many years younger than herself. The marriage, in spite of misgivings, was a happy one, providing her with 'a new world, the missing link between those already explored'. She died in 1957 at the age of eighty-four.

A niece of Alan Odle's, who knew Dorothy Richardson and Alan Odle can add some human detail to this picture. In middle age, Richardson still had a golden heap of very long hair, piled on the top of her head; she had a 'massive' face, dark brown eyes, a clear skin, and pince-nez balanced on her nose, because she was 'always reading'. She created the impression of being tall, because she was 'so stately'. Alan Odle, in fact over six feet tall, was very thin, with waist-length hair wound around the outside of his head. He never cut his hair and rarely his fingernails, but since he had 'beautifully long elegant fingers', the image he presented was not an unattractive one. He, like Dorothy, had dark brown eyes and an ascetic face. They were very controlled together, extremely calm, always sitting side by side. Dorothy talked the most and late into the night; she seemed never to do 'anything ordinary' and had a voice 'like dark brown velvet'. She spoke very slowly indeed and was 'immensely impressive as a person'. Her life seemed to be arranged 'very very carefully' and she was 'not at all spontaneous in her actions'. She could 'only work on a certain image of herself' which was 'very cerebral'. It was hard for her to deal with ordinary people. Although she and Alan were affectionate with each other, they 'didn't touch'. Dorothy always called him 'sergeant', a joke arising from the fact that after only one day's service in the army, he had been discharged on medical grounds. Dorothy, in contrast to Alan, was 'very plump, with white creamy arms and very beautiful hands'; 'as she spoke she would screw up her eyes and slightly purse her mouth and everyone would listen'.

Charles Richardson often called Dorothy his 'son', as a compensation, it seems, for his lack of a male child. Indeed there is the evidence of Richardson's own recollections, as well as the portrayal in *Pilgrimage* of Miriam's relationship with her father, to reinforce the view that much of the original stimulus of the novel was owed to Dorothy's failure to adjust to the feminine role expected of her by late nineteenth-century middle-class society. But was it a failure? Or might it be seen as a triumph? Miriam's pilgrimage is partly the journey towards the resolution of that question. Because Richardson's father used all the family resources, it was necessary for the four daughters to make their own ways and accordingly, at the age of seventeen, Richardson answered an advertisement for an English student-teacher in a German academy for girls. *Pilgrimage* begins at this point, a point at which, for Miriam, the beginning of economic autonomy corresponds with the beginning of autonomous self-consciousness. From this point until her meeting with Alan Odle, Richardson's life is paralleled by that of her protagonist Miriam. The parallels are numerous and strictly consistent, as Richardson's letters and papers confirm.

Consistent with ordinary reality, also, are the descriptions of London life at the turn of the century. And equally convincing are the detailed accounts of households, lectures, activities and even conversations. The precision of Richardson's memory at some twenty to forty years distance is itself remarkable. It should not be assumed, nevertheless, that she saw her function as a writer in traditional autobiographical terms. On the contrary, she always insisted that her task was truly appropriate to fiction and that *Pilgrimage* should be judged as fiction. The mastery with which the author is able to transform the haphazard impressions of subjective experience into a thematically organised psychological narrative is the extent to which this work of fiction achieves artistic integrity.

Miriam's consciousness is the subject matter of this novel. And it seems to her that the experiences and perceptions of women have been brutally and unreasonably discounted by men. Nor has she any mercy for the majority of women who have, in her judgment, colluded with men in the suborning of their female gifts and attributes. Such women are satirised, caricatured and eventually dismissed. On the other hand, her stance is not topical. She does not become a Suffragette. She does not argue for a recognition of the equality of the sexes. She counts it a disadvantage to be a woman only in the sense that the men who govern society refuse to recognise and to allow women's contributions. In all other respects, she affirms, implicitly and explicitly, the value of her own perceptions and judgments, which by inference Richardson would have us generalise to include an equivalent valuation of all women's experiences. The particular virtues concomitant to such a feminism are the deliberate rejection of female role-playing, an insistence on personal honesty, a passionate independence and a pilgrimage towards self-awareness. Its particular vices are correspondingly stark: an inability to compromise adequately in relationship, a tendency to categorise alternative views as ignorance or obstinacy, a not always healthy flight from confrontation and a constant temptation to egocentricity.

These failings, however, Richardson allows Miriam to demonstrate; she is not content, in her authorial role, to idealise either Miriam's moral powers or her intellectual expertise. The qualities of intelligence Richardson most prized were not abstract rationalism and analytic empiricism, but the ability to perceive relationships between phenomena and the effort to synthesize feeling and reflection. This valuation has important consequences for her fiction, since it leads to a breaking down of the structural divisions we normally impose on experience, for example, the assumption that the external world has a finite integrity which is not influenced by subjective states and the further assumption that the division of time into past, present and future is necessary and meaningful. These major structures are, for her, simply categorisations of space and of time which our culture has developed in order to define for the individual his place in nature and in society. The subjective experience of time becomes the framework within which reality exists and the corresponding task of fiction becomes the conscious bringing into relationship of meaningful moments.

The impact on her style of this effort to delineate a female consciousness was radical. She stretched the unit of the sentence sometimes to the length of a long paragraph; she dispensed with the usual rules of punctuation, often substituting a series of full stops in place of explanation or other detail; she changed from one tense to another within a single paragraph; and she changed from the first person 'I' to the third person 'she' within a single reflection. She omitted details about people and places which readers could justifiably demand to know. Yet her feminist stance is not only evident in her uncompromising adherence to the unfolding of Miriam's consciousness and the forging of a new style. Together with her rejection of the technical conventions of the realist novel went a rejection of the values which the tradition of the English novel had attested. This rejection, however, was not formulated either from the principles of aesthetics or from a general philosophical orientation. It issued primarily from her conviction that the novel was an expression of the vision, fantasies, experiences and goals of men and that only rarely in the history of the novel could a genuine account of the female half of the human condition be found.

In *Pilgrimage*, Miriam often argues with Hypo Wilson about the male bias of the novel and in most of these exchanges the main burden of her argument is that authors seek to aggrandise themselves by constructing elaborate edifices which promise to reveal truths about life but which really reveal truths about the author. Nevertheless, like all radicals, Richardson is ambivalent at heart, recognising that a work of fiction must take its place among its predecessors. Therefore, in her own terms, she is forced to make an assessment of the tradition and to take a theoretical stand on the question of the structure and function of the novel. And because of her conviction that the traditional conventions express an overwhelmingly masculine world view, she must transform those conventions to accommodate Miriam's world view. For Richardson, therefore, words themselves become highly charged with ambivalence. The higher insights are above and beyond language.

There is in *Pilgrimage* a direct connection between Miriam's alienation from male consciousness and her distrust of language. Since style is necessary to a structured use of language, it must be acquired. However, she argues in *Deadlock*, style, because of its 'knowingness', is the property of men and of male writers in particular; men who feel 'the need for phrases'. For Miriam, the trouble with language is that it sets things 'in a mould that was apt to come up again'. The fear of things 'coming up again' can be seen as a fear of commitment, which later prompts the extravagance 'silence is reality'. That may, indeed, be true, but it is an impossible position for a writer to hold. Miriam is compelled, therefore, to rationalise her ambivalence by trying to understand how men use language.

Clearly in a work of such length, which owes less than is usual to previous models, there is bound to be some unevenness in technical control, an inevitability Richardson was fully aware of. In fact she often singled out particular sections of her text as failing to fulfil her intentions; such passages she marked 'I.R.', which stood for 'imperfectly realised'. Even so, *Pilgrimage* is a major contribution to our literature. Richardson's very original vision of female experience, together with her uncompromising experimental style, make the novel an extraordinary testament to the validity of female individuality. It is to be hoped that this first paperback edition of *Pilgrimage* to be published in England points to a new, rich and perceptive understanding of Richardson's achievement.

Gillian E Hanscombe, St Hugh's College, Oxford, 1979

THE TUNNEL

CHAPTER I

MIRIAM paused with her heavy bag dragging at her arm. It was a disaster. But it was the last of Mornington Road. To explain about it would be to bring Mornington Road here.

'It doesn't matter now,' said Mrs Bailey as she dropped her bag and fumbled for her purse.

'Oh, I'd better settle it at once or I shall forget about it. I'm so glad the things have come so soon.'

When Mrs Bailey had taken the half-crown they stood smiling at each other. Mrs Bailey looked exactly as she had done the first time. It was exactly same; there was no disappointment. The light coming through the glass above the front door made her look more shabby and worn. Her hair was more metallic. But it was the same girlish figure and the same smile triumphing over the badly fitting teeth. Miriam felt like an inmate returning after an absence. The smeariness of the marble-topped hall table did not offend her. She held herself in. It was better to begin as she meant to go on. Behind Mrs Bailey the staircase was beckoning. There was something waiting upstairs that would be gone if she stayed talking to Mrs Bailey.

Assuring Mrs Bailey that she remembered the way to the room, she started at last on the journey up the many flights of stairs. The feeling of confidence that had come the first time she mounted them with Mrs Bailey returned now. She could not remember noticing anything then but a large brown dinginess, one rich warm even tone everywhere in the house; a sharp contrast to the cold, harshly lit little bedroom in Mornington Road. The day was cold. But this house did not seem cold and, when she rounded the first flight and Mrs Bailey was out of sight, the welcome of the place fell upon her. She knew it well, better than any place she had known in all her wanderings—the faded umbers and browns of the

stair carpet, the gloomy heights of wall, a patternless sheen
where the staircase lights fell upon it and, in the shadowed
parts, a blurred scrolling pattern in dull madder on a brown
background; the dark landings with lofty ceilings and high dark
polished doors surmounted by classical reliefs in grimed
plaster, the high staircase windows screened by long smoke-
grimed lace curtains. On the third landing the ceiling came
down nearer to the tops of the doors. The light from above
made the little grained doors stare brightly. Patches of fresh
brown and buff shone here and there in the threadbare linoleum.
The cracks of the flooring were filled with dust and dust lay
along the rim of the skirting. Two large tin trunks standing
one upon the other almost barred the passage way. It was
like a landing in a small suburban lodging-house, a small
silent afternoon brightness, shut in and smelling of dust.
Silence flooded up from the lower darkness. The hall where
she had stood with Mrs Bailey was far away below, and below
that were basements deep in the earth. The outside of the
house, with its first-floor balcony, the broad shallow flight of
steps leading to the dark green front door, the little steep
flight running sharply down into the railed area, seemed as
far away as yesterday.

The little landing was a bright plateau. Under the skylight, shut off by its brightness from the rest of the house, the
rooms leading from it would be bright and flat and noisy with
light compared with the rest of the house. From above came
the tap-tap of a door swinging gently in a breeze and behind
the sound was a soft faint continuous murmur. She ran up
the short twisting flight of bare stairs into a blaze of light.
Would her room be a bright suburban bedroom? Had it
been a dull day when she first called? The skylight was blue
and gold with light, its cracks threads of bright gold. Three
little glaring yellow-grained doors opened on to the small
strip of uncovered dusty flooring; to the left the little box-loft,
to the right the empty garret behind her own and, in front of
her, her own door ajar; tapping in the breeze. The little brass
knob rattled loosely in her hand and the hinge ran up the scale
to a high squeak as she pushed open the door, and down

again as it closed behind her neatly with a light wooden sound.
The room was half dark shadow and half brilliant light.

She closed the door and stood just inside it looking at the
room. It was smaller than her memory of it. When she had
stood in the middle of the floor with Mrs Bailey, she had looked
at nothing but Mrs Bailey, waiting for the moment to ask about
the rent. Coming upstairs she had felt the room was hers
and barely glanced at it when Mrs Bailey opened the door.
From the moment of waiting on the stone steps outside the
front door, everything had opened to the movement of her
impulse. She was surprised now at her familiarity with the
detail of the room . . . that idea of visiting places in dreams.
It was something more than that . . . all the real part of your
life has a real dream in it; some of the real dream part of you
coming true. You know in advance when you are really following your life. These things are familiar because reality is here.
Coming events cast *light*. It is like dropping everything and
walking backwards to something you know is there. However
far you go out, you come back. . . . I am back now where I was
before I began trying to do things like other people. I left home
to get here. None of those things can touch me here.
    . . . The room asserted its chilliness. But the dark yellow
graining of the wall-paper was warm. It shone warmly in
the stream of light pouring through the barred lattice window.
In the further part of the room, darkened by the steep slope
of the roof, it gleamed like stained wood. The window space
was a little square wooden room, the long low double lattice
breaking the roof, the ceiling and walls warmly reflecting its
oblong of bright light. Close against the window was a firm
little deal table covered with a thin, brightly coloured printed
cotton table-cloth. When Miriam drew her eyes from its
confusion of rich fresh tones, the bedroom seemed very dark.
The bed, drawn in under the slope, showed an expanse of
greyish white counterpane, the carpet was colourless in the
gloom. She opened the door. Silence came in from the

landing. The blue and gold had gone from the skylight. Its sharp grey light shone in over the dim colours of the thread-bare carpet and on to the black bars of the little grate and the little strip of tarnished yellow-grained mantelpiece, running along to the bedhead where a small globeless gas bracket stuck out at an angle over the head of the bed. The sight of her luggage piled up on the other side of the fireplace drew her forward into the dimness. There was a small chest of drawers, battered and almost paintless, but with two long drawers and two small ones and a white cover on which stood a little looking-glass framed in polished pine . . . and a small yellow wardrobe with a deep drawer under the hanging part, and a little drawer in the rickety little washstand and another above the dusty cupboard of the little mahogany sideboard. I'll paint the bright part of the ceiling; scrolls of leaves. . . . Shutting the quiet door she went into the brilliance of the window space. The outside world appeared; a long row of dormer windows and the square tops of the larger windows below them, the windows black or sheeny grey in the light, cut out against the dinginess of smoke-grimed walls. The long strip of roof sloping back from the dormers was a pure even dark grey. She bent to see the sky, clear soft heavy grey, striped by the bars of her window. Behind the top rim of the iron framework of the bars was a discoloured roll of window blind. Then the bars must move. . . . Shifting the table she pressed close to the barred window. It smelt strongly of rust and dust. Outside she saw grey tiles sloping steeply from the window to a cemented gutter, beyond which was a little stone parapet about two feet high. A soft wash of madder lay along the grey tiles. There must be an afterglow somewhere, just out of sight. Her hands went through the bars and lifted the little rod which held the lattice half open. The little square four-paned frame swung free and flattened itself back against the fixed panes, out of reach, its bar sticking out over the leads. Drawing back grimed fingers and wrists striped with grime, she grasped the iron bars and pulled. The heavy framework left the window frame with a rusty creak and the sound of paint peeling and cracking. It was very heavy, but it came up and up until her arms were straight above her head, and looking up she saw a stout iron ring in a little trapdoor in the wooden ceiling and a hook in the centre of the endmost bar in the iron framework.

Kneeling on the table to raise the frame once more and fix it to the ceiling, she saw the whole length of the top row of windows across the way and wide strips of grimy stucco placed across the house fronts between the windows.

The framework of the freed window was cracked and blistered, but the little square panes were clean. There were four little windows in the row, each with four square panes. The outmost windows were immovable. The one next to the open one had lost its bar, but a push set it free and it swung wide. She leaned out, holding back from the dusty sill, and met a soft fresh breeze streaming straight in from the west. The distant murmur of traffic changed into the clear plonk plonk and rumble of swift vehicles. Right and left at the far end of the vista were glimpses of bare trees. The cheeping of birds came faintly from the distant squares and clear and sharp from neighbouring roofs. To the left the trees were black against pure grey, to the right they stood spread and bunched in front of the distant buildings blocking the vista. Running across the rose-washed façade of the central mass she could just make out 'Edwards's Family Hotel' in large black letters. That was the distant view of the courtyard of Euston Station. . . . In between that and the square of trees ran the Euston Road, by day and by night, her unsleeping guardian, the rim of the world beyond which lay the northern suburbs, banished.

From a window somewhere down the street out of sight came the sound of an unaccompanied violin, clearly attacking and dropping and attacking a passage of half a dozen bars. The music stood serene and undisturbed in the air of the quiet street. The man was following the phrase, listening; strengthening and clearing it, completely undisturbed and unconscious of his surroundings. 'Good heavens,' she breathed quietly, feeling the extremity of relief, passing some boundary, emerging strong and equipped in a clear medium. . . . She turned back into the twilight of the room.

Twenty-one and only one room to hold the richly renewed consciousness, and a living to earn, but the self that was with her in the room was the untouched tireless self of her seventeenth year and all the earlier time. The familiar light moved within the twilight, the old light. . . . She might as well wash the grime from her wrists and hands. There was a scrap of soap in the soap dish, dry and cracked and seamed with dirt. The washstand rocked as she washed her hands; the toilet things did not match, the towel-horse held one small thin face-towel and fell sideways against the wardrobe as she drew off the towel. When the gas was on she would be visible from the opposite dormer window. Short skimpy faded Madras muslin curtains screened a few inches of the endmost windows and were caught back and tied up with tape. She untied the tape and disengaged with the curtains a strong smell of dust. The curtains would cut off some of the light. She tied them firmly back and pulled at the edge of the rolled up blind. The blind, streaked and mottled with ironmould, came down in a stifling cloud of dust. She rolled it up again and washed once more. She must ask for a bath towel and do something about the blind, sponge it or something; that was all.

A light had come in the dormer on the other side of the street. It remained unscreened. Watching carefully she could see only a dim figure moving amongst motionless shapes. No need to trouble about the blind. London could come freely in day and night through the unscreened happy little panes; light and darkness and darkness and light.

London, just outside all the time, coming in with the light, coming in with the darkness, always present in the depths of the air in the room.

The gas flared out into a wide bright flame. The dingy ceiling and counterpane turned white. The room was a

square of bright light and had a rich brown glow, shut brightly
in by the straight square of level white ceiling and thrown up
by the oblong that sloped down, white, at the side of the big
bed almost to the floor. She left her things half unpacked
about the floor and settled herself on the bed under the gas
jet with *The Voyage of the Beagle*. Unpacking had been a
distraction from the glory, very nice, getting things straight.
But there was no *need* to do anything or think about anything
. . . ever, here. No interruption, no one watching or speculating or treating one in some particular way that had to be
met. Mrs Bailey did not speculate. She knew, everything.
Every evening here would have a glory, but not the same kind
of glory. Reading would be more of a distraction than unpacking. She read a few lines. They had a fresh attractive *meaning*.
Reading would be real. The dull adventures of the *Beagle*
looked real, coming along through reality. She put the book on
her knee and once more met the clear brown shock of her room.

The carpet is awful, faded and worn almost to bits. But
it is right, in this room. . . . This is the furnished room; one
room. I have come to it. 'You could get a furnished room
at about seven shillings rental.' The awful feeling, no tennis,
no dancing, no house to move in, no society. The relief at
first when Bennett found those people . . . maddening endless
roads of little houses in the east wind . . . their kind way of
giving more than they had undertaken, and smiling and waiting
for smiles and dying all the time in some dark way without
knowing it; filling the rooms and the piano and the fern on
the serge table-cloth and the broken soap-dish in the bathroom
until it was impossible to read or think or play because of them,
the feeling of them stronger and stronger till there was nothing
but crying over the trays of meals and wanting to scream. The
thought of the five turnings to the stations, all into long little
roads looking alike and making you forget which was which
and lose your way, was still full of pain . . . the *relief* of moving
to Granville Place still a relief, though it felt a mistake from

the first.   Mrs Corrie's old teacher liking only certain sorts of
people knew it was a mistake, with her peevish silky old face
and her antique brooch.   But it had been the beginning of
London. . . .   Bond Street that Sunday morning in the thick
fog; these sudden pictures gleaming in a window, filmy . . .
von Hier.   Adelina Compayne, hanging out silk stockings on
the top balustrade.   'I *love* cawfy' . . . that was the only
real thing that had been said downstairs.   There was no need
to have been frightened of these two women in black silk
evening dress.   None of these clever things were real.   They
said young Asquith is a really able man, to hide their thoughts.
The American Academy pupils talked together to keep everybody off, except when they made their clever jokes . . . 'if
any one takes that top bit there 'll be murder, Miss Spink.'
When they went out of the room, they looked silly.   The
young man was real somewhere else.

The little man talking about the wonders of the linotype
in the smoking-room. . . .   How did I get into the smoking-
room?   Someone probably told Miss Spink I talked to him
in the smoking-room and smoked a cigarette.   Perhaps his
wife.   If they could have seen.   It was so surprising to hear
anybody suddenly talking.   Perhaps he began in the hall and
ushered me into the smoking-room.   There was no one there
and I can't remember anything about the linotype, only the
quiet and the talking face and suddenly feeling in the heart
of London.   But it was soon after that they all began being
stand-offish; before Mr Chamberlayne came; before Adela
began playing Esther Summerson at the Kennington.   They
approved of my going down to fetch her, until he began coming
too.   The shock of seeing her clumsy heavy movements on
the stage and her face looking as though it were covered with
starch. . . .   I can *think* about it all, here, and not mind.

She *was* beautiful.   It was happiness to sit and watch her
smoking so badly, in bed, in the strip of room, her cloud of

hair against the wall in the candlelight, two o'clock . . . the
Jesuit who had taught her chess . . . and Michael Somebody,
the little book *The Purple Pillar*. He was an *author* and he
wanted to marry her and take her back to Ireland. Perhaps
by now she was back from America and had gone, just
out of kindness. She was strong and beautiful and good,
sitting up in her chemise, smoking. . . . I've got that
photograph of her as Marcia somewhere. I must put it
up. Miss Spink was surprised that last week, the students
getting me into their room . . . the dark clean shining
piano, the azaleas and the muslin-shaded lamp, the way
they all sat in their evening dresses, lounging and stiff, with
stiff clean polished hair. . . . 'Miss Dust here's going to
be the highest soprano in the States.' . . . 'None of that,
Miss Thicker.' . . . 'When she caught that top note and
the gold medal she went right up top, to stay there, that
minute.'

She was surprised when Mrs Potter took me to hear
Melba. I heard Melba. I don't remember hearing her.
English opera houses are small; there are fine things all over
the world. If you see them all you can compare one with the
other; but then you don't see or hear anything at all. It
seems strange to be American and at the same time stout
and middle-aged. It would have got more and more difficult
with all those people. The dreadful way the Americans got
intimate and then talked or hinted openly, everywhere, about
intimate things. No one knew how intimate Miss O'Veagh
was. I shall remember. There is something about being
Irish Roman Catholic that makes *happiness*. She did not
seem to think the George Street room awful. She was
surprised when I talked about the hole in the wall and the cold
and the imbecile servant and the smell of ether. 'We are
brought up from the first to understand that we must never
believe anything a man says.' She *came* and sat and talked
and wrote after she had gone . . . 'good-bye—sweet blessed little rose of Mary' . . . she tried to make me think
I was young and pretty. She was sorry for me without
saying so.

I should never have gone to Mornington Road unless I had been nearly mad with sorrow . . . if Miss Thomas disapproved of germs and persons who let apartments why did she come and take a room at George Street? She must have seen she drove me nearly mad with sorrow. The thought of Wales full of Welsh people like her, makes one mad with sorrow. . . . Did she think I could get to know her by hearing all her complaints? She's somewhere now, sending someone mad.

I was mad already when I went to Mornington Road.

'You'll be all right with Mrs Swanson . . .' the awful fringes, the *horror* of the ugly clean little room, the horror of Mrs Swanson's heavy old body moving slowly about the house, a heavy dark mountain, fringes, bugles, slow dead eyes, slow dead voice, slow grimacing evil smile . . . housekeeper to the Duke of Something and now moving slowly about, heavy with disapproval. She thought of me as a business young lady.

Following advice is certain to be wrong. When you don't follow advice there may be awful things. But they are not arranged beforehand. And when they come you do not know that they are awful until you have half got hold of something else. Then they change into something that has not been awful. Things that remain awful are in some way not finished. . . . Those women are awful. They will get more and more awful, still disliking and disapproving till they die. I shall not see them again. . . . I will never again be at the mercy of such women or at all in the places where they are. That means keeping free of all groups. In groups sooner or later one of them appears, dead and sightless and bringing blindness and death . . . although they seem to like brightness and children and the young people they approve of. I run away from them because I must. They kill me. The thought of their death is awful. Even in heaven no one could explain anything to them, if they remain as they are.

Wherever people advise you to go there is in the end one of those women. . . .

When she turned out the gas the window spaces remained faintly alight with a soft light like moonlight. At the window she found a soft bluish radiance cast up from below upon the opposite walls and windows. It went up into the clear blue darkness of the sky.

When she lay down the bed smelt faintly of dust. The air about her head under the sharply sloping ceiling was still a little warm with the gas. It was full of her untrammelled thoughts. Her luggage was lying about, quite near. She thought of washing in the morning in the bright light on the other side of the room . . . leaves crowding all round the lattice and here and there a pink rose . . . *several pink roses* . . . the lovely air chilling the water . . . the basin quite up against the lattice . . . dew splashing off the rose bushes in the little garden almost dark with trellises and trees, crowding with Harriett through the little damp stiff gate, the sudden lineny smell of Harriett's pinafore and the thought of Harriett in it, feeling the same, sudden bright sunshine, two shouts, great cornfields going up and up with a little track between them . . . up over Blewburton . . . *Whittenham Clumps*. Before I saw Whittenham Clumps I had always known them. But we saw them before we knew they were called Whittenham Clumps. It was a surprise to know anybody who had seen them and that they had a name.

St Pancras bells were clamouring in the room; rapid scales, beginning at the top, coming with a loud full thump on to the fourth note and finishing with a rush to the lowest which was hardly touched before the top note hung again in the air, sounding outdoors clean and clear while all the other notes still jangled together in her room. Nothing had changed.

The night was like a moment added to the day; like years going backwards to the beginning; and in the brilliant sunshine the unchanging things began again, perfectly new. She leaped out of bed into the clamorous stillness and stood in the window rolling up the warm hair that felt like a shawl round her shoulders. A cup of tea and then the bus to Harriett's. A bus somewhere just out there beyond the morning stillness of the street. What an *adventure* to go out and take a bus without having to face anybody. They were all out there, away somewhere, the very thought and sight of them, disapproving and deploring her surroundings. She listened. There they were. There were their very voices, coming plaintive and reproachful with a held-in indignation, intonations that she knew inside and out, coming on bells from somewhere beyond the squares — another church. She withdrew the coloured cover and set her spirit lamp on the inkstained table. Strong bright light was standing outside the window. The clamour of the bells had ceased. From far away down in the street a loud hoarse voice came thinly up. '*Referee—Lloyd's—Sunday Times—People*—pypa. . . .' A front door opened with a loud crackle of paint. The voice dropped to speaking tones that echoed clearly down the street and came up clear and soft and confidential. '*Referee? Lloyd's?*' The door closed with a large firm wooden sound and the harsh voice went on down the street.

St Pancras bells burst forth again. Faintly interwoven with their bright headlong scale were the clear sweet delicate contralto of the more distant bells playing very swiftly and reproachfully a five-finger exercise in a minor key. That must be a very high-Anglican church; with light coming through painted windows on to carvings and decorations.

As she began on her solid slice of bread and butter, St Pancras bells stopped again. In the stillness she could hear the sound of her own munching. She stared at the surface of the table that held her plate and cup. It was like sitting up to the nursery table. 'How frightfully happy I am,' she thought with bent head. Happiness streamed along her arms and from her head. St Pancras bells began playing a hymn tune, in single firm beats with intervals between that left each note standing for a moment gently in the air. The first two lines were playing carefully through to the distant accompaniment of the rapid weaving and interweaving in a regular unbroken pattern of the five soft low contralto bells of the other church. The third line of the hymn ran through Miriam's head, a ding-dong to and fro from tone to semitone. The bells played it out, without the semitone, with a perfect, satisfying falsity. Miriam sat hunched against the table listening for the ascending stages of the last line. The bells climbed gently up, made a faint flat dab at the last top note, left it in the air askew above the decorous little tune and rushed away down their scale as if to cover the impropriety. They clamoured recklessly mingling with Miriam's shout of joy as they banged against the wooden walls of the window space.

CHAPTER II

'BEEN to church?' said Gerald, digging his shoulders into his chair.

'No. Have you?'

'We 've not been for weeks. . . . Everybody thinks us awful heathens.'

'P'raps you are.'

'It 's Curls. She says she 's hanged if she 's going any more.'

'I can't stand the vicar,' said Harriett. 'He doesn't believe a word he says.'

Fancy Harriett! . . .

'Besides, what 's the good?'

'Oh, there you are.'

'There 's nothing the matter with church once in a way to my way of thinking, if it 's a decent high musical service.'

'Even Eve hardly ever goes now—and nobody could possibly be more goody than she is.'

This was disquieting. It was one thing to be the agnostic of the family—but Eve and Harriett. Miriam pondered resentfully while Gerald smoked and flicked his clothing and Harriett sat upright and pursed and untroubled in her great chair. She wondered whether she ought to say something about Unitarianism. But after all there might not be anything in it, and they might not feel the relief of the way it cleared up the trouble about Christ. Besides there was no worry here in the room. A discussion would lead nowhere. They could all three look at each other if they wanted to, and laugh everything off. In the middle of a sleepy Sunday afternoon, with nothing to do, sitting in three huge chairs and looking at each other, they were all right. Harriett's strength and scorn were directed against everything in the world, but not against herself . . . never against herself. Harriett often

24

thought her grumpy and ill-tempered, but she approved of
her. She was approving now.

'After all, Frills, it 's good form to go,' Gerald said idly.
'Go on. Smart people go to show their clothes.'

'Well, we 've shown ours.'

Harriett flew out of her chair and daintily kicked him.

He grabbed and missed and sank back wailing, his face
hidden in a cushion. Her dainty foot flew out once more and
he smothered a shriek.

'Shut up,' said Harriett curling herself up in her chair.

Gerald wailed on.

'Do we smoke in here?' said Miriam, wanting the scene
to drop or change while it was perfect. She would tell them
now about her change of lodgings.

'Yes,' said Harriett absently, with an eye on Gerald.

'I 've changed my diggings,' began Miriam formally.
fumbling for her packet of cigarettes. Harriett was hurling
a cushion. Gerald, crumpled into the depths of his chair and
sobbed aloud, beating with his arms.

'Stop it, silly,' piped Harriett, blushing.

'I 've changed my diggings,' repeated Miriam uncomfortably. Harriett's face flashed a response. Gerald's loud wail-
ings were broken by beseeching cries. Masquerade, but real,
absolutely real and satisfying. Miriam answered them from
some far deep in herself as if they were her own cries. Harry
was embarrassed. Her bright strength was answering. She
was ashamed at being seen answering.

Miriam got up conversationally and began looking about
for matches in the soft curtained drawing-room light. There
were swift movements and Harriett's voice busily chiding.
When she turned Gerald was sitting on the floor at Harriett's
knee, beating it gently with his head.

'Got a match, G?' she said, seeing in imagination the flare
of the match in the soft greenish glare of the room. There
was bright light all round the house and a glare of brightness
in the garden, beyond the curtains. 'Rather,' said Gerald,
'dozens.' He sat up and handed out a box. Leaning back
against Harriett's knee he began intoning a little poem of

appeal. There was a ring at the front door bell. Miriam got herself to the piano, putting cigarettes and matches behind a vase on the mantelshelf. 'That's old Tremayne,' said Gerald cheerfully, shooting his linen and glancing in the strip of mirror in the overmantel. The door opened admitting the light from the hall. The curtains at the open french windows swayed forward, flooding the room with the bright garden light. Into the brightness stepped Mr Tremayne, grey-clad and with a pink rose in his buttonhole.

Over tea they heard the story of his morning and how it had been interrupted by the man on the floor above who had come down in his dressing-gown to tell him about a birthday party . . . the two men sitting telling each other stories about drinks and people seeing each other home. After tea he settled back easily in his chair and went on with his stories. Miriam found it almost impossible to follow him. She grew weary of his bantering tone. It smeared over everything he touched and made him appear to be saying one thing over and over again in innuendo. Something he could not say out and could never get away from. He made little pauses and then it gleamed horribly about all his refinement of dress and bearing and Gerald laughed encouragingly and he went on, making a story that was like a play, that looked like life did when you looked at it, a maddening fussiness about nothing and people getting into states of mind. He went on into a story about business life . . . people getting the better of each other. It made her feel sick with apprehension. Anybody in business might be ruined any minute, unless he could be sure of getting the better of someone else. She had never realized that before. . . . It pressed on her breathing and made her feel that she had had too much tea. . . . She hated the exponent sitting there so coolly. It made the cool green-lit afternoon room an island amongst horrors. But it was that to him too . . . he felt the need of something beyond the everlasting innuendo of social life and the everlasting smartness of business life. She felt it was true that he spent Sunday mornings picking out hymn tunes with one finger, and liked 'Sabbath music' and remembered the things his mother used to play to him. He wanted a home, something away from business life and away from social life. He saw her as a woman in a home, nicely dressed in a quiet drawing-room, lit by softly screened clear fresh garden daylight. . . . 'Business is business. . . .' 'Man's love is of man's life a thing apart—'tis woman's whole existence.' Byron did not know what he was saying when he wrote it in his calm patronizing way. Mr Tremayne would admire it as a 'great truth'—thinking it like a man in the way Byron thought it. What a hopeless thing a man's consciousness was. How awful to have nothing but a man's consciousness. One could test it so easily if one were a little careful, and know exactly how it would behave. . . .

Opening a volume of Mendelssohn she played, from his point of view, one of the *Songs without Words* quietly into the conversation. The room grew still. She felt herself and Mr Tremayne as duplicates of Harriett and Gerald, only that she was a very religious, very womanly woman, the ideal wife and mother and he was a bad fast man who wanted to be saved. It was such an easy part to play. She could go on playing it to the end of her life, if he went on in business and made enough money, being a 'gracious silence,' taking an interest in his affairs, ordering all things well, quietly training the servants, never losing her temper or raising her voice, making the home a sanctuary of rest and refreshment and religious aspiration, going to church. . . . She felt all these things expressing themselves in her bearing. At the end of her piece she was touched to the heart by the look of adoration in his eyes, the innocent youthfulness shining through his face. There was something in him she could have and guard and keep if she chose. Something that would die if there were no woman to keep it there. There was nothing in his life of business and music halls to keep it there, nothing but the memory of his mother and he joined her on to that memory. His mother and his wife were sacred . . . apart from life. But he could not be really happy with a woman unless he could also despise her. Any interest in generalities, any argument or criticism or opposition would turn him into a towering bully. All men were like that in some way. They had each a set of notions and fought with each other about them, whenever they were together and not eating or drinking. If a woman opposed them they went mad. He would like one or two more Mendelssohns and then supper. And if she kept out of the conversation and listened and smiled a little, he would go away adoring. She played the Duetto; the chords made her think of Beethoven and play the last page carelessly and glance at Harriett. Harriett had felt her response to the chords and knew she was getting away from Mendelssohn. Mr Tremayne had moved to a chair quite close to the piano, just behind her. She found the Beethoven and played the first movement of a sonata. It leapt about the piano breaking up her pose, using her body as the instrument of its gay wild shapeliness, spreading her arms inelegantly, swaying her, lifting her from the stool with the crash and vibration of its chords. . . . 'Go on,' said Harriett when it came to an end. The *Largo* came with a single voice, deep and broad and quiet; the great truth behind the fuss of things. She felt her hearers grow weary of its reiterations and dashed on alone recklessly into the storm of the last movement. Through its tuneless raging, she could hear the steady voice and see the steady shining of the broad clear light. Daylight and gaiety and night and storm and a great song and truth, the great truth that was bigger than anything. Beethoven. She got up, charged to the fingertips with a glow that transfigured all the inanimate things in the room. The party was wrecked . . . a young lady who banged the piano till her hair nearly came down. . . . Mr. Tremayne had heard nothing but noise. . . . His eyes smiled, and his uneasy mouth felt for compliments.

'Why didn't you ask him to supper, La Fée?'
'The Bollingdons are coming round, silly.'
'Well?'
'With one small chicken and a blancmange.'
'Heaven help us.'
When they sat down to play halfpenny nap after supper,

Miriam recovered her cigarette from its hiding-place. She did not know the game. She sat at Harriett's new card-table wrapped in the unbroken jesting of the Bollingdons and the Ducaynes, happily learning and smoking and feeling happily wicked. The Bollingdons taught her simply, with a complete trustful friendliness, Mrs Bollingdon leaning across in her pink satin blouse, her clear clean bulging cheeks and dark velvet hair, like a full-blown dark rose. Between the rounds they poured out anecdotes of earlier nap parties, all talking at once. The pauses at the fresh beginnings were full of the echoes of their laughter. Miriam, in the character of the Honourable Miss Henderson, had just accepted Lord Bolling-don's invitation to join the Duke and Duchess of Ducayne and himself and Lady Bollingdon, in an all-day party to Wembley Park in a break and four on Easter Monday, and had lit a second cigarette and accepted a small whisky and soda when Mr Grove was announced. Harriett's face flushed jocular consternation.

When the party subsided after Mr Grove's spasmodic handshakings, Miriam got herself into a chair in a far corner, smoking her cigarette with burning cheeks. Sitting isolated with her cigarette and her whisky while he twice sent his low harsh clearly murmuring voice into the suddenly empty air to say that he had been to evensong at the Carmelites and was on his way home, she examined the relief in his presence and the nature of her farewell. Mr Bollingdon responded to him, remarking each time on the splendour of the evening.

Strolling home towards midnight along the narrow pave-ment of Endsleigh Gardens, Miriam felt as fresh and un-troubled as if it were early morning. When she had got out of her Hammersmith omnibus into the Tottenham Court Road, she had found that the street had lost its first terrifying impression and had become part of her home. It was the borderland of the part of London she had found for herself; the part where she was going to live, in freedom, hidden, on her pound a week. It was all she wanted. That was why she was young and glad; that was why fatigue had gone out of her life. There was nothing in the world that could come nearer to her than the curious half twilight half moonlight effect of lamplit Endsleigh Gardens opening out of Gower Place; its huge high trees, their sharp shadows on the little pavement running by the side of the railings, the neighbouring gloom of the Euston Road dimly lit by lamps standing high in the middle of the roadway at long intervals, the great high quiet porched houses, black and still, the shadow mass of St Pancras church, the great dark open space in front of the church, a shadowy figure-haunted darkness with the vague stream of the Euston Road running to one side of it and the corridor of Woburn Place opening on the other. The harsh voice of an invisible woman sounded out from it as she turned off into her own street. . . . 'Dressed up—he was—to the bloody death. . . .' The words echoed about her as she strolled down the street controlling her impulse to flinch and hurry. The woman was there, there and real, and that was what she had said. Resentment was lurking about the street. The woman's harsh voice seemed close. Miriam pictured her glaring eyes. There was no pretence about her. She felt what she said. She belonged to the darkness about St Pancras church . . . people had been garrotted in that part of the Euston Road not so very long ago. . . . Tansley Street was a soft grey gloaming after the darkness. When she rattled her key into the keyhole of number seven, she felt that her day was beginning. It would be perpetually beginning now. Nights and days were all one day; all hers, unlimited. Her life and work at Wimpole Street were something extra, thrown in with her own life of endless day. Sarah and Harriett, their lives and friends, her own friends, the Brooms, the girls in Kennett Street, all thrown in. She lit her table lamp and the gas and two candles, making her little brown room brilliant under a brilliant white ceiling, and sat down, eager to tell someone of her wealth and freedom.

Someone must know she was in London, free, earning her own living. Lilla? She would not see the extraordinary

freedom; earning would seem strange and dreadful to her . . .
someone who would understand the extraordinary freedom.
. . . Alma. *Alma!* Setting forth the London address in a
heavy careless hand at the head of a post card, she wrote from
the midst of her seventeenth year, 'Dear A. Where are you?'

Walking home along the Upper Richmond Road; not liking
to buy sweets; not enjoying anything to the full—always afraid
of her refinements; always in a way wanting to be like her;
wanting to share her mysterious knowledge of how things were
done in the world and the things one had to do to get on in
some clever world where people were doing things. Never
really wanting it, because the mere thought took the beauty
from the syringa and made it look sad. Never being able to
explain why one did not want to do reasonable clever things
in a clever brisk reasonable way; why one disliked the way she
went behaving up and down the Upper Richmond Road, with
her pretty neat brisk bustling sidling walk, keeping her secret
with a sort of prickly brightness. The Upper Richmond Road
was heaven, pure heaven; smelling of syringa. She liked
flowers but she did not seem to know. . . . *Syringa.* I had
forgotten. That is one of the things I have always wanted
to stop and remember. . . . What was it all about? What
was she doing now? Anyhow the London post card would
be an answer. A letter, making her see Germany and bits of
Newlands and what life was now would answer everything,
all her snubs and cleverness and bring back the Upper Richmond Road and make it beautiful. She will know something
of what it was to me then. Perhaps that was why she liked
me, even though she thought me vulgar and very lazy and
stupid.

CHAPTER III

THERE was a carriage at the door. West-end people, after late nights, managing to keep nine o'clock appointments—in a north wind. Miriam pressed the bell urgently. The scrubbed chalky mosaic and the busy bright brass plate reproached her for her lateness during the long moment before the door was opened. . . . It must be someone for Mr Orly; an appointment made since last night; that was the worst of his living in the house. He was in his surgery now, with the patient. The nine-fifteen patient would come almost at once. He would discover that his charts were not out before there was any chance of getting at his appointment book. . . . As the great door swung open she saw Mr Hancock turn the corner of the street, walking very rapidly before the north wind. . . . Mr Orly's voice was sounding impatiently from the back of the hall. . . . 'Where's Miss Hends? . . . Oh—here y' are Miss Hends, I say, call up Chalk for me will ya, get him to come at once, I 've got the patient waiting.' His huge, frock-coated form swung round into his surgery without waiting for an answer. Miriam scurried through the hall past Mr Leyton's open surgery door and into her room. Mr Leyton plunged out of his room as she was flinging down her things and came in briskly. 'Morning, pater, got a gas case?'

'M'm,' said Miriam. 'I 've got to call up Chalk and I haven't a second to do it.'

'Why Chalk?'

'Oh, I don't know. He said "Chalk,"' said Miriam angrily, seizing the directory.

'I 'll call him up if you like.'

'You are a saint. Tell him to come at once—sooner,' said Miriam, dabbing at her hair as she ran back through the hall and upstairs. As she passed the turn of the staircase, Mr Hancock was let in at the front door. She found his kettle

furiously boiling on its wrought-iron stand near the chair.
The stained-glass window just behind it was dim with steam.
She lowered the gas, put a tumbler in the socket of the spittoon,
lit the gas burner on the bracket table and swiftly pulled open
its drawers one by one. The instruments were all right . . .
the bottles—no chloroform, the carbolic bottle nearly empty and
its label soaked and defaced. Gathering the two bottles in
her hand, she turned to the instrument cabinet, no serviettes,
no rubber dam, clamps not up from the workshop. The top
of the cabinet still to be dusted. Dust and scraps of amalgam
were visible about the surfaces of the paper lining the instrument drawers. No saliva tubes in the basin. She swung
round to the bureau and hurriedly read through the names of
the morning's patients. Mr Hancock came quietly in as she
was dusting the top of the instrument cabinet by pushing
the boxes and bottles of materials that littered its surface
to the backmost edge. They were all lightly coated with
dust. It was everlasting, and the long tubes and metal
body of the little furnace were dull again. 'Good morning,' they said simultaneously, in even tones. There were
sounds of letters being opened and the turning of the pages
of the appointment book. The chain of Mr Hancock's gold
pencil case rattled softly as he made notes on the corners of
the letters.

'Did you have a pleasant week-end?'

'Very,' said Miriam emphatically.

There was a squeak at the side of the cabinet. 'Yes,' said
Miriam down the speaking tube. . . . 'Thank you. Will you
please bring up some tubes and serviettes?'

'Mr Wontner.'

'Thank you. . . .' 'Mrs Hermann is "frightfully shocked"
at the amount of her account. What did we send it in for?'

'Seventy guineas. It's a reduction, and it's two years'
work for the whole family.' The bell sounded again. . . .
'Lady Cazalet has bad toothache and can you see her at once?'

'*Confound.* . . . Will you go down and talk to her and see
if you can get one of the others to see her?'

'She won't.'

'Well then, she must wait. I'll have Mr Wontner up.'
Miriam rang. Mr Hancock began busily washing his hands.
The patient came in. He greeted him over his shoulder.
Miriam gathered up the sheaf of annotated letters and the
appointment book and ran downstairs. 'Has Mr Leyton a
patient, Emma?' 'Miss Jones just gone in, miss.' 'Oh,
Emma, will you ask the workshop for Mr Hancock's rubber
and clamps?' She rang through to Mr Leyton's room.
'There's a patient of Mr Hancock's in pain, can you see them
if I can persuade them?' she murmured. 'Right, in ten
minutes,' came the answering murmur. Mr Hancock's bell
sounded from her room. She went to his tube in the hall.
'Can I have my charts?' Running into her room she hunted
out the first chart from a caseful and ran upstairs with it.
Mr Hancock's patient was sitting forward in the chair urging
the adoption of the decimal system. Running down again,
she went into the waiting-room. The dark, Turkey-carpeted
oak-furnished length seemed full of seated forms. Miriam
peered and Lady Cazalet, with her hat already off, rose from
the deep arm-chair at her side. 'Can he see me?' she said in
a clear trembling undertone, her dark eyes wide upon Miriam's.
Miriam gazed deep into the limpid fear. What a privilege.
How often Captain Cazalet must be beside himself with
unworthiness. 'Yes, if you can wait a little,' she said dropping
her eyes and standing with arms restrained. 'I think it won't
be very long,' she added, lingering a moment as the little form
relapsed into the chair.

'Lady Cazalet will wait until you can see her,' she tubed up
to Mr Hancock.

'Can't you make her see one of the others?'

'I'm afraid it's impossible; I'll tell you later.'

'Well, I'll see her as soon as I can. I'm afraid she'll have
to wait.'

Miriam went back to her room to sort out the remaining
charts. On her table lay a broken denture in a faded morocco
case; a strip of paper directed 'five-thirty sharp,' in Mr Orly's
handwriting. Mr Leyton's door burst open. He came with
flying coat-tails.

''V' I got to see that patient of Mr Hancock's?' he asked breathlessly.

'No,' said Miriam 'she won't.'

'Right,' he said swinging back. 'I 'll keep Miss Jones on.' Mr Hancock's bell sounded again. Miriam flew to the tube. 'My clamps please.'

'Oh yes,' she answered, shocked, and hurried back to her room.

Gathering up the broken denture, she ran down the stone steps leading to the basement. Her cheap unyielding shoes clattered on the unyielding stones. The gas was on in the lunch room, Mrs Willis scrubbing the floor. The voices of the servants came from the kitchens in the unknown background. She passed the lunch room and the cellar and clamped on across the stone hall to the open door of the workshop.

Winthrop was standing at the small furnace in the box-lined passage way. It was roaring its loudest. Through its open door, the red light fell sharply on his pink-flushed face and drooping fair moustache and poured down over his white apron. 'Good ph-morning,' he said pleasantly, his eye on the heart of the furnace, his foot briskly pumping the blower.

From the body of the room came sounds of tapping and whistling . . . the noise of the furnace prevented their knowing that any one had come in. . . . Miriam drew near to the furnace, relieved at the shortness of her excursion. She stared at the tiny shape blazing red-gold at the heart of the glare. Winthrop gathered up a pair of tongs and drew the mould from the little square of light. The air hissed from the bellows and the roaring of the flames died down. In a moment he was standing free with hot face and hot patient ironic eyes, gently taking the denture from her hands. 'Good morning,' said Miriam. 'Oh, Mr Winthrop, it 's a repair for Mr Orly. It 's urgent. Can you manage it?' 'It 's ph—ph—sure to be urgent,' said Winthrop examining the denture with a short-sighted frown. Miriam waited anxiously. The hammering and whistling had ceased. 'It 'll be all right, Miss ph-Henderson,' said Winthrop encouragingly. She turned to the door. The clamps. . . . Gathering herself together, she went down the passage and stood at the head of the two stone steps leading down into the body of the room. A swift scrubbing of emery paper on metal was going on at the end of the long bench, lit by a long skylight, from which the four faces looked up at her with a chorus of good mornings in response to her greeting. 'Are Mr Hancock's clamps ready?' she asked diffidently. 'Jimmy . . .' The figure nearest to her glanced down the row of seated forms. The small bullet-headed boy at the end of the bench scrubbed vigorously and ironically with his emery stick. 'He won't be a minute, Miss Henderson,' said the near pupil comfortingly.

Miriam observed his spruce grey suit curiously masked by the mechanic's apron, the quiet controlled amused face, and felt the burden of her little attack as part of the patient prolonged boredom of his pupillage. The second pupil, sitting next to him, kept dog-like sympathetic eyes on her face, waiting for a glance. She passed him by, smiling gently in response without looking at him while her eyes rested upon the form of the junior mechanic, whose head was turned in the direction of the scrubbing boy. The head was refined, thin and clear cut, thatched with glossy curls. Its expression was servile— the brain eagerly seeking some flowery phrase—something to decorate at once the occasion and the speaker, and to give relief to the mouth strained in an arrested, obsequious smile. Nothing came and the clever meticulous hands were idle on the board. It seemed absurd to say that Mr Hancock was waiting for the clamps while Jimmy was scrubbing so busily. But they had obviously been forgotten. She fidgeted.

'Will somebody send them up when they 're done?'

'Jimmy, you 're a miserable sinner, hurry up,' said the senior pupil.

'They 're done,' said Jimmy in a cracked bass voice. 'Thank goodness,' breathed Miriam, dimpling. Jimmy came round and scattered the clamps carefully into her outstretched hand, with downcast eyes and a crisp dimpling smile.

'Rule Britannia,' remarked the junior pupil, resuming his

work as Miriam turned away and hurried along the passage and through the door held open for her by Winthrop. She flew up to Mr Hancock's room, three steps at a time, tapped gently at the door, and went in. He came forward across the soft grey green carpet to take the clamps and murmured gently, 'Have you got my carbolic?'

Miriam looked out the remainder of the charts and went anxiously through the little pile of letters she had brought down from Mr Hancock's room. All but three were straightforward appointments to be sent. One bore besides the pencilled day and date the word 'Tape' . . . she glanced through it—it was from a university settlement worker, asking for an appointment for the filling of two front teeth. . . . She would understand increasing by one thickness per day until there were five, to be completed two days before the appointment falls due so that any tenderness may have passed off. Mrs Hermann's letter bore no mark. She could make a rough summary in Mr Hancock's phraseology. The third letter enclosed a printed card of appointment with Mr Hancock which she had sent without filling in the day and hour. She flushed. Mr Hancock had pencilled in the missing words. Gathering the letters together, she put them as far away as her hand would reach, leaving a space of shabby ink-stained morocco clear under her hands. She looked blindly out of the window; hand-painted, they are hand-painted, forget-me-nots and gold tendrils softly painted, not shining, on an unusual shape, a merry Christmas. Melly Klismas. In this countree heapee lain, chiney man lun home again, under a red and green paper umbrella in the pouring rain, that was not a hand-painted one, but better, in some *strange* way, close bright colours drawing everything *in*; a shock. I stayed in there. There was something. Chinee man lun *home* again. Her eye roamed over the table; everything but the newly-arrived letters shabby under the high wide uncurtained window. The table fitted the width of the window. There was something to be done before anything could be done. Everything would look different if something were done. The fresh letters could lie neatly on the centre of the table in the midst of something. They were on the address books, spoiled by them. It would take years to check the addresses one by one till the old books could be put away. If the day-books were entered up to date, there would still be those, disfiguring everything. If everything were absolutely up to date, and all the cupboards in perfect order and the discounts and decimals always done in the depot-books to time, there would be time to do something. She replaced the letters in the centre of the table and put them back again on the address books. His nine-forty-five patient was being let in at the front door. In a moment his bell would ring and something must be said about the appointment card. 'Mr Orly?' A big booming elderly voice, going on heavily murmuring into the waiting-room. She listened tensely to the movements of the servant. Was Mr Orly in 'the den' or in his surgery? She heard the maid ring through to the surgery and wait. No sound. The maid came through her room and tapped at the door leading from it. 'Come in,' sang a voice from within, and Miriam heard the sound of a hammer on metal as the maid opened the door. She flew to the surgery. Amidst the stillness of heavy oak furniture and dark Turkey carpet floated in the confirming smell. There it was, all about the spittoon and the red-velvet-covered chair and the bracket table, a horrible confusion—and blood stains, blood-clotted serviettes, forceps that made her feel sick and faint. Summoning her strength, she gathered up the serviettes and flung them into a basket behind the instrument cabinet. She was dabbing at the stains on the American cloth cover of the bracket when Mr Orly came swinging in, putting on his grey frock-coat and humming *Gunga Din* as he came. 'Regular field day,' he said cheerfully. 'I shan't want those things —just pop 'em out of sight.' He turned up the cupboard gas and in a moment a stream of boiling water hissed down into the basin filling the room with steam. 'I say, has this man got a chart? Don't throw away those teeth. Just look at this—how's that for twisted? Just look here.' He took

up an object to which Miriam forced reluctant eyes, grotesquely
formed fangs protruding from the enclosing blades of a huge
forceps. 'How's that, eh?' Miriam made a sympathetic
sound. Gathering the many forceps he detached their contents, putting the relic into a bottle of spirit and the rest into
the hidden basket. The forceps went head first into a jar of
carbolic and Miriam breathed more freely. 'I'll see to those.
I say, has this man got a chart?' 'I'll see,' said Miriam
eagerly making off with the appointment book. She returned
with the chart. Mr Orly hummed and looked. 'Right.
Tell 'em to send him in. I say, 'v' I got any gold and tin?'
Miriam consulted the box in a drawer in the cabinet. It was
empty. 'I'm afraid you haven't,' she said guiltily. 'All
right, I'll let y' know. Send 'im in,' and he resumed *Gunga
Din* over the wash-hand basin. Mr Hancock's bell was ringing in her room and she hurried off, with a sign to the little
maid waiting with raised eyebrows in the hall. Darting into
her room, she took the foils from the safe, laid them on a clean
serviette amongst the litter on her table, and ran upstairs.
Mr Leyton opened his door as she passed: 'I say, can you feed
for me,' he asked breathlessly, putting out an anxious head.
'I'll come down in a minute,' promised Miriam from the
stairs. Mr Hancock was drying his hands. He sounded his
bell as she came in. The maid answered. 'I'm so sorry,'
began Miriam. 'Show up Mr Green,' said Mr Hancock down
the speaking-tube. 'You remember there's Lady Cazalet?'
said Miriam relieved and feeling she was making good her
carelessness in the matter of the appointment card.

'Oh, con*found*.' He rang again hurriedly. 'Show up Lady
Cazalet.' Miriam swept from the bracket table the litter of
used instruments and materials, disposing them rapidly on
the cabinet, into the sterilizing tray, the waste basket and the
wash-hand basin, tore the uppermost leaf from the headrest
pad, and detached the handpiece from the arm of the motor
drill while the patient was being shown upstairs. Mr Hancock
had cleared the spittoon, set a fresh tumbler, filled the kettle
and whisked the debris of amalgam and cement from the
bracket table before he began the scrubbing and cleansing of

his hands, and when the patient came in Miriam was in her
corner reluctantly handling the instruments, wet with the
solution that crinkled her finger-tips and made her skin brittle
and dry. Everything was in its worst state. She began the
business of drying and cleansing, freeing fine points from
minute closely adhering fragments, polishing instruments on
the leather pad, repolishing them with the leather, scraping
the many little burs with the fine wire brush, scraping the
clamps, clearing the obstinate amalgam from slab and spatula.
The tedium of the long series of small, precise, attention-
demanding movements was aggravated by the prospect of a
fresh set of implements already qualifying for another cleansing; the endless series to last as long as she stayed at Wimpole
Street . . . Were there any sort of people who could do this
kind of thing patiently, without minding? . . . the evolution
of dentistry was wonderful, but the more perfect it became the
more and more of this sort of thing there would be . . . the
more drudgery workers, at fixed salaries . . . it was only
possible for people who were fine and nice . . . there must be,
everywhere, women doing this work for people who were not
nice. They *could* not do it for the work's sake. Did some of
them do it cheerfully, as unto God? It was wrong to work
unto man. But could God approve of this kind of thing? . . .
was it right to spend life cleaning instruments? . . . the blank
moment again, of gazing about in vain for an alternative . . .
all work has drudgery. That is not the answer. . . . Blessed
be Drudgery, but that was housekeeping, not someone else's
drudgery. . . . As she put the things back in the drawers,
every drawer offered tasks of tidying, replenishing, and re-
papering of small boxes and grooves and sections. She had
remembered to bring up Lady Cazalet's chart. It looked at
her, propped against the small furnace. Behind it were the
other charts for the day, complete. The drug bottles were
full, there was plenty of amadou pulled soft and cut ready for
use, a fair supply of both kinds of Japanese paper. None of
the bottles and boxes of stopping materials were anywhere
near running short and the gold drawer was filled. She
examined the drawers that held the less frequently used

fittings and materials, conducting her operations noiselessly, without impeding Mr Hancock's perpetual movements to and fro between the chair and the instrument cabinet. Meanwhile the dressing of Lady Cazalet's painful tooth went quietly on and Mr Leyton was waiting, hoping for her assistance downstairs. There was no excuse for waiting upstairs any longer. She went to the writing table and hung over the appointment book.

It was a busy day. Mr Hancock would hardly have half an hour for lunch. . . . She examined the names carefully, one by one, and wrote against one 'Ask address,' underlined, and against another 'Inquire for brother—ill.' Lady Cazalet drew a deep sigh . . . she had been to other dentists. But perhaps they were good ones. Perhaps she was about thirty . . . had she ever gone through a green baize door and seen a fat common little man with smooth sly eyes standing waiting for her in a dark stuffy room smelling of creosote? Even if she had always been to good ones, they were not Mr Hancock. They were dentists. Cheerful ordinary men with ordinary voices and laughs, thinking about all manner of things. Or apparently bland, with ingratiating manners. Perhaps a few of them, some of his friends and some of the young men he had trained, were something like him. Interested in dentistry and the way it was all developing, some of them more enthusiastic and interested in certain special things than he was. But no one could be quite like him. No other patients had the lot of his patients. No other dentist was so completely conscious of the patient all the time, as if he were in the chair himself. No other dentist went on year after year remaining sensitive to everything the patient had to endure. No one else was so unsparing of himself . . . children coming eagerly in for their dentistry, sitting in the chair with slack limbs and wide open mouths and tranquil eyes . . . small bodies braced and tense, fat hands splayed out tightly on the too-big arms of the chair, in determination to bear the moment of pain bravely for him. . . . She wandered to the corner cupboard and opened it and gazed idly in. But none of them knew what it cost. . . . 'I think you won't have any more pain with that; I 'll just put in a dressing for the present'—she was Lady Cazalet again, without toothache, and that awful feeling that you know your body won't last . . . they did not know what it cost. What always doing the best for the patient *meant*. Perhaps they knew in a *way*; or knew something and did not know what it was . . . there would be something different in Mr Hancock's expression, especially in the three-quarters view when his face was turned away towards the instrument cabinet, if he saved his nerves and energy and money by doing things less considerately, not perpetually having the instruments sharpened and perpetually buying fresh outfits of sharp burs. The patient would suffer more pain . . . a dentist at his best ought to be more delicately strong and fine than a doctor . . . like a fine engraving . . . a surgeon working amongst live nerves . . . and he would look different himself. It was *in* him. It was keeping to that, all day, and every day, choosing the best difficult tiresome way in everything that kept that radiance about him when he was quietly at work . . . I mustn't stay here thinking these thoughts . . . it 's that evil thing in me, keeping on and on, always thinking thoughts, nothing getting done . . . going through life like—a stuck pig. If I went straight on, things would come like that just the same in flashes—bang, bang, in your heart, everything breaking into light just in front of you, making you almost fall off the edge into the expanse coming up before you, flowers and light stretching out. Then you shut it down, letting it go through you with a leap that carries you to the moon—the sun, and makes you bump with life like the little boy bursting out of his too small clothes and go on choking with song to do the next thing deftly. That 's right. Perhaps that is what they all *do*? Perhaps that 's why they won't stop to remember. Do you realize? Do you realize you 're in Brussels? Just *look* at the white houses there, with the bright green trees against them in the light. It 's the *air*, the clearness. Sh—If they hear you, they 'll put up the rent. They were just Portsmouth and Gosport people,

staying in Brussels and fussing about Portsmouth and Gosport
and aunt this and Mr that. . . . I shan't realize Brussels
and Belgium for years because of that.   They hated and killed
me because I was like that. . . . I must be like that . . .
something comes along, *golden*, and presently there is a thought.
I can't be easy till I 've said it in my mind, and I 'm sad till
I have said it somehow . . . and sadder when I have said it.
But nothing gets done.   I must stop thinking, from now, and
be fearfully efficient.   Then people will understand and like
me.   They will hate me too, because I shall be absurd, I shan't
be really in it.   Perhaps I shall.   Perhaps I shall get in.   The
wonder is they don't hate me more.   There was a stirring in
the chair and a gushing of fresh water into the tumbler.   *Why*
do I meet such nice people?   One after another.   'There,'
said Mr Hancock, 'I don't think that will trouble you any more.
We will make another appointment.'   Miriam took the
appointment book and a card to the chair-side and stayed
upstairs to clear up.

When she reached the hall Mr Orly's door was standing
wide.   Going into the surgery she found the head parlourmaid
rapidly wiping instruments with a soiled serviette.   'Is it all
right, James?' she said vaguely, glancing round the room.
'Yes, miss,' answered James briskly emptying the half-
filled tumbler and going on to dry and polish it with the
soiled serviette . . . the housemaid spirit . . . the dry corner
of a used serviette probably appeared to James much too
good to wipe anything with.   Telling her would not be any
good.   She would think it waste of time. . . . Besides, Mr
Orly himself would not really mind; and the things were
'mechanikly clean' . . . that was a good phrase of Mr Leyton's . . . with his own things always soaking, even his
mallets, until there was no polish left on the handles; and his
nailbrush in a bath of alcohol. . . . Mr Orly came in, large
and spruce.   He looked at his hands and began combing his
beard, standing before the overmantel.   'Hancock busy?'

'Frightfully busy.'

Miriam looked judicially round the room. James hovered. The north wind howled. The little strip of sky above the outside wall that obscured the heavily stained glass of the window seemed hardly to light the room and the little light there was was absorbed by the heavy dull oak furniture and the dark heavy Turkey carpet and dado of dull red and tarnished gold.

'It *is* dark for April,' murmured Miriam. 'I'll take away your gold and tin box if I may.'

'Thank ye,' said Mr Orly nervously, wheeling about with a harsh sigh to scan the chair and bracket-table; straightening his waistcoat and settling his tie. 'I got through without it —used some of that new patent silicate stuff of Leyton's. All right—show in the countess.'

James disappeared. Miriam secured the little box and made off. On her table was a fresh pile of letters, annotated in Mr Orly's clear stiff upright rounded characters. She went hurriedly through them. Extricating her blotter she sat down and examined the inkstand. Of course one of her pens had been used and flung down still wet with its nib resting against the handle of the other pens. . . . Mr Leyton . . . his gold filling; she ought to go in and see if she could help . . . perhaps he had finished by now. She wiped away the ink from the nib and the pen-handles.

Tapping at Mr Leyton's door, she entered. He quickly turned a flushed face, his feet scrabbling noisily against the bevelled base of the chair with the movement of his head. 'Sawl right Miss Henderson. I've finished. 'V' you got any emery strips?—mine are all worn out.'

Back once more in her room she heard two voices talking both at once excitedly in the den. Mrs Orly had a morning visitor. She would probably stay to lunch. She peered into the little folding mirror hanging by the side of the small mantelpiece and saw a face flushed and animated so far. Her hair was as unsatisfactory as usual. As she looked she became conscious of its uncomfortable weight pinned to the back of her head and the unpleasant warm feeling of her thick fringe. By lunch-time her face would be strained and yellow with sitting at work in the cold room with her feet on the oil-cloth under the window. She glanced at the oil-lamp standing in the little fireplace, its single flame glaring nakedly against the red-painted radiator. The telephone bell rang. Through the uproar of mechanical sounds that came to her ear from the receiver she heard a far-off faint angry voice in incoherent reiteration. 'Hallo, hallo,' she answered encouragingly. The voice faded but the sounds went on, punctuated by a sharp angry popping. Mr Orly's door opened and his swift heavy tread came through the hall. Miriam looked up apprehensively, saying 'Hallo' at intervals into the angry din of the telephone. He came swiftly on humming in a soft light baritone, his broad forehead, bald rounded crown, and bright fair beard shining in the bloom of the hall. A crumpled serviette swung with his right hand. Perhaps he was going to the workshop. The door of the den opened. Mrs Orly appeared and made an inarticulate remark abstractedly, and disappeared. 'Hallo, hallo,' repeated Miriam busily into the telephone. There was a loud report and the thin angry voice came clear from a surrounding silence. Mr Orly came in on tiptoe, sighed impatiently and stood near her, drumming noiselessly on the table at her side. 'Wrong number,' said Miriam, 'will you please ring off?'

'What a lot of trouble they givya,' said Mr Orly. 'I say, what's the name of the American chap Hancock was talking about at lunch yesterday?'

Miriam frowned.

'Can y' remember? About sea-power.'

'Oh,' said Miriam relieved. 'Mahan.'

'Eh?'

'Mahan. May-ann.'

'That's it. You've got it. Wonderful. Don't forget to send off Major Moke's case sharp, will ye?'

Miriam's eyes scanned the table and caught sight of a half-hidden tin box.

'No. I'll get it off.'

'Right. It's in a filthy state, but there's no time to clean it.'

He strode back through the hall murmuring 'Mahan.' Miriam drew the tin from its place of concealment. It contained a mass of dirty cotton-wool upon which lay a double denture coated with tartar and joined by tarnished gold springs. 'Eleven-thirty, sharp,' ran the instruction on an accompanying scrap of paper. No address. The name of the patient was unfamiliar. Mrs Orly put her head through the door of the den.

'What did Ro want?'

Miriam turned towards the small sallow eager face and met the kind sweet intent blue glint of the eyes. She explained, and Mrs Orly's anxious little face broke into a smile that dispelled the lines on the broad strip of low forehead leaving it smooth and sallow under the smoothly brushed brown hair.

'How funny,' said Mrs Orly hurriedly. 'I was just comin' out to ask you the name of that singer. You know. Mark something. Marksy. . . .'

'Mar-kaysie,' said Miriam.

'That's it. I can't think how you remember.' Mrs Orly disappeared and the two voices broke out again in eager chorus. Miriam returned to her tin. Mastering her disgust she removed the plate from the box, shook the cotton-wool out into the paper-basket, collected fresh wool, packing paper, sealing-wax, candle and matches and set to work to make up the parcel. She would have to attack the workshop again, and get them to take it out. Perhaps they would know the address. When the case was half packed she looked up the patient's name in the ledger. Five entries in about as many years—either repairs or springs—how simple dentistry became when people had lost all their teeth. There were two addresses, a town and a country one, written in a long time ago in ink; above them were two in pencil, one crossed out. The newest of the address books showed those two addresses, one in ink, neither crossed out. What had become of the card and letter that came with the case? In the den with Mrs Orly and her guest. . . .

Footsteps were coming neatly and heavily up the basement stairs. Winthrop. He came in smiling, still holding his long apron gathered up to free his knees. 'Ph—ph—Major Moke's case ready?' he whispered cheerfully.

'Almost—but I don't know the address.'

'It's the ph—ph—*Buck*inham Palace Otel. It's to go by hand.'

'Oh, thank goodness,' laughed Miriam sweeping the scissors round the uneven edge of the wrapping-paper.

'My *word*,' said Winthrop, 'What an eye you've got, I couldn't do that to ph-save melife, and I'm supposed to be a ph-mechanic.'

'Have I?' said Miriam surprised. 'I shan't be two minutes; it'll be ready by the time anybody's ready to go. But the letters aren't.'

'All right. I'll send up for them when we go out to lunch,' said Winthrop consolingly, disappearing.

Miriam found a piece of fine glazed green twine in her string box and tied up the neat packet—sealing the ends of the string with a neat blob on the upper side of the packet, and the folded paper at each end. She admired the two firmly flattened ends of string close together. Their free ends united by the firm red blob were a decorative substitute for a stamp on the white surface of the paper. She wrote in the address in an upright rounded hand with firm rotund little embellishments. Poring over the result she examined it at various distances. It was delightful. She wanted to show it to someone. It would be lost on Major Moke. He would tear open the paper to get at his dreadful teeth. Putting the stamps on the label, she regretfully resigned the packet and took up Mr Orly's day-book. It was in arrears—three, four days not entered in the ledger. 'Major Moke repair—one guinea,' she wrote. Mr Hancock's showing-out bell rang. She took up her packet and surveyed it upside down. The address looked like Chinese. It was really beautiful . . . but handwriting was doomed . . . short-hand and typewriting . . . she ought to know them, if she were ever to make more than a pound a week as a secretary . . . awful. What a good thing Mr Hancock thought them unprofessional

. . . yet there were already men in Wimpole Street who had
their correspondence typed.   What did he mean by saying that
the art of conversation was doomed?   He did not like conversation.   Jimmie came in for the parcel and scuttled downstairs with it.   Mr Hancock's patient was going out through
the hall.   He had not rung for her to go up.   Perhaps there
was very little to clear and he was doing it himself.

He was coming downstairs.   Her hands went to the pile of
letters and busily sorted them.   Through the hall.   In here.
Leisurely.   How are you getting on?   Half amused.   Half
solicitous.   The first weeks.   The first day.   She had only
just come.   Perhaps there would be the hand on the back of
the chair again, as before he discovered the stiffness like his
own stiffness.   He was coming right round to the side of the
chair into the light, waiting, without having said anything.
She seemed to sit through a long space waiting for him to
speak, in a radiance that shaped and smoothed her face as she
turned slowly and considered the blunted grave features, their
curious light, and met the smiling grey eyes.   They were not
observing the confusion on the table.   He had something to
say that had nothing to do with the work.   She waited startled
into an overflowing of the curious radiance, deepening the light
in which they were grouped.   'Are you busy?'   'No,' said
Miriam in quiet abandonment.   'I want your advice on a
question of decoration,' he pursued, smiling down at her with
the expression of a truant schoolboy and standing aside as she
rose.   'My patient's put off,' he added confidentially, holding
the door wide for her.   Miriam trotted incredulously upstairs
in front of him and in at the open surgery door and stood contemplating the room from the middle of the great square of
soft thick grey-green carpet, with her back to the great triple
window and the littered remains of a long sitting.
Perhaps a question of decoration meant altering the positions
of some of the pictures.   She glanced about at them, enclosed
in her daily unchanging unsatisfying impressions—the green

landscape plumy with meadow-sweet, but not letting you through to wander in fields, the little soft bright coloury painting of the doorway of St Mark's—San Marco, painted by an Englishman, with a procession going in at the door and beggars round the doorway, blobby and shapeless like English peasants in Italian clothes . . . bad . . . and the man had worked and studied and gone to Italy and had a name and still worked and people bought his things . . . an engraving very fine and small of a low bridge in a little town, quiet, sharp cheering lines; and above it another engraving, a tiresome troubled girl, all a sharp film of fine woven lines and lights and shadows in a rich dark liny filmy interior, neither letting you through nor holding you up, the girl worrying there in the middle of the picture, not moving, an obstruction . . . Maris . . . the two little watercolours of Devonshire, a boat with a brown sail and a small narrow piece of a street zigzagging sharply up between crooked houses, by a Londoner—just to say how crooked everything was . . . that thing in this month's *Studio* was better than any of these . . . her heart throbbed suddenly as she thought of it . . . a narrow sandy pathway going off, frilled with sharp greenery, far into a green wood. . . . Had he seen it? The *Studios* lay safely there on the polished table in the corner, the disturbing bowl of flowers from the country, the great pieces of pottery, friends, warm and sympathetic to touch, never letting you grow tired of their colour and design . . . standing out against the soft dull gold of the dado and the bold soft green and buff of the wall-paper. The oil painting of the cousin was looking on a little superciliously . . . centuries of 'fastidious refinement' looking forth from her child's face. If she were here, it would be she would be consulted about the decoration; but she was away somewhere in some house, moving about in a dignified way under her mass of gold hair, saying things when speech became a necessity in the refined fastidious half-contemptuous tone, hiding her sensitive desire for companionship, contemptuous of most things and most people. To-day she had an interested look, she was half jealously setting standards for him all the time. . . . Miriam set her aside. The Chinese figures staring down ferociously from the narrow shelf running along

the base of the high white frieze where more real to her.   They
belonged to the daily life here, secure from censure.

From the brown paper wrappings emerged a large plaque of
Oriental pottery. Mr Hancock manœuvred it upright, holding
it opposite to her on the floor, supported against his knees.
'There—what do you think of that?' he murmured bending over
it.   Miriam's eyes went from the veinings on his flushed forehead to the violent soft rich red and blue and dull green covering
the huge concave disk from side to side. It appeared to
represent a close thicket of palm fronds, thin flat fingers,
superimposed and splaying out in all directions over the
deep blue background. In the centre appeared the head
and shoulders of an enormous tiger, coming sinuously forward,
one great paw planted on the greenery near the foremost
middle edge of the plaque.
'M'm,' said Miriam staring.
Mr Hancock rubbed the surface of the plaque with his forefinger. Miriam came near and ran her finger down across the
rich smooth reliefs.
'Where shall I put it?' said Mr Hancock.
'I should have it somewhere on that side of the room, where
the light falls on it.'
Mr Hancock raised the plaque in his arms and walked with
it to the wall raising it just above his head and holding it in
place between the two pictures of Devonshire. They faded
to a small muddled dinginess, and the buff and green patterning
of the wall-paper showed shabby and dim.
'It looks somehow too big or too small or something. . . .
I should have it down level with the eyes, so that you can look
straight into it.'
Mr Hancock carefully lowered it.
'Let me come and hold it so that you can look,' said Miriam
advancing.
'It's too heavy for you,' said Mr Hancock, straining his head
back and moving it from side to side.

'I believe it would look best,' said Miriam, 'across the corner of the room as you come in—where the corner cupboard is—I'm sure it would,' she said eagerly and went back to the centre of the carpet.

Mr Hancock smiled towards the small oak cupboard fixed low in the angle of the wall.

'We should have to move the cupboard,' he said dubiously and carried the heavy plate to the indicated place.

'That's simply lovely,' said Miriam in delight as he held the plaque in front of the long narrow façade of black oak.

Mr Hancock lowered the plaque to the floor and propped it crosswise against the angle.

'It would be no end of a business fixing it up,' he murmured crossing to her side. They stood looking at the beautiful surface; blurred a little in the light by its backward tilt. They gazed fascinated as the plaque slid gently forward and fell heavily, breaking into two pieces.

They regarded one another quietly and went forward to gather up the fragments. The broken sides gritted together as Miriam held hers steady for the other to be fitted to it. When they were joined the crack was hardly visible.

'That'll be a nice piece of work for Messrs Nikkoo,' said Mr Hancock with a little laugh, 'we'd better get it in back behind the sofa for the present.' They spread the brown paper over the brilliant surfaces and stood up. Miriam's perceptions raced happily along. How had he known that she cared for things? She was not sure that she did . . . not in the way that he did. . . . How did he know that she had noticed any of his things? Because she had blurted out 'Oh what a perfectly lovely picture,' when he showed her the painting of his sister? But that was because he admired his sister and her brother had painted the picture and he admired them both and she had not known about this when she spoke.

'Did you see this month's *Studio*?' she asked shyly.

He turned to the table and took up the uppermost of the pile.

'There's a lovely green picture,' said Miriam, 'at least I like it.'

Mr Hancock turned pages ruminatively.

'Those are good things,' he said flattening the open page.

'Japanese Flower Decorations,' read Miriam looking at the reproduced squares of flowering branches arranged with a curious naturalness in strange flat dishes. They fascinated her at once—stiff and real, shooting straight up from the earth and branching out. They seemed coloured. She turned pages and gazed.

'How nice and queer.'

Mr Hancock bent smiling. 'They've got a whole science of this, you know,' he said; 'it takes them years to learn it; they apprentice themselves and study for years. . . .'

Miriam looked incredulously at the simple effects—just branches placed 'artistically' in flat dishes and fixed somehow at the base amongst little heaps of stones.

'It looks easy enough.'

Mr Hancock laughed. 'Well—you try. We'll get some broom or something, and you shall try your hand. You'd better read the article. Look here—they've got names for all the angles. . . . "Shin,"' he read with amused admiring delight, '"sho-shin" . . . there's no end of it.'

Miriam fired and hesitated. 'It's like a sort of mathematics. . . . I'm no good at mathematics.'

'I expect you could get very good results . . . we'll try. They carry it to such extraordinary lengths because there's all sorts of social etiquette mixed up with it—you can't have a branch pointing at a guest for instance—it would be rude.'

'No wonder it takes them years,' said Miriam.

They laughed together, moving vaguely about the room.

Mr Hancock looked thoughtfully at the celluloid tray of hairpins on the mantelshelf, and blew the dust from it . . . there was something she remembered in some paper, very forcibly written, about the falsity of introducing single specimens of Japanese art, the last results of centuries of an artistic discipline, that was it, that had grown from the life of a secluded people living isolated in a particular spot under certain social and natural conditions, into English household decoration. . . . *Gleanings in Buddha Fields*, the sun on

rice-fields . . . and Fujiyama—Fuji-no-San, in the distance . . .
but he did not like Hearn—'there's something in the chap that
puts me off' . . . puts off—what a good phrase . . . 'something sensuous in him' . . . but you could never forget
Buddha Fields. It made you know you were in Japan, in the
picture of Japan . . . and somebody had said that all good
art, all great art, had a sensuous element . . . it was dreadful,
but probably true . . . because the man had observed it and was
not an artist, but somebody looking carefully on. Mr Hancock,
Englishman, was 'put off' by sensuousness, by anybody taking
a delight in the sun on rice fields and the gay colours of Japan
. . . perhaps one ought to be 'put off' by Hearn . . . but Mr
Hancock liked Japanese things and bought them and put them
in with his English things, that looked funny and tame beside
them. What he did not like was the expression of delight. It
was queer and annoying somehow . . . especially as he said
that the way English women were trained to suppress their
feelings was bad. He had theories and fixed preferences and
yet always seemed to be puzzled about so many things.

'D'you think it right to try to introduce single pieces of
Japanese art into English surroundings?' she said tartly, beginning on the instruments.

'East is East and West is West and never the twain can
meet?'

'That's a dreadful idea—I don't believe it a bit.'

Mr Hancock laughed. He believed in those awful final
dreary-weary things . . . some species are so widely dif-
ferentiated that they cannot amalgamate—awful . . . but if
one said that he would laugh and say it was beyond him . . .
and he liked and disliked without understanding the curious
differences between people—did not know why they were
different—they put him off or did not put him off and he was
just. He liked and reverenced Japanese art and there was an
artist in his family. That was strange and fine.

'I suppose we ought to have some face-powder here,' mused
Mr Hancock.

'They'll take longer than ever if we do.'

'I know—that's the worst of it; but I commit such fearful

depredations . . . we want a dressing-room . . . if I had my
way we 'd have a proper dressing-room downstairs. But I
think we must get some powder and a puff. . . . Do you think
you could get some . . . ?' Miriam shrank. Once in a
chemist's shop, in a strong Burlington Arcade west-end mood,
buying some scent, she had seized and bought a little box . . .
La Dorine de Poche . . . Dorin, Paris . . . but that was different
to asking openly for powder and a puff . . . la Dorine de Dorin,
Paris was secret and wonderful. . . . 'I 'll try,' she said
bravely and heard the familiar little sympathetic laugh.

Lunch would be ready in a few minutes and none of the
letters were done. She glanced distastefully at the bold hand-
writings, scrawling, under impressive stamped addresses with
telephone numbers, and names of stations and telegraphic
addresses, across the well-shaped sheets of expensive note-
paper, to ask in long, fussy, badly-put sentences for expensive
appointments. Several of the signatures were unfamiliar to
her and must be looked up in the ledger, in case titles might be
attached. She glanced at the dates of the appointments—they
could all go by the evening post. What a good thing Mr
Hancock had given up overlooking the correspondence. Mrs
Hermann's letter he should see . . . but that could not anyhow have been answered by return. The lunch-bell rang.
. . . Mr Orly's letters! There was probably a telegram or
some dreadful urgent thing about one or other of them that
ought to have been dealt with. With beating heart she
fumbled them through—each one bore the word 'Answered' in
Mrs Orly's fine pointed hand. Thank goodness. Opening a
drawer she crammed them into a crowded clip . . . at least a
week's addresses to be checked or entered. . . . Mr Hancock's
unanswered letters went into the same drawer, leaving her
table fairly clear. Mr Leyton's door burst open, he clattered
down the basement stairs. Miriam went into his room and
washed her hands in the corner basin under the patent unleaking
taps. Everything was splashed over with permanganate of

potash. The smell of the room combined all the dental drugs with the odour of leather—a volunteer officer's accoutrements lay in confusion all over on the secretaire. Beside them stood an open pot of leather polish. Mr and Mrs Orly passed the open door and went downstairs. They were alone. The guest had gone.

'Come and share the remains of the banquet, Miss Hens'n.'

'*Do* have just a bit of somethin', Ro darling, a bit of chicking or somethin'.'

'Feeling the effects?' remarked Mr Leyton cheerfully munching. 'I've got a patient at half past,' he added, nervously glancing up as if to justify his existence as well as his remark. Miriam hoped he would go on; perhaps it would occur to Mrs Orly to ask him about the patient.

'*You*'d feel the effects, my boy, if you hadn't had a wink the whole blessed night.'

'Hancock busy, Miss Hens'?' Miriam glanced at the flushed forehead and hoped that Mr Orly would remain with his elbows on the table and his face hidden in his hands. She was hungry, and there would be no peace for anybody if he were roused.

'Too many whiskies?' inquired Mr Leyton cheerfully, shovelling salad on to his plate.

'Too much whisking and frisking altogether, captain,' said Mr Orly incisively, raising his head.

Mrs Orly flushed, and frowned at Mr Orly.

'Don't be silly, Ley—you know how father hates dinner parties.'

Mr Orly sighed harshly, pulling himself up as Miriam began a dissertation on Mr Hancock's crowded day.

'Ze got someone with him now?' put in Mrs Orly perfunctorily.

'Wonderful man,' sighed Mr Orly harshly, glancing at his son.

'Have a bit of chicking, Ro.'

'No, my love, no, not all the perfumes of Araby—not all the

chickens of Cheshire. Have some pâté, Miss Hens'—No?
despise pâté?'

A maid came briskly in and looked helpfully round.

'Who's your half-past-one patient, Ley?' asked Mrs Orly
nervously.

'Buck,' rapped Mr Leyton. 'We going to wait for Mr
Hancock, mater?'

'No, of course not. Keep some things hot, Emma, and
bring in the sweets.'

'Have some more chicken, Miss Hens'. Emma!'—he indicated his son with a flourish of his serviette—'wait upon Mr
Leyton, serve him speedily.'

Emma, arrested, looked helpfully about, smiled in brisk
amusement, seized some dishes, and went out.

Mrs Orly's pinched face expanded. 'Silly you are, Ro.'
Miriam grinned, watching dreamily. Mr Leyton's flushed face
rose and dipped spasmodically over the remains of his salad.

'Bucking for Buck'—laughed Mr Orly in a soft falsetto.

'Ro, you *are* silly, who's Buck, Ley?'

'Don't question the officer, Nelly.'

'Ro, you *are* absurd,' laughed Mrs Orly.

'Help the *jellies*, dearest,' shouted Mr Orly in a frowning
whisper. 'Have some jelly, Miss Hens'. It's all right,
Ley . . . glad you so busy, my son. . How many did you have
this morning?' Mopping his brow and whisking his person
with his serviette, he glanced sidelong.

'Two,' said Mr Leyton, noisily spooning up jelly. 'Any more
of that stuff, mater? how about Hancock?'

'There's plenty here,' said Mrs Orly helping him. Miriam
laboured with her jelly and glanced at the dish. People wolfed
their food. It would seem so conspicuous to begin again when
the fuss had died down; with Mr Orly watching as if feeding
were a contemptible self-indulgence.

'Had a beastly gold case half the morning,' rapped Mr
Leyton and drank, with a gulp.

'Get any help?' said Mr Orly, glancing at Miriam.

'No,' said Mr Leyton in a non-committal tone, reaching
across the table for the cheese.

'Hancock too busy?' asked Mr Orly. 'Have some more jelly, Miss Hens'n.'

'No thank you,' said Miriam.

'A bit of cheese; a fragment of giddy Gorgonzola.'

'No thanks.'

Mrs Orly brushed busily at her bodice, peering down with indrawn chin. The room was close with gas. If Mr Hancock would only come down, and give her the excuse of attending to his room.

'What you doing s'aafnoon?' asked Mr Leyton.

'I, my boy, I don't know,' said Mr Orly with a heavy sigh, 'string myself up, I think.'

'You'd much better string yourself round the Outer Circle and take Lennard's advice.'

'Good advice, my boy—if we all took good advice . . . eh, Miss Hens'n? I've taken twenty grains of phenacetin this morning.'

'Well, you go and get a good walk,' said Mr Leyton clattering to his feet. ''Scuse me, mater.'

'Right, my boy! Excellent! A Daniel come to judgment! All right, Ley—get on with you. Buck up and see Buck. Oh-h-h, my blooming head. Excuse my language Miss Hens'n. Ah! Here's the great man. Good morning Hancock. How are you? D'they know you're down?'

Mr Hancock murmured his greetings and sat down opposite Miriam with a grave preoccupied air.

'Busy?' asked Mr Orly turning to face his partner.

'Yes—fairly,' said Mr Hancock pleasantly.

'Wonderful man. . . . Ley's gone off like a bee in a gale. D'they know Hancock's down, Nelly?'

Miriam glanced at Mr Hancock, wishing he could lunch in peace. He was tired. Did he too feel oppressed with the gas and the pale madder store cupboards? . . . glaring muddy hot pink?

'I've got a blasted head on . . . excuse my language. Twenty of 'em, twenty to dinner.'

'Oh, yes?' said Mr Hancock shifting in his chair and glancing about.

'*Nelly!* D' they know he's down? Start on a pâté, Hancock. The remains of the banquet.'

'Oh . . . well, thanks.'

'You never get heads, do ye?'

Mr Hancock smiled, and began a murmuring response as he busied himself with his pâté.

'Poor Ro, he's got a most awful head. . . . How's your uncle, Mr Hancock?'

'Oh—thank you. . . . I'm afraid he's not very flourishing.'

'He's better than he used to be, isn't he?'

'Well—yes, I think perhaps on the whole he is.'

'You ought to have been there, Hancock. Cleave came. He was in no end of form. Told us some fine ones. Have a biscuit and butter Miss Hens'n.'

Miriam refused and excused herself.

On her way upstairs she strolled into Mr Leyton's room. He greeted her with a smile—polishing instruments busily.

'Mr Hancock busy?' he asked briskly.

'M'm.'

'You busy? I say, if I have Buck in will you finish up these things?'

'All right, if you like,' said Miriam, regretting her sociable impulse. 'Is Mr Buck here?' She glanced at the appointment book.

'Yes, he's waiting.'

'You haven't got anybody else this afternoon,' observed Miriam.

'I know. But I want to be down at headquarters by five in full kit if I possibly can. Has the pater got anybody?'

'No. The afternoon's marked off—he's going out, I think. Look here, I'll clear up your things afterwards, if you want to go out. Will you want all these for Mr Buck?'

'Oh—all right, thanks; I dunno. I've got to finish him off this afternoon and make him pay up.'

'Why pay up? Isn't he trustworthy?'

'Trustworthy? A man who's just won three hundred pounds on a horse and chucked his job on the strength of it.'

'What a fearfully insane thing to do.'

'Lost his head.'

'Is he very young?'

'Oo—'bout twenty-five.'

'H'm.   I spose he'll begin the rake's progress.'

'That's about it.   You've just about hit it,' said Mr Leyton
with heavy significance.

Miriam lingered.

'I boil every blessed thing after he's been . . . if that's any
indication to you.'

'*Boil* them!' said Miriam vaguely distressed and pondering
over Mr Leyton standing active and aseptic between her and
some horror . . . something infectious . . . it must be that
awful mysterious thing . . . how awful for Mr Leyton to have
to stop his teeth.

'Boil 'em,' he chuckled knowingly.

'Why on earth?' she asked.

'Well—there you are,' said Mr Leyton—'that's all I can
tell you.   I *boil* 'em.'

'Crikey,' said Miriam half in response and half in comment
on his falsetto laugh, as she made for the door.   'Oh, but I
say, I don't understand your boiling apparatus, Mr Leyton.'

'All right, don't you worry.   I'll set it all going and shove
the things in.   You've only to turn off the gas and wipe 'em.
I dare say I shall have time to do them myself.'

When she had prepared for Mr Hancock's first afternoon
patient Miriam sat down at her crowded table in a heavy
drowse.   No sound came from the house or from the den.
The strip of sky above the blank wall opposite her window was
an even cold grey.   There was nothing to mark the movement
of the noisy wind.   The room was cold and stuffy.   Shivering
as she moved, she glanced round at the lamp.   It was well
trimmed.   The yellow flame was at its broadest.   The
radiator glared.   The warmth did not reach her.   She was
cold to the waist, her feet without feeling, on the strip of
linoleum; her knees protruding into the window space felt as

if they were in cold water. Her arms crept and flushed with cold at every movement, strips of cold wrist disgusted her, showing beyond her skimpy sleeves and leading to the hopelessness of her purplish red hands swollen and clammy with cold. Her hot head and flushed cheeks begged for fresh air. Warm rooms, with carpets and fires; an even, airy warmth. . . . There were people who could be in this sort of cold and be active, with cool faces and warm hands, even just after lunch. If Mr Leyton were here he would be briskly entering up the books—perhaps with a red nose; but very brisk. He was finishing Buck off; briskly, not even talking. Mr Hancock would be working swiftly at well-up-to-date accounts, without making a single mistake. Where had he sat doing all those pages of beautiful spidery book-keeping? Mr Orly would be rushing things through. What a drama. He knew it. He *knew* he had earned his rest by the fire . . . doing everything, making and building the practice . . . people waiting outside the surgery with basins for him to rush out and be sick. Her sweet inaccurate help in the fine pointed writing on cheap paper . . . the two cheap rooms they started in. . . . *The Wreck of the 'Mary Gloucester'* . . . 'and never a doctor's brougham to help the missis unload.' They had been through everything together . . . it was all there with them now . . . rushing down the street in the snow without an overcoat to get her the doctor. They were wise and sweet; in life and wise and sweet. They had gone out and would be back for tea. Perhaps they had gone out. Everything was so quiet. Two hours of cold before tea. Putting in order the materials for the gold and tin she propped her elbows on the table and rested her head against her hands and closed her eyes. There was a delicious drowsiness in her head, but her back was tired. She rose and wandered through the deserted hall into the empty waiting-room. The clear blaze of a coal fire greeted her at the doorway and her cold feet hurried in on to the warm Turkey carpet. The dark oak furniture and the copper bowls and jugs stood in a glow of comfort. From the centre of the great littered table a bowl of daffodils asserted the movement of the winter and pointed forward and away from the winter stillness of the old room. The long faded rich crimson rep curtains obscured half the width of each high window, and the London light, screened by the high opposing houses, fell dimly on the dingy books and periodicals scattered about the table. Miriam stood by the mantelpiece, her feet deep in the black sheepskin rug, and held out her hands towards the fire. They felt cold again the instant she withdrew them from the blaze. The hall clock gonged softly twice. The legal afternoon had begun. Any one finding her in here now would think she was idling. She glanced at the deep dark shabby leather arm-chair near by and imagined the relief that would come to her whole frame, if she could relax into it for five undisturbed minutes. The ringing of the front door bell sent her hurrying back to her room.

The sound of reading came from the den—a word-mouthing, word-slurring monotonous drawl — thurrah-thurrah-thurrah; thurrah thurrah . . . a single beat, on and on, the words looped and forced into it without any discrimination, the voice dropping uniformly at the end of each sentence . . . *thrah*. . . . An Early Victorian voice, giving reproachful instruction to a child . . . a class of board-school children reciting. . . . Perhaps they had changed their minds about going out. . . . Miriam sat with her hands tucked between her knees, musing, with her eyes fixed on the thin sheets of tin and gold . . . extraordinary to read any sort of text like that . . . but there was something in it, something nice and good . . . listening carefully you would get most of the words. It would be better to listen to than a person who read with intelligent modulations, as if they had written the thing themselves; like some men read . . . and irritatingly intelligent women . . . who knew they were intelligent. But there ought to be clear . . . enunciation. Not expression—that was like commenting as you read; getting at the person you were reading to . . . who might not want to comment in the same way. Reading, with expression, really hadn't any expression. How wonderful — of course. Mrs Orly's reading had an expression; a shape. It was exactly like the way they looked at things; exactly; everything was there; all the things they agreed about, and the things

he admired in her . . . things that by this time she knew he
admired. . . . She was conscious of these things . . . that
was the difference between her and her sister, who had exactly
the same things but had never been admired . . . standing
side by side exactly alike, the sister like a child—clear with a
sharp fresh edge; Mrs Orly with a different wisdom . . .
softened and warm and blurred . . . conscious, and always
busy distracting your attention, but with clear eyes like a
child, too.

Presently the door opened quietly and Mrs Orly appeared
in the doorway. 'Miss Hens'n,' she whispered urgently.
Miriam turned to meet her flushed face. 'Oh, Miss Hens'n,'
she pursued absently, 'if Mudie's send, d' you mind lookin'
and choosin' us something nice?'

'Oh,' said Miriam provisionally with a smile.

Mrs Orly closed the door quietly and advanced confidently
with deprecating bright wheedling eyes. 'Isn't it tahsome,'
she said conversationally. 'Ro's asleep and the carriage is
comin' round at half past. Isn't it tahsome!'

'Can't you send it back?'

'I want him to go out; I think the drive will do him good.
I say, d' you mind just lookin'—at the books?'

'No, I will; but how shall I know what to keep? Is there a
list?'

Mrs Orly looked embarrassed. 'I 've got a list somewhere,'
she said hurriedly, 'but I can't find it.'

'I 'll do my best,' said Miriam.

'*You* know—anythin' historical . . . there 's one I put
down, *The Sorrows of a Young Queen*. Keep that if they send
it and anything else you think.'

'Is there anything to go back?'

'Yes, I 'll bring them out. We 've been reading an awful
one—awful.'

Miriam began fingering her gold-foil. Mrs Orly was going
to expect her to be shocked. . . .

'By that awful man Zola. . . .'

'Oh, yes,' said Miriam, dryly.

'Have you read any of his?'

'Yes,' said Miriam carefully.

'*Have* you? Aren't they shockin'?'

'Well I don't know. I thought *Lourdes* was simply wonderful.'

'Is that a nice one—what's it about?'

'Oh you know—it's about the Madonna of Lourdes, the miracles, in the south of France. It begins with a crowded trainload of sick people going down through France on a very hot day . . . it's simply stupendous . . . you feel you're in the train, you go through it all'—she turned away and looked through the window overcome . . . 'and there's a thing called *Le Rêve*,' she went on incoherently with a break in her voice, 'about an embroideress and a man called Félicien— it's simply the most *lovely* thing.'

Mrs Orly came near to the table.

'You understand about books, don't you,' she said wistfully.

'Oh, no,' said Miriam. 'I've hardly read anything.'

'I wish you'd put those two down.'

'I don't know the names of the translations,' announced Miriam conceitedly.

A long loud yawn resounded through the door.

'Better, boysie?' asked Mrs Orly turning anxiously towards the open door.

'Yes, my love,' said Mr Orly cheerfully.

'I *am* glad, boy—I'll get my things on—the carriage'll be here in a minute.'

She departed at a run and Mr Orly came in and sat heavily down in a chair set against the slope of the wall close by and facing Miriam.

'Phoo,' he puffed, 'I've been taking phenacetin all day; you don't get heads, do you?'

Miriam smiled and began preparing a reply.

'How's it coming in? Totting up, eh?'

'I think so,' said Miriam uneasily.

'What's it totting up to this month? Any idea?'

'No; I can see if you like.'

'Never mind, never mind. . . . Mrs O.'s been reading
. . . phew! You're a lit'ry young lady—d'you know that
French chap—Zola—Emmil Zola——' Mr Orly glanced
suspiciously.

'Yes,' said Miriam.

'Like 'im?'

'Yes,' said Miriam firmly.

'Well—it's a matter of taste and fancy,' sighed Mr. Orly
heavily. 'Chacun à son goût—shake an ass and go, as they
say. One's enough for me. I can't think why they do it
myself—sheer, well to call a spade a spade sheer bestiality those
French writers—don't ye think so, eh?'

'Well no. I don't think I can accept that as a summary of
French literature.'

'Eh, well, it's beyond me. I suppose I'm not up to it.
Behind the times. Not cultured enough. Not cultured
enough I guess. Ready dearest?' he said, addressing his wife
and getting to his feet with a groan. 'Miss Hens'n's a great
admirer of Emmil Zola.'

'She says some of his books are pretty, didn't you, Miss
Hens'n? It isn't fair to judge from one book, Ro.'

'No, my love, no. Quite right. Quite right. I'm wrong—
no doubt. Getting old and soft. Things go on too fast for
me.'

'Don't be so silly, Ro.'

Drowsily and automatically Miriam went on rolling tin and
gold—sliding a crisp thick foil of tin from the pink-tissue-
paper-leaved book on to the serviette . . . a firm metallic
crackle . . . then a silent layer of thin gold . . . then more
tin . . . adjusting the three slippery leaves in perfect super-
position without touching them with her hands, cutting the
final square into three strips, with the long sharp straight-
bladed scissors—the edges of the metal adhering to each other
as the scissors went along—thinking again with vague distant
dreamy amusement of the boy who cut the rubber tyre to mend

it—rolling the flàt strips with a fold of the serviette, deftly, until they turned into neat little twisted crinkled rolls— wondering how she had acquired the knack. She went on and on lazily, unable to stop, sitting back in her chair and working with outstretched arms, until a small fancy soap box was filled with the twists—enough to last the practice for a month or two. The sight filled her with a sense of achievement and zeal. Putting on its lid, she placed the soap box on the second chair. Lazily, stupidly, longing for tea—all the important clerical work left undone, Mr Orly's surgery to clear up for the day—still, she was working in the practice. She glanced approvingly at the soap box . . . but there were ages to pass before tea. She did not dare to look at her clock. Had the hall clock struck three? Bending to a drawer she drew out a strip of amadou— offended at the sight of her red wrist coming out of the harsh cheap black sleeve and the fingers bloated by cold. They looked lifeless; no one else's hands looked so lifeless. Part of the amadou was soft and warm to her touch, part hard and stringy. Cutting out a soft square, she cut it rapidly into tiny cubes, collecting them, in a pleasant flummery heap on the blotting paper—Mr Hancock should have those; they belonged to his perfect treatment of his patients; it was quite just. Cutting a strip of the harsher part, she pulled and teased it into comparative softness and cut it up into a second pile of frag- ments. Amadou, gold, and tin . . . Japanese paper? A horrible torpor possessed her. Why did one's head get into such a hot fearful state before tea? . . . grey stone wall and the side of the projecting glass-roofed peak of Mr Leyton's surgery . . . grey stone wall . . . wall . . . railings at the top of it . . . cold—a cold sky . . . it was their time—nine to six—no doubt those people did best who thought of nothing during hours but the work—cheerfully—but they were always pretending—in and *out* of work hours they pretended. There was something wrong in them and something wrong in the people who shirked. 'La—te—ta—te—te—ta,' she hummed, searching her table for relief. Mr Hancock's bell sounded and she fled up to the warmth of his room. In a moment Mudie's cart came and the maid summoned her. There was a pile of books in the hall. . . . She glanced curiously at the titles, worried with the responsibility — *The Sorrows* — that was all right. *Secrets of a Stormy Court* . . . that was the sort of thing . . . 'you can't make a silk purse out of a sow's ear' . . . one day she must explain to Mr Orly that that was really 'sousière' a thing to hold halfpence. *My Reminiscences* by Count de Something. Perhaps that was one they had put down. The maid presented the volumes to be returned. Taking them, Miriam asked her to ask Mr Hancock if he had anything to change. *Cock Lane and Common Sense* she read . . . there was some sort of argument in that . . . the 'facts' of some case . . . it would sneer at something, some popular idea . . . it was probably by some doctor or scientific man . . . but that was not the book. . . . *The Earth* . . . Émile Zola. She flapped the book open and hurriedly read a few phrases. The hall pulsated curiously. She flushed all over her body. 'There's nothing for Mr Hancock, miss.' 'All right; these can go and these are to be kept,' she said indistinctly. Wandering back to her room she repeated the phrases in her mind in French. They seemed to clear up and take shelter— somehow they were terse and acceptable and they were secret and secure—but English people ought not to read them; in English. It was — outrageous. Englishmen. The Frenchman had written them simply . . . French logic . . . Englishmen were shy and suggestive about these things—either that or breezy . . . 'filth,' which was almost worse. The Orlys ought not to read them at all . . . it was a good thing the book was out of the house . . . they would forget. But she would not forget. Her empty room glanced with a strange confused sadness; the clearing up upstairs was not quite done; but she could not go upstairs again yet. Three-fifteen; the afternoon had turned; her clock was a little slow, too. The warm, quiet, empty den was waiting for the tea-tray. Clearing the remnants from her table, she sat down again. The heavy stillness of the house closed in. . . . She opened the drawer of stationery. Various kinds of notepaper lay slid together in confusion; someone had been fumbling there. The correspondence cards propped against the side of the drawer would never stay in their proper places. With comatose meticulousness she put the whole drawer in order, replenishing it from a drawer of reserve packets, until it was so full that nothing could slide. She surveyed the result with satisfaction; and shut the drawer. She would tidy one drawer every afternoon. . . . She opened the drawer once more and looked again. To keep it like that, would mean, never using the undermost cards and notepaper. That would not do . . . change them all round sometimes. She sat for a while inertly, and presently lazily roused herself with the idea of going upstairs. Pausing in front of a long three-shelved whatnot filling the space between the door and the narrow many-drawered specimen case that stood next her table, she idly surveyed its contents. Nothing but piles of *British Dental Journals*, *Proceedings of the Odontological Society*, circulars from the dental manufacturing companies. Propping her elbows on the upper shelf of the whatnot she stood turning leaves.

'Tea up?'

'Don't know,' said Miriam irritably, passing the open door. He could see she had only just come down and could not possibly know. The soft jingling of the cups shaken together on a tray by labouring footsteps came from the basement stairs. Mr Leyton's hurried clattering increased. Miriam waited impatiently by her table. The maid padded heavily through, swinging the door of the den wide with her elbow. When she had retired, Miriam sauntered, warm and happy almost before she was inside the door, into the den. With her eyes on the tea-tray she felt the afternoon expand. . . . 'There's a Burma girl a settin' and I know she thinks of me.' . . . 'Come you *back*, you British soldier, come you *back* to Mandalay.' Godfrey's tune was much the best; stiff, like the words, the other was only singsong. Pushing off the distraction she sat down near the gently roaring blaze of the gas fire in a low little chair, upholstered in cretonne almost patternless with age. The glow of the fire went through and through her. If she had tea at once, everything would be richer and richer, but

things would move on and, if they came back, she would have
finished and would have to go.   The face of the railway clock
fixed against the frontage of the gallery at the far end of the
room said four-fifteen.   They had evidently ordered tea to be
a quarter of an hour late and might be in any minute . . . this
curious feeling that the room belonged to her more than to the
people who owned it, so that they were always intruders. . . .
Leaving with difficulty the little feast untouched . . . a
Dundee cake from Buszard's . . . she browsed rapidly, her
eyes roaming from thing to thing . . . the shields and assegais
grouped upon the raised dull gold papering of the high opposite wall, the bright beautiful coloured bead skirts spread out
amongst curious carved tusks and weapons, the large cool
placid gold Buddha reclining below them with his chin on
his hand and his elbow on a red velvet cushion, on the Japanese
cabinet; the Japanese cupboard fixed above Mrs Orly's writing
table, the fine firm carved ivory on its panels; the tall vase of
Cape gooseberries flaring on the top of the cottage piano under
the shadow of the gallery; the gallery with its upper mystery,
the happy clock fastened against its lower edge, always at something after four, the door set back in the wall, leading into her
far-away midday room, the light falling from the long high
frosted window along the confusion of Mr Orly's bench, noisy
as she looked at it with the sound of metal tools falling with a
rattle, the drone and rattle of the motor lathe, Mr Orly's cheerful hummings and whistlings.   Mr Orly's African tobacco
pouch bunched underneath the lamp on the edge of the bench
near the old leather arm-chair near to the fire, facing the assegais; the glass-doored bookcase on either side of the fireplace,
the strange smooth gold on the strips of Burmese wood fastened
along the shelves, the clear brown light of the room on the gold,
the curious lettering sweeping across the gold.

  'Tea?   Good.'

Mr Leyton pulled up a chair and plumped into it digging
at his person and dragging out the tails of his coat with one
hand, holding a rumpled newspaper at reading length.   When
his coat-tails were free he scratched his head and scrubbed
vigorously at his short brown beard.

'You had tea?' he said to Miriam's motionlessness, without looking up.

'No—let's have tea,' said Miriam. Why should he assume that she should pour out the tea. . . .

'I *say*, that's a *nasty* one,' said Mr Leyton hysterically and began reading in a high hysterical falsetto.

Miriam began pouring out. Mr Leyton finished his passage with a little giggling shriek of laughter and fumbled for bread and butter with his eyes still on the newspaper. Miriam sipped her hot tea. The room darkled in the silence. Everything intensified. She glanced impatiently at Mr Leyton's bent unconscious form. His shirt and the long straight narrow ends of his tie made a bulging curve above his low-cut waistcoat. The collar of his coat stood away from his bent neck and its tails were bunched up round his hips. His trousers were so hitched up that his bent knees strained against the harsh crude Rope Brothers cloth. The ends of his trousers peaked up in front, displaying loose rolls of black sock and the whole of his anatomical walking-shoes. Miriam heard his busily masticating jaws and dreaded his operations with his tea-cup. A wavering hand came out and found the cup and clasped it by the rim, holding it at the edge of the lifted newspaper. She busied herself with cutting stout little wedges of cake. Mr Leyton sipped, gasping after each loud quilting gulp; a gasp, and the sound of a moustache being sucked. Mr Hancock's showing-out bell rang. Mr Leyton plunged busily round, finishing his cup in a series of rapid gulps. 'Kike?' he said.

'M'm,' said Miriam, 'jolly kike—did you finish Mr Buck?'

'More or less——'

'Did you boil the remains?'

'Boiled every blessed thing—and put the serviette in k'bolic.'

Miriam hid her relief and poured him out another cup.

Mr Hancock came in through the open door and quickly up to the tea-tray. Pouring out a cup he held the teapot suspended. 'Another cup?'

'No, thanks, not just at present,' said Miriam getting to her feet with a morsel of cake in her fingers.

'Plenty of time for my things,' said Mr Hancock sitting down in Mr Orly's chair with his tea; his flat compact slightly wrinkled and square-toed patent leather shoes gleamed from under the rims of his soft, dark grey, beautifully cut trousers with a pleasant shine as he sat back comfortable and unlounging, with crossed knees in the deep chair.

Mr Leyton had got to his feet.

'Busy?' he said rapidly munching. 'I say, I've had that man Buck this afternoon.'

'Oh yes,' said Mr Hancock brushing a crumb from his knee.

'*You* know—that case I told you about.'

'Oh yes?' said Mr Hancock with a clear glance and a slight tightening of the face.

Miriam made for the door. Mr Hancock was not encouraging the topic. Mr Leyton's cup came down with a clatter. 'I'm fearfully rushed,' he said. 'I must be off.' He caught Miriam up in the hall. 'I say, tea must have been fearfully late. I've got to get down to headquarters by five *sharp*.'

'You go on first,' said Miriam standing aside.

Mr Leyton fled up through the house three steps at a time.

When she came down again intent on her second cup of tea in the empty brown den, a light had been switched on, driving the dark afternoon away. The crayon drawings behind the piano shone out on the walls of the dark square space under the gallery as she hesitated in the doorway. There was someone in the dim brightness of the room. She turned noiselessly towards her table.

'Come and have some more tea, Miss Hens'n.'

Miriam went in with alacrity. The light was on in the octagonal brass-framed lantern that hung from the skylight and shed a soft dim radiance through its old glass. Mrs Orly, still in her bonnet and fur-lined cape, was sitting drinking tea in the little old cretonne chair. She raised a tired flushed face and smiled brightly at Miriam as she came down the room.

'I 'm dying for another cup; I had to fly and clear up Mr Hancock's things.'

'Mr Hancock busy? Have some cake, it 's rather a nice one.' Mrs Orly cut a stout little wedge.

Clearing away the newspaper, Miriam took possession of Mr Leyton's chair.

Mr Orly swung in shutting the door behind him and down the room, peeling off his frock coat as he came.

'Tea, darling?'

'Well, m' love, since you're so pressing.'

Mr Orly switched on the lamp on the corner of the bench and subsided into his chair, his huge bulk poised lightly and alertly, one vast leg across the other knee.

''Scuse my shirt-sleeves, Miss Hens'n. I say, I 've got a new song—like to try it presently, or are ye too busy?'

Poised between the competing interests of many worlds, Miriam basked in the friendly tones.

'Well, I *have* got rather a fearful lot of things to do.'

'Come and try it now, d' ye mind?'

'Have your tea, Ro, darling.'

'Right, my love, right, right, always right—Hancock busy?'

'Yes; he has two more patients after this one.'

'Marvellous man.'

'Mr Hancock never gets rushed or flurried, does he? He 's always been the same ever since we 've known him.'

'He 's very even and steady, outwardly,' said Miriam indifferently.

'You think it 's only outward?'

'Well, I mean he 's really frightfully sensitive.'

'Just so; it 's his coolness carries him through, self-command, I wish I 'd got it.'

'You 'd miss other things, boysie; you can't have it both ways.'

'Right, m' love—right. I don't understand him. D' you think any one does, Miss Hens'n—really, I mean? D' you understand him?'

'Well, you see I haven't known him very long——'

'No—but you come from the same district and know his relatives.'

'The same Berkshire valley, and his cousins happened to be my people's oldest friends.'

'Well, don't ye see, that makes all the difference.—I say, I heard a splendid one this afternoon. D' you think I could tell Miss Hens'n that one, Nelly?—you 're not easily shocked, are you?'

'I 've never been shocked in my life,' said Miriam getting to her feet.

'Must ye go? Shall we just try this over?'

'Well, if it isn't too long.'

'Stop and have a bit of dinner with us, can ye?'

Miriam made her excuse, pleading an engagement, and sat down to the piano. The song was a modern ballad with an easy impressive accompaniment, following the air. The performance went off easily and well, Mr Orly's clear trained baritone ringing out persuasively into the large room. Weathering a second invitation to spend the evening, she got away to her room.

Her mind was alight with the sense of her many beckoning interests, aglow with fullness of life. The thin piercing light cast upon her table by the single five-candle-power bulb, drawn low and screened by a green glass shade, was warm and friendly. She attacked her letters, dispatching the appointments swiftly and easily in a bold convincing hand, and drafted a letter to Mrs Hermann that she carried with a glow of satisfaction to Mr Hancock's room. When his room was cleared in preparation for his last patient, it was nearly six o'clock. She began entering his day-book in the ledger. The boy coming up for the letters brought two dentures to be packed and dispatched by registered post from Vere Street before six o'clock. 'They 'll be ready by the time you 've got your boots on,' said Miriam and packed her cases brilliantly in a mood of deft-handed concentration. Jimmy clattered up the stairs as she was stamping the labels. When he fled with them, she gave a general sigh and surveyed the balance of her day with a responsible cheerful wicked desperation; her mind leaping forward to her evening. The day books would not be done, even Mr Hancock's would have to go up unentered; she had not the courage to investigate the state of the cash book; Mr Leyton's room was ready for the morning; she ran through to Mr Orly's room and performed a rapid perfunctory tidying up; many little things were left; his depleted stores must be refilled in the morning; she glanced at his appointment book, no patient so far until ten. She left the room with her everyday guilty consciousness that hardly anything in it was up to the level of Mr Hancock's room . . . look after Hancock, I'm used to fending for myself . . . but he knew she did not do her utmost to keep the room going. There were times when he ran short of stores in the midst of a sitting. That could be avoided.

When Miriam entered his room at half past six, Mr Hancock was switching off the lights about the chair. A single light shone over his desk. The fire was nearly out.

'Still here?'

'Yes,' said Miriam switching on a light over the instrument cabinet.

'I should leave those things to-night if I were you.'

'It isn't very late.'

She could go on, indefinitely, in this confident silence, preparing for the next day. He sat making up his daybook and would presently come upon Mrs Hermann's letter. As long as he was there, the day lingered. Its light had left the room. The room was colourless and dark except where the two little brilliant circles of light made bright patches of winter evening. Their two figures quietly at work meant the quiet and peace of the practice; the full, ended day, to begin again to-morrow in broad daylight in this same room. The room was full of their quiet continuous companionship. It was getting very cold. He would be going soon.

He stood up, switching off his light. 'That will do excellently,' he said with an amused smile, placing Mrs Hermann's letter on the flap of the instrument cabinet and wandering into the gloomy spaces.

'*Well.* I'll say good night.'

'Good night,' murmured Miriam.

Leaving the dried instruments in a heap with a wash-leather flung over them she gathered up the books, switched the room into darkness, felt its promise of welcome, and trotted downstairs through the quiet house. The front door shut quietly on Mr Hancock as she reached the hall. She flew to get away. In five minutes the books were in the safe and everything locked up. The little mirror on the wall, scarcely lit by the single bulb over the desk just directed the angle of her hat and showed the dim strange eager outline of her unknown face. She fled down the hall past Mr Leyton's room and the opening to the forgotten basement, between the heavy closed door of Mr Orly's room and the quiet scrolled end of the balustrade and past the angle of the high dark clock staring with its unlit face down the length of the hall, between the high oak chest and the flat oak coffer confronting each other in the glooms thrown by Mrs Orly's tall narrow striped Oriental curtains; she saw them standing in straight folds, the beautiful height and straightness of their many-coloured stripes, as they must have been before the outside stripe of each had been cut and used as a tie-up; and was out beyond the curtains in the brightly-lit square facing the door. The light fell on the rich edge of the Turkey carpet and the groove of the bicycle stand. In the corner stood the blue and white pipe, empty of umbrellas. Her hand grasped the machine-turned edge of the small flat circular knob that released the door . . . brahma; that was the word, at last. . . . The door opened and closed with its familiar heavy wooden firmness, neatly, with a little rattle of its chain. Her day scrolled up behind her. She halted, trusted and responsible, for a long second, in the light flooding the steps from behind the door.

The pavement was under her feet and the sparsely lamplit night all round her. She restrained her eager steps to a walk. The dark houses and the blackness between the lamps were elastic about her.

CHAPTER IV

WHEN she came to herself she was in the Strand. She walked
on a little and turned aside to look at a jeweller's window and
consider being in the Strand at night. Most of the shops
were still open. The traffic was still in full tide. The jeweller's
window repelled her. It was very yellow with gold, all the
objects close together and each one bearing a tiny label with
the price. There was a sort of commonness about the Strand,
not like the cheerful commonness of Oxford Street, more like
the City with its many sudden restaurants. She walked on.
But there were theatres also, linking it up with the West End,
and streets leading off it where people like Bob Greville had
chambers. It was the tailing off of the West End and the
beginning of a deep dark richness that began about Holywell.
Mysterious important churches crowded in amongst little
brown lanes . . . the little dark brown lane. . . . She
wondered what she had been thinking since she left Wimpole
Street, and whether she had come across Trafalgar Square
without seeing it or round by some other way. They were
fighting; sending out suffocation and misery into the surrounding air . . . she stopped close to the two upright
balanced threatening bodies, almost touching them. The
men looked at her. 'Don't,' she said imploringly and hurried
on trembling. . . . It occurred to her that she had not seen
fighting since a day in her childhood when she had wondered
at the swaying bodies and sickened at the thud of a fist against
a cheek. The feeling was the same to-day, the longing to
explain somehow to the men that they *could* not fight. . . .
Half-past seven. Perhaps there would not be an A.B.C. so
far down. It would be impossible to get a meal. Perhaps the
girls would have some coffee. An A.B.C. appeared suddenly
at her side, its panes misty in the cold air. She went confidently in. It seemed nearly full of men. Never mind, City

75

men; with a wisdom of their own which kept them going and
did not affect anything, all alike and thinking the same thoughts;
far away from anything she thought or knew. She walked confidently down the centre, her plaid-lined golf-cape thrown back;
her small brown boat-shaped felt hat suddenly hot on her head
in the warmth. The shop turned at a right angle showing a
large open fire with a fireguard, and a cat sitting on the hearthrug in front of it. She chose a chair at a small table in front of
the fire. The velvet settees at the sides of the room were more
comfortable. But it was for such a little while to-night, and it
was not one of her own A.B.Cs. She felt as she sat down as if
she were the guest of the City men, and ate her boiled egg and
roll and butter and drank her small coffee in that spirit, gazing
into the fire and thinking her own thoughts unresentful of the
uncongenial scraps of talk that now and again penetrated her
thoughts; the complacent laughter of the men amazed her;
their amazing unconsciousness of the things that were written
all over them.

The fire blazed into her face. She dropped her cape over
the back of her chair and sat in the glow; the small pat of
butter was not enough for the large roll. Pictures came out
of the fire, the strange moment in her room, the smashing of
the plaque, the lamplit den; Mr Orly's song, the strange, rich,
difficult day and now her untouched self here, free, unseen, and
strong, the strong world of London all round her, strong free
untouched people, in a dark lit wilderness, happy and miserable
in their own way, going about the streets looking at nothing,
thinking about no special person or thing, as long as they were
there, being in London.

Even the business people who went about intent, going to
definite places, were in the secret of London and looked free.
The expression of the collar and hair of many of them said they
had homes. But they got away from them. No one who had
never been alone in London was quite alive. . . . I'm free—
I've got free—nothing can ever alter that, she thought, gazing
wide-eyed into the fire, between fear and joy. The strange
familiar pang gave the place a sort of consecration. A strength
was piling up within her. She would go out unregretfully at

closing time and up through wonderful unknown streets, not her own streets, till she found Holborn and then up and round through the squares.

On the hall table lay a letter . . . from Alma; under the shadow of the bronze soldier leaning on his gun. Miriam gathered it up swiftly. No one knew her here . . . no past and no future . . . coming in and out unknown, in the present secret wonder. Pausing for a moment near the smeary dimly-lit marble slab, the letter out of sight, she held this consciousness. There was no sound in the house . . . its huge high thick walls held all the lodgers secure and apart, fixed in richly enclosed rooms in the heart of London; secure from all the world that was not London, flying through space, swinging along on a planet spread with continents—Londoners. Alma's handwriting, the same as it had been at school, only a little larger and firmer, broke into that. Of course Alma had answered the post card . . . it had been an impulse, a cry of triumph after years of groping about. But it was like pulling a string. Silly. And now this had happened. But it was only a touch, only a finger laid on the secret hall table that no one had seen. The letter need not be answered. Out of sight it seemed to have gone away . . . destroyed unopened it would be as if it had never come and everything would be as before. . . . Enough, more than enough without writing to Alma. An evening-paper boy was shouting raucously in the distance. The letter-box brought his voice into the hall as he passed the door. Miriam moved up on the many flights.

Upstairs, she found herself eagerly tearing open the letter. . . . 'I 've just heard from an old schoolfellow,' she heard herself saying to the girls in Kennett Street. There was something exciting in the letter . . . at the end 'Alma Wilson (officially Mrs G. Wilson)' . . . strange people in the room . . . Alma amongst them; looking out from amongst dreadfulness. *Married*. She had gone in amongst the crowd already—for ever. How clever of her . . . deceitful . . . that little spark of Alma in her must have been deceitful . . . sly, at some moment. Alma's eyes glanced at her with a new, more preoccupied and covered look . . . she used to go sometimes to theatres with large parties of people with money and the usual dresses who never thought anything about anything . . . perhaps that was part of the reason, perhaps Alma was more that than she had thought . . . marrying in the sort of way she went to theatre-parties—clever. The letter was full of excitement . . . Alma leaping up from her marriage and clutching at her . . . not really married: dancing to some tune in some usual way like all those women and jumping up in a way that fizzled and could not be kept up. . . .

'You dear old thing! . . . fell out of the sky this morning . . . to fill pages with "you dear old thing!" . . . see you at *once*! *Immediately* ! . . . come up to town and meet you . . . some sequestered tea-shop . . . our ancient heads together . . . tell you all that has happened to me since those days . . . next Thursday . . . let you know how really really rejoiced I am . . . break the very elderly fact that I am married . . . but that makes no difference. . . .' That would not be so bad—seeing Alma alone in a tea-shop in the West End; in a part of the new life, that would be all right; nothing need happen, nothing would be touched, 'all I have had the temerity to do . . .' what did that mean ?

Unpinning the buckram-stiffened black velvet band from her neck, she felt again with a rush of joy that her day was beginning and moved eagerly about amongst the strange angles and shadows of her room, the rich day all about her. Somebody had put up her little varnished oak bookshelf just in the right place, the lower shelf in a line with the little mantelpiece. When the gas bracket was swung out from the wall, the naked flame shone on the backs of the indiscriminately arranged books . . . the calf-bound Shakespeare could be read now comfortably in the immense fresh dark night under the gas flame; the Pernes' memorial edition of Tennyson. . . . She washed her face and hands in hard cold water at the little rickety washstand, yellow-grained, rich, beloved, drying them on the thin holey face towel hurriedly. Lying neatly folded amongst the confusion of oddments in a top drawer was her lace tie. Holding it out to its full length she spread it against her neck, crossed the ends at the back bringing them back round her neck to spread in a narrow flat plastron to her waist, kept in place by a brooch at the top and a pin fastened invisibly half-way down. Her face shone fresh and young above the creamy lace . . . the tie was still fairly new and crisp . . . when it had to be washed it would be limp . . . but it would go on some time just for evenings transforming her harsh black John Doble half-guinea costume into evening dress. For some moments she contemplated its pleasant continuous pattern and the way the rounded patterned ends fell just below the belt. . . .

The top-floor bell would not ring. After some hesitation, Miriam rang the house bell. The door was opened by a woman in a silk petticoat and a dressing jacket. Miriam gazed dumbly into large clear blue eyes gazing at her from a large clean clear fresh face, feathered with little soft natural curls, cut out sharply against the dark passage.

'Are you for the top?' inquired the woman in a smooth serene sleepy voice.

'Yes,' announced Miriam eagerly coming in and closing the door, her ears straining to catch the placid words spoken by the woman as she disappeared softly into a softly-lit room. She went tremulously up the dark stairs into a thick stale odour of rancid fried grease and on towards a light that glimmered from the topmost short flight of steep uncarpeted winding stairs. 'They're in,' said her thoughts with a quick warm leap. 'Hallo,' she asserted, ascending the stairs.

'Hallo,' came in response a quick challenging voice . . . a soft clear reed-like happy ring that Miriam felt to her knees while her happy feet stumbled on.

'Is that the Henderson?'

'It's me,' said Miriam, emerging on a tiny landing and going through the open door of a low-ceiled lamplit room. 'It's me, it's me,' she repeated from the middle of the floor. An eager face was turned towards her from a thicket of soft dull wavy hair. She gazed. The small slippered feet planted firmly high up against the lintel, the sweep of the red dressing-gown, the black patch of the Mudie book with its yellow label, the small ringed hand upon it, the outflung arm and hand, the little wreath of smoke about the end of the freshly lit cigarette, the cup of coffee on the little table under the lamp, the dim shapes about the room lit by the flickering blaze. . . .

Miriam smiled into the smiling steel blue of the eyes turned towards her, and waited smiling for the silver reed of tone to break again. 'I'm so glad you've come. I wanted you. Sit down and shut the door, my child. . . . I don't mind which you do first, but—do—them—both,' she tinkled, stretching luxuriously and bringing her feet to the ground with a swing.

Miriam closed the door. 'Can I take off my things?'

'Of course, child . . . take them all off; you know I admire you most draped in a towel.'

'I've got such awful feet,' said Miriam hugging the compliment as she dropped her things in a distant arm-chair.

'It's not your feet, it's your extraordinary shoes.'

'M'm.'

'How beautiful you look. You put on ties better than any one I know. I wish I could wear things draped round my neck.'

Miriam sat down in the opposite wicker chair.

'Isn't it cold?—my feet are freezing; it's raining.'

'Take off your shoes.'

Miriam got off her shoes and propped them in the fender to dry.

'What is that book?'

'Eden Phillpotts's *Children of the Mist*,' fluted the voice reverently. 'Read it?'

'No,' said Miriam expectantly.

The eager face turned to an eager profile with eyes brooding into the fire. 'He's so wonderful,' mused the voice and Miriam watched eagerly. Mag read books—for their own sake; and could judge them and compare them with other books by the same author . . . but all this wonderful knowledge made her seem wistful; knowing all about books and plays and strangely wistful and regretful; the things that made her eyes blaze and made her talk reverently, or in indignant defence, always seemed sad in the end . . . wistful hero worship . . . raving about certain writers and actors as if she did not know they were people.

'He's so wonderful,' went on the voice with its perpetual modulations, 'he gets all the atmosphere of the west country— perfectly. You *live* there while you're reading him.'

With a little chill sense of Mag in this wonderful room alone, living in the west country and herself coming in as an interruption, Miriam noted the name of the novelist in her mind . . . there was something about it, she knew she would not forget it; soft and numb with a slight clatter and hiss at the end, a rain-storm, the atmosphere of Devonshire and the mill-wheel.

'Devonshire people are all consumptive,' she said decisively.

'Are they?'

'Yes, it's the mild damp air. They have lovely complexions; like the Irish. There must be any amount of consumption in Ireland.'

'I suppose there is.'

Miriam sat silent and still watching Mag's movements as she sipped and puffed, so strangely easy and so strangely wistful in her wonderful rich Bloomsbury life—and waiting for her next remark.

'You look very happy to-night, child; what have you been doing?'

'Nothing.'

'You look as happy as a bird.'

'Are birds happy?'

'Of *course* birds are happy.'

'Well — they prey on each other — and they're often frightened.'

'How wise we are.'

Brisk steps sounded on the little stairs.

'Tell me what you have been doing.'

'Oh, I don't know. Weird things have been happening.
. . . Oh, weird things.'

'Tell your aunt at once.' Mag gathered herself together
as the brisk footsteps came into the room. 'Hoh,' said a
strong resonant voice, 'it's the Henderson. I thought as
much.'

'Yes. Doesn't she look pretty?'

'Yes—she has a beautiful lace tie.'

'I wish I could wear things like that round my neck, don't
you, von Bohlen?'

'I *do*. She can stick *anything* round her neck—and look
nice.'

'Anything; a garter or a—a *kipper*. . . .'

'Don't be so cracked.'

'She says weird things have been happening to her. I say,
I didn't make any coffee for you and the spirit lamp wants
filling.'

'Damn you—Schweinhund.'

Miriam had been gazing at the strong square figure in the
short round fur-lined cloak and sweeping velvet hat, the
firm decisive movements, and imagining the delicate pointed
high-heeled shoes. Presently those things would be off and
the door closed on the three of them.

'There's some Bass.'

'I'm going to have some suppe. Have some suppe,
Henderson.'

'Non, merci.'

'She's proud. Bring her some. What did you have for
supper, child?'

'Oh, we had an enormous lunch. They'd had a dinner-
party.'

'What did you have for supper?'

'Oh, lots of things.'

'Bring her some suppe. I'm not sure I won't have a basin
myself.'

'All right. I'll put some on.' The brisk steps went off and a voice hummed in and out of the other rooms.

Watching Mag stirring the fire, giving a last pull at her cigarette end and pushing back the hair from her face . . . silent and old and ravaged, and young and animated and powerful, Miriam blushed and beamed silently at her reiterated demands for an account of herself.

'I say, I saw an extraordinary woman downstairs.'

Mag turned sharply and put down the poker.

'Yes?'

'In a petticoat.'

'Frederika Elizabeth! She's seen the Pierson!'

'Hoh! Has she?' The brisk footsteps approached and the door was closed. The dimly shining mysteries of the room moved about Miriam, the outside darkness flowing up to the windows moved away as the tall dressing-gowned figure lowered the thin, drab, loosely rattling Venetian blinds; the light seemed to go up and distant objects became more visible; the crowded bookshelf, the dark littered table under it, the empty table pushed against the wall near the window—the bamboo bookshelf between the windows above a square mystery draped to the ground with a table cover—the little sofa behind Mag's chair, the little pictures, cattle gazing out across a bridge of snow, cattish complacent sweepy women—Albert . . . ? Moore?—the framed photographs of Dickens and Irving, the litter on the serge-draped mantelpiece in front of the mirror of the bamboo overmantel, silver candlesticks, photographs of German women and Canon Wilberforce . . . all the riches of comfortable life.

'You are late.'

'Yes, I am fearfully late.'

'Why are you late, Frederika Elizabeth von Bohlen?'

The powerful rounded square figure was in the leather arm-chair opposite the blaze, strongly moulded brown-knickered, black-stockinged legs comfortably crossed, struck firmly out between the heavy soft folds of a grey flannel dressing gown. The shoes had gone, grey woollen bedroom slippers blurred all but the shapely small ankles. Mag was lighting another

cigarette, von Bohlen was not doing needlework, the room
settled suddenly to its best rich exciting blur.

'To-night I must smoke or die.'

'*Must* you, my dear.'

'Why.'

'To-*nate*—a, ay must smoke—a, or *daye*.'

'Es ist bestimmt, in Gottes Rath.'

'Tell us what you think of the Pierson, child.'

'She was awfully nice.　Is it your landlady?'

'Yes—isn't she nice?　We think she's extraordinary—all
things considered.　You know we hadn't the least idea what
she was, when we came here.'

'What is she?'

'Well—er—you embarrass me, child, how shall we put it to
her, Jan?'

'D' you mean to say she's improper?'

'Yes—she's improper.　We hadn't the faintest notion of it
when we came.'

'How extraordinary.'

'It is extraordinary.　We're living in an improper house—
the whole street's improper, we're discovering.'

'How absolutely awful.'

'*Now* we know why Mother Cosway hinted, when we left her
her to come here, that we wanted to be free for devil's mirth.'

'How did you find out?'

'Henriette told us; you see she works for the Pierson.'

'What did she tell you?'

'Well—she told us.'

'Six,' laughed Mag, quoting towards Jan.

'Six,' trumpeted Jan, 'and if not six, seven.'

They both laughed.

'In one evening,' trumpeted Jan.

'I say, are you going to leave?'　The thought of the improper street was terrible and horrible; but they might go right
away to some other part of London.　Mag answered instantly,
but the interval had seemed long and Miriam was cold with
anxiety.

'No; we don't see why we should.'

Miriam gazed dumbly from one to the other, finding herself admiring and wondering more than ever at their independence and strength.

'You see the woman's so absolutely self-respecting.'

'Much more so than we are!'

'Out of doors she's a model of decorum and good style.'

'We're ashamed when we meet her.'

'We are. We skip into the gutter.'

'We babble and slink!'

'Indoors she's a perfect landlady. She's been awfully good to us.'

'A perfect brick!'

'She doesn't drink; she's most exquisitely clean. There's nothing whatever to—to indicate the er—nature of her profession.'

'Except that she sits at the window.'

'But she does not tire her hair and look forth.'

'Or fifth.'

'*Fool.*'

Miriam giggled.

'Really, Miriam, she *is* rather wonderful, you know. We like her.'

'Henriette is devoted to her.'

'And so apparently is her husband.'

'Her *husband*?'

'Yes—she has a husband—he appears at rare intervals—and a little girl at boarding school. She goes to see her, but the child never comes here. She tells us quite frankly that she wants to keep her out of harm's way.'

'How amazing!'

'Yes, she's extraordinary. She's Eurasian. She was born in India.'

'That accounts for a good deal. Eurasians are awful; they've got all the faults of both sides. '

'East is East and West is West and never the two shall meet.'

'Well, we like her.'

'So we have decided to ignore her little peccadillos.'

'I don't see that it's our business.   Frankly I can't see that
it has anything whatever to do with us.   Do you?'

'Well, I don't know; I don't suppose it has really.'

'What would you do in our place?'

'I don't know . . . I don't believe I should have found out.'

'I don't believe you would; but if you had?'

'I think I should have been awfully scared.'

'You would have been afraid that the sixth——'

'Or the seventh——'

'Might have wandered upstairs.'

'No; I mean the whole idea.'

'Oh; the idea. . . .'

'London, my dear Miriam, is full of ideas.'

'I will go and get the suppe.'

Jan rose; her bright head and grey shoulders went up above
the lamplight, darkening to steady massive outlines, strongly
moving as she padded and fluttered briskly out of the room.

The rich blur of the room, free of the troubling talk and the
swift conversational movements of the two, lifted and was
touched with a faint grey, a suggestion of dawn or twilight, as
if coming from the hidden windows.   Mag sat motionless in
her chair, gazing into the fire.

'. . . Wise and happy infant, I want to ask your opinion.'

Miriam roused herself and glanced steadily across.   The
outlines of things grew sharp.   She could imagine the room
in daylight and felt a faint sharp sinking; hungry.

'I'm going to state you a case.   I think you have an extraordinarily sharp sense of right and wrong.'

'Oh, *no*.'

'You have an extraordinarily sharp sense of right and wrong.
Imagine a woman.   Can you imagine a woman?'

'Go on.'

'Imagine a woman engaged to a man.   Imagine her allowing
—another man—to kiss her.'

Miriam sat thinking.   She imagined the two, the snatched
caress, the other man alone and unconscious.

'Would you call that treachery to the other person?'

'It would depend upon which she liked best.'

'That's just the difficulty.'

'*Oh!* That's awful.'

'Don't you think a kiss, just a kiss—might be—well— neither here not there?'

'Well, if it's nothing, there nothing in the whole thing. If there *is* anything—you can't talk about just kisses.'

'Dreadful Miriam.'

'Do you believe in blunted sensibilities?' How funny that Mag should have led up to that new phrase . . . but this was a case.

'You mean——'

'Whether if a sensibility is blunted it can ever grow sharp again.'

'No. I suppose that's it. How can it?'

'I don't know. I'm not sure. It's a perfectly awful idea, I think.'

'It is awful—because we are all blunting our sensibilities all the time—are we not?'

'That's just it—whether we ought.'

'Does one always know?'

'Don't you think so? There's a feeling. Yes I think one always knows.'

'Suppe, children.'

Miriam took her bowl with eager embarrassment . . . the sugar-basin, the pudding basin and the slop bowl together on a tray, the quickly produced soup—the wonderful rich life the girls lived in their glowing room—each room with a different glow. . . . Jan's narrow green clean room, with its suite and hair brushes and cosmetics and pictures of Christ, Mag's crowded shadowy little square, its litter and its many photographs, their eiderdowns and baths and hot-water bottles; the kitchen alive with eyes and foreheads—musicians, artists, philosophers pasted on the walls . . . why? Why? . . . Jan with wonderful easy knowledge of the world's great people . . . and strange curious intimate liking for them . . . the sad separate effect of all those engraved faces . . . the perfectly beautiful blur they made all together in patches on the walls . . . the sitting-room, Mag, nearly all Mag, except the photographs on the mantelpiece . . . the sight of the rooms from the top of the stairs . . . her thoughts folded down; they were not going away; not; that was certain.

'I say, I can't go on for ever eating your soup.'

'*Drink* it then for a change, my child.'

'No, but really.'

'This is special soup; there is a charge; one guinea a basin.'

'Use of room, two guineas.'

'Intellectual conversation——'

'One-and-eleven-three.'

Miriam flung out delighted admiring glances and laughed unrestrainedly. Mag's look saying 'it does not take much to keep the child amused,' took nothing from her mirthful joy. Their wit, or was it humour?—always brought the same happy shock . . . they were so funny; there was a secret in it.

'It's awfully good soup.'

'Desiccated——'

'A penny a packet.'

'Thickened with pea flour——'

'Twopence a packet.'

'Was she your favourite schoolfellow?'

Miriam's jarred mind worked eagerly. The girls thought this was a revival of some great school friendship . . . they would not be in the least jealous; they were curious and interested, but they must understand . . . they must realize that Alma was wonderful . . . something to be proud of . . . in the strange difficult scientific way; something they knew hardly anything about, Mag almost not at all, and Jan only in a general way in her neat wide education; but not in Alma's way of being rigid and reverent and personally interested about, so that every other way of looking at things made her angry. But they must understand, they must in some quite certain way be quickly made to understand at the same time that she was outside . . . an extra . . . a curious bright distant resource, nothing whatever to do with the wonderful present . . . the London life was sacred and secret, away from everything else in the world. It would disappear if one had ties outside . . . anything besides the things of holidays and week-ends that they all three had, and brought back from outside to talk about. It would be easy and exciting to meet Alma if that were clear, and to come back and tell the girls about it.

'I don't think so.'

They both looked up, stirring in their quick way, and waited.

Miriam moved her head uneasily. It was painful. They were using a sort of language . . . that was the trouble . . . your favourite flower . . . your favourite colour . . . it was just the sort of pain that came in trying to fill up confession albums. This bit of conversation would be at an end presently. Her anger would shut it up, and they would put it away without understanding, and Mag would go on to something else.

'No—I don't think she was. She was very small and pretty —petite. She had the most wonderful, limpid eyes.'

Mag was sitting forward, with her elbows on her knees and her little clasped hands sticking out into the air. A comfortable tinkling chuckle shook her shoulders. Miriam tugged and wrenched.

'I don't think she cared for me, really . . . she was an only child.'

Mag's chuckle pealed up into a little festoon of clear laughter.

'She doesn't care for you because—she's—an—only—child,' she shook out.

'One of the sheltered ones.' Jan returned to her chiffon pleats. She was making conversation. She did not care how much or how little Alma mattered.

'She 's sheltered now, anyhow—she 's married.'

'Oh—she's married. . . .'

'She 's married, is she ?'

Polite tones . . . they were not a bit surprised . . . both faces looked calm and abstracted. The room was dark and clear in the cold entanglement. It must be got over now, as if she had not mentioned Alma. She felt for her packet of

cigarettes with an uneasy face, watching Mag's firm movements as she rearranged herself and her dressing-gown in her
chair.

'How old is she?'

'About my age.'

'Oh—about nine; that's early to begin the sheltered life.'

'You can't begin the sheltered life too early; if you are going
to begin it at all.'

'Why begin it at all, Jan?'

'Well, my dear little Miriam, I think there is a good deal to
be said for the sheltered life.'

'Yes'—Mag settled more deeply into her chair, burrowing
with her shoulders and crossing her knees with a fling—'and
if you don't begin it jolly early it's too late to begin it at all. . . .'

Then Mag meant to stay always as she was . . . oh, good,
good . . . with several people interested in her . . . what a
curious worry her engagement must be . . . irrelevant . . . and
with her ideas of loyalty. 'Don't you think soh?' Irritating—
why did she do it?—what was it?—not a provincialism—some
kind of affectation as if she were on the stage. It sounded
brisk and important—soh—as if her thoughts had gone on and
she was making conversation with her lips. Why not let them,
and drop it . . . there was something waiting, always something waiting just outside the nag of conversation.

'I can't imagine anything more awful than what you call the
sheltered life,' said Miriam with a little pain in her forehead.
Perhaps they would laugh and that would finish it and something would begin.

'For us, yes. Imagine either of us coming down to it in
the morning; the regular breakfast table, the steaming coffee,
the dashes of rishers . . . dishers of rashes I mean, the eggs. . . .'

'You are alluding, I presume, to the beggs and acon.'

'Precisely. We should die.'

'Of boredom.'

'Imagine not being able to turn up on Sunday morning in
your knickers, with your hair down.'

'I love Sundays. That first cigarette over the *Referee*——'

'Is like nothing on earth.'

'Or in heaven.'

'Well, or in heaven.'

'The first cigarette anyhow, with or without the *Referee*. It's just pure absolute bliss, that first bit of Sunday morning; complete well-being and happiness.'

'While the sheltered people are flushed with breakfast-table talk——'

'Or awkward silences.'

'The deep damned silence of disillusionment.'

'And thinking about getting ready for church.'

'The men smoke.'

'Stealthily and sleepily in arm-chairs, like cats—ever seen a cat smoke?—like cats—with the wife or somebody they are tired of talking to, on the doormat—as it were—tentatively, I speak *ten*tatively . . . in a dead-alley—Dedale—Dedalus—coming into the room any minute, in Sunday clothes——'

'To stand on the hearthrug.'

'No, hanging about the room. If there's any hearthrug standing it's the men who do it, smoking blissfully alone, and trying to look weary and wise and important if any one comes in.'

'Like Cabinet ministers?'

'Yes; when they are really—er——'

'Cabinets.'

'Footstools; office stools; you never saw a sheltered woman venture on to the hearthrug, except for a second if she's short-sighted, to look at the clock.' Miriam sprang to the hearthrug and waved her cigarette. 'Con-fu-sion to the sheltered life!' The vast open of London swung, welcoming, before her eyes.

'Hoch! Hoch!'

'Banzai!'

'We certainly have our compensations.'

'Com-pen-*sa*-tions?'

'Well—for all the things we have to give up.'

'What things?'

'The things that belong to us. To our youth. Tennis, dancing—er, irresponsibility in general. . . .'

'I've never once thought about any of those things; never

once since I came to town,' said Miriam grappling with little
anxious pangs that assailed her suddenly; dimly seeing the
light on garden trees, hearing distant shouts, the sound of
rowlocks, the lapping of water against smoothing swinging
sculls. But all that life meant people, daily association with
sheltered women and complacent abominable men, there half
the time and half the time away on their own affairs which
gave them a sort of mean advantage, and money. There was
nothing really to regret. It was different for Mag. She did
not mind ordinary women. Did not know the difference; or
men.

'Yes, but anyhow. If we were in the sheltered life we
should either have done with that sort of thing and be married
—or still keeping it up and anxious about not being married.
Besides anyhow; think of the awful *people*.'

'Intolerant child.'

'Isn't she intolerant? What a good thing you met us.'

'Yes of course; but I 'm not intolerant. And look here.
Heaps of those women envy us. They envy us our freedom.
What we 're having is wanderyahre; the next best thing to
wanderyahre.'

'Women don't want wanderyahre.'

'I do, Jan.'

'So do I. I think the child's quite right there. Freedom
is life. We may be slaves all day and guttersnipes all the rest
of the time but, ach Gott, we are free.'

'What a perfectly extraordinary idea.'

'I know. But I don't see how you can get away from it,'
mused Miriam, dreamily holding out against Jan's absorbed
sewing and avoiding for a moment Mag's incredulously
speculative eyes; 'if it 's true,' she went on, the rich blur of the
warm room becoming, as she sent out her voice evenly,
thinking eagerly on, a cool clear even daylight, 'that everything
that can possibly happen does happen, then there must be,
somewhere in the universe, every possible kind of variation of
us and this room.'

'D' you mean to say,' gurgled Mag with a fling of her knickered leg and an argumentative movement of the hand that hung loosely dangling a cigarette over the fireside arm of the chair, 'that there are millions of rooms exactly like this each with one thing different—say the stem of one narcissus broken instead of whole, for instance?'

'My dear Miriam, infinitude couldn't hold them.'

'Infinitude can hold anything—of course I can see the impossibility of a single world holding all the possible variations of everything at once—but what I mean is that I can think it, and there must be something corresponding to it in life—anything that the mind can conceive is realized, somehow, all possibilities must come about, that's what I mean, I think.'

'You mean you can see, as it were in space, millions of little rooms—a little different,' choked Mag.

'Yes, I can—quite distinctly—solid—no end to them.'

'I think it's a perfectly horrible idea,' stated Jan complacently.

'It isn't—I love it and it's true . . . you go on and on and on, filling space.'

'Then space is solid.'

'It is solid. People who talk of empty space don't think . . . space is more solid than a wall . . . yes . . . more solid than a diamond—girls, I'm sure.'

'Space is full of glorious stars. . . .'

'Yes, I know, but that's such a tiny bit of it. . . .'

'Millions and trillions of miles.'

'Those are only words. Everything is words.'

'Well, you *must* use words.'

'You ought not to think in words. I mean—you can think in your brain, by imagining yourself going on and on through it, endless space.'

'You can't grasp space with your mind.'

'You don't GRASP it. You go through it.'

'I see what you mean. To me it is a fearful idea. Like eternal punishment.'

'There's no such thing as eternal punishment. The idea is too silly. It makes God a failure and a fool. It's a man's idea. The men who take the hearthrug. Sitting on a throne judging everybody and passing sentence, is a thing a man would do.'

'But humanity is wicked.'

'Then God is. You can't separate God and humanity, and that includes women who don't really believe any of those things.'

'*But*. Look at the churches. Look at women and the parsons.'

'Women like ritual and things and they like parsons, *some* parsons, because they are like women, penetrable to light, as Wilberforce said the other day, and understand women better than most men do.'

'Miriam, are you a pantheist?'

'The earth, the sea, and the sky——'

'The sun, the moon, and the stars——'

'Are not these, O soul——'

'That's the Higher Pantheism.'

'Nearer is he than breathing, closer than hands and feet. It doesn't matter what you call it.'

'If you don't accept eternal punishment, there can't be eternal happiness.'

'Oh, punishment, happiness; tweedledum, tweedledee.'

'Well—look here, there's remorse. That's deathless. It must be. If you feel remorseful about anything, the feeling must last as long as you remember the thing.'

'Remorse is real enough. I know what you mean. But it may be short-sightedness. Not seeing all round a thing. Is that Tomlinson? Or it may be cleansing you. If it were *complete*, Mag, it would *kill* you outright. I can believe that. I can believe in annihilation. I am prepared for it. I can't think why it doesn't happen to me. That's just it.'

'I should like to be annihilated.'

'Shut up, von Bohlen; you wouldn't. But look here, Miriam child, do you mean to say you think that as long as there is something that keeps on and on, fighting its way on in spite of everything, one has, well, a right to exist?'

'Well, that may be the survival of the fittest, which doesn't mean the ethically fittest as Huxley had to admit. We kill the ethically fittest at present. We killed Christ. They go to heaven. All of us who survive, have things to learn down here in hell. Perhaps this is hell. There seems something, ahead.'

'Ourselves. Rising on the ashes of our dead selves. Lord, it's midnight——'

The chill of the outside night, solitude and her cold empty room. . . .

'I'm going to bed.'

'So am I. We shall be in bed, Miriam, five minutes after you have gone.'

Jan went off for the hot-water bottles.

'All right, I'm going——' Miriam bent for her shoes. The soles were dry, scorching; they scorched her feet as she forced on the shoes; one sole cracked across as she put her foot to the ground . . . she braced the muscles of her face and said nothing. It must be forgotten before she left the room that they were nearly new and her only pair; two horrid ideas, nagging and keeping things away.

Outside in the air, daylight grew strong and clear in Miriam's mind. Patches of day came in a bright sheen from the moonlit puddles, distributed over the square. She crossed the road to the narrow pathway shadowed by the trees that ran round the long oblong enclosure. From this dark pathway the bright-ness of the wet moonlit roadway was brighter, and she could see façades that caught the moonlight. There was something trying to worry her, some little thing that did not matter at all, but that some part of her had put away to worry over and was now wanting to consider. Mag's affairs . . . no, she had decided about that. It might be true about blunted sensi-bilities; but she had meant for some reason to let that other man kiss her, and people never ask advice until they have made up their minds what they are going to do, and Mag was Mag quite apart from anything that might happen. She would still be Mag if she were old . . . or mad. That was a firm settled real thing, real and absolute in the daylight of the moonlit square. She wande.ed slowly on humming a tune; every inch of the way would be lovely. The figure of a man in an overcoat and a bowler hat loomed towards her on the narrow pathway and stopped. The man raised his hat, and his face showed smiling, with the moonlight on it. Miriam had a moment's fear; but the man's attitude was deprecating and there was her song; it was partly her own fault. But why, why . . . fierce anger at the recurrence of this kind of occurrence seized her. She wanted him out of the way and wanted him to know how angry she was at the interruption.

'Well,' she snapped angrily, coming to a standstill in the moonlit gap.

'Oh,' said the man a little breathlessly in a lame broken tone, 'I thought you were going this way.'

'So I am,' retorted Miriam in a loud angry shaking tone, 'obviously.'

The man stepped quickly into the gutter and walked quickly away across the road. St Pancras church chimed the quarter.

Miriam marched angrily forward with shaking limbs that steadied themselves very quickly . . . the night had become suddenly cold; bitter and penetrating; a north-east wind, of course. It was frightfully cold, after the warm room; the square was bleak and endless; the many façades were too far off to keep the wind away; the pavement was very cold under her right foot; that was it; the broken sole was the worry that had been trying to come up; she could walk with it; it would not matter if the weather kept dry . . . an upright gait, hurrying quickly away across the moonlit sheen; just the one she had summoned up anger and courage to challenge, was not so bad as the others . . . they were not so bad; that was not it; it was the way they got in the way . . . figures of men, dark, in dark clothes, presenting themselves, calling attention to themselves and the way they saw things, mean and suggestive, always just when things were loveliest. Couldn't the man see the look of the square and the moonlight? . . . that afternoon at Hyde Park Corner . . . just when everything flashed out after the rain . . . the sudden words

close to her ear . . . my beauty . . . my sweet . . . you
sweet girl . . . the puffy pale old face, the puffs under the
sharp brown eyes. A strange . . . *conviction* in the trembling
old voice . . . it was deliberate; a sort of statement; done on
purpose, something chosen that would please most. It was
like the conviction and statement there had been in Bob
Greville's voice. Old men seemed to have some sort of
understanding of things. If only they would talk about other
things with the same conviction as there was in their tone when
they said those personal things. But the things they said were
worldly—generalizations, like the things one read in books that
tired you out with trying to find the answer, and made books
so awful . . . things that might look true about everybody at
some time or other, and were not really true about anybody
—when you knew them. But people liked those things and
thought them clever and smiled about them. All the things
the old men said about life and themselves and other people,
about everything but oneself, were sad; disappointed and sad
with a glint of far-off youth in their faces as they said them . . .
something moving in the distance behind the blue of their eyes.
. . . 'Make the best of your youth, my dear, before it flies.'
If it all ended in sadness and envy of youth, life was simply a
silly trick. *Life* could not be a silly trick. Life cannot be a
silly trick. That is the simple truth . . . a certainty. Whatever happens, whatever things look like, life is not a trick.

Miriam began singing again when she felt herself in her own
street, clear and empty in the moonlight. The north wind
blew down it unobstructed and she was shivering and singing
. . . spring is *co*-ming a-and the *swa*-llows—have come *back*
to te-ell me *so*.' Spring could not be far off. At this moment
in the dark twilight behind the thick north wind, the squares
were green.

Her song, restrained on the doorstep and while she felt her
already well-known way in almost insupportable happiness
through the unlit hall and through the moonlight up the

seventy-five stairs, broke out again when her room was reached and her door shut; the two other doors had stood open showing empty moonlit spaces. She was still alone and unheard on the top floor. Her room was almost warm after the outside cold. The row of attic and fourth-floor windows visible from her open lattice were in darkness, or burnished blue with moonlight. Warm blue moonlight gleamed along the leads sloping down to her ink-black parapet. The room was white and blue lit, with a sweet morning of moonlight. She had a momentary impulse towards prayer, and glanced at the bed. To get so far and cast herself on her knees and hide her face in her hands against the counterpane, the bones behind the softness of her hands meeting the funny familiar round shape of her face, the dusty smell of the counterpane coming up, her face praying to her hands, her hands praying to her face, both throbbing separately with their secret, would drive something away. Something that was so close in everything in the room, so pouring in at the window that she could scarcely move from where she stood. She flung herself more deeply into her song and passed through the fresh buoyant singing air to light the gas. The room turned to its bright evening brown. *Prayer*. Being so weighed down and free with happiness was the time . . . sacrifice . . . the evening *sacrifice* of praise and prayer. That is what that means. To toss all the joys and happiness away and know that you are happy and free without anything. That you cannot escape being happy and free. It always comes.

Why am I so happy and free? she wondered, with tears in her eyes. Why? Why do lovely things and people go on happening? To *own* that something in you had no right. But not crouching on your knees . . . standing and singing till everything split with your joy and let you through into the white white brightness.

To *see* the earth whirling slowly round, coloured, its waters catching the light. She stood in the middle of the floor hurriedly discarding her clothes. They were old and worn, friendly and alive with the fresh strength of her body. Other clothes would be got somehow; just by going on and working . . . there's so much—eternally. It's stupendous. I've no right to be in it; but I'm in. Someone means me to be in. *I* can't help it. Fancy people being alive. You would think every one would go mad. She found herself in bed, sitting up in her flannellette dressing jacket. The stagnant air beneath the sharp downward slope of the ceiling was warmed by the gas. The gaslight glared beautifully over her shoulder down on to the page. . . .

All that has been said and known in the world is in *language*, in words; all we know of Christ is in Jewish words; all the dogmas of religion are words; the meaning of words change with people's thoughts. Then no one *knows* anything for certain. Everything depends upon the way a thing is put, and that is a question of some particular civilization. Culture comes through literature, which is a half-truth. People who are not cultured are isolated in barbaric darkness. The Greeks were cultured; but they are barbarians . . . why? Whether you agree or not, language is the only way of expressing anything and it dims everything. So the Bible is not true; it is a culture. Religion is wrong in making word-dogmas out of it. Christ was something. But Christianity which calls Him divine and so on, is false. It clings to words which get more and more wrong . . . then there's nothing to be afraid of and nothing to be quite sure of rejoicing about. The Christians are irritating and frightened. The man with side-whiskers understands something. But——

CHAPTER V

THEN all these years they might have been going sometimes to those lectures. Pater talking about them—telling about old Rayleigh and old Kelvin as if they were his intimates—flinging out remarks as if he wanted to talk and his audience were incapable of appreciation . . . light, heat, electricity, sound-waves; and *never* saying that members could take friends or that there were special lectures for children . . . Sir Robert Ball . . . 'a fascinating Irish fellow with the gift of the gab who made a volcano an amusing reality,' Krakatoa . . . that year of wonderful sunsets and afterglows . . . the air half round the world, full of fine dust . . . it seemed cruel . . . deprivation . . . all those years; all that wonderful knowledge, just at hand. And, now it was coming, the Royal Institution . . . this evening. She must find out whether one had to dress and exactly how one got in. Albemarle Street. . . . It all went on in *Albemarle* Street.

'We might meet,' said Mr Hancock, busily washing his hands and lifting them in the air to shake back his coat sleeves. Miriam listened from her corner behind the instrument cabinet, stupid with incredulity; he *could* not be speaking of the lecture . . . he must be . . . he had meant all the time that he was going to be with her at the lecture.

'. . . in the library, at half past eight.'

'Oh, yes,' she replied casually.

To sit hearing the very best in the intellectual life of London, the very best science there was; the inner circle suddenly open . . . the curious quiet happy laughter that went through the world with the idea of the breaking up of air and water and rays of light; the strange *love* that came suddenly to them all in the object-lesson classes at Banbury Park. That was to begin again . . . but now not only books, not the strange heavenly difficult success of showing the children the things that had been found out; but the latest newest things from the men themselves—there would be an audience, and a happy man with a lit face talking about things he had just found out. Even if one did not understand there would be that. Fancy Mr Hancock being a member and always going and not talking about it . . . at lunch. He must know an enormous number of things besides the wonders of dentistry and pottery and Japanese art.

It was education . . . a liberal education. It made up for only being able to say one was secretary to a dentist at a pound a week . . . it sounded strange at the end of twelve years of education and five months in Germany and two teaching posts —to people who could not see how wonderful it was from the inside; and the strange meaning and rightness there was; there had been a meaning in Mr Hancock from the beginning, a sort of meaning in her privilege of associating with fine rare people, so different from herself and yet coming one after another, like questions into her life, and staying until she understood . . . somebody struggled all night with the angel . . . I will not let thee go until thou bless me . . . and there was some meaning —of course, meanings everywhere . . . perhaps a person inside a life could always feel meanings . . . or perhaps only those who had moved from one experience to another could get that curious feeling of a real self that stayed the same through thing after thing.

'This is the library,' said Mr Hancock, leading Miriam along from the landing at the top of the wide red-carpeted staircase. It seemed a vast room—rooms leading one out of the other, lit with soft red lights and giving a general effect of redness, dull crimson velvet in a dull red glow and people, standing in groups and walking about—a quite new kind of people. Miriam glanced at her companion. He looked in place; he was in his right place; these were his people; people with gentle enlightened faces and keen enlightened faces. They were all alike in some way. If the room caught fire there would be no panic. They were gentle, shyly gentle or pompously gentle, but all the same and in agreement because they all knew everything, the real important difficult things. Some of them were discussing and disagreeing; many of the women's faces had questions and disagreements on them, and they were nearly all worn with thought; but they would disagree in a way that was not quarrelsome, because every one in the room was sure of the importance of the things they were discussing . . . they were all a part of science. . . . 'Science is always right and the same, religion cannot touch it or be reconciled with it, theories may modify or cancel each other, but the methods of science are one and unvarying. To question that fundamental truth is irreligious' . . . these people were that in the type of their minds —one and unvarying; always looking out at something with gentle intelligence or keen intelligence . . . this was Alma's world . . . it would be something to talk to Alma about.

There was something they were not. They were not . . . jolly. They could not be. They would never stop 'looking.' Culture and refinement; with something about it that made them quite different from the worldly people, a touch of rawness, raw school harshness about them that was unconscious of itself and could not come to life. Their shoulders and the back of the heads could never come to life. It gave them a kind of deadness that was quite unlike the deadness of the worldly people, not nearly so dreadful—rather funny and likeable. One could imagine them all washing, very carefully, in an abstracted way, still looking and thinking, and always with the advancement of science on their minds; never really aware of anything behind or around them because of the wonders of science. Seeing these people changed science a little. They were almost something tremendous; but not quite.

'That's old Huggins,' murmured Mr Hancock, giving Miriam's arm a gentle nudge as a white-haired old man passed close by them with an old woman at his side, with short white hair, exactly like him. 'The man who invented spectrum analysis—and that's his wife; they're both great fishermen.' Miriam gazed. *There*, was the splendid thing. . . . In her mind blazed the coloured bars of the spectrum. In the room was the light of the beauty, the startling *life* these two old people shed from every part of their persons. The room blazed in the light they shed. She stood staring, moving to watch their gentle living movements. They moved as though the air through which they moved was a living medium—as though everything were alive all round them—in a sort of hushed vitality. They were young. She felt she had never seen any one so young. She longed to confront them just once, to stand for a moment the tide in which they lived.

'*Ah*, Meesturra Hancock—you *are* a faceful votary.'

That's German, thought Miriam, as the flattering, deep, caressing gutturals rebounded dreadfully from her startled consciousness. What a determined intrusion. How did he come to know such a person? Glancing she met a pair of swiftly calculating eyes fixed full on her face. There was fuzzy black hair lifted back from an anxious, yellowish, pre-occupied little face. Under the face came the high collar-band of a tightly-fitting, dark claret-coloured ribbed silk bodice, fastened from the neck to the end of the pointed peak by a row of small round German buttons, closely decorated with a gilded pattern. Mr Hancock was smiling an indulgent, depre-cating smile. He made an introduction and Miriam felt her hand tightly clasped and held by a small compelling hand, while she sought for an answer to a challenge as to her interest in science. 'I don't really know anything about it,' she said vaguely, strongly urged to display her knowledge of German. The eyes were removed from her face and the little lady, boldly planted and gazing about her, made announcements to Mr Hancock—about the fascinating subject of the lecture and her hopes of a large and appreciative audience.

What did she want? She could not possibly fail to see that Mr Hancock was telling her that he could see through her social insincerities. It was dreadful to find that even here there were social insincerities. She was like a busy ambassador for things that belonged somewhere else, and that he was laughing at in an indulgent, deprecating way that must make her blaze with an anger that she did not show. Looking at her, as her eyes and mouth made and fired their busy sentences, Miriam suddenly felt that it would be easy to deal with her, take her into a corner and talk about German things, food and love affairs and poetry and music. But she would always be breaking away to make a determined intrusion on somebody she knew. She could not really know any English person. What was she doing, bearing herself so easily in the inner circle of English science? Treating people as if she knew all about them and they were all alike. How surprised she must often be, and puzzled.

'That was Miss Teresa Szigmondy,' said Mr Hancock, reproducing his amused smile as they took their seats in the dark theatre.

'Is she German?'

'Well . . . I think, as a matter of fact, she's part Austro-Hungarian and part—well, *Hebrew*.' A Jewess . . . Miriam left her surroundings, pondering over a sudden little thread of memory. An eager, very bright-eyed, curiously dimpling school-girl face peering into hers, and a whispering voice— 'D' you know why we don't go down to prayers? 'Cus we're *Jews*'—they had always been late; fresh-faced and shiny-haired and untidy and late, and clever in a strange brisk way, and talkative and easy and popular with the teachers. . . . Their guttural voices ringing out about the stairs and passages, deep and loud and stronger than any of the voices of the other girls. The Hyamson girls—they had been foreigners, like the Siggs and the de Bevers, but different . . . what was the difference in a Jew? Mr Hancock seemed to think it was a sort of disgraceful joke . . . what was it? Max Sonnenheim had been a Jew, of course, the same voice. Banbury Park 'full of Jews' . . . the Brooms said that in patient contemptuous voices. But what *was* it? What did everybody mean about them?

'Is she scientific?'

'She seems to be interested in science,' smiled Mr Hancock.

'How funny of her to ask me to go to tea with her, just because you told her I knew German.'

'Well, you go; if you 're interested in seeing notabilities, you 'll meet all kinds of wonderful people at her house. She knows everybody. She's the niece of a great Hungarian poet. I believe he 's to be seen there sometimes. They 're all coming in now.' Mr Hancock named the great names of science one by one as the shyly gentle and the pompously gentle little old men ambled and marched into the well of the theatre and took their seats in rows at either end of the central green table.

'*There*'s a pretty lady,' said Mr Hancock, conversationally, just as the light was lowered. Miriam glanced across the half-circle of faintly shining faces and saw an effect, a smoothly coiffured head and smooth neck and shoulders draped by a low deep circular flounce of lace rising from the gloom of a dark dress, sweep in through a side door, bending and swaying—'or a pretty dress at any rate'—and sat through the first minutes of the lecture, recalling the bearing and manner of the figure, with sad fierce bitterness. Mr Hancock admired 'feminine' women . . . or at any rate he was bored by her own heavy silence, and driven into random speech by the sudden dip and sweep of the lace appearing in the light of the doorway. He was surprised, himself, by his sudden speech and half corrected it . . . 'or a pretty dress.' . . . But anyhow he, even he, was one of those men who do not know that an effect like that was just an effect, a deliberate 'charming' feminine effect. But if he did not know that, did not know that it was a trick and the whole advertising manner, the delicate, plunging fall of the feet down the steps—'I am late; look how nicely and quietly I am doing it; look at me being late and apologetic and interested'— out of place in the circumstances, then what was he doing here at all? Did he *want* science, or would he really rather be in a drawing-room with 'pretty ladies' advertising effects and being 'arch' in a polite, dignified, lady-like manner? How dingy and dull and unromantic and unfeminine he must find her. She sat in a lively misery, following the whirling circle of thoughts round and round, stabbed by their dull thorns, and trying to drag her pain-darkened mind to meet the claim of the platform, where, in a square of clear light, a little figure stood talking eagerly and quietly in careful slow English. Presently the voice of the platform won her—clear and with its curious, even, unaccented rat-tat-tat flowing and modulated with pure passion, the thrill of truth and revelation running alive and life-giving through every word. That, at least, she was sharing with her companion . . . 'development-in-thee-method-of-in-taircepting-thee-light.' 'Daguerre' . . . a little Frenchman, stopping the sunlight, breaking it up, making it paint faces in filmy black and white on a glass. . . . There would only be a few women like the one with the frill in an audience like this . . . 'women will talk shamelessly at a concert or an opera, and chatter on a mountain top in the presence of a magnificent panorama; their paganism is incurable.' Then men mustn't stare at them, and treat them as works of art. It was entirely the fault of men . . . perfectly reasonable that the women who got that sort of admiration from men should assert themselves in the presence of other works of art. The thing men called the noblest work of God must be bigger than the work by a man. Men plumed themselves and talked in a clever expert way about women and never thought of their own share in the way those women went on . . . unfair, unfair; men were stupid complacent idiots. But they were wonderful with their brains. The life and air and fresh breath coming up from the platform amongst the miseries and uncertainties lurking in the audience, was a man . . . waves of light which would rush through the film at an enormous speed and get away into space without leaving any impression, were stopped by some special kind of film and went surging up and down in confinement—making strata . . . 'supairposeetion of strata' . . . no Englishman could move his hands with that smoothness, making you see. 'Violet subchloride of silver.' That would interest Mr Hancock's chemistry. She glanced at the figure sitting very still, with bent head, at her side. He was asleep. Her thoughts recoiled from the platform and bent inwards, circling on their miseries. That was the end, for him, of coming to a lecture, with her. If she had been the frilled lady, sitting forward with her for-ward-falling frill, patronizing the lecture and 'exhibiting' her interest, he would not have gone to sleep.

When the colour photographs came, Miriam was too happy for thought. Pictures of stained glass, hard crude clear brilliant opaque flat colour, stood in miraculous squares on the screen, and pieces of gardens, grass and flowers and trees, shining with a shadeless blinding brilliance.

She made vague sounds. 'It's a wonderful achievement,' said Mr Hancock, smiling with grave delighted approval to-wards the screen. Miriam felt that he understood, as her ignorance could not do, exactly what it all meant scientifically; but there was something else in the things as they stood, blinding, there, that he did not see. It was something that she had seen somewhere, often.

'They 'll never touch pictures.'

'Oh, no—there's no atmosphere; but there's something else; they 're exactly like something else. . . .'

Mr Hancock laughed, a little final crushing laugh, and turned away sceptical of further enlightenment.

Miriam sat silent, busily searching for something to express the effect she felt. But she could not tell him what she felt. There was something in this intense hard rich colour like some-thing one sometimes *saw* when it wasn't there, a sudden brightening and brightening of all colours till you felt some-thing must break if they grew any brighter—or in the dark, or in one's mind, suddenly, at any time, unearthly brilliance. He would laugh and think one a little insane; but it was the real certain thing; the one real certain happy thing. And he would not have patience to hear her try to explain; and by that he robbed her of the power of trying to explain. He was not interested in what she thought. Not interested. His own thoughts were statements, things that had been agreed upon and disputed and that people bandied about, competing with each other to put them cleverly. They were not *things*. It was only by pretending to be interested in these statements and taking sides about them that she could have conversation with him. He liked women who thought in these statements. They always succeeded with men. They had a reputation for wit. Did they really think and take an interest in the things they said, or was it a trick, like 'clothes' and 'manners'—or was it that the women brought up with brothers or living with husbands, got into that way of thinking and speaking? Perhaps there was something in it. Something worth cultivating; a fine talent. But it would mean hiding so much, letting so much go; all the real things. The things men never seemed to know about at all. Yet he loved beautiful things; and worried about religion and had found comfort in *Literature and Dogma*, and wanted her to find comfort in it, assuming her difficulties were the same as his own; and knowing the dreadfulness of them. The brilliant unearthly pictures remained in her mind, supporting her through the trial of her consciousness of the stuffiness of her one long-worn dress. Dresses should be fragrant in the evening. The Newlands evening dress was too old-fashioned. Things had changed so utterly since last year. There was no money to have it altered. But this was awful. Never again could she go out in the evening, unless alone or with the girls. That would be best, and happiest, really.

CHAPTER VI

MIRIAM sat on a damp wooden seat at the station. Shivering with exhaustion, she looked across at the early morning distance, misty black and faint misty green. . . . Something had happened to it. It was not beautiful; or anything. It was not anything. . . . That was the punishment. . . . The landscape was dead. All that had come to an end. Her nimble lifeless mind noted the fact. There was dismay in it. Staring at the landscape she felt the lifelessness of her face; as if something had brushed across it and swept the life away, leaving her only sight. She could never feel any more.

Behind her fixed eyes, something new seemed moving forward with a strange indifference. Suddenly the landscape unrolled. The rim of the horizon was no longer the edge of the world. She lost sight of it in the rolling out of the landscape in her mind, out and out, in a light easy stretch, showing towns and open country and towns again, seas and continents on and on; empty and still. *No*thing. Everywhere in the world, nothing. She drifted back to herself and clung, bracing herself. She was somebody. If she were somebody who was going to do something . . . not roll trolleys along a platform. The train swept busily into the landscape; the black engine, the brown, white-panelled carriages, warm and alive in the empty landscape. Her strained nerves relaxed. In a moment she would be inside it, being carried back into her own world. She felt eagerly forward towards it. Heartsease was there. She would be able to breathe again. But not in the same way; unless she could forget. There were other eyes looking at it. They were inside her; not caring for the things she had cared for, dragging her away from them.

They are not my sort of people. Alma does not care for me, personally. Little cries and excitement and affection.

She wants to; but she does not care for any one, personally.
Neither of them do. They live in a world . . . 'Michael
Angelo' and 'Stevenson' and 'Hardy' and 'Dürer' and that
other man . . . Alma . . . popping and sweeping gracefully
about with little cries and clever sayings and laughter, trying
to be real; in a bright outside way, showing all the inside
things because she kept crushing them down. It was so
tiring that one could not like being with her. She seemed
to be carrying something off all the time; and to be as if
she were afraid if the talk stopped for a moment, it would
be revealed.

In the tea-shop with Alma alone it had been different; all the
old school-days coming back as she sat there. Her eager story.
It was impossible to do anything but hold her hands and admire
her bravery and say you did not care. But it was not quite
real; it was too excited and it was wrong, certainly wrong, to go
down not really caring. I need not go down again.

Cold and torpid she got up and stepped into an empty
carriage. Both windows were shut and the dry stuffy air
seemed almost warm after her exposure. She let one down
a little; sheltered from the damp the little stream of outside
air was welcome and refreshing. She breathed deeply, safe,
shut in and moving on. With an unnecessarily vigorous swing
of her arms, she hoisted her pilgrim basket on to the rack. Of
course, she murmured smiling, of *course* I shall go down again
. . . ra*ther*.

That extraordinary ending of fear of the great man at the
station. Alma and the little fair square man not much taller
than herself, looking like a grocer's assistant with a curious,
kind, confidential . . . unprejudiced eye . . . they had come,
both of them, out of their house to the station to meet her . . .
'this is Hypo' and the quiet shy walk to the house, he asking
questions by saying them—statements. You caught the elusive
three-fifteen. This is your bag. We can carry it off without

waiting for the . . . British porter. You 've done your
journey brilliantly. We haven't far to walk.

The strange shock of the bedroom, the strange new thing
springing out from it . . . the clear soft bright tones, the
bright white light streaming through the clear muslin, the
freshness of the walls . . . the flattened dumpy shapes of
dark green bedroom crockery gleaming in a corner; the little
green bowl standing in the middle of the white spread of the
dressing-table cover . . . wild violets with green leaves and
tendrils put there by somebody, with each leaf and blossom
standing separate . . . touching your heart; joy, looking from
the speaking pale mauve little flowers to the curved rim of the
green bowl and away to the green crockery in the corner;
again and again the fresh shock of the violets . . . the little
cold change in the room after the books, strange fresh bindings
and fascinating odd shapes and sizes, gave out their names
. . . *The White Boat—Praxiter—King Chance—Mrs Prendergast's Palings* . . . the promise of them in their tilted
wooden case by the bedside table from every part of the room,
their unchanged names, the chill of the strange sentences inside
like a sort of code written for people who understood, written
at something, clever raised voices in a cold world. In *Mrs
Prendergast's Palings* there were cockney conversations spelt
as they were spoken. None of the books were about ordinary
people . . . three men, seamen, alone, getting swamped in a
boat in shallow water in sight of land . . . a man, and a
girl he had no right to be with, wandering on the sands, the
cold wash and sob of the sea; her sudden cold salt tears; the
warmth of her shuddering body. *Praxiter* beginning without
telling you anything, about the thoughts of an irritating contemptuous superior man, talking at the expense of everybody.
Nothing in any of them about anything one knew or felt;
casting you off . . . giving a chill ache to the room. To sit
. . . alone, reading in the white light, amongst the fresh
colours—but not these books. To go downstairs was a sacrifice: coming back, there would be the lighting of the copper

candlestick, twisting beautifully up from its stout stem. What made it different from ordinary candlesticks? *What?* It was like . . . a gesture.

'You knew Susan at school.' The brown, tweed-covered arm of the little square figure handed a tea-cup. The high, huskily hooting voice . . . what was the overwhelming impression? A common voice, with a cockney twang. Overwhelming. 'What was Susan like at school?' The voice was saying two things; that was it; doing something deliberately; it was shy and determined, and deliberate and expectant. Miriam glanced incredulously, summoning all her forces against her sense of strange direct attack, pushing through and out to some unknown place, dreading her first words, not taking in a further remark of the live voice. She could get up and go away for ever; or speak, and whatever she spoke would keep her there for ever. Alma, sitting behind the tea-tray in a green Alma dress with small muslin cuffs and collars, had betrayed her into this. Alma had been got by this and had brought her to the test of it. The brown walls, brown paper all over, like parcel paper, and Japanese prints; nothing else, high-backed curious-shaped wooden chairs all with gestures, like the candlestick, and the voice that was in the same difficult, different world as the books upstairs. . . . Alma had betrayed her, talking as if they were like other people and not saying anything about this strange cold difference. Alma had come to it and was playing some part she had taken up . . . there was some wrong hurried rush somewhere within the beautiful room. Stop, she wanted to say, you 're all wrong. You 've dropped something you don't know anything about, deliberately. Alma ought to have told you. Hasn't she told you?

'Alma hasn't changed,' she said, desperately questioning the smooth soft movements of the smooth soft hands, the quiet controlled pose of the head. Alma had the same birdlike wide blink and flash of her limpid brown eyes, the same tight crinkle and snicker when she laughed, the same way of saying nothing, or only the clever superficially true things men said. Alma had agreed with this man and had told him nothing, or only things in the clever way he would admire.

He made little sounds into his handkerchief. He was nonplussed at a dull answer. It would be necessary to be brilliant and amusing to hold his attention—in fact to tell lies. To get on here, one would have to say clever things in a high bright voice.

The little man began making statements about Alma. Sitting back in his high-backed chair, with his head bent and his fine hands clasping his large handkerchief, he made little short statements, each improving on the one before it and coming out of it, and little subdued snortings at the back of his nose in the pauses between his sentences as if he were afraid of being answered or interrupted before he developed the next thing. Alma accompanied his discourse with increasing snickerings. Miriam, after eagerly watching the curious mouthing half hidden by the drooping straggle of moustache and the strange, concentrated gleam of the grey-blue eyes staring into space, laughed outright. But how could he speak so of her? He met the laughter with a minatory outstretched forefinger, and raised his voice to a soft squeal ending, as he launched with a little throw of the hand his final jest, in a rotund crackle of high hysterical open-mouthed laughter. The door opened and two tall people were shown in; a woman with a narrow figure and a long, dark-curtained, sallow, horse-like face, dressed in a black-striped cream serge coat and skirt, and a fair florid troubled fickle smiling man in a Norfolk tweed and pale blue tie. 'Hullo,' said the little man propelling himself out of his chair with a neat swift gesture, and standing small and square in the room making cordial sounds and moving his arms about as if to introduce and seat his guests without words and formalities. Alma's thin excited hubbub and the clearly enunciated, obviously prepared facetiousnesses of the newcomers—his large and tenor and florid . . . a less clever man than Mr Wilson . . . and hers bass and crisp and contemptuous . . . nothing was hidden from her; she would *like* the queer odd people who went about at Tansley Street—

was broken into by the entry of three small young men, all three dark and a little grubby and shabby looking. The foremost stood with vivid, eager eyes, wide open, as if he had been suddenly checked in the midst of imparting an important piece of news. Alma came forward to where they stood herded and silent just inside the door, and made little faint encouraging maternal sounds at them as she shook hands.

As she did this, Miriam figured them in a flash coming down the road to the house; their young men's talk and arguments, their certainty of rightness and completeness, their sudden embarrassment and secret anger with their precipitate rescuer. Mr Wilson was on his feet again, not looking at them nor breaking up the circle already made, but again making his sociable sounds and circular movements with his arms as if to introduce and distribute them about the room. The husband and wife kept on a dialogue in strained social voices as if they were bent on showing that their performance was not dependent on an audience. Miriam averted her eyes from them, overcome by painful visions of the two at breakfast, or going home after social occasions. The three young men retreated to the window alcove behind the tea-table, one of them becoming Miriam's neighbour as she sat in the corner near the piano, whither she had fled from the centre of the room when the husband and wife came in.

It was the young man with the important piece of news. He sat bent forward, holding his cup and plate with outstretched arms. His headlong expression remained unchanged. Wisps of black hair stood eagerly out from his head, and a heavy thatch fell nearly to his eyebrows. 'Did anybody see anything of Mrs Binks at the station?' asked Alma from her table. 'Oh, my dear,' she squealed gently as the maid ushered in a little lady in a straight dress of red flannel, frilled with black chiffon at the neck and wrists, 'we were all afraid you weren't coming.' 'Don't anybody move'—the deep reedy voice reverberated amongst the standing figures; the firm compact undulating figure came across the room to Alma. Its light-footed swiftness and easy certainty filled Miriam with envy. The envy evaporated during the embracing of Alma

and the general handshaking. The low strong reedy voice
went on saying things out into the silence of the room in a
steady complete way. There was something behind it all that
did not show, or showed in the brilliant ease, something that
Miriam did not envy. She tried to discover what it was as the
room settled, leaving Mrs Binkley on a low chair near to Alma,
taking tea and going on with her monologue, each of her pauses
punctuated by soft appreciative sounds from Alma and little
sounds from Mr Wilson. She was popular with them. Mr
Wilson sat surveying her. Did they know how hard she was
working? Perhaps they did, and admired or even envied it.
But what was it for? Surely she must feel the opposition in
the room? Alma and Mr Wilson approved and encouraged
her exhibition. She was in their curious league for keeping
going high-voiced clever sayings. So had the husband appeared to be, at first. Now he sat silent with a kind polite
expression about his head and figure. But his mouth was
uneasy, he was afraid of something or somebody and was
staring at Mrs Binkley. The wife sat in a gloomy abstraction
smoking a large cigarette . . . she was something like Mrs
Kronen, in her way; only instead of belonging to South
Africa she had been a hard-featured English schoolgirl; she
was still a hard-featured English schoolgirl, with the oldest
eyes Miriam had ever seen.

'Why not write an article about a lamp-post?' said one of
the young men suddenly, in a gruff voice, in answer to a
gradually growing murmur of communications from one of his
companions. Miriam breathed easier air. The shameful irritating tension was over. It was as if fresh wonderful life-
giving things that were hovering in the room, driven back into
corners, pressing up and away against the angles of the ceiling
and about the window-door behind the young men and against
the far-away door of the room, came back, flooding all the
spaces of the room. Mr Wilson moved in his chair, using his
handkerchief towards the young men with an eye on the speaker.
'Or a whole book,' murmured the young man farthest from
Miriam, in an eager cockney voice. The two young men were
speaking towards Mr Wilson, obviously trying to draw him

in bringing along one of his topics; something that had been
discussed here before. There would be talk, men's talk,
argument and showing off; but there would be something
alive in the room. In the conflict there would be ideas,
wrong ideas, men taking sides, both right and both wrong;
men showing off; but wanting with all their wrongness to
get at something. Perhaps somebody would say something.
She regretted her shy refusal of a cigarette from Mr Wilson's
large full box. It stood open now by the side of the tea-tray.
He would not offer it again. Cigarettes and talk. . . . What
would Mr Hancock think? 'People do not meet together for
conversation, nowadays.' . . . There was going to be conversation, literary conversation, and she was going to hear it
. . . be in it. Clever literary people trying to say things well;
of course they were all literary; they were all the same set,
knowing each other, all calling Mr Wilson 'Hypo'; talk about
books was the usual Saturday afternoon thing here; and she
was in it and would be able to be in it again, any week. It
was miraculous. All these people were special people, emanci-
pated people. Probably they all wrote, except the women.
There were too many women. Somehow or other she must
get a cigarette. Life, suddenly full of new things made her
bold. Presently, when the conversation was general she
would beg one of the young man at her side. Mr Wilson
would not turn to her again. She had failed twice already in
relation to him; but after her lame refusal of a cigarette, which
he had accepted instantly and sat down with, he had glanced
sharply at her in a curious personal way, noticing the little
flat square of white collarette—the knot of violets upon it, the
long-sleeved black nun's-veiling blouse, the long skirt of her
old silkette evening dress. These items had made her sick
with anxiety in their separate poverty as she put them on for
the visit; but his eyes seemed to draw them all together.
Perhaps there in the dark corner they made a sort of whole.
She rejoiced gratefully in the memory of Mag's factory girl,
in her own idea of having the sleeves gauged at the wrists in
defiance of fashion, to make frills extending so as partly to
cover her large hands; over the suddenly realized possibility of

wearing the silkette skirt as a day skirt. She must remain in the corner, not moving, all the afternoon. If she moved in the room the bright light would show the scrappiness of her clothes. In the evening it would be all right. She sat back in her corner, happy, and forgetful. She had not had so much tea as she wanted. She had refused the cigarette against her will. Now she was alive. These weak things would not happen again, and the next time she would bring her own cigarettes. To take out a cigarette and light it here, at home amongst her own people. These were her people. There was something here in the exciting air that she did not understand; something that was going to tax her more than she had ever been taxed before. She had found her way to it through her wanderings; it had come; it was her due. It corresponded to something in herself, shapeless and inexpressible; but there. She knew it by herself, sitting in her corner; her own people would know it, if they could see her here; but no one here would find it out. Every one here was doing something; or the wife of somebody who did something. They were like a sort of secret society . . . all agreed about something . . . about what? *What* was it Mr Wilson was so sure about? . . . They would despise everybody who was living an ordinary life, or earning a living in anything but something to do with books. Seeing her here, they would take for granted that she, too, was somebody . . . and she was, somehow, within herself somewhere; although she had made herself into a dentist's secretary. She was better qualified to be here and to understand the strange secret here, in the end, than any one else she knew. But it was a false position, unless they all knew what she was. If she could say clever things they would like her; but she would be like Alma and Mrs Binkley; pretending; and without any man to point to as giving her the right to be about here. It was a false position. It was as if she were here as a candidate to become an Alma or a Mrs Binkley; imitating the clever sayings of men, or flattering them.

'*Do* it, Gowry,' said Mr Wilson . . . 'a book' . . . he made his little sound behind his nose as he felt for the phrases that were to come after his next words . . . 'a—er—book; about a

lamp-post. You see,' he held up his minatory finger to keep
off an onslaught, and quench an eager monologue that began
pouring from Miriam's nearest neighbour, and went on in
his high weak husky voice. The young men were quiet.
For a few moments the red lady and Alma made bright conversation as if nothing were happening; but with a curious hard
emptiness in their voices, like people rehearsing and secretly
angry with each other. Then they were silent, sitting posed
and attentive, with uneasy intelligent smiling faces; their
costumes and carefully arranged hair useless on their hands.
Mrs Binkley did not suffer so much as Alma; her corsetless
eager crouch gave her the appearance of intentness, her hair
waved naturally, had tendrils and could be left to look after
itself; her fresh easy strength was ready for the next opportunity. It was only something behind her face that belied her
happy pose. Alma was waiting in some curious fixed single-
ness of tension; her responses hovered fixed about her mouth,
waiting for expression, she sat fixed in a frozen suspension of
deliberate amiability and approval, approval of a certain chosen
set of things; approval which excluded everything else with
derision . . . it was Alma's old derision, fixed and arranged
in some way by Mr Wilson.

'There will be books—with all that cut out—him and her—
all that sort of thing. The books of the future will be clear of
all that,' he was saying.

Miriam sat so enclosed in her unarmed struggle with this
new definition of a book, that the entry of the newcomers left
her unembarrassed. Two rotund ruddy men in mud-spotted
tweeds, both fair, one with a crest like a cockatoo standing
straight up from his forehead above a smooth pink face, the
other older than anybody in the room, with a shaggy head and
a small pointed beard. They came in talking aloud, and
stumped about the room, making their greetings. Miriam
bowed twice and twice received a sturdy handclasp and the
kindly gleam of blue eyes, one pair large, mild, and owl-like

behind glasses; the other fierce and glinting, a shaft of whimsical blue light. The second pair of eyes surely would not agree with what Mr Wilson had been saying. But their coming in had broken a charm; the overwhelming charm of the way he put things; so that even while you hated what he was saying, and his way of stating things as if they were the final gospel and no one else in the world knew anything at all, you wanted him to go on; only to go on and to keep on going on. It was wrong somehow; he was all wrong; 'though I speak with the tongues of men and of angels'; it was wrong and somehow wicked; but it caught you, it had caught Alma and all these people; and in a sense he despised them all, and was talking to something else; the thing he knew; the secret that made him so strong, even with his weak voice and weak mouth; strong and fascinating. It was wrong to be here; it would be wrong to come again; but there was nothing like it anywhere else; no other such group of things; and thought and knowledge of things. More must be heard. It would be impossible not to risk everything to hear more.

Alma ordered fresh tea; Mr Wilson and the husband and the two new men were standing about. The elder man was describing, in a large shouting voice, a new mantelpiece—a Tudor mantelpiece. What was a Tudor mantelpiece? . . . to buy a *house* to put round it. What a clever idea. . . . Little Mr Wilson seemed to be listening; he squealed amendments of the jests between the big man's boomings . . . buy a *town* to put round it. . . . What a lovely idea . . . buy a NATION to put round it . . . there was a burst of guffaws. Mr Wilson's face was crimson; his eyes appeared to be full of tears. The big man went on. Mrs Binkley kept uttering deep reedy caressing laughs. Two of the young men were leaning forward talking eagerly with bent heads. Miriam's neighbour sat upright with his hands on his knees, his eyes glaring as if . . . as if he were just going to jump out of his skin. Hidden by the increased stir made by the re-entry of the maid, and encouraged by the extraordinary clamour of hilarious voices, Miriam ventured to ask him if he would perform an act of charity by allowing her to rob him of one of his cigarettes. She liked her unrecognizable voice. It was pitched deep, but strong; a little like Mrs Binkley's. The young man started and turned eagerly towards her, stammering and muttering and fumbling about his person. 'I swear,' he brought out, 'I could cut my throat . . . my *God* . . . oh, here we are.' Seizing the open box from the tea-table he swung round with his crossed legs extended across her corner so that she was cut off from the rest of the room, and held the box eagerly towards her. They both took cigarettes and he lit them with matches obtained from his neighbour. 'Thank you,' said Miriam blissfully drawing 'that has saved my life.' Precipitately restoring the matches he swung round again leaning forward with his elbow on his knee, blocking out Miriam's view. Before it was blocked, she had caught the eye of Mr Wilson who was standing facing her in the little group of men about the tea-table and still interpolating their hubbub with husky squeals of jocularity, quietly observing the drama in her corner. For the moment she did not wish to listen; Alma's appreciative squeals were getting strained and the big man was a bore. Seen sitting in profile taking his tea, he reminded her of Mr Staple-Craven; her eye caught and recoiled from weak patches, touches of frowsy softness here and there about the shaggy head. Cut off from the room, safe in the extraordinary preoccupation of the young man whose eager brooding was moving now towards some tremendous communication—she had undisturbed knowledge of what she had done. Speech and action had launched her, for good or ill, into the strange tide running in this house. Its cold waters beat against her breast. She was no longer quite herself. There was something in it that quickened all her faculties, challenged all the strength she possessed. By speech and action she had accepted something she neither liked, nor approved nor understood; refusal would have left its secret unplumbed, standing aside in her life, tormenting it. The sense of the secret intoxicated her . . . perhaps I am selling my soul to the devil. But she was glad that Mr Wilson had witnessed her launching.

'You are magnificent,' gasped the young man glaring at the wall. 'I mean you are simply magnificent.' He flashed unconscious eyes at her—*he* had no consciousness of the cold tide with its curious touch of evil; it was hand in hand with him and his simplicity that she had stepped down into the water—and hurried on. 'An angel of dreams. Dreams . . . you know—I say,' he spluttered incoherently, 'I *must* tell you.' His working, preoccupied face turned to face hers with a jerk that brought part of the heavy sheaf of hair across one of his eyes. 'I 've been doing the best work this week I ever did in my life!' Red flooded the whole of his face and the far-away glare of his one visible eye became a blaze of light, near, and smiling a guilty delighted smile. He was demanding *her* approval, *her* sympathy, just on the strength of her being there. It was a moment of consenting to Alma that had brought this. However it had come, she would have been unable to withstand it. He wanted approval and sympathy; someone here had some time or other shut him up; perhaps he was considered second-rate, perhaps he was second-rate; but he was innocent as no one else in the room was innocent. '*Oh*, I *am* glad,' she replied swiftly. Putting his cigarette on the edge of the piano he seized one of her hands and crushed it between his own. His face perspired and there were tears in his eye. '*Do* tell me about it,' she said with bold uneasy eagerness, hoping he would drop her hand when he spoke. 'It 's a play,' he shouted in a low whisper, a spray of saliva springing through his lips, 'a play—it 's the finest stuff I ever rout.' Were all these people either cockney or with that very bland Anglican cultured way of speaking—like the husband and the man with the Tudor mantelpiece?

'I can of course admit that the growth of corn was, at first, accidental and unconscious, and that even after the succession of processes began to be grasped and the soil methodically cultivated, the success of the crop was supposed to depend upon the propitiation of a *god*. I can see that the discovery of the possibility of growing *food* would enormously alter the savage's conception of God, by introducing a new set of attributes into his *consciousness* of him; but in defining the God of the Christians as a *corn* deity you and Allen are putting the cart before the horse.'

That was it, that was it—that was right somehow; there was something in this big red-faced man that was not *in* Mr Wilson; but why did his talk sound so lame and dull, even while he was saving God—and Mr Wilson's, while he made God from the beginning a nothing created by the fears and needs of man, so thrilling and convincing, so painting the world anew? He was wrong about everything and yet while he talked everything changed in spite of yourself.

The earlier part of the afternoon looked a bright happy world behind the desolation of this conflict; the husband and wife and the young men and Mrs Binkley and the bright afternoon light, dear far-off friends . . . withstanding, in their absence, the chilly light of Mr Wilson's talk. Who was Mr Wilson? But he was so certain that men had created God . . . life in that thought was a nightmare. Nothing that could happen could make it anything but a nightmare henceforth . . . it did not matter what happened, and yet he seemed pleased, amused about everything and eager to go on and 'do' things and get things done. . . . His belief about life was worse than agnosticism. There was no doubt in it. 'Mr G.' was an invention of man. There was nothing but man; man, coming from the ape, some men a little cleverer than others, men had discovered science, science was the only enlightenment, science would put everything right; scientific imagination, scientific invention. Man. Women were there, cleverly devised by nature to ensnare man for a moment and produce more men to bring scientific order out of primeval chaos; chaos was decreasing, order increasing; there was nothing worth considering before the coming of science; the business of the writer was imagination, not romantic imagination, but realism, fine realism, the truth about 'the savage,' about all the past and present, the avoidance of cliché . . . what was cliché? . . .

'Well, my dear man, you 've got the Duke of Argyll to keep you company,' sighed Mr Wilson with a smothered giggle, getting to his feet.

Miriam went from the sitting-room she had entered in another age with the bedroom violets pinned against her collarette, stripped and cold and hungry into the cold of the brightly-lit little dining-room. The gay cold dishes, the bright jellies and fruits, the brown nuts, the pretty Italian wine in thin white long-necked decanters . . . Chianti . . . Chianti . . . they all seemed familiar with the wine and the word; perhaps it was a familiar wine at the Wilson supper-parties; they spoke of it, sitting at the little feast amongst the sternness of nothing but small drawings and engravings on walls that shone some clear light tone against the few pieces of unfamiliar grey-brown furniture, like people clustering round a fire. But it was a feast of death; terrible because of their not knowing that it was a feast of death. The wife of the cockatoo had come in early enough to hear nearly the whole of the conversation, and had sat listening to it with a quiet fresh talkative face under her fresh dark hair; the large deep furrow between her eyebrows was nothing to do with anything here, it was permanent, belonging to her life. She had brought her life in with her and kept it there, the freshness and the furrow; she seemed now, at supper, to be out for the evening, to enjoy herself—at the Wilsons' . . . coming to the Wilsons' . . . for a jolly evening, just as anybody would go anywhere for a jolly evening. She did not know what was there, what it all meant. Perhaps because of the two little boys. She, with two little unseen boys and the big house so near, big and full of her and noise and things, and her freshness and the furrow of her thought about it, prevented anything from going on; the dreadful thing had to be dropped where it was, leaving the big man who had fought to pretend to be interested and amused, leaving Mr Wilson with the last word, and his quiet smothered giggle.

Alma tried to answer Mrs Pinner's loud fresh talking in the way things had been answered earlier in the afternoon, before the departure of all the other people. Everything she said was an attempt to beat things up. Every time she spoke, Miriam was conscious of something in the room that would be there with them all if only Alma would leave off being funny;

something there was in life that Alma had never yet known, something that belonged to an atmosphere she would call 'dull.' Mr Wilson knew that something . . . had it in him somewhere, but feared it and kept it out by trying to be bigger, by trying to be the biggest thing there was. Alma went on and on, sometimes uncomfortably failing, her thin voice sounding out like a corkscrew in a cork without any bottle behind it, now and again provoking a response which made things worse because it brought to the table the shamed sense of trying to keep something going. . . . The clever excitements would not come back. Mrs Binkley would have helped her. . . . Miriam sat helpless and miserable between her admiration of Alma's efforts and her longing for the thing Alma kept out. Her discomfiture at Alma's resentment of her dullness and Alma's longing for Mrs Binkley, was made endurable by her anger over Alma's obstructiveness. Mr Pinner and the big man were busily feeding. Mrs Pinner laughed and now and again tried to imitate Alma; as if she had learned how it was done by many visits to the Wilsons', and then forgot and talked in her own way, forgetting to try to say good things. Alma grew smaller as supper went on, and Mr and Mrs Pinner larger and larger. Together they were too strong for their sense of some other life and some other way of looking at things, to give the Wilson way a clear field. Mr Wilson began monologues at favourable intervals, but they tailed off for lack of nourishing response. Miriam listened eagerly and suspiciously; lost in admiration and a silent, mentally wordless opposition. She felt the big man was on her side and that the Pinners would be, if they could understand. They only saw the jokes . . . the—the—higher facetiousness . . . good phrase, that was the Chianti. And they were getting used to that; perhaps they were secretly a little tired of it.

After supper, Mr Pinner sang very neatly in a small clear tenor voice an English translation of *Es war ein König im Thule*. Miriam longed for the German words; Mr Pinner

cancelled even the small remainder of the German sentiment
by his pronunciation of the English rendering; 'There was a
king of old tame' he declared, and so on throughout the song.
Alma followed with a morsel of Chopin. The performance
drove Miriam into a rage. Mr Pinner had murdered his
German ballad innocently, his little Oxford voice and his false
vowels did not conceal the pleasure he took in singing his un-
imagined little song. Alma played her piece at her audience,
every line of her face and body proclaiming it fine music, the
right sort of music, and depreciating all the compositions that
were not 'music.' It was clear that her taste had become
cultivated, that she *knew* now, that the scales had fallen from
her eyes as they had fallen from Miriam's eyes in Germany;
but the result sent Miriam back with a rush to cheap music,
sentimental 'obvious' music, shapely waltzes, the demoralizing
chromatics of Gounod, the demoralizing descriptive passion
pieces of Chaminade, those things by Liszt, whom somebody
had called a charlatan, who wrote to make your blood leap and
your feet dance and made your blood leap and your feet dance
. . . why not? . . .

Her mind went on amazed at the rushing together of her
ideas on music, at the amount of certainty she had accumulated.
Any of these things she declared to herself played, really *played*,
would be better than Alma's Chopin. The Wilsons had discovered 'good' music, as so many English people had, but they
were all wrong about music; nearly all English people were.
Only in England would either the song or the solo have been
possible. The song was innocent, the solo was an insult. The
player's air of superiority to other music was insufferable; her
way of playing out bar by bar of the rain on the roof as if she
were giving a lesson, was a piece of intellectual snobbery.
Chopin she had never met, never felt or glimpsed. Chopin
was a shape, an endless delicate stern rhythm as stern as anything in music; all he was, came through that, could come only
through it, and she played tricks with the shape, falsified
all the values, outdid the worst trickery of the music she was
deprecating. At the end of the performance, which was applauded with a subdued reverence, Miriam eased her agony by

humming the opening phrase of the motive again and again in her brain, and very nearly aloud, it was such a perfect rhythmic drop. For long she was haunted and tortured by Alma's horrible holding back of the third note for emphasis where there was no emphasis . . . it was like . . . finding a *wart* at the dropping end of a fine tendril, she was telling herself furiously, while she fended off Alma's cajoling efforts to make her join in a game of cards. She felt too angry and too suffering—what *was* this wrong thing about music in all English people ?—even if she had not been too shy to exhibit her large hands and her stupidity at cards. So they were going to play cards, actually cards. The room felt cold to her in her long-suppressed anger and misery. She began to wish the Pinners would go. Sitting by the fire, shivering and torpid, she listened to Mrs Pinner's outcries and the elaboration, between the rounds, of jests that she felt were weekly jests. Sitting there dully listening she began to have a sort of insight into the way these jests were made. It was a thing that could be cultivated. Her tired brain experimented. Certain things she heard she knew she would remember; she felt she would repeat them—with an air of originality. They would seem very brilliant in any of her circles—though the girls did that sort of thing rather well; but in a less 'refined' way; that was true! This was the sort of thing the girls did; only their way was not half so clever . . . if she did, every one would wonder what was the matter with her; and she would not be able to keep it up, without a great deal of practice; and it would keep out something else . . . but perhaps for some people there was something in it; it was their way. It had always been Alma's way, a little. Only now she did it better. Perhaps . . . it was like Chopin's shape. . . . They do not know how angry I have been . . . they are quite amiable. I am simply horrid . . . wanting Alma to know I know she's wrong, quite as much as caring for Chopin; perhaps more . . . no; if *anybody* had *played*, I should be happy; perfectly happy . . . what does that mean . . . because real musicians are not at all nice people . . . 'a queer soft lot.' But why are the English so awful about music ? They are poets. Why are they not

musicians? I hope I shall never hear Alma play Beethoven.
As long as she plays Chopin like that, I shall never like her.
. . . Perhaps English people ought never to play, only to
listen to music. They are not innocent enough to play. They
cannot forget themselves.

At ten o'clock they trooped into the kitchen. Miriam, half
asleep and starving for food, eagerly ate large biscuits, too
hungry to care much for Alma's continued resentment of her
failure to join the card party and her unconcealed contempt of
her sudden return to animation at the prospect of nourishment.
She had never felt so hungry.

Going at last to her room she found its gleaming freshness
warm and firelit. Warm fresh deeps of softly coloured room,
that were complete before she came in with her candle. She
stood a moment imagining the emptiness. The April night
air was streaming gently in from meadows. Going across to
the windows, she hesitated near the flowered curtain. It
stirred gently; but not in that way as if moved by ghostly
fingers. The meadows here were different. They might
grow the same again. But woods and meadows were always
there, away from London. One could go to them. They
were going on all the time. All the time in London, spring
and summer and autumn were passing unseen. But this was
not the time. They were *different* here. She pulled a deep
wicker chair close up to the exciting white ash-sprinkled hearth.
The evening she had left in the flames downstairs was going on
up here. To-morrow, to-day, in a few hours she would be
sitting with them again, facing flames; no one else there. She
sat with her eyes on the flames. A clock struck two. . . . I 've
got to them at last, the people I ought to be with. The books
in the corner showed their bindings and opened their pages
here and there. They made a little sick patch on her heart.
The Wilsons approved of them. Other people approved of
things. Nothing had been done yet that anybody could
approve of . . . the *some*thing village of Grandpré . . . und

dann sagte darauf, die gute vernünftige Hausfrau. . . . It all
floated in the air. They would see it if somebody showed it.
They would be angry and amused if anybody tried to show it.
It was wrong in some way to try and show the things you were
looking at. Keep quiet about them. Then somebody else
expressed them; and those other people turned to you, and
demanded your admiration—and wondered why you were
furious. It's too long to wait, until the things come up of
themselves. You *must* attend to them. . . .

How the fragrance of the cigarette stood out upon the fresh
warm air . . . that was perique, that curious strong flavour.
They were very strong, he had said so; but downstairs, talking
like that, they had had no particular flavour, just cigarettes,
bringing the cigarette mood . . . no wonder he had been
surprised, really surprised, at her smoking so many . . . but
then he had been surprised at her eating a hard apple at midnight . . . the sitting-room had suddenly looked familiar,
going into it alone while they were seeing out the Pinners and
the big man. Strange unknown voices that perhaps she would
not hear again, going out into the night . . . their voices
jesting the last jests as the guests went down the garden,
sounding in the hall, familiar and homely, well known to her,
presently coming back into the sitting-room; the fire burning
brightly like any other fire, the exciting deep pinkness of the
shaded lamplight like nothing else in the world. Alma knew
it, rushing in . . . whirling about with Alma in that room
with that afternoon left in it; the sounds of bolting and locking
coming in from the hall.

. . . 'You looked extraordinarily pretty. . . .'
'You have come through it all remarkably well' . . . remarkable had a k in it in English, and German, merkwürdig,
and perhaps in Scandinavian languages; but not in other
languages; it was one of the things that separated England from
the south . . . remarkable . . . hard and chilly.
'You know you're awfully good stuff. You've had an

extraordinary variety of experience; you 've got your freedom; you ought to write.'

''That is what a palmist told me at Newlands. It was at a big afternoon "at home"; there was a palmist in a little dark room sitting near a lamp; she looked at nothing but your hands; she kept saying "Whatever you do, write. If you haven't written yet, write, if you don't succeed go on writing."'

'Just so, have you written?'

'Ah, but she also told me my self-confidence had been broken; that I used to be self-confident and was so no longer. It 's true.'

'Have you written anything?'

'I once sent in a thing to *Home Notes*. They sent it back but asked me to write something else and suggested a few things.'

'If they had taken your stuff you would have gone on and learnt to turn out stuff bad enough for *Home Notes*, and gone on doing it for the rest of your life.'

'But then an artist, a woman who had a studio in Bond Street and knew Leighton, saw some things I had tried to paint and said I ought to make any sacrifice to learn painting, and a musician said the same about music.'

'You could work in writing quite well with your present work.'

. . . 'Pieces of short prose; anything; a description of an old woman sitting in an omnibus . . . anything. There 's plenty of room for good work. There 's the *Academy*, always ready to consider well-written pieces of short prose. Write something and send it to me.'

Nearing London, shivering and exhausted, she recalled Sunday morning and the strangeness of it being just as it had promised to be. Happy waking with a clear refreshed brain in a tired drowsy body, like the feeling after a dance; making the next morning part of the dance, your mind full of pictures and thoughts, and the evening coming up again and again, one great clear picture in the foreground of your mind. The *evening* in the room as you sat propped on your pillows, drinking the clear pale, curiously refreshing tea left by the maid on a little wooden tray by your bedside; its fragrance drew you to

sip at once, without adding milk and sugar. It was delicious;
it steamed aromatically up your nostrils and went straight to
your brain; potent without being bitter. Perhaps it was
'China' tea; it must be. The two biscuits on the little plate
disappeared rapidly, and she poured in milk and added much
sugar to her remaining tea to appease her hunger. The
evening strayed during her deliberately perfunctory toilet; she
wanted only to be down. It began again unbroken with the
first cigarette after breakfast, when a nimble remark, thrown
out from the excited gravity of her happiness, made Mr Wilson
laugh. She was learning how to do it. It stayed on through
the day, adding the day to itself in a chain, a morning of talk,
a visit to Mr Wilson's study—the curious glimpses of pinewood
from the windows; pinewood looking strange and far away—
there were people in Weybridge to whom those woods were
real woods, where they walked and perhaps had the thoughts
that woods bring; here they were like woods in a picture book;
not real, just a curious painted background for Mr Wilson's
talk . . . all those books, in fifty years' time, burnt up by the
air; he did not seem to think it an awful idea . . . you can do
anything with English . . . and then the names of authors
who had done some of these things with English . . . making
it sing and dance and march, making it like granite or like film
and foam. Other languages were more simple and single in
texture; less flexible. . . . Gazing out at the exciting silent
pines—so dark and still, waiting, not knowing about the
wonders of English—Miriam recalled her impressions of the
authors she knew. It was true that those were their effects
and the great differences between them. How did he come to
know all about it, and to put it into words? Did the authors
know when they did it? She passionately hoped not. If they
did, it was a trick and spoilt books. Rows and rows of 'fine'
books; nothing but men sitting in studies doing something
cleverly, being very important, 'men of letters'; and looking out
for approbation. If writing meant that, it was not worth doing.
English a great flexible language; more than any other in the
world. But German was the same? Only the inflections
filled the sentences up with bits. English was flexible and

beautiful. Funny. Foreigners did not think so. Many English people thought foreign literature the best. Perhaps Mr Wilson did not know much foreign literature. But he wanted to; or he would not have those translations of Ibsen and Björnsen. German poetry marched and sang and did all sorts of things. Anyhow it was wonderful about English—but if books were written like that, sitting down and doing it cleverly and knowing just what you were doing, and just how somebody else had done it, there was something wrong, some mannish cleverness that was only half right. To write books, knowing all about style, would be to become like a man. Women who wrote books and learned these things would be absurd and would make men absurd. There was something wrong. It was in all those books upstairs. 'Good stuff' was wrong, a clever trick, not worth doing. And yet everybody seemed to want to write.

The rest of the day—secret and wonderful. Sitting about, taken for one of the Wilson kind of people, someone who was writing or going to write, by the two Scotch professors; sitting about listening to their quiet easy eager unconcerned talk, seeing them 'all round' as Mr Wilson saw them, the limits of professorship and teaching, the silly net and trick of examinations, their simplicity and their helplessness; playing the lovely accompaniment, like quiet waves, of Schubert's *Ave Maria*, the sudden, jolly, sentimental voice of Professor Ewings, his nice attentions . . . if it had been Wimpole Street, or anywhere in society, he would not have seen me. . . .

It would be wrong to try to write just because Mr Wilson had said one ought. . . . The reasons he had given for writing were the wrong ones . . . but it would be impossible to go down again without doing some writing. . . . Impossible not to go down again. . . . They knew one was 'different'; and liked it and thought it a good thing; a sort of distinction. No one had thought that before. It made them a home and a refuge. The only refuge there was, except being by oneself . . . only their kind of difference was not the same. They thought nearly every one 'futile' and 'dull'—every one who did not see things in their way was that. Presently they would

find that one was not different in the same way. He had
spoken of people who grow 'dull' as you get to know them.
Awful . . . perhaps already, he meant——

'It's all very well . . . people read Matthew Arnold's
simple profundities; er—simple profundities; and learn his
little trick; and go *about*—hcna, hcna—arm in arm with this
swell . . . hcna . . . *puffing* with illumination. All about
nothing. It's all, my dear Miss Henderson, about absolutely
nothing.'

The train stopped. Better not to go down again. There
was something all wrong in it. Wrong about everything. The
Pinners and the big man were right . . . but there was something dreadful in them, the something that is in all simple right
sort of people, who just go on, never thinking about anything.
Were they good and right? It did not enter their heads to
think that they were wrong in associating with him. . . . Here
in London it seemed wrong . . . she hurried wearily with
aching head up the long platform. The Wimpole Street people
would certainly think it wrong; if they knew about the marriage. They knew he was a coming great man; the great new
'critic'; a new kind of critic . . . they knew everybody was
beginning to talk about him. But if they knew they would not
approve. They would never understand his way of seeing
things. Impossible to convey anything to them of what the
visit had been.

The hall clock said half-past nine. The hall and the large
rooms had shrunk. Everything looked shabby and homely.
The house was perfectly quiet. Passing quietly and quickly
into her room, she found the table empty. The door into the
den was shut and no sound came from behind it. No one but
James had seen her. The holiday was still there. Perhaps

there would be time to take hold in a new way before any one discovered her and made demands. Perhaps they were all three wanting her at this moment. But the house was so still, there was nothing urgent. Perhaps she would never feel nervous at Wimpole Street again. It was really all so easy. There was nothing she could not manage, if only she could get a fair start and get everything in order and up to date. Her mind tried to encircle the book-keeping. There must be a plan for it all; so much work on the accounts, to keep the whole ledger-full sent out to date, so much on the address books, and so much on the monthly cash books—a little of all these things every day in addition to the day's work, whatever happened; that would do it. Then there would be no muddle and nothing to worry about and perhaps time to write. They must be told that she would use any spare time there was on other things. . . . They would be quite ready for that, provided the books were always up to date and the surgeries always in order. That is what a Wilson would have done from the first.

'Mr Grove to see you, miss.'
'Mr *Grove* ?'
'Yes miss; a dark gentleman.'
Miriam rose from her chair. James had gone, after a moment of sympathetic waiting, back down the basement stairs to her dinner. Miriam felt herself very tall and slender—set apart and surrounded; healed of all fighting and effort. She went quickly through the hall, thinking of nothing; herself, walking down Harriett's garden path. At the door of the waiting-room she hesitated. Mr Grove was the other side of the door, waiting for her to come in. She opened the door with a flourish, and advanced with stiffly outstretched hand. Before she said 'Teeth?' in a cheerful, breezy, professional tone that exploded into the past and scattered it, she saw the pained anxiousness of his face and the flush that had risen under his dark skin.

'No,' he said, recoiling swiftly from his limp handshake and

sitting abruptly down on the chair from which he had risen.
Miriam watched him go helplessly on to say in stiff resentful-
ness what he had come to say, while she stood apologetically
at his chair side.

'I meant to write to you—two or three times.'

'Oh why didn't you?' she responded emphatically. . . .
Why can't I be quiet and hear what he has to say? He must
have wanted to see me dreadfully to come here like this.

His eyes were fixed blindly upon the far-off window.

'Yes. I wanted to very much. How do you like your life
here?' He was flushing again. His skin still had that shiny
film over it, so unlike the clear snaky brilliance of the eyes.
They were dreadful, and all the rest flappy and floppy and
somehow feverish.

'Oh—I like it immensely.'

'That is a very good thing.'

'Do you like your life?'

He drew in his lower lip on an indrawn breath and held it
with his teeth. His eyes were thinking busily under a slight
frown.

'That is one of the things I wished to discuss with you.'

'Oh *do* discuss it with me,' cried Miriam.

'I am very glad you are getting on here so well,' he murmured thoughtfully, gazing through the window, to and fro as
if scanning the opposite house-fronts.

'Oh, I like it immensely,' said Miriam after a silence. Her
head was beginning to ache. He sat quite still, scanning to and
fro, his lip recaptured under his teeth.

'They are such nice people. I like it for so many things.'
He looked absently round at her.

'M-yes. On several occasions I thought of writing to you.'

'Yes,' said Miriam sitting down opposite to him.

He shifted a little in his chair, to keep his way clear to the
window.

For a few moments they sat silent; then he suddenly took
out his watch and stood up.

Miriam rose. 'Have you seen the Ducaynes lately?' she
asked hurriedly, moving nervously towards the door. Mur-

muring an indistinct response he led the way to the door and held it open for her.

James was coming forward with a patient. They stood aside for the patient to pass in, James waiting to escort Mr Grove to the front door. They shook hands limply and silently. Miriam stood watching his narrow, loosely knit clerical back as he plunged along through the hall and out. She turned as James turned from the door. . . . What it must have cost him to break in here and ask for me . . . how silly and how rude I was. . . . I *can't* believe he's been; it's like a dream. He's seen me in the new life, changed . . . and I'm not really changed.

CHAPTER VII

WHY must I always think of her in this place? . . . It is always worst just along here. . . . Why do I always forget there's this piece . . . always be hurrying along seeing nothing and then, suddenly, Teetgen's Teas and this row of shops? I can't bear it. I don't know what it is. It's always the same. I always feel the same. It is sending me mad. One day it will be worse. If it gets any worse I shall be mad. Just here. Certainly. Something is wearing out of me. I am meant to go mad. If not, I should not always be coming along this piece without knowing it, whichever street I take. Other people would know the streets apart. I don't know where this bit is or how I get to it. I come every day because I am meant to go mad here. Something that knows brings me here and is making me go mad because I am myself and nothing changes me.

CHAPTER VIII

THE morning went on. It seemed as though there was to be no opportunity of telling Mr Hancock until lunch had changed the feeling of the day. He knew there was something. Turning to select an instrument from a drawer she was at work upon, he had caught sight of her mirth and smiled his amusement and anticipation into the drawer before turning gravely back to the chair. Perhaps that was enough, the best, like a moment of amusement you share with a stranger and never forget. Perhaps by the time she was able to tell him, he would be disappointed. No. It was too perfect. Just the sort of thing that amused him.

He had one long sitting after another, the time given to one patient overlapping the appointment with the next, so that her clearings and cleansings were done with a patient in the chair, noiselessly and slowly, keeping her in the room, making to-day seem like a continuation of yesterday afternoon. Yesterday shed its radiance. The shared mirth made a glowing background to her toil. The duties accumulating downstairs made her continued presence in the surgery a sort of truancy. She felt more strongly than ever the sense of her usefulness to him. She had never so far helped him so deftly and easily, being everywhere and nowhere, foreseeing his needs without impeding his movements, doing everything without reminding the patient that there was a third person in the room. She followed sympathetically the long slow process of excavation and root treatment, the delicate shaping and undercutting of the walls of cavities, the adjustment and retention of the many appliances for the exclusion of moisture, the insertions of the amalgams and pastes whose pounding and mixing made a recurrent crisis in her morning. She wished again and again that the dentally ignorant, dentally ironic world could see the operator at his best; in his moments of quiet intense concentration on giving his best to his patients.

The patients suffering the four long sittings were all of the best group, leisurely and untroubled as to the mounting up of guineas, and three of them intelligently appreciative of what was being done. *They* knew all about the 'status' of modern dentistry and the importance of teeth. They were all clear serene tranquil cheerful people who probably hardly ever went to a doctor. They would rate oculists and dentists on a level with doctors, and two of them at least would rate Mr Hancock on a level with anybody. . . . To-morrow would be quite different, a rush of gas cases, that man who was sick if an instrument touched the back of his tongue; Mrs Wolff, disputing fees, the deaf-mute, the grubby little man on a newspaper . . . he ought to have no patients but these intelligent ones and really nervous and delicate people and children.

'I sometimes wish I 'd stuck to medicine.'
'Why?'
'Well—I don't know. You know they get a good deal more all round out of their profession than a dentist does. It absorbs them more. . . . I don't say it ought not to be the same with dentistry. But it isn't. I don't know a dentist who wants to go on talking shop until the small hours. I 'm quite sure I don't. Now look at Randle. He was dining here last night. So was Bentley. We separated at about midnight; and Randle told me this morning that he and Bentley walked up and down Harley Street telling each other stories, until two o'clock.'
'That simply means they talk about their patients.'
'Well—yes. They discuss their cases from every point of view. They get more human interest out of their work.'
'Of course everybody knows that medical students and doctors are famous for stories. But it doesn't really mean they know anything about *people*. *I* don't believe they do.

I think the dentist has quite as much opportunity of studying human nature. Going through dentistry is like dying. You must know almost everything about a patient who has had much done, or even a little——'

'The fact of the matter is their profession is a hobby to them as well as a profession. That's the truth of the matter. Now I think a man who can make a hobby of his profession is a very fortunate man.'

How surprised the four friendly wealthy patients, especially the white-haired old aristocrat who was always pressing invitations upon him, would have been, ignoring or treating her with the kindly consideration due to people of her station, if they could have seen inside his house yesterday and beheld her ensconced in the most comfortable chair in his drawing-room . . . talking to Miss Szigmondy.

Each time she came downstairs, she sat urgently down to the most pressing of her clerical duties and presently found her mind ranging amongst thoughts whose beginnings she could not remember. She felt equal to anything. Every prospect was open to her. Simple solutions to problems that commonly went unanswered round and round in her head, presented themselves in flashes. At intervals she worked with a swiftness and ease that astonished her, making no mistakes, devising small changes and adjustments that would make for the smoother working of the practice, dashing off notes to friends in easy expressive phrases that came without thought.

Rushing up towards lunch-time in answer to the bell, she found Mr Hancock alone. He turned from the washstand and stood carefully drying his hands. 'Are they showing up?' he murmured and seeing her, smiled his sense of her eagerness to communicate and approached a few steps, waiting and smiling with the whole of his face exactly as he would smile when the communication was made. There was really no need to tell.

Miriam glanced back for an incoming patient. 'Miss Szigmondy,' she began in a voice deep with laughter.

He laughed at once, with a little backward throw of his head,
just as the patient came in. Miriam glided swiftly into her
corner.

At tea-time she found herself happily exhausted, sitting alone
in the den waiting for the sound of footsteps. For the first
time the gas-stove was unlit. The rows of asbestos balls stood
white and bare. But a flood of sunlight came through the
western panes of the newly washed skylight. The little low
tea-table, with its fresh uncrumpled low-hanging white cover
and compact cluster of delicate china, stood in full sunshine
amidst the comfortable winter shabbiness. The decorative
confusion on the walls shone richly out of the new bright light.
It needed only to have all the skylights open, the blue of the
sky visible, the thin spring air coming in, the fire alight making
a summery glow, to be perfect; like spring tea-time in a newly
visited house. The Wilsons' sitting-room would be in an
open blaze of shallow spring sunshine. She saw it going on
day by day towards the rich light of summer . . . jealously.
One ought to be there every day. So much life would have
passed through the room. Every day last week had been full
of it, everything changed by it, and now, since yesterday, it
seemed months ago. It seemed too late to begin going down
again. One thing blots out another. You cannot have more
than one thing intensely. Quite soon it would be as if she had
never been down; except in moments now and again, when
something recalled the challenge of their point of view. They
would not want her to go down again, unless she had begun to
be different. Until yesterday she might have begun. But
yesterday afternoon they had been forgotten so completely, and
waking up from yesterday she no longer wanted to begin their
way of being different. But other people had already begun
to identify her with them. That came of talking. If she
had said nothing, nothing would have been changed; either at

Wimpole Street or with the girls. Did they really like reading *The Evolution of the Idea of God*, or were they only pretending? Sewing all the time, busily, like wives, instead of smoking and listening and thinking.

Which was the stronger? The interest of getting the whole picture there, and struggling with Mr Wilson's deductions, or the interest of getting the girls to grasp and admire his conclusions even while she herself refused them? . . .

'Why can't I keep quiet about the things that happen? It 's all me, my conceit and my way of rushing into things.' . . . But other people were the same in a way. Only there was something real in their way. They believed in the things they rushed into. 'Miss Henderson knows the great critic, intimately.' He had thought that would impress Miss Szigmondy. It did. For a moment she had stopped talking and looked surprised. There was time to disclaim, to tell them they were being impressed in the wrong way; to tell them something, to explain in some way. The moment had passed, full of terrible far-off trouble, 'decisive.'

There is always a fraction of a second when you know what you are doing. Miss Szigmondy would have gone on talking about bicycling, until Mr Hancock came back. There was no need to say suddenly, without thinking about it, 'I am dying to learn.' *Really* that sudden remark was the result of having failed to speak when they were all talking about Mr Wilson. If, then, one had suddenly said 'I am dying to learn bicycling,' or *anything*, they would have known something of the truth about Mr Wilson. It was the worrying thought of him, still there, that made one say, without thinking, 'I am dying to learn.' It was too late. It linked up with the silence about Mr Wilson and left one being a person who knew and altogether approved of Mr Wilson and wanted to learn bicycling. Altogether wrong. 'You know—I don't approve of Mr Wilson; and you might not if you heard him talk, and . . . his marriage . . . you know. . . .'

. . . If I had done that, I should have been easy and strong

and should have 'made conversation' when she began talking
about bicycling. I was like the man who proposed to the girl
at the dance because he could not think of anything to say to
her. He could not think of anything to say, because he had
something on his mind. . . .

And Miss Szigmondy would not have called this morning.

'*No* one can pgonounce my name. You had better call me
Thégèse, my dear girl. Yes, do; I want you to.' She had said
that with a worried face, a sudden manner of unsmiling intimacy. She certainly had some plan. Standing there, with
her broken-hearted voice and her anxious face, she seemed to
be separate from the room, even from her own clothes. Yet
something within her was moving so quickly that it made one
breathless. She was so intent that she was unconscious of the
appealing little figure she made, huddled in her English clothes.
She stood dressed and determined and prosperous, her smart
little toque held closely against her dark hair and sallow face
with the kind of chenille-spotted veil that was a rampart
against *everything* in the world, for an Englishwoman. But it
did not touch her or do anything for her. It gave an effect of
prison bars behind which she was hanging her head and
weeping and appealing. One could have laughed and gathered
her up. Why was she forlorn? Why did she imagine that
one was also forlorn? The sight of her made all the forlorn-
ness one had ever seen or read about seem peopled with
knowledge and sympathy and warm thoughts that flew
crowding along one's brain as close and bright as the texture of
everybody's everyday. But the eyes were anxious and preoccupied, blinking now and then in her long unswerving
appealing gaze, shutting swiftly for lightning calculations
between her rapid appealing statements. What was she
trying to do?

She tried to stand in front of everything, to put everything
aside as if it were part of something she knew. Laughing over
it with Mr Hancock would not dispose of that. After the fun
of telling him, she would still be there, with the two bicycle

lessons that were going begging. He knew already that Miss Szigmondy had called, and would assume that she had suggested things and that one was not going to do them. If one told him about the lessons he would say that is very kind and would mean it. He was always fine in thinking a 'kind' action kind . . . but she does not come because she wants me. She does not want anybody. She does not know the difference between one person and another. . . . He knows only her social manner. She has never been alone with him and come close and shown him her determination and her sorrow . . . sorrow . . . sorrow. . . .

He could never see that it was impossible, without forcibly crushing her, to get out of doing some part of what she desired . . .

If one were drawn in and did things, let oneself want to do things for any one else, there would be a change in the atmosphere at Wimpole Street. That never occurred to him. But he would feel it if it happened. If there were someone near who made distractions, there would be a difference, something that was not given to him. He was so unaware of this. He was absolutely ignorant of what it was that kept things going as they were.

CHAPTER IX

THE cycling school was out of sight and done with, and Miriam hurried down the Chalk Farm Road. If only she could see an omnibus and be in it, going anywhere down away from the north. Miss Szigmondy had brought shame and misery upon her, in Chalk Farm. There was nothing there to keep off the pain. Once back, she would never think of Chalk Farm again. How could any one think it was a place, like other places? It was torture even to be in it, going through it. . . . Of course the man had thought I should take on a course of lessons and pay for them. I have to learn everything meanly and shamefully. He thinks I'm getting all I can for nothing. The people in the bus will see me pay my fare and I shall be all right again, going down there. What an *awful* road, going on and on with nothing in it. I am shamed and helpless; *helpless*. It's no use to try and do anything. It always exposes me and brings this maddening shame and pain. It's over again this time, and I shall soon forget it altogether. I might just as well begin to stop thinking about it now. It's this part of London. It's like Banbury Park. The people are absolutely awful. They take cycling lessons quite coolly. They are not afraid of anybody. To them this part is the best bit of north London. They are that sort of people. They are all alike. All of them would dislike me. I should die of being with them.

Why is it that no one seems to know what north London is? They say it is healthy and open. Perhaps I shall meet someone who feels like I do about it, and would get ill and die there. It is not imagination. It is a real feeling that comes upon me. . . .

The north London omnibus reached the tide of the Euston Road and pulled up at Portland Road station. Miriam got out, weak and ill. The first breath of the central air revived her. Standing there, the omnibus looked like any other omnibus.

She crossed the road, averting her eyes from the north-going roads on either side of the church, and got into the inmost corner of another bus. She wanted to ride about, getting from bus to bus, inside London until her misery had passed. Opposite her was a stout woman in a rusty bonnet and shawl and dust-defaced black skirt, looking about with eyes that did not see what they looked at, all the London consciousness in her. Miriam sat gazing at her. The woman's eyes crossed her and passed unperturbed. . . .

The lane of little shops flowed away, their huddled detail crushing together, wide shop windows glittered steadily by and narrowed away. When the bus stopped at Gower Street, the tower of St Pancras church came into sight soaring majestically up, screened by trees.

The trees in Endsleigh Gardens came along, gently waving their budding branches in bright sunshine. The colour of the gardens was so intense that the sun must just be going to set behind Euston station. The large houses moved steadily behind the gardens, in blocks, bright white, with large quiet streets opening their vistas in between the blocks, leading to green freshness and then safely on down into Soho. The long square came to an end. The shrub-trimmed base of St Pancras church came heavily nearer and stopped. As Miriam got out of the bus, she watched its great body rise in clear sharp outline against the blue. Its clock was booming the hour out across the gardens through the houses and down into the squares. On this side its sound was broken up by the narrow roar of the Euston Road and the clamour coming right and left from the two great stations.

Her feet tramped happily across the square of polished roadway patterned with shadows, and along the quiet clean sunlit pavement behind the gardens. It was always bright and clean and quiet and happy there, like the pavement of a road behind a sea-front. The sound of a mail van, rattling heavily along Woburn Place, changed to a soft rumble as she turned in between the great houses of Tansley Street and walked along its silent corridor of afternoon light. Sparrows were cheeping in the stillness. To be able to go down the quiet street and on

into the squares—on a bicycle. . . . I must learn somehow to
get my balance. To go along, like in that moment when he
took his hands off the handle-bars, in knickers and a short skirt
and all the summer to come. . . . Everything shone with a
greater intensity. Friends and thought and work were nothing
compared to being able to ride alone, balanced, going along
through the air.

On the hall table was a post card. 'Come round on Sunday
if you 're in town—Irländisches Ragout. Mag.' Her heart
stirred; that settled it—the girls wanted her; Mag wanted her.
She took Alma's crumpled letter from her pocket and glanced
through it once more . . . 'such a dull Sunday and all your
fault. Why did you not come? Come on Saturday *any* time,
or Sunday morning if you can't manage the week-end.' What
a good thing she had not written promising to go. She would
be in London, safe in Kenneth Street for Sunday. Mag was
quite right; going away unsettled you for the week and you did
not *get* Sunday. She looked at her watch, five-thirty; in half
an hour the girls would probably be at Slater's; the London
week-end could begin this minute; all the people who half-
expected her, the Brooms, the Pernes, Sarah and Harriett, the
Wilsons, would be in their homes far away; she safe in Bloomsbury, in the big house, the big kind streets, Kenneth Street;
places they none of them knew; safe for the whole length of
the week-end. Saturday had looked so obstructed, with the
cycling lesson, and the visit to Miss Szigmondy, and the many
alternatives for the rest of the time. . . . 'Oh, I 've got about
fifty engagements for Saturday,' and now Saturday was clear
and she felt equal to anything for the week-end. What a discovery, standing hidden there in the London house, to drop
everything and go down, with all the discarded engagements,
all the solicitous protecting friends put aside; easy and alone
through the glimmering green squares to the end of the Strand
and find Slater's. . . . I 'll never stir out of London again.
The girls are right. It isn't worth it.

She saw the girls seated at a table at the far end of the big
restaurant, and shyly advanced.

'Hulloh child!'

'What you having?' she asked, sitting down opposite to them. The empty white table-cloth shone under a brilliant incandescent light; far away down the vista the door opened on the daylit street.

'Isn't it a glorious spring evening?' Spring? It was, of course. Every one had been saying the spring would never come, but to-day it was very warm. Spring was here, of course. Perspiring in a dusty cycling school and sitting in a hot restaurant was not spring. Spring was somewhere far away. Going to stay and talk in people's houses did not bring spring—landscapes belonging to people were *painted*; you must be alone . . . or perhaps at the Brooms'. Perhaps next week-end at the Brooms' would be in time for the spring; in their back garden, the watered green lawn and the sweetbrier, and the distant trees in the large garden beyond the fence. In London it was better not to think about the times of year.

But Mag seemed to find spring in London. Her face was all glowing with the sense of it.

'What you having?'

'Have you observed with what a remarkable brilliance the tender green shines out against the soot-black branches?' Yes, that was wonderful, but what was the joke?

'Every spring I have spent in Lonndonn, I have heard that remark at least fifty times.'

Miriam laughed politely. 'Jan, *what* have you ordered?'

'We 've ordered beef, my child, cold beefs and salads.'

'Do you think I should like salad?'

'If you *had* a brother would he like salad?'

'Do they put dressing on it? If I could have just plain lettuce.'

'Ask for it, my child, ask and it shall be given unto thee.'

A waitress brought the beef and salad, two glasses with an inch of whisky in each, and a large siphon.

Miriam ordered beef and potatoes.

'I suppose the steak and onion days are over.'

'I shan't have another steak and onions, please God, until next November.'

Miriam laughed delightedly.

'Why haven't you gone away for the week-end, child?'

'I told you she wouldn't.'

'I don't know.   I wanted to come down here.'

'Is that a compliment to us?'

'I say, I 've had a bicycle lesson.'

Both faces came up eagerly.

'You remember; that extraordinary woman I met at the Royal Institution.'

The faces looked at each other.

'Oh, you know; I *told* you about it—the two lessons she didn't want.'

'Go on, my child; we remember; go on.'

Miriam sat eating her beef.

'Go on, Miriam.   You 've really had a lesson.   I 'm delighted, my child.   Tell us all about it.'

'D' you remember the extraordinary moment when you felt the machine going along; even with the man holding the handle-bars?'

'You wait until there 's nobody to hold the handle-bars.'

'Have you been out alone yet?'

The two faces looked at each other.

'Shall we tell her?'

'You *must* tell me; es ist bestimmt in Gottes Rath.'

They leaned across the table and spoke low, one after the other.   'We went out—last night—after dark—and rode—round Russell Square—twice—in our knickers——'

'*No!*   Did you really?   How simply heavenly.'

'It *was*.   We came home nearly crying with rage at not being able to go about, permanently, in nothing but knickers. It would make life an *absolutely* different thing.'

'The freedom of movement.'

'Exactly.   You feel like a sprite you are so light.'

'And like a poet though you don't know it.'

'You feel like a sprite you are so light, and you feel so strong and capable and so broadshouldered you could knock down a policeman.   Jan and I knocked down several last night.'

'Yes; and it is not only that; think of never having to brush your skirt.'

'I know. It would be bliss.'

'I spend half my life brushing my skirt. If I miss a day I notice it—if I miss two days, the office notices it. If I miss three days the public notices it.'

'La vie est dure; pour les femmes.'

'You don't want to be a man, Jan.'

'Oh, I do, sometimes. They have the best of everything all round.'

'*I* don't. I wouldn't be a man for anything. I wouldn't have a man's—*consciousness*, for anything.'

'Why not, asthore?'

'They 're too absolutely pig-headed and silly. . . .'

'*Isn't* she intolerant?'

Miriam sat flaring. That was not the right answer. There was something; and they must know it; but they would not admit it.

'Then you can both really ride?'

'We do nothing else; we 've given up walking; we no longer walk up and down stairs; we ride.'

Miriam laughed her delight. 'I can quite understand; it alters everything. I realized that this afternoon at the school. To be able to bicycle would make life utterly different; on a bicycle you feel a different person; nothing can come near you, you forget who you are. Aren't you glad you are alive to-day, when all these things are happening?'

'What things, little one?'

'Well, cycling and things. You know, girls, when I 'm thirty I 'm going to cut my hair short and wear divided skirts.'

Both faces came up.

'Why on earth?'

'I can't face doing my hair and brushing skirts and keeping more or less in the fashion, that means about two years behind because I never realize fashions till they 're just going, even if I could afford to—all my life.'

'Then why not do it now?'

'Because all my friends and relatives would object. It would worry them too—they would feel quite sure then I should never marry—and they still entertain hopes, secretly.'

'Don't you want to marry—ever; ever?'

'Well—it would mean giving up this life.'

'Yes, I know. I agree there. That can't be faced.'

'I should think *not*. Aren't you going to have any pudding?'

'But why thirty? Why not thirty-one?'

'Because nobody cares what you do when you're thirty; they've all given up hope by that time. Aren't you two going to have any pudding?'

'No. But that is no reason why you should not.'

'What a good idea—to have just one dish and coffee.'

'That's what we think; and it's cheap.'

'Well, I couldn't have had any dinner at all, only I'm cadging dinner with you to-morrow.'

'What would you have done?'

'An egg, at an A.B.C.'

'How fond you are of A.B.C.s.'

'I love them.'

'What is it that you love about them?'

'Chiefly, I think, their dowdiness. The food is honest; not showy, and they are so blissfully dowdy.'

Both girls laughed.

'It's no good. I have come to the conclusion I like dowdiness. I'm not smart. You are.'

'This is the first we have heard of it.'

'Well, you know you are. You keep in the fashion. It may be quite right, perhaps you are more sociable than I am.'

'One is so conspicuous if one is not dressed more or less like other people.'

'That's what I hate; dressing like other people. If I could afford it I should be stylish—not smart. Perfect coats and skirts, and a few good evening dresses. But you must be awfully well off for that. If I can't be stylish I'd rather be dowdy, and in a way I like dowdiness even better than stylishness.'

The girls laughed.

'But aren't clothes awful, anyhow? I've spent four and eleven on my knickers and I can't possibly get a skirt till next year, if then, or afford to hire a machine.'

'Why don't you ask them to raise your salary?'

'After four months? Besides, any fool could do the work.'

'If I were you I should tell them. I should say "Gentlemen—I wish for a skirt and a bicycle."'

'Mag, don't be so silly.'

'I *can't* see it. *They* would benefit by your improved health and spirits. Jan and I are new women since we have learned riding. *I* am thinking of telling the governor I must have a rise to meet the increased demands of my appetite. Our housekeeping expenses, I should say, are doubled. What *will* you? Que faire?'

'You see the work I 'm doing is not worth more than a pound a week—my languages are no good there. I suppose I ought to learn typing and shorthand; but where could I find the money for the training?'

'Will you teach her shorthand, if I teach her typing?'

'Certainly, if the child wants to learn. I don't advise her.'

'Why not, Jan? *You* did. How long would it take me in evenings?'

'A year at least, to be marketable. It 's a vile thing to learn, unless you are thoroughly stupid.'

'That 's true. Jan was a perfect fool. The more intelligent you are, the longer you take.'

'You see it isn't a language. It is an arbitrary system of signs.'

'With your intelligence you 'd probably grow grey at the school. Wouldn't she, Jan?'

'Probably.'

'Besides, I can't imagine Mistress Miriam in an office.'

'Nobody would have me. I 'm not business-like enough. I am learning book-keeping at their expense. And don't forget they give me lunch and tea. I say, we are going to read *The Evolution of the Idea of God* to-night?'

'Yes. Let 's get back and get our clothes off. If I don't have a cigarette within half an hour, I shall die.'

'Oh, so shall I. I had forgotten the existence of cigarettes.'

Out in the street, Miriam felt embarrassed. The sunset glow broke through wherever there was a gap towards the north-west, and flooded a strip of the street and struck a building. The presence of the girls added a sharpness to its beauty, especially the presence of Mag, who felt the spring even in London. But both of them seemed entirely oblivious. They marched along at a great rate, very upright and swift—like grenadiers—why grenadiers? Like grenadiers, making her hurry in a way that increased the discomfort of her hard cheap down-at-heel shoes. Their high-heeled shoes were in perfect condition and they went on and on, laughing and jesting as if there were no spring evening all round them. She wanted to stroll, and stop at every turn of the road. She grew to dislike them both long before Kenneth Street was reached, their brisk gait as they walked together in step, leaving her to manœuvre the passing of pedestrians on the narrow pavements of the side streets, the self-confident set of their this-season's clothes, 'line' clothes, like every one else was wearing, every one this side of the West End; Oxford Street clothes . . . and to long to be wandering home alone through the leafy squares. Were people who lived together always like this, always brisk and joking and keeping it up? They got on so well together . . . and she got on so well, too, with them. 'No one ever feels a third,' Mag had said. I am tired, too tired. They are stronger than I am. I feel dead; and they are perfectly fresh.

'D' you know I believe I feel too played out to read,' she said at their door.

'Then come in and smoke,' said Mag taking her arm. 'The night is yet young.'

CHAPTER X

MIRIAM swung her legs from the table and brought her tilted chair to the ground. The leads sloped down as she got to her feet and the strip of sky disappeared. The sunlight made a broad strip of gold along the parapet and a dazzling plaque upon the slope of the leads. She lounged into the shadowy middle of the room and stood feeling tall and steady and easy and agile in the freedom of knickers. The clothes lying on the bed were transformed. 'I say,' she murmured, her cigarette end wobbling encouragingly from the corner of her lips as she spoke, 'they're not bad.' She strolled about the room glancing at them from different points of view. They really made quite a good whole. It was the lilac that made them a good whole, the fresh heavy blunt cones of pure colour. In the distance, the bunched ribbon looked almost all green. She drew the hat nearer to the light, and the ribbon became mauve with green shadows and green with mauve shadows as it moved. The girl had been right about bunching the ribbon a little way up the sugar-loaf and over the wide brim. It broke the papery stiffness of the lilac and the harshness of the black straw. The straw looked very harsh and black in the clearer light. Out of doors it would look almost as if it had been done with that awful shiny hat polish. If the straw had been dull and silky and some shaded tone of mauve and green, it would have been one of those hats that give you a sort of madness, taking your eyes in and in, with the effect of a misty distant woodland brought near and moving, depths of interwoven colour under your eyes. But it would not have gone with the black-and-white check. The black part of the hat was right for the tiny check. That is the idea of some smart woman. . . . I did not think of it in the shop, but I got it right somehow, I can see now. It's right. Those might be someone else's things. . . . The sight of the black suède gloves and the lace-edged handkerchief and the powder-box laid out on the chest of drawers made her eager to begin. This was dressing. The way to feel you were dressing was to put everything out first, and then come back as another person and make a grand toilet. It makes you feel free and leisurely. There had been the long strange morning. In half an hour the adventure would begin and go on and be over. The room would not be in it. Something nice, or horrible, would come back. But the room would not be changed.

She found the dark green Atlas bus standing ready by the kerb and waited until it was just about to start, looking impatiently up and down the long vistas of the empty Sunday street, and then jumped hurriedly in with the polite half-irritated resignation of the man about town who finds himself stranded in a god-forsaken part of London, and steered herself carefully, against the swaying of the vehicle, along between the rows of seated forms, keeping her eyes carefully averted and fixed upon distant splendours. Securing an empty corner she sat down provisionally, on the edge of the seat, occupying the least possible space, clear of her neighbour, her eyes, turned inwards on splendours, still raking the street, her person ready to leap up at the sight of a crawling hansom—telling herself in a drawl that she felt must somehow be audible to an observant listener, how damnable it was that there were not hansoms in these remarkable backwoods—so damned inconvenient when your own barrow is laid up at Windover's. But a hansom might possibly appear. . . . She turned to the little corner window at her side and gazed with fierce abstraction down the oncoming street. Presently she would really be in a hansom. Miss Szigmondy had mentioned hansoms . . . supposing she should have to pay her share? Her heart beat rapidly and her face flushed as she thought of the fourpence in her purse. She would not be able even to offer. But if Miss Szigmondy were alone she would take cabs. There would be no need to mention it. The ambling trit-trot of the vehicle gradually

prevailed over the mood in which she had dressed. She was
becoming aware of her companions. Presently she would be
taking them all in and getting into a world that had nothing to
do with her afternoon. Turning aside so that her face could
not be seen and her own vision might be restricted to the roadway rolling slowly upon her through the little end window, she
dreamed of contriving somehow or other to save money for
hansoms. Hansoms were a necessary part of the worldly life.
Floating about in a hansom in the West End, in the season, was
like nothing else in the world. It changed you, your feelings,
manner, bearing, everything. It made you part of a wonderful
exclusive difficult triumphant life, a streak of it, going in and
out. It cut you off from all personal difficulties, made you
drop your personality and lifted you right out into the freedom
of a throng of happy people, a great sunlit tide, singing, all the
same laughing song, wave after wave, advancing, in open sunlight. It took you on to a great stage, lit and decked, where
you were lost, everything was lost and forgotten in the masque.
Nothing personal could matter so long as you were there and
kept there, day and night. Every one was invisible and vision-
less, united in the spectacle, gilding and hiding the underworld
in a brilliant embroidery . . . continuously.

As they rumbled up Baker Street, she wondered impatiently
why Miss Szigmondy had not appointed a meeting place in the
West End. Baker Street began all right; one felt safe going up
Orchard Street, past the beautiful china shop and the Romish
richness of Burns and Oates, seeing the sequestered worldli-
ness of Granville Place and rolling through Portman Square
with its enormous grey houses masking hidden wealth; but
after that it became a dismal corridor retreating towards the
full chill of the north. If they had met in Piccadilly, they
could have driven straight down through heaven into Chelsea.
Perhaps it would not be heaven with Miss Szigmondy. She
would not know the difference in the feeling of the different
parts of London. She would drive along like a foreigner—or
a member of a provincial antiquarian society, 'intelligently'
noticing things, knowing about the buildings and the statues.
Londoners were always twitted with not knowing about

London . . . the reason why they jested about it, half proudly,
their consciousness of being Londoners, living in London, was
going about happy, the minute they were outside their houses,
looking at nothing and feeling everything, like people wandering happily from room to room in a well-known house at some
time when everybody's attention was turned away by a festival
or a catastrophe. . . . London was like a prairie. In a hansom
it would be heaven, with anybody. A hansom saved you from
your companion more than any other vehicle. You were as
much outside it in London as you were inside with your companion, if you were anywhere south of Marylebone . . . the
way the open hood framed the vista. . . .

There was a hansom waiting outside Miss Szigmondy's
garden gate. The afternoon would begin at once with a swift
drive back into the world. Miss Szigmondy met her in the
dark hall, with an outbreak of bright guttural talk, talking as she
collected her things, breaking in with shouted instructions to
an invisible servant. Her voice sounded very foreign in the
excited upper notes, but it rang, a thin wiry ring, not shrieking
and breaking like the voices of excited Englishwomen. Perhaps
that was 'voice production.'

In the cab she sat sorting her cards, reading out names.
Miriam thrilled as she heard them. Miss Szigmondy's attention was no longer on her. Her mind slipped easily back; the
intervening time fell away. She was going with her sisters
along past the Burlington Arcade, she saw the pillar box, the
old man selling papers, the old woman with the crooked black
sailor hat and the fringed shawl, sitting on a box behind her
huge basket of tulips and daffodils . . . the great grimed stone
pillars, the court-yard beyond them blazing with sunshine, the
wide stone steps at the far end of the court-yard leading up into
cool shadow, the turnstile and great hall, an archway, and the
sudden fresh blaze of colours. . . .

But the hansom had turned into the main road and was going

north. They were going even further north than Miss Szigmondy's . . . up a straight empty Sunday suburban road
between rows of suburban houses with gardens that tried to
look pretty . . . an open silly prettiness like suburban ladies
coming up to town for matinées . . . if there were artists
living up here, it would not be worth while to go and see
them. . . .

As the afternoon wore on it dawned upon Miriam that if
Miss Szigmondy were to be at the poet's house in evening dress
by half past six, they had seen nearly all they were going to see.
There could be no thought of Chelsea. But she answered
with a swift negative when Miss Szigmondy inquired, as they
were shown into their hansom outside their eighth large Hampstead house, whether she were tired. Her unsatisfied consciousness ran ahead, waiting; just beyond, round the next
corner, was something that would relieve the oppression. 'I
just want to run in and see that poor boy Gilbert Haze.' Then
it was over, and she must go on enduring whilst Miss Szigmondy paid a call; unable to get free because she was being
paid for and could not afford to go back alone. They drove for
some distance, the large houses disappeared, they were in
amongst little drab roadways like those round about Mornington Road. Perhaps if she improvised an engagement, she could
find her way to Regent's Park and get back. But they had
come so far. They must be on the outskirts of N.W., perhaps
even in N. They pulled up before a small drab villa. The sun
had gone behind the clouds, the short street was desolate. No
touch of life or colour anywhere, hardly a sign of spring in the
small parched shrub-filled front gardens, uniformly enclosed
by dusty railings. She dreaded her wait alone in the cab with
her finery and her empty afternoon, while Miss Szigmondy
visited her sick friend.

'Come along,' said Miss Szigmondy from the little garden
path; 'poor creature, you *do* look tired.' Miriam got angrily
out of the cab. Whose fault was it that she was tired? Why
did Miss Szigmondy go to these things? She had not cared,

and was not disappointed at not caring. She was just the same
as when she had started out.

'I will wait in the garden,' she said hurriedly as the door
opened on the house of sickness. A short young man with
untidy dark hair and a shabby suit stood in the doorway. His
brilliant dark eyes smiled sharply at Miss Szigmondy and shot
beyond her towards Miriam as he stood aside holding the door
wide. 'Come along,' shouted Miss Szigmondy, disappearing.
Miriam came reluctantly forward and got herself through the
door, reaping the second curious sharp smile as she passed.
The young man had an extraordinary face, cheerful and grimy,
like a street arab; he was rather like a street arab. Miss Szigmondy was talking loudly from a little room to the right of
the door. Miriam's embarrassment in the impossibility of explaining her own superfluous presence was not relieved when
she entered the room. The young man was clearly not prepared. It was a most unwarrantable intrusion. She stood at
a loss behind Miss Szigmondy who was planted, still eagerly
talking, on the small clear space of bare boards—cracked and
dusty, like a warehouse—in the middle of the room, and tried
not to see anything in particular; but her eyes already had the
sense that there was nothing to sit upon, no corner to retire
into, nothing but an extraordinary confusion of shabby dust-
covered things laid bare by the sunlight that poured through
the uncurtained window. Her eyes took refuge in the face of
the young man confronting Miss Szigmondy making replies
to her volley of questions. He had no front teeth, nothing but
blackened stumps; dreadful, one ought not to look, unless he
were going to be helped. Perhaps Miss Szigmondy was going
to help him. But he did not look ill. His bright glancing
eyes shot about as if looking at something that was not there,
and he answered Miss Szigmondy's sallies with a sort of cheerful convulsion of his whole frame. He seemed to be 'on wires';
but not weak; strong and cheerful; happy; a kind of cheerfulness and happiness she had never met before. It was quiet.
It came from him soundlessly, making within his pleasant
voice a gay noise that conquered the strange embarrassing
room. Presently, in answer to a demand from Miss Szigmondy

he opened folding doors and ushered them into an adjoining room.

Miriam stood holding the little group in her hands, longing for words. She could only smile and smile. The young man stood by looking at it and smiling, too, giving his attention to Miss Szigmondy's questions about some larger white things standing in the bare room. When he moved away towards these and she could leave off wondering whether it would do to say 'And is this really going to the Academy next week?' instead of again repeating 'How beautiful,' and her eye could run undisturbed over and over the outlines of the two horses, impressions crowded upon her. The thing moved and changed as she looked at it; it seemed as if it must break away, burst out of her hands into the surrounding atmosphere. Everything about took on a happy familiarity, as if she had long been in the bright bare plaster-filled little room. From the edges of the small white group a radiance spread, freshening the air, flowing out into the happy world, flowing back over the afternoon, bringing parts of it to stand out like great fresh bright Academy pictures. The great studios opening out within the large garden-draped Hampstead houses, rich and bright with colour in a golden light, their fur rugs and tea services on silver trays, and velvet-coated men, the wives with trailing dresses and the people standing about, at once conspicuous and lost, were like Academy pictures. It was all real now, the pictures on the great easels, scraps of the Academy blaze; the studio with the bright light, and marble, and bright clear tiger-skins on the floor, the big clean fresh tiger almost filling the canvas . . . the dark studio with antique furniture and pictures of people standing about in historical clothes. . . .

'Goodness gracious, *isn't* she a swell!'
'Are they all right?'

'Are you a millionaire my dear? Have they raised your salary?'

'Do you really like them?'

'Yes. I've never seen you look so nice. You ought always to go about in a large black hat trimmed with lilac.'

'Didn't one of the artists want to paint your portrait?'

'They all did. I've promised at least twenty sittings.'

'Come nearer to the lamp, fair child, that I may be even more dazzled by thy splendour.'

'I'm awfully glad you like them—they'll have to go on for ever.'

'Where on earth did you find the money, child?'

'Borrowed it from Harry. It was her idea. You see I shall get four pounds for my four weeks' holiday; and if I go to stay with them it won't cost me anything; so she advanced me two pounds.'

'And you got all this for two pounds?'

'Practically; the hat was ten and six and the other things twenty-seven and six, and the gloves half a crown.'

'Where did you get them?'

'Edgware Road.'

'And just put them on?'

'It is really remarkable. Do you realize how lucky you are in being a stock size?'

'I suppose I am. But you know the awful thing about it is that they will never come in for Wimpole Street.'

'Why on earth not? What could be more ladylike, more simple, more altogether suitable?'

'You see I have to wear black there.'

'What an extraordinary idea. *Why?*'

'Well they asked me to. I don't know. I believe it's the fault of my predecessor. They told me she *rustled* and wore all kinds of dresses——'

'I see—a series of explosions.'

'On silk foundations.'

'But why should they assume that you would do the same?'

'I don't know. It's an awful nuisance. You can't get black blouses that will wash; it will be awful in the summer; besides, it's so unbecoming.'

'There I can't agree. It would be for me. It makes me look dingy; but it suits you, throws up your rose-leaf complexion and your golden hair. But I call it jolly hard lines. I'd like to see the governor dictating to me what I should wear.'

'It's so expensive if one can't wear out one's best things.'

'It's intolerable. Why do you stand it?'

'What can I do?'

'Tell them you must either wear *scarlet* at the office or have a higher *screw*.'

'It isn't an office, you see. I have to be so much in the surgeries and interviewing people in the waiting-room, you know.'

'Yes—from dukes to dustmen. But would either the dukes or the dustmen disapprove of scarlet?'

'One has to be a discreet nobody. It's the professional world; you don't understand; you are equals, you two, superiors, pampered countesses in your offices.'

'Well I think it's a beastly shame. I should brandish a pair of forceps at Mr Hancock and say "Scarlet—or I leave."'

'Where should I go? I have no qualifications.'

'You wouldn't leave. They would say, "Miss Henderson, wear purple and yellow, only stay." I think it's a reflection on her taste, don't you, Jan?'

'Certainly it is. It is fiendish. But employers *are* fiends —to women.'

'I haven't found that soh.'

'Ah, you keep yours in order, you rule them with a rod of iron.'

'I do. I believe in it.'

'I envy you your late hours in the morning.'

'Ah-ha—she's had a row about that.'

'*Have* you, Mag?'

'Not a row; simply a discussion.'

'What happened?'

'Simply this. The governor begged me—almost in tears— to come down earlier—for the sake of the discipline of the office.'

'What did you say?'

'I said Herr *Epstein*; what can I do? How do you suppose I can get up, have breakfast and be down here before eleven?'

'What did he say?'

'He protested and implored and offered to pay cabs for me.'

'Good Lord, Mag, you are extraordinary.'

'I am not extraordinary and it is no concern of the Deity's. I fail to see why I should get to the office earlier than I do. I don't get my letters before half-past eleven. I am fresh and gay and rested, I get through my work before closing-time. I work like anything whilst I am there.'

'And you still go down at eleven?'

'I still go down at eleven.'

'I *do* envy you. You see my people always want me most the first thing in the morning. It's awful, if one has been up very late.'

'And what is our life worth, without late hours? The evening is the only life we have.'

'Exactly. And they are the same really. They do their work to be free of it and live.'

'Precisely; but they are waited on. They have their houses and baths and servants and meals and comforts. We get up in cold rooms untended and tired. *They* ought to be first at the office and wait upon us.'

'She is a queen in her office; waited upon hand and foot.'

'Well—why not? I do them the honour of bringing my bright petunia-clad feminine presence into their dingy warehouse; I expect some acknowledgment of the honour.'

'You don't allow them either to spit or swear.'

'I do not; and they appreciate it.'

'Mine are beasts. I defy any one to do anything with them. I *loathe* the city man.'

Miriam sighed. In neither of these offices, she felt sure, could she hold her own—and yet, compared to her own long day, what freedom the girls had—ten to five and eleven to six and any clothes they found it convenient to wear. But city men . . . no restrictions were too high a price to pay for the privileges of her environment; the association with gentlemen, her quiet room, the house, the perpetual interest of the patients, the curious exciting streaks of social life, linking up with the past and carrying it forward on a more generous level. The girls had broken with the past and were fighting in the world. She was somehow between two worlds, neither quite sheltered, nor quite free . . . not free as long as she wanted, in spite of her reason, to stay on at Wimpole Street and please the people there. Why did she want to stay? What future would it bring? Less than ever was there any chance of saving for old age. She could not for ever go on being secretary to a dentist. . . . She drove these thoughts away; they were only one side of the matter; there were other things; things she could not make clear to the girls; nor to any one who could not see and feel the whole thing from inside, as she saw and felt it. And even if it were not so, if the environment of her poorly paid activities had been trying and unsympathetic, at least it gave seclusion, her own room to work in, her free garret and her evening and week-end freedom. But what was she going to do with it?

'Tell us about the *show*, Miriam. Cease to gaze at Jan's relations; sit down, light a cigarette.'

'These German women fascinate me,' said Miriam swinging round from the mantelshelf; 'they are so like Jan and so utterly different.'

'Yes; Jan is Jan and they are Minna and Erica.'

Taking a cigarette from Mag's case, Miriam lit it at the lamp. Before her eyes the summer unrolled—concerts with Miss Szigmondy, going in the cooling day in her new clothes, with a thin blouse, from daylight into electric light and music, taking off the zouave inside and feeling cool at once, the electric light mixing with the daylight, the cool darkness to walk home in alone, full of music that would last on into the next day; Miss Szigmondy's musical at-homes, evenings at Wimpole Street, week-ends in the flowery suburbs, windows and doors open, cool rooms, gardens in the morning and evening, week-ends in the country, each journey like the beginning of the summer holiday, week-ends in town, Sunday afternoons at Mr Hancock's and Miss Szigmondy's—all taking her away from

Kenneth Street. All these things yielded their best reality in this room. Glowing brightly in the distance they made this room like the centre of a song. But a week-end taken up was a week-end missed at Kenneth Street. It meant missing Slater's on Saturday night, the week-end stretching out ahead immensely long, the long evening with the girls, its lateness protected by the coming Sunday, waking lazily fresh and happy and easy-minded on Sunday morning, late breakfast, the cigarette in the sunlit window space, its wooden sides echoing with the clamour of St Pancras bells, the three voices in the little rooms, irländisches ragout, the hours of smoking and talking out and out on to strange promontories where everything was real all the time, the faint gradual coming of the twilight, the evening untouched by the presence of Monday, no hurry ahead, no social performances, no leave-taking, no railway journey.

'Yes; Jan is Londonized; she looks German; her voice suggests the whole of Germany; these girls are Germany untouched, strong, cheerful, musical, tree-filled Germany, without any doubts. They've got Jan's sense of humour without her cynicism.'

'Is that so, Jan?'

'Yes, I think perhaps it is. They are sweet simple children.' Yes, sweet—but maddening too. German women were so sure and unsuspicious and practical about life. Jan had some of that left. But she was English too, more transparent and thoughtful.

'The show! The show!'

She told them the story of the afternoon in a glowing précis, calling up the splendours upon which she felt their imaginations at work, describing it as they saw it and as, with them, in retrospect, she saw it herself. Her descriptions drew Mag's face towards her, glowing, rapt and reverent. Jan sat sewing with inturned eyes and half open, half smiling appreciative face. They both fastened upon the great gold-framed pictures, asking for details. Presently they were making plans to visit the Academy, and foretelling her joy in seeing them again and identifying them. She had not thought of that; certainly, it would be delightful; and perhaps seeing the pictures in freedom and alone she might find them wonderful.

'Why do you say their wives were all like cats?'

'They were.' She called up the unhatted figures moving about among the guests in trailing gowns—keeping something up, pretending to be interested, being cattishly nice to the visitors, and thinking about other things all the time. . . . I can't *stand* them, oh, I *can't* stand them. . . . But the girls would not have seen them in that way; they would have been interested in them and their dresses, they would have admired the prettiness of some of them and found several of them 'charming' . . . if Mag were an artist's wife she would behave in the way those women behaved. . . .

'Were they all a*like*?' That was half sarcastic. . . .

'Absolutely. They were all *cats*, simply.'

'Isn't she *extraordinary*?'

'It's the cats who are extraordinary. Why do they do it, girls! *Why* do they do it?' She flushed, feeling insincere. At this moment she felt that she knew that Mag, in social life, would conform and be a cat. She had never thought of her in social life; here, in poverty and freedom, she was herself.

'Do *phwatt*, me dear?'

'Oh, let them go. It makes me tired, even to think of them. The thought of the sound of their voices absolutely wears me out.'

'I'm not laaazy—I'm tie-erd—I was *born* tie-erd.'

'I say, girls, I want to ask you something.'

'Well?'

'Why don't you two write?'

'*Write?*'

'Write what?'

'Us?'

'Just as we are, without one'——

'Flea—I know. No. *Don't* be silly. I'm perfectly serious. I mean it. Why don't you write things—both of you. I thought of it this morning.'

Both girls sat thoughtful. It was evident that the idea was not altogether unfamiliar to them.

'Someone kept telling me the other day I ought to write and it suddenly struck me that if any one ought it's you two. Why don't you, Mag?'

'Why should I? Have I not already enough on my fair young shoulders?'

'*Jan*, why don't *you*?'

'I, my dear? For a most excellent reason.'

'What reason?' demanded Miriam in a shaking voice. Her heart was beating; she felt that a personal decision was going to be affected by Jan's reason, if she could be got to express it. Jan did not reply instantly, and she found herself hoping that nothing more would be said about writing, that she might be free to go on cherishing the idea, alone and unbiased.

'I do not write,' said Jan slowly, 'because I am perfectly convinced that anything I might write would be mediocre.'

Miriam's heart sank. If Jan, with all her German knowledge and her wit and experience of two countries, felt this, it was probably much truer of herself. To think about it, to dwell upon the things Mr Wilson had said, was simply vanity. He had said *any one* could learn to write. But he was clever and ready to believe her clever in the same way, and ready to take ideas from him. It was true she had material, 'stuff,' as he called it, but she would not have known it, if she had not been told. She could see it now, as he saw it, but if she wrote at his suggestion, a borrowed suggestion, there would be something false in it, clever and false.

'Yes—I think Jan's right,' said Mag cheerfully. 'That is an excellent reason, and the true one.'

It was true. But how could they speak so lightly and cheerfully about writing? . . . the thing one had always wanted to do, that every one probably secretly wanted to do, and the girls could give up the idea without a sigh. They were right. It would be wrong to write mediocre stuff. Why was she feeling so miserable? Of course, because neither of them had suggested that she should write. They knew her better than Mr Wilson and it never occurred to them that she should write. That settled it. But something moved despairingly in the void.

Do you think it would be *wrong* to write mediocre stuff?' she asked huskily.

'It would be worse than *wrong*, child—it would be foolish; it wouldn't sell.'

CHAPTER XI

EVERYTHING was ready for the two o'clock patient. There was no excuse for lingering any longer. Half past one. Why did they not come up? On her way to the door she opened the corner cupboard and stood near the open door hungry, listening for footsteps on the basement stairs, dusting and ranging the neat rows of bottles. At the end of five minutes she went guiltily down. If he had finished his lunch, they would wonder why she had lingered so long. If she had hurried down as soon as she could, no one would have known that she hoped to have lunch alone. Now, because she had waited deliberately someone would read her guilt. She wished she were one of those people who never tried to avoid anything. The lunch-room door opened and closed as she reached the basement stairs. James's cheerful footsteps clacked along—neat high-heeled shoes—towards the kitchen. She had taken something in. They were still at lunch, unconsciously, just in the same way. No. She was glad she was not one of those people who just went on—not avoiding things. . . .

Mr Hancock was only just beginning his second course. He must have lingered in the workshop. . . . He was helping himself to condiments; Mr Orly proffered the wooden peppermill; 'Oh—thank you'; he screwed it with an air of embarrassed appreciativeness. There was a curious fresh lively air of embarrassment in the room, making a stirring warmth in its cellar-like coolness. Miriam slipped quietly into her place, hoping she was not an interloper. At any rate every one was too much engrossed to ponder over her lateness. Mr Orly was sitting with his elbows on the table and his serviette crumpled in his hands, ready to rise from the table, beaming mildness and waiting. Mrs Orly sat waiting and smiling with her elbows on the table.

'Ah,' said Mr Orly gently as Miriam sat down, 'here comes the clerical staff.'

Miriam beamed and began her soup. It was James waiting to-day too, with her singing manner; a happy day.

Mrs Orly asked a question in her happiest voice. They were fixing a date. . . . They were going . . . to a *theatre* . . . together. Her astonished mind tried to make them coalesce . . . she saw them sitting in a row, two different worlds confronted by one spectacle . . . there was not a scrap of any kind of performance that would strike them both in the same way.

'Got anything on on Friday, Miss Henderson?'

The sudden question startled her. Had it been asked twice? She answered, stammering, in amazed consciousness of what was to follow and accepted the invitation in a flood of embarrassment. Her delight and horror and astonishment seemed to flow all over the table. Desperately she tried to gather in all her emotions behind an easy appreciative smile. She felt astonishment and dismay coming out of her hair, swelling her hands, making her clumsy with her knife and fork. Far away, beyond her grasp was the sense she felt she ought to have, the sense of belonging; socially. It was being offered. But something or someone was fighting it. Always, everywhere someone or something was fighting it.

Mr Orly had given a ghostly little chuckle. 'Like dining at restaurants?' he asked kindly and swiftly.

'I don't think I ever have.'

'Then we shall have the pleasure of initiating you. Like caviare?'

'I don't even know what it is,' said Miriam trying to bring gladness into her voice.

'Oh—this is great. Caviare to the million, eh?—oh, I ought not to have put it like that, things one would rather have said otherwise—no offence intended—none taken, I hope—don't yeh know really?—Sturgeon's roe, y' know.'

'Oh, I know I don't like *roe*,' said Miriam gravely.

'Chalk it up. Miss Henderson doesn't like roe.'

Miriam flushed. Pressing back through her anger to what had preceded, she found inspiration.

'My education has been neglected.'

'Quite so, but now's your chance. Seize your opportunity; carpe diem. See?'

'I thought it was caviare, not carp,' said Mr Hancock quietly.

Was it a rescue, or a sacrifice to the embarrassing occasion? She had never heard him jest with the Orlys. Mrs Orly chuckled gleefully, flashing out the smile that Miriam loved. It took every line from her care-fashioned face and lit it with a most extraordinary radiance. She had smiled like that as a girl, in response to the jests of her many brothers . . . her eyes were sweet; there was a perfect sweetness in her somewhere.

'Bravo, Hancock, that's a good one. . . . Ye gods and fishes large and small, listen to *that*,' he murmured half turning towards the door.

The clattering of boots on the stone stairs was followed by the rattling of the loose door knob and the splitting open of the door. Mr Leyton shot into the room, searching the party with a swift glance and taking his place in the circle in a state of headlong silent volubility. By the way he attacked his lunch it was clear he had a patient waiting, or imminent. It occurred to Miriam to wonder why he did not always arrange his appointments round about lunch-time . . . but any such manœuvre would be discovered and things would be worse than ever. Mr Orly watched quietly while he refused Mrs Orly's offer to ring for soup, devouring bread and butter until she should have carved for him—and then extended his invitation to his son.

'Oh, is this the annual?' asked Mr Leyton gruffly. 'What's the show?'

'My dear, will you be so good as to inform Mr Leyton of ——'

'Don't be silly, Ro,' said Mrs Orly trying to laugh, 'we're going to *Hamlet*, Ley.'

'We have the honour of begging Mr Leyton's company on the occasion of our visit, dinner included, to——'

'What's the date?' rapped Mr Leyton with his tumbler to his lips.

'The date, ascertained as suited to all present with the

exception of your lordship—oh my God, Ley,' sighed Mr Orly, hiding his face in his serviette, his huge shoulders shaking.

'What have I done now?' asked Mr Leyton, gasping after his long drink.

'Don't be so silly, Ley. You haven't answd fathez queshun.'

'How can I answer till I'm told the *date*?'

'Don't be silly, you can come any evening.'

'*Friday*,' whispered Miriam.

'*What?*' said Mr Orly softly, emerging from his serviette, 'a traitor in the camp?'

'Friday is it? Well, then it's pretty certain I *can't* come.'

'Don't be silly, Ley—you haven't any engagements.'

'*Haven't I?* There's a sing-song at headquarters Friday.'

'Enough, my dear, enough, press him no more,' said Mr Orly rising. 'Far be it from us to compete. Going to sing, Ley, or to song, eh? Never mind, boy, sorry you can't come,' he added, sighing gustily as he left the room.

'You'll be able to come, Ley, won't you?' whispered Mrs Orly, impatiently lingering.

'If you'd only let me know the date beforehand instead of springing it on me.'

'Don't be si'y, Ley, it vexes father so. You needn't go to the si'y sing-song.'

'I don't see how I can get out of it. It's rather a big function; as an officer I ought to be there.'

'Oh never mind; you'd better come.'

Mr Orly called from the stairs.

'All right darling,' she said, in anxious cheerful level tones, hurrying to the door. 'You *must* come, Ley, you can manage, somehow.'

Miriam sat feeling wretchedly about in her mind. Mr Leyton was busily finishing his lunch. In a moment Mr Hancock would reassert himself by some irrelevant insincerity. She found courage to plunge into speech, on the subject of her two lessons at the school. Her story strove strangely against the echoes and fell, impeded. It was an attempt to create a quiet diversion. . . . It should have been done violently . . . how many times had she seen it done, the speaker violently pushing off what had gone before and protruding his diversion, in brisk animated deliberately detached tones. But it was never really any good. There was always a break and a wound, something left unhealed, something standing unlearned . . . something that can only grow clear in silence. . . .

'You 'll never learn cycling like *that*,' said Mr Leyton with the superior chuckle of the owner of a secret, as he snatched up a biscuit and made off. She clung fearfully to his cheerful harassed departing form. There was nothing left now in the room but the echoes. Mr Hancock sat munching his biscuit and cheese with a look of determined steely preoccupation in his eyes that were not raised above the level of the spread of disarray along the table; but she could hear the busy circulation of his thoughts. If now she could endure for a moment. But her mind flung hither and thither, seeking with a loathed servility some alien neutral topic. She knew anything she might say with the consciousness of his thoughts in her mind would be resented and slain. To get up and go quietly away with some murmured remark about her work, would be to leave him with his judgment upon him. What he wanted was to give her an instruction about something in a detached professional voice and get rid of her, believing that she had gone unknowing, and remaining in his circle of reasonable thoughts. She hit out with all her force, coming against the buttress of silent angry forehead with random speech.

'I can't believe that it 's less than two months to the longest day.'

'Time flies,' responded Mr Hancock grimly. She recoiled exhausted by her effort and quailed under the pang in the mid-day gaslit room of realization of the meaning of her words. Her eye swept over the grey-clad form and the blunted features, seeking some power that would stay the inexorable consumption of the bright passing days.

' "Tempus fugit," I suppose one ought to say,' he said with a little laugh, getting up.

'Oui,' said Miriam angrily, 'le temps s'envole; die Zeit vergeht, in other words.'

CHAPTER XII

RUNNING upstairs to Mr Hancock's room a quarter of an hour before his arrival in the morning, Miriam found herself wishing that she lived altogether at Wimpole Street. They were all so kind. Life would be simplified if she could throw in her lot with them. Coming in to breakfast after the lesson had been a sort of home-coming. There were pleasant noises about the house; the family shouted carelessly to each other on the stairs, the schoolboy slid down the banisters; the usual subdued manner of the servants was modified by an air of being a possession of the house and liking it. They rushed quietly and happily about. The very aroma of the coffee seemed tranquilly to feed one. At breakfast every one was cheerful and kind. It was home. They were so sympathetic and amused over the adventure. The meeting in the freshness of the morning made everything easier to handle. It gave the morning a beginning and shed its brightness over the professional hush that fell upon the house at nine o'clock. It would make lunch-time more easy; and, at the end of the day, if asked, she would join the family party again.

While Mr Hancock was looking through his letters, she elaborately suppressed a yawn.

'How did you get on?' he asked, with prompt amusement, his eyes on a letter.

'Well, I couldn't get off; that was just it,' murmured Miriam quietly, enjoying her jest; how strong she felt after her good breakfast. . . .

He turned an amused inquiring face, and they both laughed.

Everything in the room was ready for the day's work. She polished the already bright set of forceps, with a luxurious sense of leisure.

'It was perfectly awful. When we got to the Inner Circle, Mr Leyton simply put me on the bicycle and sent me off. *He* rode round the other way and I had to go on and on. He scorched about and kept passing me.'

Mr Hancock waited, smiling, for the more that stood in her struggling excited voice.

'There were people going round on horseback and a few other people on bicycles.'

'I expect they all gave you a pretty wide berth.'

'They *did*; except one awful man, an old gentleman sailing along looking at nothing.'

'What happened?' laughed Mr Hancock delightedly.

'It was awful, I was most fearfully rude—I shouted "*Get* out of the way" and *I* was on the wrong side of the road; but miles off, only I *knew* I couldn't get back. I had forgotten how to steer.'

'What did he do?'

'He swept round me looking very frightened and disturbed.'

'Hadn't you a bell?'

'Yes, but it meant sliding my hand along. I daren't do that; nobody seemed to want it, they all glided about; they were really awfully nice. I *had* to go on, because I couldn't get off. I can wobble along, but I can't mount or dismount. I was never so frightened in my life.'

'I'm afraid you've had a very drastic time.'

'I fell off in the end, I was so dead beat.'

'But this is altogether too drastic. Where was Leyton?'

'Rushing round and round, meeting me and then overtaking me, startling me out of my wits by ringing behind for me to get to the side. Nobody else did that. It was awfully kind. I went tacking about from side to side.'

'I'm afraid you've had a very drastic time. I think you'd better come up this evening and learn getting on and off on the lawn; that's the way to do it.'

'Oh,' said Miriam gratefully; 'but I have no machine. Mrs Orly lent me hers.'

'I dare say we can hire a machine.'

CHAPTER XIII

MIRIAM found it difficult to believe that the girl was a dental
secretary. She swept about among Miss Szigmondy's guests
in a long Liberty dress, her hands holding her long scarf about
her person as if she were waiting for a clear space to leap or run,
staying nowhere, talking here and there with the assurance of
a successful society woman, laughing and jesting, swiftly talking
down the group she was with and passing on, with a shouted
remark about herself, as she had done in the library on the
night of Lord Kelvin's lecture. . . . 'I 'm tired of being good;
I 'm going to try being naughty for a change.' Mr Hancock
had stood planted before her, in laughing admiration, waiting
for the next thing that she might say. How could he, of all
men in the world, be taken out of himself by an effective trick?
He had laughed more spontaneously than Miriam had ever
seen him do. What *was* this effective thing? An appearance
of animation. That, it seemed, could make any man, even Mr
Hancock, if it were free from any suggestion of loudness or
vulgarity, stand gaping and disarmed. Why had he volun-
teered the information that she was eighteen, and secretary to
his friend in Harley Street? 'You don't seem very *keen*'; that
was her voice from the other end of the room; using the new
smart word with a delicate emphasis, pretending interest in
something, meaning nothing at all. She was a middle-aged
woman, she would never be older than she was now. She saw
nothing and no one, nor ever would. In all her life she would
never be arrested by anything. Nice kind people would call
her 'a charming girl.' . . . 'Charming girls' were taught to
behave effectively, and lived in a brilliant death, dealing death
all round them. Nothing could live in their presence. No
natural beauty, no spectacle of art, no thought, no music. They
were uneasy in the presence of these things, because their
presence meant cessation of 'charming' behaviour—except at

such moments as they could use the occasion to decorate themselves. *They had no souls*. Yet, in social life, nothing seemed to possess any power but their surface animation.

There was real power in that other woman. Her strong young comeliness was good, known to be good. It was strange that a student of music should be known for her work among the poor. The serene large outlines of her form gave out light in the room; and the light on her white brow, unconscious above her deliberately kind face, was the loveliest thing to be seen; the deliberately kind face spoiled it, and would presently change it; unless some great vision came to her, it would grow furrowed over 'the housing problem' and the face would dry up, its white life cut off at a source; at present she was at the source; one could tell her anything. Mr Hancock recognized her goodness, spoke of her with admiration and respect. What was she doing here, among all these worldly musicians? *She* would never be a musician, never a first-class musician. Then she had ambition. She was poor. Someone was helping her . . . Miss Szigmondy! Why? She must know she would never make a musician. Miriam cowered in her corner. The good woman was actually going to sing before all these celebrities. What a fine great free voice. . . . '*When* shall we meet—*refined* and free, amongst the moorland *brack-en* . . .' if Mr Hancock could have heard her sing that, surely his heart must have gone out to her? She knew, to her inmost being, what that meant. She *longed* for cleansing fires, even she with her radiant forehead; her soul flew out along the sustained notes towards its vision, her dark eyes were set upon it as she sang, the clear tones of her voice called to the companion of her soul for the best that was in him. She was the soul of truth, counting no cost. She would attain her vision, though the earthly companion she longed for might pass her by. The pure beauty of the moorland would remain for her, would set itself along the shores of her life for ever. . . .

But she could not sing. It was the worst kind of English singing, all volume and emphasis and pressure. Was there that in her goodness too . . . deliberate kindness to everybody? Was it a method—just a social method? She was one of those people about whom it would be said that she never spoke ill of any one. But was not indiscriminate deliberate conscious goodness to everybody an insult to humanity? People who were like that never knew the difference between one person and another. 'Philanthropic' people were never sympathetic. They pitied. Pity was not sympathy. It was a denial of something. It assumed that life was pitiful. Yet her clear eyes would see through anything, any evil thing to the human being behind. But she knew it, and practised it like a doctor. She had never been amazed by the fact that there were any human beings at all . . . and with all her goodness she had plans and ambitions. She wanted to be a singer—and she was thinking about somebody. Men were dazzled by the worldly little secretary, and they reverenced the singer and her kind. Irreligious men would respect religion for her sake— and would wish, thinking of her, to live in a particular kind of way; but she would never lead a man to religion, because she had no thoughts and no ideas.

The surprise of finding these two women here, and the pain of observing them, was a just reward for having come to Miss Szigmondy's At Home without a real impulse—just to see the musicians and to be in the same room with them. All that remained was to write to someone about them by name. There was nothing to do but mention their names. There was no wonder about them. They were all *fat*. Not one of them was an artist and they all hated each other. It was like a ballad concert. They all sang in the English way. They were not in the least like the instrumentalists; or St James's Hall Saturday afternoon audiences, not that kind of 'queer soft lot'; not shadowy grey or dead white or with that curious transparent look; they all looked ruddy or pink, and sleek; they had the same sort of kindly common sense as Harriett's Lord and Lady Bollingdon . . . perhaps to keep a voice going it was necessary to be fat.

CHAPTER XIV

'IT was simply heavenly going off—all standing in the hall in evening dress, while the servants blew for hansoms. I wore my bridesmaid's dress with a piece of tulle arranged round the top of the bodice. It was wrong at the back so I had to sit very carefully the whole evening to prevent it going up like a muffler, but never mind; it was heavenly, I tell you. We bowled off down through the West End in three hansoms, one behind the other, in the dark. You know the gleam and shine inside a hansom sprinting along a dark empty street where the lamps are few and dim (see *The Organist's Daughter*); and then came the bright streets all alight and full of dinner and theatre people in evening dress, in hansoms, and you kept getting wedged in between other hansoms with people talking and laughing all round you; and it took about ten minutes to get from the end of Regent Street across to the other side of Piccadilly, where we dined in wicked Rupert Street. Just as the caviare was brought in, we heard that the Prince of Wales had won the Derby. Shakespeare is extraordinary. I had no idea *Hamlet* was so full of quotations.'

Miriam flushed as the last words ran automatically from her pen. The sense of the richly moving picture that had filled her all the morning, and now kept her sitting happily under the hot roof at her small dusty table in the full breadth of Saturday afternoon, would be gone if she left that sentence. She felt a curious painful shock at the tips of her fingers as she re-read it; a current, singing within her, was driven back by it. . . . Mrs Orly's face had been all alive and alight when she had leant forward across Mr Hancock and said the words that had seemed so meaningless and irritating. Perhaps she too had felt something she wanted to express and had lost it at that moment. Certainly both she and Mr Orly would feel the beauty of Shakespeare. But the words had shattered the spell

of Shakespeare, and writing them down like that was spoiling
the description of the evening, though Harriett would not
think so.

But anyhow the letter would not do for Harriett—even if
words could be found to express 'Shakespeare.' That would
not interest Harriett. She would think the effort funny and
Miriamish, but it would not mean anything to her. She had
been to Shakespeare because she adored Ellen Terry and put
up with Irving for her sake. . . . People in London seemed to
think that Irving was just as great as Ellen Terry. . . . Perhaps
now Irving would seem different. Perhaps Irving was great.
. . . I will go and hear Irving in Shakespeare . . . no money
and no theatres except with other people. . . . The rest of the
letter would simply hurt Harriett, because it would seem like a
reflection on theatres with her. Theatres with her had had a
magic that last night could not touch . . . sitting in the front
row of the pit, safely in after the long wait, the walls of the
theatre going up, softly lit buff and gold, fluted and decorated
and bulging with red-curtained boxes, the clear view across
the empty stalls of the dim height of fringed curtain hanging
in long straight folds, the certainty that Harriett shared the
sense of the theatre, that for her, too, when the orchestra began,
the great motionless curtain shut them in in a life where
everything else in the world faded away and was forgotten, the
sight of the perfection of happiness on Harriett's little buff-
shadowed face, the sudden running ripple, from side to side,
of the igniting footlights . . . the smoothly clicking rustle of
the withdrawing curtain . . . the magic square of the lit
scene . . . the daily growth of the charm of these things
during that week when they had gone to a theatre every night,
so that on looking back, the being in the theatre with the certainty of the moving changing scenes ahead was clearer than
either of the plays they had seen. . . . She sat staring through
the open lattice. . . . The sound of the violin from the house
down the street, that had been a half-heard obbligato to her
vision of last night, came in drearily, filling the space whence
the vision had departed, with uneasy questions. She turned
to her letter to recapture the impulse with which she had sat

down. . . . If she turned it into a letter to Eve, all the description of the evening would have to be changed; Eve knew all about grandeurs, with the Greens's large country house and their shooting-boxes and visits to London hotels; the bright glories must go—overwhelming and unexpressed. Why did that make one so sad? Was it because it suggested that one cared more for the gay circumstances than for the thing seen? What was it they had seen? Why had they gone? What *was* Shakespeare? Her vision returned to her, as she brooded on this fresh problem. The whole scene of the theatre was round her once more; she was sitting in the half darkness gazing at the stage. What had it been for her? What was it that came from the stage? Something—*real* . . . to say that drove it away. She looked again and it clustered once more, alive. The gay flood of the streets, the social excitements and embarrassments of the evening were a conflagration; circling about the clear bright kernel of moving lights and figures on the stage. She gazed at the bright stage. Moments came sharply up, grouped figures, spoken words. She held them, her contemplation aglow with the certainty that something was there that set her alight with love, making her whole in the midst of her uncertainty and ignorance. Words and phrases came, a sentence here and there that had suddenly shaped and deepened a scene. Perhaps it was only in seeing Shakespeare acted that one could appreciate him? But it was *not* the acting. No one could act. They all just missed it. It was all very well for Mag to laugh. They *did* just miss it. . . . 'Why, my child? In what way?' 'They act at the audience, they take their cues too quickly, and have their emotions too abruptly; and from outside not inside.' 'But if they felt at all, all the time, they would go mad or die.' 'No, they would not. But even if they did not feel it, if they looked, it would be enough. They don't *look* at the thing they are doing.' It was not the acting. Nor the play. The characters of the story were always tiresome. The ideas, the wonderful quotations, if you looked closely at them, were every one's ideas; things that everybody knew. To read Shakespeare carefully all through, would only be to find all the general things somewhere or other. But that did not matter. Being ignorant of him and of history did not matter, as long as you heard him. Poetry! The poetry of Shakespeare . . .? Primers of literature told one that. It did not explain the charm. Just the sound. Music. Like Beethoven. Bad acting cannot spoil Shakespeare. Bad playing cannot destroy Beethoven. It was the *sound* of Shakespeare that made the scenes real—that made *Winter's Tale*, so long ago and so bewildering, remain in beauty. . . . 'Dear Eve, Shakespeare is a sound . . .' She tore up the letter. The next time she wrote to Eve, she must remember to say that. The garret was stifling. Away from the brilliant window, the room was just as hot; the close thick smell of dust sickened her. She came back to the table, sitting as near as possible to the open. The afternoon had been wasted trying to express her evening, and nothing had been expressed. The thought of last night was painful now. She had spoiled it in some way. Her heart beat heavily in the stifling room. Her head ached and her eyes were tired. She was too tired to walk; and there was no money; barely enough for next week's A.B.C. suppers. There was no comfort. It was May . . . in a stuffy dusty room. May. Her face quivered and her head sank upon the hot table.

CHAPTER XV

NEARLY all the roses were half-opened buds; firm and stiff. Larger ones put in here and there gave the effect of mass. Closest contemplation enhanced the beauty of the whole. Each rose was perfect. The radiant mass was lovely throughout. The body of the basket curved firmly away to its slender hidden base; the smooth sweep of the rim and the delicate high arch of the handle held the roses perfectly framed. It was a perfect gift. . . . It had been quite enough to have the opportunity of doing little things for Mrs Berwick . . . the surprise of the roses. The *surprise* of them. Roses, roses, roses . . . all the morning they had stood, making the morning's work happy; visible all over the room. Every one in the house had had the beautiful shock of them. And they were still as they had been when they had been gathered in the dew. If they were in water, by the end of the afternoon the buds would revive and expand . . . even after the hours in the Lyceum. If they were thrown now into the waste-paper basket it would not matter. They would go on being perfect—to the end of life. 'And as long; as my heart is bea-ting; as long; as my eyes; have; tears.'

Winthrop came up punctually at one o'clock, as he had promised. 'It would save you comin' down if I was to ph—come up.' It would go on then. He had thought about it and meant to do it. She opened the cash box quickly and deftly in her gratitude and handed him his four sovereigns and the money for the second mechanic and the apprentices. He waited gently while she counted it out. Next Saturday she would have it ready for him. 'Thank you Miss ——; ph—ph *good* afternoon,' he said cheerfully. 'Good afternoon Mr Winthrop,' she responded busily, with all her heart, and listened as he clattered away downstairs. A load was lifted from Saturday mornings, for good. No more going down to run the gauntlet of the row of eyes and get herself along the bench, depositing the various sums. Nothing in future but the letters, the overhauling of Mr Hancock's empty surgery, the easy lunch with Mr Leyton, and the week-end. She entered the sums in the petty-cash book. There was that. They would always be that, week after week. But to-day the worrying challenge of it disappeared in the joy of the last entry. 'Self,' she wrote, the light across the outspread prospect of her life steadying and deepening as she wrote, 'one pound, five.' The five, written down, sent a thrill from the contemplated page. Taking the customary sovereign from the cash-box she placed it carefully in the middle pocket of her purse and closed the clip. The five shillings she distributed about the side-pockets; half a crown, a shilling, two sixpenny bits and six coppers. The purse was full of money. By September she would have about four pounds five in hand, and two pounds ten of her month's holiday money still unspent; six pounds fifteen; she could go to a matinée every week and still have about half the four pounds five; about four pounds fifteen altogether; enough to hire a bicycle for the month and buy some summer blouses for the holiday. . . . She pocketed the heavy purse. Why was there always a feeling of guilt about a salary? It was the same every week. The life at Wimpole Street was so full and so interesting; she was learning so much and seeing so much. Salary was out of place—a payment for leading a glorious life, half of which was entirely her own. The extra five shillings was a present from the Orlys and Mr Hancock. She could manage on the pound. The new sum was wealth, superfluity. They would expect more of her in future. Surely it would be possible to give more; with so much money; to find the spirit to come punctually at nine; always to have everything in complete readiness in all three surgeries; to keep all the books up to date. . . . But they would not have given her the rise at the end of five months, if they had not felt she was worth it. . . . It would make all the difference to the summer. Hopefully she took a loose sheet of paper and made two lists of the four pages of the week's entries—dissecting them under the heads of workshop and surgery. About fifteen pounds had been spent. Again and again with heating head she added her pages of small sums, getting each time slightly different results, until at last they balanced with the dissected lists— twice in succession. The hall clock struck one and Mr Leyton came downstairs rattling, and rattled into her room. 'How d' you like this get-up?' The general effect of the blue-grey uniform and brown leather belt and bandolier was pleasing. 'Oh, *jolly*,' she said abstractedly to his waiting figure. He clattered downstairs to lunch. *Everybody* had outside interests. Mr Hancock would be on the Broads by now. Her afternoon beckoned, easy with the superfluity of money. Anxiously she counted over the balance in the cash box. It was two and ninepence short. Damnation. Damnation. 'Put it down to stamps—or miscellanea; not accounted for.' She looked back through her entries. Stamps, one pound, at the beginning of the week. Stamps, ten shillings yesterday. It could not be that. It was some carelessness—something not entered—or a miscalculation. Something she had paid out to the workshop in the middle of a rush, and forgotten to put down. She went back through her entries one by one with flaring cheeks; recovering the history of the week and recalling incidents. Nothing came that would account for the discrepancy. It was simply a mistake. Something had been put down wrong. The money had been spent. But was it a workshop or a surgery expense that had gone wrong? 'Postage, etc.: two and nine,' would make it all right—but the account would not be right. Either the workshop or the surgery account must suffer. It would be another of those little inaccurate spots that came every few weeks; that she would always have to remember . . . her mind toiled, goaded and hot. . . . Mr Orly had borrowed five pounds to buy tools at Buck & Hickman's, and come back with the money spent and some of the tools to be handed to the practice. Perhaps it was in balancing that up that the mistake had occurred . . . or the electric lamp account; some for the house, some for the practice, and some for the workshop. Thoroughly miserable, she made a provisional entry of the sum against surgery, in pencil, and left the account unbalanced. Perhaps on Monday it would come right. When the ledgers were all in place and the safe and drawers locked, she stretched her limbs and forced away her misery. The roses reproached her, but only for a moment. They understood, in detail, as clearly as she did, all the difficulties. They took her part. Standing there waiting, they too felt that there was nothing now but lunch and Irving.

With the basket of roses over her arm she walked as rapidly as possible down to Oxford Circus, taking the first turning out of Wimpole Street to hurry the more secretly and conveniently. A bus took her to Charing Cross, where she jumped off as soon as it began pulling up and ran down the Strand. As soon as she felt herself flying towards her bourne, the fears that last week's magic would have disappeared left her altogether. Last week had been wonderful, an adventure, her first deliberate piece of daring in London. Inside the theatre the scruples and the daring had been forgotten. To-day, again, everything would be forgotten, everything; to-day's happiness was more secure; it would not mean going almost foodless over the week-end and without an egg for supper all next week; there was no anticipation of disapproving eyes in the theatre this week; the sense of the impropriety of going alone had gone; it would never return; the feeling of selfishness in spending money on a theatre alone was still there, but a voice within answered that —saying that there was no one at hand to go, and no one she knew who would find at the Lyceum performance just what she found, no one to whom it would mean much more than a theatre; like any other theatre and a play, amongst other plays, with a celebrated actor taking the chief part . . . except Mag. Mag had been with her as she gazed. Mag was with her now. Mag, fulfilling one or other of her exciting Saturday afternoon engagements, would sit at her side.

Easy and happy, she fled along . . . her heart greeting each passenger in the scattered throng she threaded, her eyes upon

the traffic in the roadway. A horseless brougham went by,
moving smoothly and silently amongst the noisy traffic—the
driver looked as though he were fastened to the front of the
vehicle, a little tin driver on a clockwork toy; there was nothing
between him and the road but the platform of the little tank
on which his feet were set. He looked as if he were falling off.
If anything ran into him there was nothing to protect him. It
left an uncomfortable memory . . . it would only be for
carriages; the well-loved horse omnibuses would go on . . . it
must be somewhere near here . . . 'Lyceum Pit,' there it
was, just ahead, easily discernible. Last week when she had
had to ask, she had not noticed the words printed on the side
of the passage that showed as you came down the Strand. The
pavement was clear for a moment, and she rounded the near
angle and ran home down the passage without slackening her
pace, her half-crown ready in her hand, a Lyceum pittite.

The dark pit seemed very full as she entered the door at
the left-hand corner; dim forms standing at the back told her
there were no seats left; but she made her way across to the
right and down the incline, hoping for a neglected place somewhere on the extreme right. Her vain search brought her
down to the barrier, and the end of her inspection of the serried
ranks of seated forms to her left swept her eyes forward. She
was just under the overhanging balcony of the dress circle; the
well of the theatre opened clear before her as she stood against
the barrier, the stalls half full and filling with dim forms gliding
in right and left, the upward sweep of the theatre walls covered
with boxes from which white faces shone in the gloom, a soft
pervading saffron light, bright light heavily screened. There
was space all round her, the empty gangway behind, the gangway behind the stalls just in front of the barrier, the view clear
away to the stage over the heads of the people sitting in the
stalls. . . . Why not stay here? If people stood at the back
of the pit they might stand in front. She retreated into the
angle made by the out-curving wall of the pit and the pit

barrier. Putting down the basket of roses on the floor at her side she leaned against the barrier with her elbows on its rim.

He was there before he appeared . . . in the orchestra, in the audience, all over the house. Presently, in a few moments, he was going to appear, moving and speaking on the stage. Someone might come forward and announce that he was ill or dead. He would die; perhaps only years hence; but long before one was old . . . death of Henry Irving. No more thoughts of that; he is there—perhaps for twenty years; coming and going, having seasons at the Lyceum. He knew he must die; he did not think about it. He would turn with a smile and go straight up, in a rosy chariot . . . well done, thou good and faithful and happy servant. He would go, closing his eyes upon the vision that was always in them, upon something they saw, something they gave out every moment. Whom the gods love die young . . . not always young in years, but young always; trailing clouds of glory. It is always the unexpected that happens. Things you dread never happen. That is Weber—or Meyerbeer. Who chooses the music? Perhaps he does.

The orchestration brought back last week's performance. It was all there, behind the curtain. Shylock, swinging across the stage with his halting dragging stride; halting, standing with bent head; shut-in, lonely sweetness. She looked boldly now, untrammelled in her dark corner, at the pictures which had formed part of her distant view all last week in the far-away life at Wimpole Street; the great scenes . . . beautifully staged; 'Irving always *stages* everything perfectly'—and battled no longer against her sympathy for Shylock. It no longer shocked her to find herself sharing something of his longing for the blood of the Christians. It was wrong; but were not they, too, wrong? They must be; there must be some reason for this certainty of sympathy with Shylock and aversion from Antonio. It might be a wrong reason, but it was there in her. Mag said 'that's his genius; he makes you sympathize even

with Shylock. . . .' He shows you that you *do* sympathize
with Shylock; Mag thinks that is something to admit shame-
facedly. Because those other people were to her just 'people.'
Antonio—was it not just as wrong to get into debt and raise
money from the Jews as to let money out on usury? But it
was his friend. He was innocent. Never mind. They were
all, all, smug and complacent in their sunshine. Polished lustful man, with his coarse lustful men friends. Portia and Nerissa
were companions in affliction. Beautiful first of all; as lovely
and wandering and full of visions as Shylock, until their lovers
came. Hearn was right. English lovers would shock any
Japanese. Not that the Japanese were prudish. According
to him they were anything but . . . they would not talk as
Englishmen did, among themselves, and, in mixed society, in a
sort of code; thinking themselves so clever; any one could talk
a code who chose to descend to a mechanical trick.

How much more real was the relation between Portia and
Nerissa than between either of the sadly jesting women and
their complacently jesting lovers. Did a man *ever* speak in a
natural voice—neither blustering, nor displaying his cleverness,
nor being simply a lustful slave? Women always despise men
under the influence of passion or fatigue. What horrible old
men those two would be—still speaking in put-on voices to
hide their shame, pompous and philosophizing. . . . 'Man's
love is of man's life a thing apart . . .' so much the worse for
man; there must be something very wrong with his life. But
it would go on, until men saw and admitted this. . . . Portia
was right when she preached her sermon—it made every one
feel sorry for all harshness—then one ought not to be harsh to
the blindness of men . . . somebody had said men would lose
all their charm if they lost their vanity and childish cocksure-
ness about their superiority—to force and browbeat them into
seeing themselves would not help—but that is what I want to
do. I am like a man in that, overbearing, bullying, blustering.
I am something between a man and a woman; looking both
ways. But to pretend one did not see through a man's voice,
would be treachery. Nearly all men will hate me—because I
can't play up for long. Harshness must go; perhaps that was

what Christ meant. But Portia only wanted to save Antonio's life; and did it by a trick. It was not a Daniel come to judgment; it showed the folly of law; pettifogging; the abuse of the letter of the law. She was harsh to Shylock. Which is most cruel, to take life or to torture the living? The Christians were so self-satisfied; going off to their love-making; that spoiled the play. Their future was much more dark and miserable than the struggle between the sensual Englishman and the wily Jew. The play ought to have ended there, with the woman in the cap and gown pleading, showing something that could not be denied—ye are all together in one condemnation. In that moment Portia was great, her red robe shone and lit the world. She ought to have left them all, and gone through all the law courts of the world; showing up the law. Wit. Woman's wit. Men at least bowed down to that; though they did not know what it was. 'Wit' used to mean knowledge —'inwit,' conscience. The knowledge of woman is larger, bigger, deeper, less wordy and clever than that of men. Certainly. But why do not men acknowledge this? They talk about mother-love and mother-wit and instinct, as if they were mysterious tricks. They have no real knowledge, but of things; a sort of superiority they get by being free to be out in the world amongst things; they do not understand people. If a woman is good it is all right; if she is bad it is all wrong. Cherchez la femme. Then everything in life depends upon women? 'A civilization can never rise above the level of its women.' Perhaps if women became lawyers, they would change things. Women do not respect law. No wonder, since it is folly, an endless play on words. Portia? She had been quite complacent about being unkind to the Jew. She had been invented by a man. There was no reality in any of Shakespeare's women. They please men because they show women as men see them. All the other things are invisible; nothing but their thoughts and feelings about men and bothers. Shakespeare did not know the meaning of the words and actions of Nerissa and Portia when they were alone together, the beauty they knew and felt and saw, holy beauty everywhere. Shakespeare's plays are 'universal' because they are about the

things that everybody knows and hands about, and they do not
trouble anybody. They make every one feel wise. It isn't
what he says, it's the way he says all these things that don't
matter and leave everything out. It's all a sublime fuss.

Italians! Of course. Well—Europeans. It is the difference between the Europeans and the Japanese that Hearn
had meant.

Then there *is* tragedy! Things are not simple right and
wrong. There are a million sides to every question; as many
sides as there are people to see and feel them, and in all big
national struggles two clear sides, both right and both wrong.
The man who wrote *The Struggle against Absolute Monarchy*
was a Roundhead; and he made me a Roundhead; Green's
History is Roundhead. I never saw Charles's point of view
or thought about it; but only of the unjust levies and the dis-
solution of Parliament and the dissoluteness of the Court. If
I had seen Irving then, it would have made a difference. He
could never have been Cromwell. He is Charles. Things
happen. People tell him things and he cannot understand.
He believes in divine right . . . sweet and gentle, with perfect
manners for all . . . perfect in private life . . . the first gentleman in the land, the only person free to have perfect manners;
the representative of God on earth. 'Decaying feudalism.'
But they ought not to have killed him. He cannot *understand*.
He is the scapegoat. Freedom looks so fine in your mind.
Parliaments and Trial by Jury and the abolition of the Star
Chamber and the triumph of Cromwell's visionaries. But it
means this gentle velvet-coated figure with its delicate ruffled
hands, its sweetness and courtesy, going with bandaged eyes—
to death. Was there no way out? Must one either be a
Royalist or a Roundhead. Must monarchies decay? Then
why did the Restoration come? What do English people
want? 'A limited monarchy'; a king controlled by Parliament. As well not have a king at all. Who would not rather
live with Charles than with Cromwell? Charles would have

entertained a beggar royally. Cromwell was too busy with 'affairs of state' to entertain beggars. Charles dying for his faith was more beautiful than Cromwell fighting for his reason. Yet the people must be free; there must be justice. Kings ought to be taught differently. He did not understand. No one believing in divine right can understand. Was the idea of divine right a mistake? Can no one be trusted? Cromwell's son was a weak fool. How can a country be ruled? People will never agree. What ought one to be if one can neither be quite a Roundhead nor quite a Cavalier? They worshipped two gods. Are there two Gods? . . . Irving . . . walking gently about inside Charles, feeling, as Charles felt the beauty of the sunlit garden, the delicate clothes, the refinement of fine living, the charm of perfect association, the rich beauty of each day as it passed. . . . Charles died with all that in his eyes, *knowing* it *good*. Cromwell was a farmer. Christ was a carpenter. Christ did not bother about kings. 'Render unto Caesar.'

CHAPTER XVI

THEY had walked swiftly and silently along through the bright evening daylight of the Finchley Road. Miriam held her knowledge suspended, looking forward to the enclosure at the end of the few minutes' walk. But the conservatoire was not enclosed. The clear bright light flooding the rows and rows of seated summer-clad Hampstead people, and lighting up every corner of the level square hall was like the outside evening daylight. The air seemed as pure as the outside air. She followed Mr Hancock to their seats at the gangway end of the fourth row, passing between the sounds echoing thinly from the platform and the wave of attention sweeping towards the platform from the massed rows of intelligent faces. As they sat down, the chairman's voice ceased and the lights were lowered; but so slightly that the hall was still perfectly exposed and clear. The people still looked as though they were out of doors or in their large houses. This was modern improvement—hard clear light. Their minds and their thoughts and their lives and their clothes were always in it. She stared at the screen. A large slide was showing, lit from behind. It made a sort of stage scenery for the rest of the scene, all in one light. She fixed her attention. An enormous vessel with its side stove in, yes, 'stove in'; in a dock. They got *information* at any rate, and then, perhaps, got free and thought their own thoughts. No. They would follow and think and talk intelligently about the information. Rattling their cultured voices. Mad with pretences. . . . In *dry* dock, going to be repaired. Gazing sternly at the short man with the long pointer talking in an anxious high thin voice, his head with its upstanding crest of hair half-turned towards the audience, she suppressed a giggle. Folding her hands she gazed, shaking in every limb, not daring to follow what he said, for fear of laughing aloud. Shreds of his first long sentence caught in her thoughts and gave her his meaning, shaking her into giggles. Her features quivered under her skin as she held them, in forcing her eyes towards the distances of sky beyond the ship. Her customary expletives shot through her mind in rapid succession. With each one, the scarves and silk and velvet of the audience grew brighter about the edge of her circle of vision.

She was an upstart and an alien and here she was. It was more extraordinary in this Hampstead clarity than at a theatre or concert in town. It was a part of his world . . . and theirs; one might get the manner and still keep alive. . . . Was he out of humour because he had realized what he had done or because she had been late for dinner? Was he thinking what his behaviour amounted to, in the eyes of his aunt and cousins; even supposing they did not know that the invitation to dinner and the lecture had been given only this afternoon? He must have known it was necessary to go home and tidy up. When he said the conservatoire was so near that there would be plenty of time, was not that as good as saying she might be a little late? Why had he not said they were staying with him? Next week was full of appointments for their teeth. So he knew they were coming . . . and then to go marching into the midst of them, three-quarters of an hour late, and to be so dumbfounded as to be unable to apologize . . . my dear, I shall *never* forget the faces of those women. I could not imagine, at first, what was wrong. He was looking so strange. The women barely noticed me—barely noticed me. 'I'm afraid dinner will be spoiled,' he said, in his way. They had all been sitting round the fire three mortal quarters of an hour waiting for *me*! How they would talk. Their thoughts and feelings about employees could be seen at a glance. It was bad enough for them to have a secretary appearing at dinner, the first evening of their great visit. And now they were sitting alone round the fire and she was at the lecture alone, unchaperoned, with him, 'she had the effrontery to come to dinner three-quarters of an hour late . . .' feathery hair and periwinkle eyes and white noses; gentle die-away voices. Perhaps the thought of his favourite cousins coming next week buoyed him up. No wonder he wanted to get away to the lecture. He had come, reasonably; not seeing why he should not; just as he would have gone if they had not been there. Now he saw it as they saw it. There he sat. She gazed at the shifting scenes . . . ports and strange islands in distant seas, sunlit coloured mountains tops peaking up from forests. The lecturing voice was far away, irrelevant and unintelligible. Peace flooded her.

CHAPTER XVII

THE patient sat up with a groan of relief. His dark strong positive liverish profile turned away towards the spittoon. There was a clean broad gap of neck between the strong inturned ending of his hair and the narrow strip of firm, heavily glazed blue-white collar fitting perfectly into the collar of the well-cut grey coat clothing the firm bulk of his body. 'To my mind, there's no reason why they shouldn't do thoroughly well,' he said into the spittoon. All the hospitals would employ 'em in the end. They're more natty and conscientious than men, and there's nothing in the work they can't manage.'

'No, I think that's so.'

Miriam cleared her throat emphatically. They had no right to talk in that calm disposing way, in the presence of a woman. Mr Hancock felt that too. That kind of man was always nice to women. Strong and cheerful and helping them; but with his mind full of quotations and generalizations. He would bring them out, anywhere. It would never occur to him that the statement of them could be offensive. His newspaper office would be full of little girls. 'It's those little ph'girls.' But the Amalgam Company probably had quite uneducated girls. Nobody ought to be asked to spend their lives calculating decimal quantities. The men who lived on these things had their drudgery done for them. They did it themselves first. Yes, but then it meant their *future*. A woman clerk never becomes a partner. There was no hope for women in business. That man's wife would be wealthy and screened and looked after all her days; he working. He would live as long as she—a little old slender nut-brown man.

'What was the employment Mr Dolland was speaking of?'

'Dispensing. I think he's quite right. And it's not at all badly paid.'

'It ought not to be. Think of the responsibility and anxiety.'

'It's a jolly stiff exam, too.'

'I like the calm way he talks, as if it were his business to decide what is suitable.'

Mr Hancock laughed. 'He's a very influential man, you know,' he said going to the tube. 'Yes?—Oh, show them up.'

Miriam detected the note that meant a trial ahead, and went about her clearing with quiet swift busy sympathy. But Mr Dolland had been a good introduction to the trying hour. Her thoughts followed his unconsciousness down to his cab. She saw the spatted boot on the footplate, the neat strong swing of the body, the dip of the hansom, the darkling face sitting inside under the shiny hat . . . the room had become dreadful; empty and silent; pressed full with a dreadful atmosphere; those women from Rochester—but they always sat still. These people were making little faint fussings of movement, like the creakings of clothes in church, and the same silent hostile feeling; people being obliged to be with people. There were two or three besides the figure in the chair. Mr Hancock had got to work with silent assiduity. His face when he turned to the cabinet was disordered, separate from the room and from his work; a most curious expression. He turned again, busily. It was something in the mouth, resentful, and a bad-tempered look in the eyes; a look of discomposed youth. Of course. The aunt and cousins. Had she cut them, standing with her back to the room, or they her? She moved sideways with her bundle of cleaned instruments to the cabinet, putting them all on the flap and beginning to open drawers, standing at his elbow as he stood turned away from the chair mixing a paste.

'You might leave those there for the present,' he murmured. She turned and went down the room between the unoccupied seated figures, keeping herself alert to respond to a greeting. They sat vacant and still. Ladies in church. Acrimonious. Querulously dressed in pretty materials and colours that would keep fresh only in the country. She went to the door lingeringly. It was so familiar. There had been all that at Babington.

It was that that was in these figures straggling home from
school, in pretty successful clothes, walking along the middle
of the sunlit road . . . *May-bell* deah . . . not balancing along
the row of drain-pipes nor pulling streaks of Berkshire goody
through their lips. This was their next stage. When she
reached the stairs, she felt herself wrapped in their scorn. It
was true; there was something impregnable about them. They
sat inside a little fortress, letting in only certain people. But
they did not know she could see everything inside the fortress,
hear all their thoughts much more clearly than the things they
said. To them, she was a closed book. They did not want
to open it. But if they had wanted to they could not have read.

The *insolence* of it. Her social position had been identical
with theirs and his. Her early circumstances a good deal more
ambitious and generous. . . . 'A moment of my consciousness
is wider than any of theirs will be in the whole of their lives.'
. . . If she could have stayed in all that, she would have been
as far as possible just the same, sometimes . . . for certain
purposes. A little close group, loyal and quarrelsome for ends
that any woman could see through. Fawning and flattering
and affectionate to each other and getting half-maddened by
the one necessity. The girls would repeat the history of their
mother, and get her sour-faced, pretty, delicate refinement.
They were so exquisite, now, to look at—the flower-like edges
of their faces, unchanging from morning to night; warmth and
care and cleanliness and rich clean food; no fatigue or worry
or embarrassment, once they had learned how to sit and move
and eat. To many men, they would appear angels. They
would not meet many in the Berkshire valley. But their mother
would manœuvre engagements for them and their men would
see them as angels fresh from their mother's hands; miracles
of beauty and purity. . . .

Refined shrews, turning in circles, like moths on pins; brain-
less, mindless, heartless, the prey of the professions; priests,
doctors, and lawyers. These two groups kept each other

going. There was something hidden in the fact that these women's men always entered professions.

Large portions of the mornings and afternoons of that week were free from visits to the upstairs surgery. From Tuesday morning, she kept it well filled with supplies; guessing that she was to be saved further contact with the aunt and cousins; and drew from the stimulus of their comings and goings, the sound of their voices in the hall and on the stairs, a fund of energy that filled her unexpected stretches of leisure with unceasing methodical labour. Uninterrupted work on the ledgers awakened her interest in them, the sense that the books were nearly all up to date, the possibility of catching up altogether before the end of the week, brought a relief and a sense of mastery that made the June sunshine gay morning after morning as she tramped through it along the Euston Road. Every hour was full of a strange excitement. Wide vistas shone ahead. On the first of September shone a blinding radiance. She would get up that morning in her dusty garret in the heat and dust of London, with nothing to do for a month; and ride away, somewhere, ride away through the streets, free, out to the suburbs, like a Sunday morning ride, and then into the country. She had weathered the winter and the strange beginnings and would go away to come back; the rest of the summer till then would go dancing, like a dream. There was all that coming; making her heart leap when she thought of it, unknown Wiltshire—with Leader landscapes for a week, and then something else. And meanwhile Wimpole Street. She went about her work, borne along unwearied upon a tide that flowed out in glistening sunlit waves over the sunlit shore of the world. The doors and windows of her cool shaded room opened upon a life that spread out before her fanwise towards endless brilliant distances. Moments of fatigue, little obstinate knots and tangles of urgent practical affairs, did their utmost to convince her that life was a perpetual conflict, nothing certain and secure but the thwarting and discrediting of the dream-vision;

every contact seemed to end in an assurance of her unarmed resourceless state. Pausing now and again to balance her account, to try to find a sanction for her joy, she watched and felt the little stabs of the actual facts as they would be summarized by some disinterested observer, and again and again saw them foiled. Things danced, comically powerless against some unheard piping; motes, funny and beloved, in the sunbeam of her life. . . . Next week, and the coming of the favourite cousins, made a bright barrier across the future and a little fence round her labours. Everything must be ordered and straight before then. She must be free and reproachless for the wonders and terrors of their visit. . . . Perhaps there might be only the one meeting; the evening already arranged might be all the week's visit would bring. The week would pass unseen by her and everything would be as before. As before; was not that enough, and more than enough?

Her rare visits to the surgery were festivals. Free from the usual daily fatigue of constant standing for reiterated clearances and cleansings of small sets of instruments, she swept full of cheerful strength, her mind free for method, her hands steady and deft, upon the accumulations left by long sittings, rapping out her commentary upon his prolonged endurance by emphatic bumpings of basins and utensils; making it unnecessary for him to voice the controlled exasperation that spoke for her from every movement and tone. Once or twice she felt it wavering towards speech, and whisked about and bumped things down with extra violence. Once or twice he smiled into her angry face, and she feared he was going to speak of them.

CHAPTER XVIII

IT was a sort of formality. They all three seemed to be waiting for something to begin. They were not at ease. Perhaps they had come to the end of everything they had to say to each other, and had only the memory of their common youth to bind them to each other. Members of the same family never seemed to be quite at ease sitting together doing nothing. These three met so seldom that they were obliged when they met to appear to be giving their whole attention to each other, sitting confronted and trying to keep talk going all the time. That made every one speak and smile and look self-consciously. Perhaps they reminded each other, by their mutual presence, that the dreams of their youth had not been fulfilled. And the cousins were formal. Like the other cousins, they belonged to the prosperous provincial middle class that always tries to get its sons into professions. Without the volume of Sophocles, one would have known he was part of a school and she could have been nothing but the wife or daughter or sister of an English professional man. It was always the same world; once the only world that was worthy of one's envious admiration and respect; changed now . . . 'hardworked little text-book people and here and there an enlightened thwarted man.' . . . Was Mr Canfield thwarted? There was a curious look of lonely enlightenment about his head. At the university, and now and again with a head master or a fellow assistant-master, he had had moments of exchange and been happy for a moment and seen the world alight. But his happiest times had been in loneliness, with thoughts coming to him out of books. They had been his solace and his refuge since he was fifteen; and in spite of the hair greying his temples he was still fifteen; within him were all the dreams and all the dreadful crudities of boyhood . . . he had never grown to man's estate. . . . He had

199

understood at once. 'It always seems unnecessary to explain things to people; you feel while you are explaining that they will meet the same thing themselves, perhaps in some different form; but certainly, because things are all the same.' 'Oh, yes; that 's certainly so.' He had looked pleased and lightened. Darkness and cold had come in an instant, with Mrs Canfield's unexpected reverent voice. 'I don't quite understand what that means; tell me.' She had put down her fancy work and lifted her flowerlike face, not suspiciously as the other cousins would have done, but with their type of gentle formal refinement and something of their look. She could be sour and acid if she chose. She could curl her lips and snub people. What was the secret of the everlasting same awfulness of even the nicest of refined sheltered middle-class Englishwoman? He had stumbled and wandered through a vague statement. He knew that all the long loneliness of his mind lay revealed before one—and yet she had been the dream and wonder and magic of his youth and was still his dear companion. The 'lady' was the wife for the professional Englishman—simple, sheltered, domesticated, trained in principles she did not think about, and living by them; revering professional and professionally successful men; never seeing the fifth-form schoolboys they all were. No woman who saw them as they were, with their mental pride and vanity and fixity, would stay with them; no woman who saw their veiled appetites. . . . But where could all these wives go?

Throughout the evening, she was kept quiet and dull and felt presently very weary. Her helpless stock-taking made it difficult to face the strangers, lest painful illumination and pity and annoyance should stream from her too visibly. . . . Perhaps they, too, took stock and pitied; but they were interested, a little eager in response and, though too well bred for questions, obviously full of unanswered surmises, which perhaps presently they would communicate to each other. There were people who would say she was too egoistic to be interested in them, a selfish, unsocial, unpleasant person, and they were kind charming people, interested in everybody. That might be true. . . .

But it was also true that they were eager and interested because their lives were empty of everything but principles and a certain fixed way of looking at things; and one could be fond of their niceness and respectful to their goodness but never interested, because one knew everything about them, even their hidden thoughts and the side of them that was not nice or good, without having any communication with them. . . . He had another side; but there was no place in his life which would allow it expression. It could only live in the lives of people met in books; in sympathies here and there for a moment; in people who passed 'like ships in the night'; in moments at the beginning and end of holidays when things would seem real, and as if henceforth they were going to be real every day. If it found expression in his life, it would break up that life. Any one who tried to make it find personal expression would be cruel; unless it were to turn him into a reformer or the follower of a reformer. That could happen to him. He was secretly interested in adventurers and adventuresses.

CHAPTER XIX

IT had evidently been a great festival. One of the events of
Mr Hancock's summer; designed by him for the happiness and
enjoyment of his friends, and enjoyed by him in labouring to
those ends. It was *beautiful* to look back upon; in every part;
the easy journey, the approach to the cottage along the mile of
green-feathered river, the well-ordered feast in the large clean
cottage; the well-thought-out comfort of the cottage bedrooms,
the sight of the orchard lit by Chinese lanterns, the lantern-lit
boats, the drifting down the river in the soft moonlit air; the
candle-lit supper table, morning through the cottage windows,
upstairs and down, far away from the world, people meeting
at breakfast like travellers in a far-off country, pleased to see
well-known faces . . . the morning on the green river . . .
the gentleness and kindliness and quiet dignity of everybody,
the kindly difficult gently jesting discussion of small personal
incidents; the gentle amiable strains; the mild restrained self-
effacing watchfulness of the women; the uncompeting mutual
admiration of the men; the general gratitude of the group when
one or other of the men filled up a space of time with a piece
of modestly narrated personal reminiscence. . . .

Never, never could she belong to that world. It was a
perfect little world; enclosed; something one would need to be
born and trained into; the experience of it as an outsider was
pure pain and misery; admiration, irritation, and resentment
running abreast in a fever. Welcome and kindliness could do
nothing; one's own straining towards it, nothing; a night of
sleepless battering at its closed doors, nothing. There was a
secret in it, in spite of its simple-seeming exterior; an undesired
secret. Something to which one could not give oneself up.

Its terms were terms on which one could not live. That girl could live on them, in spite of her strenuous different life in the East End settlement . . . in spite of her plain dull dress and red hands. She knew the code; her cheap straw hat waved graciously, her hair ruffled about her head in soft clouds. Why had he never spoken of her uncle's cottage so near his own? She must be always there. When she appeared in the surgery she seemed to come straight out of the East End . . . his respect for workers amongst the poor . . . his general mild revulsion from philanthropists; but down here she was not a philanthropist . . . outwardly, a girl with blowy hair and a wavy hat, smiling in boats, understanding botany and fishing . . . inwardly a designing female, her mind lit by her cold intellectual 'ethical'—hooooo—the very *sound* of the word— 'ethical Pantheism'; cool and secret and hateful. 'Rather a nice little thing'; 'pretty green dress'; *nice!*

CHAPTER XX

MIRIAM turned swiftly in her chair and looked up. But Mr Hancock was already at the door. There was only a glimpse of his unknown figure, arrested for a moment with its back to her as he pulled the door wide enough to pass through. The door closed crisply behind him and his crisp unhastening footsteps went away out of hearing along the thickly carpeted hall.

'*Dear* me!' she breathed through firmly held lips, standing up. Her blood was aflame. The thudding of her heart shook the words upon her breath. She was fighting against something more than amazement. She knew that only part of her refused to believe. In a part of her brain illumination, leaving the shock already far away in the past, was at work undisturbed, flowing rapidly down into thoughts set neatly in the language of the world. She held them back, occupying herself irrelevantly about the room, catching back desperately at the familiar trains of reverie suggested by its objects; cancelling the incident and summoning it again and again without prejudice or afterthought. Each time the shock recurred unchanged, firmly registered, its quality indubitable. She sat down at last to examine it and find her thoughts. Taking a pencil in a trembling hand, she began carefully adding a long column of figures. A system of adding that had been recommended to her by the family mathematician now suggested itself for the first time in connection with her own efforts. . . .

How *dare* he?

It was deliberate. A brusque casual tone, deliberately put on; a tone he sometimes used to the boys downstairs, or to cabmen. How did he dare to use it to her? It must cease instantly. It was not to be suffered for a moment. Not for a moment could she hold a position which would entitle any one, particularly any man, to speak to her in that—outrageous —*official* tone. Why not? It was the way of business people and officials all the world over. . . . Then he should have begun as he meant to go on. . . . I won't endure it now. No one has ever spoken to me in that way—and no one shall, with impunity. I have been fortunate. They have spoiled me. . . . I should never have come, if I had found they had that sort of tone. It was his difference that made me come.

Those two had talked to him and made him think. The aunt and cousins had prepared the way. But their hostility had been harmless. These two had approved. That was clear at the week-end. They must have chaffed him, and given him their blessing. Then, for the first time, he had thought, sitting alone and pondering reasonably. It was he himself who had drawn back. He was quite right. He belonged to that side of society and must keep with them and go their way. Very wise and right . . . but damn his insolent complacency. . . .

'Everything a professional man does must stabilize his position.' Perhaps that is true. But then his business relationships must be business relationships from the first . . . that was expected. The wonder of the Wimpole Street life was that it had not been so. Instead of an employer there had been a sensitive isolated man; prosperous and strong outwardly, and as suffering and perplexed in mind as any one could be. He had not hesitated to seek sympathy.

Any fair-minded onlooker would condemn him. Any one who could have seen the way he broke through resistance to social intercourse outside the practice. He may have thought he was being kind to a resourceless girl. It was *not* to resourcelessness that he had appealed. It was not that. That was not the truth.

He would have cynical thoughts. The truth was that something came in and happened of itself before one knew. A

woman always knows first. It was not clear until Babington.
But there was a sharp glimpse then. He must have known
how amazed they would be at his cycling over after he had
neglected them for years, on that one Sunday. They had con-
cealed their amazement from him. But it was they who had
revealed things. There was nothing imaginary, after that, in
taking one wild glance and leaving things to go their way.
Nothing. No one was to blame. And now he knew and had
considered, and had made an absurd reasonable decision and
taken ridiculous prompt action.

A business relationship . . . by *all* means. But he shall
acknowledge and apologize. He shall explain his insulting
admission of fear. He shall admit in plain speech what has
accounted for his change of manner.

Then that little horror is also condemned. *She* is not a
wealthy efficient woman of the world.

Men are simply paltry and silly—all of them.

In pain and fear, she wandered about her room, listening for
her bell. It had gone; the meaning of their days had gone;
trust and confidence could never come back. A door was
closed. His life was closed on her for ever. . . .

The bell rang softly in its usual way. The incident had
been an accident; an illusion. Even so; she had been prepared for it, without knowing she was prepared, otherwise she
would not have understood so fully and instantly. If she had
only imagined it, it had changed everything, her interpretation
of it was prophetic; just as before he had not known where they
were, so now the rupture was imminent whether he knew it or
no. She found herself going upstairs breathing air thick with
pain. This was dreadful. . . . She could not bear much of
this. . . . The patient had gone. He would be alone. They

would be alone.   To be in his presence would be a relief . . .
this was appalling.   This pain could not be endured.   The
sight of the room holding the six months would be intolerable.
She drew her face together, but her heart was beating noisily.
The knob of the door handle rattled in her trembling hand . . .
large flat brass knob with a row of grooves to help the grasp
. . . she had never observed that before.   The door opened
before her.   She flung it wider than usual and pushed her way,
leaving it open . . . he was standing impermanently with a
sham air of engrossment at his writing table, and would turn
on his heel and go the moment she was fairly across the room.
Buoyant with pain, she flitted through the empty air towards
the distant bracket-table.   Each object upon it stood marvel-
lously clear.   She reached it and got her hands upon the
familiar instruments . . . no sound; he had not moved.   The
flame of the little spirit-lamp burned unwavering in the complete stillness . . . now was the moment to drop thoughts and
anger.   Up here was something that had been made up here,
real and changeless and independent.   The least vestige of
tumult would destroy it.   It was something that no one could
touch; neither his friends nor he nor she.   They had not made
it and they could not touch it.   Nothing had happened to it;
and he had stood quietly there long enough for it to re-assert
itself.   Steadily, with her hands full of instruments, she
turned towards the sterilizing tray.   The room was empty.
Pain ran glowing up her arms from her burden of nauseating
relics of the needs of some complacent patient . . . the room
was stripped, a West End surgery, among scores of other West
End surgeries, a prison claiming her by the bonds of the loathsome duties she had learned.

CHAPTER XXI

To-day the familiar handwriting brought no relief. This letter must be the final explanation. She opened it, standing by the hall table. 'Dear Miss Henderson—you are very persistent.' She folded the letter up and walked rapidly out into the sunshine. The way down to the Euston Road was very long and sunlit. It was radiant with all the months and weeks and days. She thought of going on with the unread letter and carrying it into the surgery, tearing it up into the waste-paper basket and saying 'I have not read this. It is all right. We will not talk any more.' One thing would have gone. But there would be a tremendous cheerfulness and independence, and the memory of the things in the other letters. The letter once read, two things would have gone, everything. She paused at the corner of the gardens, looking down at the pavement. There was, in some way that would not come quite clear, so much more at stake than personal feelings about the insulting moment. It was something that stuck into everything, made everything intolerable until it was admitted and cancelled. As long as he went on hedging and pretending it was not there, there could be no truth anywhere. It was something that must go out of the world, no matter what it cost. It would be smiling and cattish and behaving to drop it. Explained, it would be wiped away, and everything else with it. To accept his assertions would be to admit lack of insight. That would be treachery. The continued spontaneity of manner which it would ensure would be the false spontaneity that sat everywhere . . . all over that woman getting into the bus; brisk cheerful falsity. She glanced through to the end of the letter . . . 'foolish gossip which might end by making your position untenable.' *Idiot*. Charming chivalrous gentleman.

I want to have it both ways. To keep the consideration and flout the necessity for it. No one shall dare to protect me from gossip. To prove myself independent and truth-demanding

I would break up anything. That's damned folly. Never mind. Why didn't he admit it at once? He hated being questioned and challenged. He may have thought that manner was 'the kindest way.' It is not for him to choose ways of treating me. This cancels the past. But it admits it. Not to admit the past would be to go on for ever in a false position. He still hides. But he knows that I know he is hiding. Where we have been we have been. It may have been through a false estimate of me, to begin with. That does not matter. Where we have been we have been. That is not imagination. One day he will know it is not imagination. There is something that is making me very glad. A painful relief. Something forcing me back upon something. There is something that I have smashed, for some reason I do not know. It's something in my temper, that flares out about things. Life allows no chance of getting at the bottom of things. . . .

I have nothing now but my pained self again, having violently rushed at things and torn them to bits. It's all my fault from the very beginning. But I stand for something. I would dash my head against a wall rather than deny it. I make people hate me by *knowing* them and dashing my head against the wall of their behaviour. I should never make a good chess-player. Is God a chess-player? I shan't leave until I have proved that no one can put me in a false position. There is something that is untouched by positions. . . .

I did not know what I had. . . . Friendship is fine fine porcelain. I have sent a crack right through it. . . .

Mrs Bailey . . . numbers of people I never think of would like to have me always there. . . .

The sky, fitting down on the irregular brown vista, bore an untouched life. . . . There were always mornings; at work. I am free to work zealously and generously with and for him.

At *least* I have broken up his confounded complacency.

He will be embarrassed. *I* shan't.

CHAPTER XXII

'. . . And at fifty, when a woman is beginning to sit down intelligently to life—behold, it is beginning to be time to take leave. . . .'

That woman was an elderly woman of the world; but a dear. She understood. She had spent her life in amongst people, having a life of her own going on all the time; looking out at something through the bars, whenever she was alone and sometimes in the midst of conversations; but no one would see it, but people who *knew*. And now she was free to step out and there was hardly any time left. But there was a little time. Women who *know* are quite brisk at fifty. 'A man must never be silent with a woman unless he wishes for the quiet development of a relationship from which there is no withdrawing . . . if ordinary social intercourse cannot be kept up he must fly . . . in silence a man is an open book and unarmed. In speech with a man a woman is at a disadvantage—because they speak different languages. She may understand his. Hers he will never speak nor understand. In pity, or from other motives, she must therefore, stammeringly, speak his. He listens and is flattered and thinks he has her mental measure when he has not touched even the fringe of her consciousness. . . . Outside the life relationship men and woman can have only conversational, and again conversational, interchange.' . . . That's the truth about life. Men and women never meet. Inside the life relationship you can see them being strangers and hostile; one or the other or both, completely alone. That was the world. Social life. In social life no one was alive but the lonely women keeping up half-admiring half-pitying endless conversations with men, with one little ironic part of themselves . . . until they were fifty and had done their share of social life. But outside the world—one could be alive always. Fifty. Thirty more years. . . .

When I woke in the night I felt nothing but tiredness and regret for having promised to go. Now, I never felt so strong and happy. This is how Mag is feeling. Their kettle is bumping on their spirit lamp, too. She loves the sound just in this way, the Sunday morning sound of the kettle, with the air full of coming bells and the doors opening—I'm half-dressed, without any effort—and shutting up and down the streets is *perfect*, again, and again; at seven o'clock in the silence, with the air coming in from the squares smelling like the country, is bliss. 'You know, little child, you have an extraordinary capacity for happiness.' I suppose I have. Well; I can't help it. . . . I *am* frantically, frantically happy. I'm up here alone, frantically happy. Even Mag has to *talk* to Jan about the happy things. Then they go, a little. The only thing to do is either to be silent or make cheerful noises. Bellow. If you do that too much, people don't like it. You can only keep on making cheerful noises if you are quite alone. Perhaps that is why people in life are always grumbling at 'annoyances' and things; to hide how happy they are . . . 'there is a dead level of happiness all over the world'—hidden. People go on about things, because they are always trying to remember how happy they are. The worse things are, the more despairing they get, because they are so happy. You know what I mean. It's there—there's nothing else there. . . . But some people *know* more about it than others. Intelligent people. I suppose I am intelligent. I can't *help* it. I don't want to be different. Yes, I do—oh Lord, yes, I *do*. Mag knows. But she goes in amongst people and the complaints and the fuss, and takes sides. But they both come out again; to be by themselves and talk about it all . . . they sit down intelligently to life. . . . They do things that have nothing to do with their circumstances. They were always doing things like this all the year round. Spring and summer and autumn and winter things.

They had done, for years. The kind of things that made independently elderly women, widows and spinsters who were free to go about, have that look of intense appreciation . . . 'a heart at leisure from itself to soothe and sympathize'; no, that type was always inclined to revel in other people's troubles. It was something more than that. Never mind. Come on. Hurry up. Oh—for a man, oh for a man, *oh* for a man—*sion* in the skies. . . . Wot a big voice I 've got, mother.

'Cooooooo—ooo—er, Bill.' The sudden familiar sound came just above her head. Where was she? *What* a pity. The boys had wakened her. Then she had been asleep! It was perfect. The footsteps belonging to the voice had passed along just above her head; nice boys, they could not help chiking when they saw the sleeping figures, but they did not mean to disturb. They had wakened her from her first daytime sleep. Asleep! She had slept in broad sunlight, at the foot of the little cliff. Waking in the daytime is *perfect* happiness. To wake suddenly and fully, nowhere; in paradise; and then to see sharply with large clear strong eyes the things you were looking at when you fell asleep. She lay perfectly still. Perhaps the girls were asleep. Presently they would all be sitting up again, and she would have to begin once more the tiring effort to be as clever as they were. But it would be a little different now that they had all lain stretched out at the foot of the cliffs, asleep. She was changed. Something had happened since she had fallen asleep disappointed in the east-coast sea and the little low cliff, wondering why she could not see and feel them like the seas and cliffs of her childhood. She could see and feel them now, as long as no one spoke and the first part of the morning remained far away. She closed her eyes and drifted drowsily back to the moment of being awakened by the sudden cry. In the instant before her mind had slid back, and she had listened to the muffled footsteps thudding along the turf of the low cliff above her head, waiting angrily and anxiously for further disturbance, she had been perfectly alive, seeing; perfect things all round her, no beginning or ending . . . there had been moments like that, years ago, in gardens, by seas and cliffs. Her mind wandered back amongst these; calling up each one with perfect freshness. They were all the same. In each one she had felt exactly the same; out-side life, untouched by anything, free. She had thought they belonged to the past, to childhood and youth. In childhood she had thought each time that the world had just begun and would always be like that; later on, she now remembered, she had always thought when such a moment came that it would be the last, and had clung to it with wide desperate staring eyes until tears came and she had turned away from some great open scene, with a strong conscious body flooded suddenly by a strong warm tide, to the sad dark world to live for the rest of her time upon a memory. But the moment she had just lived was the same, it was exactly the *same* as the first one she could remember, the moment of standing, alone, in bright sunlight on a narrow gravel path in the garden at Babington between two banks of flowers, the flowers level with her face, and large bees swinging slowly to and fro before her face from bank to bank, many sweet smells coming from the flowers and, amongst them, a strange pleasant smell like burnt paper. . . . It was the same moment. She saw it now in just the same way; not remembering going into the garden or any end to being in the bright sun between the blazing flowers, the two banks linked by the slowly swinging bees, nothing else in the world, no house behind the little path, no garden beyond it. Yet she must somehow have got out of the house and through the shrubbery and along the plain path between the lawns.

All the six years at Babington were that blazing alley of flowers without beginning or end, no winters, no times of day or changes to be seen. There were other memories, quarrelling with Harriett in the nursery, making paper pills, listening to the bells on Sunday afternoon, a bell and a pomegranate, a bell or a pomegranate round about the hem of Aaron's robe, the

squirting of water into one's aching ear, the taste of an egg after
scarlet fever, the witch in the chimney, cowslip balls, a lobster
walking upstairs on its tail, dancing in a ring with grown-ups,
the smell of steam and soap, the warm smell of the bath towel,
Martha's fingers warming one's feet, her lips kissing one's back,
something going to happen to-morrow, crackling green paper
clear like glass and a gold paper fringe in your hand before the
cracker went off; an eye blazing out of the wall at night, 'Thou
God seest me,' apple pasties in the garden; coming up from the
mud pies round the summer-house to bed, being hit on the nose
by a swing and going indoors screaming at the large blots of
blood on the white pinafore, climbing up the cucumber frame
and falling through the glass at the top, blowing bubbles in the
hay-loft and singing *Rosalie the Prairie Flower*, and whole
pieces of life indoors and out, coming up bit by bit as one
thought, but all mixed with sadness and pain and bothers with
people. They did not come first, or without thought. The
blazing alley came first without thought or effort of memory.
The flowers all shining separate and distinct and all together,
indistinct in a blaze. She gazed at them . . . sweet-williams
of many hues, everlasting flowers, gold and yellow and brown
and brownish purple, pinks and petunias and garden daisies
white and deep crimson . . . then *memory* was happiness,
one happiness linked to the next. . . . It was the same already
with Germany . . . the sunny happy beautiful things came
first . . . in a single glance, the whole of the time in Germany
was beautiful, golden happy light, and people happy in the
golden light, garlands of music, and the happy ringing certainty
of voices, no matter what they said, the way the whole of life
throbbed with beauty when the hush of prayer was on the
roomful of girls . . . the wonderful house, great dark high
wooden doors in the distance thrown silently open, great silent
space of sunlight between them, high windows, alight against
the shadows of rooms; the happy confidence of the open scene.
. . . Germany was a party, a visit, a gift. It *had* been, in spite
of everything in the difficult life, what she had dreamed it when
she went off; all woods and forests and music . . . Hermann
and Dorothea happiness in the summer twilight of German

villages. It had become that now. The heart of a German town was that, making one a little homesick for it. . . . The impulse to go and the going had been right. It was part of something . . . with a meaning; perhaps there is happiness only in the things one does deliberately, without a visible reason; drifting off to Germany, because it called; coming here to-day . . . in freedom. If you are free, you are alive . . . nothing that happens in the part of your life that is not free, the part you do and are paid for, is alive. To-day, because I am free I am the same person as I was when I was there, but much stronger and happier because I know it. As long as I can sometimes feel like this nothing has mattered. Life is a chain of happy moments that cannot die.

'Damn those boys—they woke me up.'

'Did they, Mag? so they did me; did you dream?' Perhaps Mag would say something . . . but people never seemed to think anything of 'dropping off to sleep.'

'I drempt that I dwelt in Marble Halls; you awake von Bohlen?'

'I don't quite know.'

'But speaking tentatively . . .'

'A long lean mizzerable *tent*ative——'

'I perceive that you are still asleep. Shall I sing it?—"I *durr-r*-empt, I da-*we*-elt, in ma-ha-har-ble halls."'

'Cooooo—oooo—er, Bill.' The response sounded faintly from far away on the cliffs.

'Cooooo—ooo—er, Micky,' warbled Miriam. 'I like that noise. When they are further off I shall try doing it very loud, to get the proper crack.'

'I think we'd better leave her here, don't you von Bohlen?'

Was it nearly tea-time? Would either of them soon mention tea? The beauty of the rocks had faded. Yet, if they ceased being clever and spoke of the beauty, it would not come back. The weariness of keeping things up went on. When the gingernuts and lemonade were at last set out upon the sand, they shamed Miriam with the sense of her long preoccupation with them. The girls had not thought of them. They never seemed to flag in their way of talking. Perhaps it was partly their regular meals. It was dreadful always to be the first one to want food. . . .

But she was happier down here with them than she would have been alone.

Going alone for a moment in the twilight across the little scrub, as soon as she had laughed enough over leaving the room in the shelter of a gorse bush, she recovered the afternoon's happiness. There was a little fence, bricks were lying scattered about, and half-finished houses stood along the edge of the scrub. But a soft land-breeze was coming across the common carrying the scent of gorse; the silence of the sea reminded her of its presence beyond the cliffs; her own gorse-scented breeze, and silent sea and sunlit cliffs.

CHAPTER XXIII

COOL with sound short sleep, she rose early, the memory of yesterday giving a Sunday leisure to the usual anxious hurry of breakfast. She was strong with her own possessions. Wimpole Street held nothing but her contract of duties to fulfil. These she could see in a clear vexatious tangle, against the exciting oncoming of everybody's summer; an excitement that was enough in itself. Patients were pouring out of town—in a fortnight the Orlys would be gone; all Mr Orly's accounts must be out by then. In a month, Mr Hancock would go. For a month before her own holiday there would be almost nothing to do. If every one's accounts were examined before then, she could get them off at leisure during that month . . . then for this month there was nothing to do but the lessening daily duties and to get every one to examine accounts; then the house to herself, with only Mr Leyton there; the cool ease of summer in her room, and her own month ahead.

The little lavatory with its long high window sending in the light from across the two sets of back-to-back tree-shaded Bloomsbury gardens, its little shabby open sink cupboard facing her with its dim unpolished taps and the battered enamel cans on its cracked and blistered wooden top, became this morning one of her own rooms, a happy little corner in the growing life that separated her from Wimpole Street. There were no corners such as this in the beautiful clever Hampstead house; no remote shabby happy corners at all; nothing brown and old and at peace. Between him and his house were his housekeeper and servants; between him and his life was his profession . . . and the complex group of people with whom he must perpetually deal, with whom he dealt in alternations of intimacy and formality. He was still at his best in his practice. That was still his life. There was nothing more real, as yet, in his life than certain times and moments in his room at Wimpole Street. . . . Life had answered no other questions for him. . . . His thought-life and his personal life were troubled and dark and cold . . . in spite of his attachment to some of his family group . . . he could buy beautiful things, and travel freely in his leisure . . . perhaps that, those two glorious things, were sufficient compensation. But there was something wrong about them; they gave a false sense of power . . . the way all those people smiled at each other when they went about and bought things, picked up a fine thing at a bargain, or gave a price whose size they were proud of . . . thinking other people's thoughts . . . apart from this worldly side of his life, he was entirely at Wimpole Street; the whole of him; an open book; there was nothing else in his life, yet . . . his holiday with those two men—even the soft-voiced sensuous one who would quote poetry and talk romantically and cynically about women in the evenings—would bring nothing else. Yet he was counting upon it so much that he could not help unbending about his boat and his boots and his filters . . . perhaps all that was the best of the holiday—men were never tired of talking about the way they did this and that . . . clever difficult things that made all the difference; but they missed all the rest. Even when they sat about smoking, their minds were fussing. The women in their parties dressed, and smiled and appreciated. There would be no real happiness in such a party . . . except when the women were alone, doing the things with no show about them. Supposing I were able to go anywhere on this page . . . Ippington . . . 295 m.; pop. 760 . . . trains to Tudworth and thence two or three times daily . . . Spray Bay Hotel . . . A sparrow cheeped on the window sill and fluttered away. The breath of happiness poured in at the high window; all the places in the railway guide told over their charms; mountains and lakes and rivers, innumerable strips of coast, village streets to walk along for the first time, leading out . . . going, somewhere, in a train. Standing on tiptoe, she gazed her thoughts across the two garden spaces towards the grimed backs of the large brown houses. Why was one allowed to be so utterly happy? There it was . . . happily here and happily going away . . . away.

CHAPTER XXIV

'There; how d' ye like that, eh? A liberal education in
twelve volumes, with an index. Read them when ye want to.
See?' . . .

They looked less, set up like that in a row, than when they
had lain about on the floor of the den . . . taking up Dante
and Beethoven at tea time.

'Books posted? I wonder I 'm not more rushed. I say—
v'you greased all Hancock's and the pater's instruments?'

He knows I 'm slacking . . . he 'll tell the others when they
come back. . . .

Mr Leyton's door shut with a bang. He would be sitting
reading the newspaper until the next patient came. The
eternal sounds of laughter and dancing came up from the
kitchen. The rest of the house was perfectly still. Her
miserable hand reopened the last page of the index. There
were five or six more entries under 'Woman.'

If one could only burn all the volumes; stop the publication
of them. But it was all books, all the literature in the world,
right back to Juvenal . . . whatever happened, if it could all
be avenged by somebody in some way, there was all that . . .
the classics, the finest literature—'unsurpassed.' Education
would always mean coming in contact with all that. Schoolboys got their first ideas. . . . *How* could Newnham and
Girton women endure it? How could they go on living and
laughing and talking?

And the modern men were the worst . . . 'We can now,

with all the facts in our hands, sit down and examine her at our leisure.' There was no getting away from the scientific facts . . . *inferior*; mentally, morally, intellectually, and physically . . . her development arrested in the interest of her special functions . . . reverting later towards the male type . . . old women with deep voices and hair on their faces . . . leaving off where boys of eighteen began. If that is true everything is as clear as daylight. 'Woman is not undeveloped man but diverse' falls to pieces. Woman is undeveloped man . . . if one could die of the loathsome visions . . . I *must* die. I can't go on living in it . . . the whole world full of *creatures*; half-human. And I am one of the half-human ones, or shall be, if I don't stop now.

Boys and girls were much the same . . . women stopped being people and went off into hideous processes. What for? What was it all for? Development. The wonders of science. The wonders of science for women are nothing but gynaecology —all those frightful operations in the *British Medical Journal* and those jokes—the hundred golden rules. . . . Sacred functions . . . highest possibilities . . . sacred for what? The hand that rocks the cradle rules the world? The Future of the Race? What world? What race? Men. . . . Nothing but men; for ever.

If, by one thought, all the men in the world could be stopped, shaken, and slapped. There *must*, somewhere, be some power that could avenge it all . . . but if these men were right, there was not. Nothing but Nature and her decrees. Why was nature there? Who started it? If nature 'took good care' this and that . . . there must be somebody. If there was a trick, there must be a trickster. If there is a god who arranged how things should be between men and women, and just let it go and go on I have no respect for him. I should like to give him a piece of my mind. . . .

It will all go on as long as women are stupid enough to go on bringing men into the world . . . even if civilized women stop the colonials and primitive races would go on. It is a nightmare.

They invent a legend to put the blame for the existence of humanity on woman and, if she wants to stop it, they talk about the wonders of civilization and the sacred responsibilities of motherhood. They can't have it both ways. They also say women are not logical.

They despise women and they want to go on living—to reproduce — themselves. None of their achievements, no 'civilization,' no art, no science can redeem that. There is no pardon possible for man. The only answer to them is suicide; all women ought to agree to commit suicide.

The torment grew as the August weeks passed. There were strange interesting things unexpectedly everywhere. Streets of great shuttered houses, their window boxes flowerless, all grey, cool and quiet and untroubled, on a day of cool rain; the restaurants were no longer crowded; torturing thought ranged there unsupported, goaded to madness, just a mad feverish swirling in the head, ranging out, driven back by the vacant eyes of little groups of people from the country. Unfamiliar people appeared in the parks and streets, talking and staring eagerly about, women in felt boat-shaped hats trimmed with plaid ribbons—Americans. They looked clever—and ignorant of worrying thoughts. Men carried their parcels. But it was just the same. It was impossible to imagine these dried, yellow-faced women with babies. But if they liked all the fuss and noise and talk as much as they seemed to do. . . . If they did *not*, what were they doing? What was everybody *doing*? So busily.

Sleeplessness, and every day a worse feeling of illness. Every day the new torture. Every night the dreaming and tossing in the fierce, stifling, dusty heat, the awful waking, to know that presently the unbearable human sounds would begin again; the torment of walking through the streets, the solitary torment of leisure to read again in the stillness of the office; the moments of hope of finding a fresh meaning; hope of having misread.

There was nothing to turn to. Books were poisoned. Art. All the achievements of men were poisoned at the root. The beauty of nature was tricky femininity. The animal world was cruelty. Humanity was based on cruelty. Jests and amusements were tragic distractions from tragedy. Religion was the only hope. But even there there was no hope for women. No future life could heal the degradation of having been a woman. Religion in the world had nothing but insults for women. Christ was a man. If it was true that he was God taking on humanity—he took on *male* humanity . . . and the people who explained him, St Paul and the priests, the Anglicans and the Nonconformists, it was the same story everywhere. Even if religion could answer science and prove it wrong there was no hope, for women. And no intelligent person can prove science wrong. Life is poisoned, for women, at the very source. Science is true and will find out more and more, and things will grow more and more horrible. Space is full of dead worlds. The world is cooling and dying. Then why not stop *now*?

'Nature's great Salic Law will never be repealed.' 'Women can never reach the highest places in civilization.' Thomas Henry Huxley. With side-whiskers. A bouncing complacent walk. Thomas Henry Huxley. (*Thom*as *Bab*ington Ma*cau*lay.) The same sort of walk. Eminent men. Revelling in their cleverness. 'The Lord has delivered him into my hand.' He did not believe in any future for anybody. But he built his life up complacently on home and family life while saying

all those things about women, lived on them and their pain,
ate their food, enjoyed the comforts they made . . . and wrote
conceited letters to his friends about his achievements and his
stomach and his feelings.

What is it in me that stands back? Why can't it explain?
My head will burst if it can't explain. If I die now in wild
anger it only makes the thing more laughable on the whole.
. . . That old man lives quite alone in a little gas-lit lodging.
When he comes out, he is quite alone. There is nothing
touching him anywhere. He will go quietly on like that till he
dies. But he is me. I saw myself in his eyes that day. But
he must have money. He can live like that with nothing to do
but read and think and roam about, because he has money. It
isn't fair. Some woman cleans his room and does his laundry.
His thoughts about women are awful. It 's the best way . . .
but I 've made all sorts of plans for the holidays. After that,
I will save and never see anybody and never stir out of Bloomsbury. The woman in black works. It 's only in the evenings
she can roam about seeing nothing. But the people she works
for know nothing about her. She knows. She is sweeter than
he. She is sweet. I like her. But he is more me.

CHAPTER XXV

THE room still had the same radiant air. Nothing looked
worn. There was not a spot anywhere. Bowls of flowers
stood about. The Coalport tea-service was set out on the
little black table. The drawn-thread work table cover. . . .
She had arranged the flowers. That was probably all she did;
going in and out of the garden, in the sun, picking flowers.
The Artist's Model and *The Geisha* and the *Strand Musicals*
still lay about; the curious new smell still came from the inside
of the piano. But there was this dreadful tiredness. It was
dreadful that the tiredness should come nearer than the thought
of Harriett. A pallid worried disordered face looked back from
the strip of glass in the overmantel. No need to have looked.
Always now, away from London, there was this dreadful
realization of fatigue, dreadful empty sense of worry and hurry
. . . feeling so *strong* riding down through London, everything dropping away, nothing to think of; off and free, the
holiday ahead, nothing but lovely, lonely freedom all round one.

Perhaps Harriett would be nervous and irritable. She had
much more reason to be. But even if she were, it would be no
good. It would be impossible to conceal this frightful fatigue
and nervousness. Harriett *must* understand at once how
battered and abject one was. And it was a misrepresentation.
Harriett knew nothing of all one had come from; all one was
going to in the distance. Maddening. . . . Lovely; how rich
and good they looked, more honest than those in the London
shops. Harriett or Mrs Thimm or Emma had ordered them
from some confectioner in Chiswick. Fancy being able to
buy anything like that without thinking. How well they went
with the black piano and the Coalport tea-service and the

garden light coming in.   Gerald did not think that women were
inferior or that Harriett was a dependent. . . . But Gerald
did not think at all. He knew nothing was too good for Harriett.
Oo, *I* dunno, she would say with a laugh.   She thought all
men were duffers. Perhaps that was the best way. Selfish
babies. But Gerald was not selfish. He would never let
Harriett wash up, if he were there. He would never pretend
to be ignorant of 'mysteries' to get out of doing things. I get
out of doing things—in houses. But women won't let me do
things. They all know I want to be mooning about. How do
they know it? What is it? But they like me to be there.
And now in houses there's always this fearful worry and tiredness. What is the meaning of it?

Heavy footsteps came slowly downstairs.

'I put tea indoors.   I thought Miss Miriam'd be warm
after her ride.'

A large undulating voice with a shrewd consoling glance in
it. She must have come to the kitchen door to meet Harriett
in the hall.

'Yes, I'ke spect she will.' It was the same voice Harriett
had had in the nursery, resonant with practice in speaking to
new people.   Miriam felt tears coming.

'Hallo, you porking?   Isn't it porking?'

'Simply porked to death, my dear. Porked to *Death*,'
bawled Miriam softly, refreshed and delighted. Harriett was
still far off, but she felt as if she had touched her. Even the
end of the awful nine months was not changing her. Her
freshly shampooed hair had a leisurely glint. There was
colour in her cheeks. She surreptitiously rubbed her own hot
face. Her appearance would improve now, with every hour.
By the evening she would be her old self. After tea she would
play *The Artist's Model* and *The Geisha*.

'Let's have tea. I was asleep. I didn't hear you come.'

She sank into one of the large chairs, her thin accordion-
pleated black silk tea-gown billowing out round her squared
little body. Even her shoulders looked broader and squarer.
From the little pleated white chiffon chemisette, her radiant
firm little head rose up, her hair glinting under the light of the

window behind her. She looked so fine—such a 'fine spectacle'—and seemed so strong. How did she feel? Mrs
Thimm brought the teapot. The moment she had gone,
Harriett handed the rich cakes. Mrs Thimm *beaming*, shedding strong beams of happiness and approval. . . .

'Come on,' said Harriett. 'Let's tuck in. There's some
thin bread and butter somewhere, but I can't eat anything
but these things.'

'Can't you?'

'The last time I went up to town, Mrs Bollingdon and I had
six between us at Slater's and when we got back we had another
tea.'

'Fancy *you*!'

'I know. I can't 'elp it.'

'I can't 'elp it, Micky. *Love*lay b-hird.'

The fourth cup of creamy tea; Harriett's firm ringed hand;
the gleaming serene world; the sunlit flower-filled garden,
shaded at the far end by the large tree the other side of the
fence, coming in, one with the room; the sun going to set and
bring the evening freshness and rise to-morrow. Twenty-
eight leisurely teas, twenty-eight long days; a feeling of strength
and drowsiness. Nothing to do but clean the bicycle and
pump up the tyres on the lawn, to-morrow. Nothing—after
carrying the bicycle from the coal cellar up the area steps and
through the house into the Tansley Street back yard. Nothing
more but setting out after two nights of sleep in a cool room.

'That your machine in the yard, Mirry?'

'Yes; I've hired it, thirty bob for the whole month.'

'Well, if you're going a sixty-mile ride on it, I advise you to
tighten up the nuts a bit.'

'I will if you'll show me where they are. I've got a lovely
spanner. Did you look in the wallet?'

'I'll have a look at it all over, if you like.'

'Oh, Gerald, you saint. . . .'

'Now he's happy,' said Harriett, as Gerald's white-flannelled figure flashed into the sunlight and disappeared through the yard gate.

'Ph—how hot it is; it 's this summer-house.'

'Let 's go outside if you like,' said Miriam lazily, 'it seems to me simply perfect in here.'

'It 's all right—ph—it 's hot everywhere,' said Harriett languidly. She mopped her face. Her face emerged from her handkerchief fever-flushed, the eyes large and dark and brilliant; her lips full and drawn in and down at the corners with a look of hopeless anxiety.

Anger flushed through Miriam. Harriett at nineteen, in the brilliant beauty of the summer afternoon, facing hopeless fear.

'That 's an awfully pretty dress,' she faltered nervously.

Harriett set her lips and stretched both arms along the elbows of her basket chair.

'You could have it made into an evening gown.'

'I loathe the very sight of it. I shall burn it the minute I 've done with it.'

It was awful that anything that looked so charming could seem like that.

'D' you feel bad? Is it so awful?'

'I 'm all right, but I feel as if I were bursting. I wish it would just hurry up and be over.'

'I think you 're simply splendid.'

'I simply don't think about it. You don't think about it, except now and again when you realize you 've got to go through it, and then you go hot all over.'

'The head 's a bit wobbly,' said Gerald riding round the lawn.

'Does that matter?'

'Well, it doesn't make it any easier to ride, especially with this great bundle on the handle-bars. You want a luggage-carrier.'

'I dare say. I say, Gerald, show me the nuts to-morrow, not now.'

The machine was lying upside down on the lawn, with its back wheel revolving slowly in the air.

'The front wheel 's out of the true.'

'What do you think of the saddle?'

'The saddle's all right enough.'

'It's a Brooks's, B 40; about the best you can have. It's my own, and so's the Lucas's Baby bell.'

'By Jove, she's got an adjustable spanner.'

'That's not mine, nor the repair outfit; Mr Leyton lent me those.'

'And vaseline on the bearings.'

'Of course.'

'I don't think much of your gear-case, my dear.'

'Gerald, do you think it's all right on the whole?'

'Well, it's sound enough as far as I can see; bit squiffy and wobbly. I don't advise you to ride it in traffic, or with this bundle.'

'I *must* have the bundle. I came down through Tottenham Court Road and Oxford Street and Bond Street and Piccadilly all right.'

'Well, there's no accounting for tastes. Got any oil?'

'There's a little oil can in the wallet, wrapped up in the rag. It's lovely; perfectly new.'

CHAPTER XXVI

THERE was a strong soft grey light standing at the side of the blind . . . smiling and touching her as it had promised. She leaped to the floor and stood looking at it, swaying with sleep. Ships sailing along with masts growing on them, poplars streaming up from the ships, all in a stream of gold. . . . Last night's soapy water poured away, and the fresh poured out ready standing there all night, everything ready. . . . I must not forget the extra piece of string. . . . Je-ru-sa-*lem* the Gol-den, with-milk-and-hun-ny—blest. . . . Sh, not so much noise . . . beneath thy con, tem, *pla*, tion, sink, heart, and, voice, o, ppressed.

I *know* not, oh, I, *know*, not.

Sh—Sh . . . hark hark my soul angelic songs are swelling O'er earth's green fields, and ocean's wave-beat shore . . . damn—blast where are my bally knickers? Sing us sweet fragments of the songs above.

The green world everywhere, inside and out . . . all along the dim staircase, waiting in the dim cold kitchen.

No blind, brighter. Cool grey light, a misty windless morning. Shut the door.

They STAND *those* HALLS *of* ZI-ON
ALL JUBILANT *with* SONG.

As she neared Colnbrook the road grew heavier and a closer mist lay over the fields. It was too soon for fatigue, but her knees already seemed heavy with effort. Getting off at the level crossing she found that her skirt was sodden and her zouave spangled all over with beads of moisture. She walked shivering across the rails and remounted rapidly, hoisting into the saddle a draggled person that was not her own, and riding doggedly on beating back all thoughts but the thought of sunrise.

'Is this Reading?'

The cyclist smiled as he shouted back. He knew she knew. But he liked shouting too. If she had yelled Have you got a *soul*, it would have been just the same. If every one were on bicycles all the time you could talk to everybody, all the time, about anything . . . sailing so steadily along with two free legs . . . how much easier it must be with your knees going so slowly up and down . . . how *funny* I must look with my knees racing up and down in lumps of skirt. But I'm here, at the midday rest. It must be nearly twelve.

Drawing into the kerb near a confectioner's, she thought of buying two bars of plain chocolate. There *was* some sort of truth in *The Swiss Family Robinson*. If you went on, it was all right. There was only death. People frightened you about things that were not there. I will never listen to anybody again; or be frightened. That cyclist knew, as long as he was on his bicycle. Perhaps he has people who make him not himself. He can always get away again. Men can always get away. I am going to lead a man's life, always getting away. . . .

Wheeling her machine back to the open road, she sat down on a bank and ate the cold sausage and bread and half of the chocolate and lay down to rest on a level stretch of grass in front of a gate. Light throbbed round the edges of the little high white fleecy clouds. She swung triumphantly up. The earth throbbed beneath her with the throbbing of her heart . . . the sky steadied and stood further off, clear, peaceful, blue, with light neat soft bunches of cloud drifting slowly across it. She closed her eyes upon the dazzling growing distances of blue and white, and felt the horizon folding down in a firm clear sweep round her green cradle. Within her eyelids fields swung past green, cornfields gold and black, fields with coned clumps of harvested corn, dusty gold, and black, on either side of the bone-white grass-trimmed road. The road ran on and on, lined by low hedges and the strange everlasting back-flowing fields. Thrilling hedges and outstretched fields of distant light, coming on mile after mile, winding off, left behind . . . 'It's the Bath Road I shall be riding on; I'm going down to Chiswick to see which way the wind is on the Bath Road. . . .' Trees appeared, golden and green and shadowy, with warm cool strong shaded trunks coming nearer and larger. They swept by, their shadowy heads sweeping the lower sky. Poplars shot up, drawing her eyes to run up their feathered slimness and sweep to the top of the pointed plumes piercing the sky. Trees clumped in masses round houses leading to villages that shut her into little corridors of hard hot light . . . the little bright sienna form of the hen she had nearly run over; the land stretching serenely out again, rolling along, rolling along in the hot sunshine with the morning and evening freshness at either end . . . sweeping it slowly in and out of the deeps of the country night . . . eyelids were transparent. It was *light* coming through one's eyelids that made that clear soft buff; soft buff light filtering through one's body . . . little sounds, insects creeping and humming in the hedge, sounds from the grass. Sudden single quiet sounds going up from distant fields and farms, lost in the sky.

I've got my sea-legs . . . this is *riding*—not just straining along trying to forget the wobbly bicycle, but feeling it wobble and being able to control it . . . being able to look about easily . . . there will be a harvest moon this month, rolling up huge and hot, suddenly over the edge of a field; the last moon. I shall see that anyhow, whatever the holiday is like. It will be cold again in the winter. Perhaps I shan't feel so cold this winter.

She recognized the figure the instant she saw it. It was as if she had been riding the whole day to meet it. Completely forgotten, it had been all the time at the edge of the zest of her ride. It had been everywhere all the time and there it was at

last, dim and distant and unmistakable . . . coming horribly
along, a murk in the long empty road. She slowed up looking
furtively about. The road had been empty for so long. It
stretched invisibly away behind, empty. There was no sound
of anything coming along; nothing but the squeak squeak of
her gear-case; bitter empty fields on either side, greying away
to the twilight, the hedges sharp and dark, enemies; nothing
ahead but the bare road, carrying the murky figure; there all
the time; and bound to come. She rode on at her usual pace,
struggling for an absorption so complete as to make her invisible, but was held back by her hatred of herself for having
wondered whether he had seen her. The figure was growing
more distinct. Murky. Murk from head to foot. Wearing
openly like a coat the expression that could be seen hidden
inside everybody. She had made an enemy of him. It was
too late. The voice in her declaring sympathy, claiming
kinship, faded faint and far away within her . . . hullo old
boy, isn't it a bloody world . . . he would know it had come
too late. He came walking along, slowly walking like someone
in a procession or a quickly moving funeral; like someone in a
procession, who must go on. He was surrounded by people,
pressed in and down by them, wanting to kill every one with a
look and run, madly, to root up trees and tear down the landscape and get outside . . . he is myself. . . . He stood still.
Her staring eyes made him so clear that she saw his arrested
face just before he threw out an arm and came on, stumbling.
Measuring the width of the roadway she rode on slowly along
the middle of it, pressing steadily and thoughtlessly forward,
her eyes fixed on the far-off spaces of the world she used to
know, towards a barrier of swirling twilight. He was quite
near, slouching and thinking and silently talking, on and on.
He was all right, poor thing. She put forth all her strength and
shot past him in a sharp curve, her eye just seeing that he turned
and stood, swaying.

What a blessing he was drunk, what a blessing he was drunk,
she chattered busily, trying to ignore her trembling limbs.
Again and again as she steadied and rode sturdily and blissfully on, came the picture of herself saying with confidential

eagerness as she dismounted: 'I *say*—make haste—there's a madman coming down the road—get behind the hedge till he's gone—I'm going for the police.' A man would not have been afraid. Then men *are* more independent than women. Women can never go very far from the protection of men— because they are physically inferior. But men are afraid of mad bulls. . . . They have to resort to tricks. What was that I was just thinking? Something I ought to remember. Women have to be protected. But men explain it the wrong way. It was the same thing. . . . The polite protective man was the same; if he relied on his strength. The world is the most sickening hash. . . . I'm so sorry for you. *I* hate humanity too. *Isn't* it a lovely day? *Isn't* it? Just look.

The dim road led on into the darkness of what appeared to be a private estate. The light from the lamp fell upon wide gates fastened back. The road glimmered on ahead with dense darkness on either side. There had been no turning. The road evidently passed through the estate. She rode on and on between the two darknesses, her light casting a wobbling radiance along her path. Rustling sounded close at hand, and quick thuddings startled her, making her heart leap. The hooting of an owl echoed through the hollows amongst the trees. Stronger than fear, was the comfort of the dense darkness. Her own darkness by right of riding through the day. Leaning upon the velvety blackness she pushed on, her eyes upon the little circle of light, steady on the centre of the pathway, wobbling upon the feet of the trees emerging in slow procession on either side of the way.

The road began to slope gently downwards. Wearily back-pedalling, she crept down the incline, her hand on the brake, her eyes straining forward. Hard points of gold light—of course. She had put them there herself. Marlborough . . . the prim polite lights of Marlborough; little gliding moving lights, welcoming, coming safely up as she descended. They disappeared. There must have been a gap in the trees. Presently she would be down among them.

'*Good* Lord—it's a woman.'
She passed through the open gate into the glimmer of a descending road. Yes. Why not? Why that amazed stupefaction? Trying to rob her of the darkness and the wonderful coming out into the light. The man's voice went on with her down the dull safe road. A young lady, taking a bicycle ride in a daylit suburb. That was what she was. That was all he would allow. It's something in men.

'You don't think of riding up over the downs at this time of night?' It was like an at-home. Everybody in the shop was in it, but she was not in it. Marlborough thoughts rattling in all the heads; with Sunday coming. They had sick and dying relations. But it was all in Marlborough. Marlborough was all round them all the time, the daily look of it, the morning coming each day excitingly, all the people seeing each other again and the day going on. They did not know that that was it; or what it was they liked. Talking and thinking, with the secret hidden all the time even from themselves. But it was that that made them talk and make such a to-do about everything. They had to hide it because, if they knew, they would *feel* fat and complacent and wicked. They were fat and complacent because they did not know it.
'Oh yes I do,' said Miriam in feeble husky tones.
She stood squarely in front of the grating. The people became angrily gliding forms; cheated; angry in an eternal resentful silence; pretending. The man began thoughtfully ticking off the words.
'How far have you come?' he asked, suddenly pausing and looking up through the grating.
'From London.'
'Then you've just come down through the Forest.'
'Is that a forest?'
'You must have come through Savernake.'

'I didn't know it was a forest.'

'Well, I don't advise you to go on up over the downs at this time of night.'

If only she had not come in, she could have gone on without knowing it was 'the downs.'

'My front tyre is punctured,' she said conversationally, leaning a little against the counter.

The man's face tightened. 'There's Mr Drake next door would mend that for you, in the morning.'

'Next door. Oh, thank you.' Pushing her sixpence under the rail, she went down the shop to the door seeing nothing but the brown dusty floor leading out to the helpless night.

Why did he keep making such impossible suggestions? The tyre was absolutely flat. How much would a hotel cost? How did you stay in hotels . . . hotels . . . her hands went busily to her wallet. She drew out the repair outfit and Mr Leyton's voice sounded, emphatic and argumentative, 'You know where you are and they don't rook you.' There was certain to be one in a big town like this. She swished back into the shop and interrupted the man with her eager singing question.

'Yes,' came the answer, 'there's a quiet place of that sort up the road, right up against the Forest.'

'Has my telegram gone? Can I alter it?'

'No, it's not gone, you're just in time.'

It was the loveliest thing that could have happened. The day was complete, from morning to night.

Someone brought in the meal and clattered it quietly down, going away and shutting the door without a word. A door opened and the sound of departing footsteps ceased. She was shut in with the meal and the lamp in the little crowded world. The musty silence was so complete that the window hidden behind the buff-and-white blinds and curtains must be shut. The silence throbbed. The throbbing of her heart shook the room. Something was telling the room that she was the happiest thing in existence. She stood up, the beloved little

room moving as she moved, and gathered her hands gently
against her breast, to . . . get through, through into the soul
of the musty little room. . . . 'Oh! . . .' She felt herself
beating from head to foot with a radiance, but her body within
it was weak and heavy with fever. The little scene rocked,
crowding furniture, antimaccassars, ornaments, wool mats.
She looked from thing to thing with a beaming, feverish,
frozen smile. Her eyes blinked wearily at the hot crimson
flush of the mat under the lamp. She sank back again, her
heavy light limbs glowing with fever. 'By Jove, I 'm tired.
. . . I 've had nothing since breakfast m—but a m-bath *bun*
and an acidulatudd *drop*.' . . . She laughed and sat whistling
softly . . . Jehoshaphat—Manchester—Mesopotamia—beloved
—you sweet, sweet thing—Veilchen, unter Gras versteckt—
out of it all—here I am. I shall always stay in hotels. . . .
Glancing towards the food spread out on a white cloth near the
globed lamp, she saw behind the table a little stack of books.
Ham and tea and bread and butter. . . . Leaning unsteadily
across the table . . . battered and ribbed green binding and
then a short moral story or natural history—blue, large and
fat, a 'story-book' of some kind . . . she drew out one of the
undermost volumes. . . . *Robert Elsmere!* Here, after all
these years in this little outlandish place. She poured out
some tea and hurriedly slid a slice of ham between two pieces
of bread and butter and sat back with the food drawn near, the
lamplight glaring into her eyes, the printed page in exciting
shadow. Everything in the room was distinct and sharp—
morning strength descended upon her.

How he must have liked and admired. It must have amazed
him; a woman setting forth and putting straight the muddles
of his own mind. 'Powerful,' he probably said. It was a half-
jealous keeping to himself of a fine, good thing. If he could
have known that it would have been, just at that very moment,
the answer to my worry about Christ, he would have been
jealous and angry quite as much as surprised and pleased and

sympathetic . . . he was afraid *himself* of the idea that any one can give up the idea of the divinity of Christ and still remain religious and good. He ought to have let me read it. . . . If he could have stated it himself as well, that day by the gate he would have done so . . . 'a very reasonable dilemma, my dear.' He knew I was thinking about things. But he had not read *Robert Elsmere* then. He was jealous of a thunderbolt flung by a woman. . . .

And now I 've got beyond *Robert Elsmere.* . . . That 's Mrs Humphry Ward and Robert Elsmere; that 's gone. There 's no answering science. One must choose. Either science or religion. They can't both be true. This is the same as *Literature and Dogma.* . . . Only in *Literature and Dogma* there is that thing that is perfectly true—that thing—what is it? What was that idea in *Literature and Dogma*?

I wonder if I 've strained my heart. This funny feeling of sinking through the bed. Never mind. I 've done the ride. I 'm alive and alone in a strange place. Everything 's alive all round me in a new way. Nearer. As the flame of the candle had swelled and gone out under her blowing, she had noticed the bareness of everything in the room—a room for chance travellers, nothing that any one could carry away. She could still see it as it was when she moved and blew out the candle, a whole room swaying sideways into darkness. The more she relinquished the idea of harm and danger, the nearer and more intimate the room became. . . . No one can prevent my being alone in a strange place, near to things and loving them. It 's more than worth half killing yourself. It makes you ready to die. I 'm not going to die, even if I have strained my heart. 'Damaged myself for life.' I am going to sleep. The dawn will come, no one knowing where I am. Because I have no money, I must go on and stay with these people. But I have been alive here. There 's hardly any time. I *must* go to sleep.

CHAPTER XXVII

BEING really happy or really miserable makes people like you and like being with you. They need not know the cause. Someone will speak now, in a moment. . . . Miriam tried to return to the falling rain, the soft light in it, the soft light on the greenery, the intense green glow everywhere . . . misty green glow. But her eyes fell and her thoughts went on. They would have seen. Her face must be speaking of their niceness in coming out on the dull day, so that she might drive about once more in Lord Lansdowne's estate. Someone will speak. Perhaps they had not found forgetfulness in the green through the rain under the grey. Moments came suddenly in the lanes between the hedges, like that moment that always came where the lane ran up and turned, and the fields spread out in the distance. But usually you could not forget the chaise and the donkey and the people. In here amongst the green, something always came at once and stayed. Perhaps they did not find it so, or did not know they found it, because of their thoughts about the 'fine estate.' They seemed quite easy driving in the lanes, as easy as they ever seemed when one could not forget them. What were they doing when one forgot them? They knew one liked some things better than others; or suddenly liked everything very much indeed . . . she said you were apathetic . . . what does that mean? . . . what did she mean? . . . with her, one could see nothing and sat waiting . . . I said I don't think so, I don't think she is apathetic at all. Then they understood when one sat in a heap. . . . They had been pleased this morning because of one's misery at going away. They did not know of the wild happiness in the garden before breakfast, nor that the garden had been so lovely because the strain of the visit was over, and London was coming. They did not know that the happiness of being in amongst the greenery to-day, pouring out one's heart in farewell to the great trees, had grown so intense because the feeling of London and freedom was there. They could not see the long rich winter, the lectures and books, out of which something was coming. . . .

'It's a pity the rain came.'

Ah no, that is not rain. It is not raining. What is 'raining'? What do people *think* when they say these things?

'We are like daisies, *drenched* in dew.' She pursed up her face towards the sky.

They laughed and silence came again. Heavy and happy.

'I'm glad you came up. I want to ask you what is to be done about Hendie.'

Miriam looked about the boudoir. Mrs Green had hardly looked at her. She was smiling at her fancy work. But if one did not say something soon, she would speak again, going on into things from her point of view. Doctor and medicine. Eve liked it all. She *liked* Mrs Green's clever difficult fancy work, and the boudoir smell of Tonquin beans, and the house and garden and the bazaars and village entertainments, and the children's endless expensive clothes and the excitements and troubles about that fat man. Down here she was in a curious flush of excitement all the time herself. . . .

'I think she wants a rest.'

'I told her so. But resting seems to make her worse. We all thought she was worse after the holidays.'

Miriam's eyes fell before the sudden glance of Mrs Green's blue-green eye. She must have seen her private vision of life in the great rich house . . . misery, death with no escape. But they had Eve. Eve did not know what was killing her. She liked being tied to people.

'She is very nervous.'

'Yes. I know it's only nerves. I've told her that.'

'But you don't know what nerves are. They're not just nothing. . . .'

'*You*'re not nervous.'

'Don't you think so?'

'Not in the way Hendie is. You're a solid little person.'

Miriam laughed, and thought of Germany and Newlands and Banbury Park. But this house would be a thousand times worse. There was no one in it who knew anything about anything. That was why, when she was not too bad, Eve thought it was good for her to be there.

'I think she's very happy here.'

'I'm glad you think that. But something must be done. She can't go on with these perpetual headaches and sleeplessness and attacks of weepiness.'

'I think she wants a long rest.'

'What does she do with her holidays? Doesn't she rest then?'

'Yes, but there are always *worries*,' said Miriam desperately.

'You have had a good deal of worry—how is your father?'

How much do you know about that. . . . How does it strike you. . . .

'He is all right, I think.'

'He lives with your eldest sister.'

'Yes.'

'That's very nice for him. I expect the little grandson will be a great interest.'

'Yes.'

'And your youngest sister has a little girl?'

'Yes.'

'Do you like children?'

'Yes.'

'I expect you spend a good deal of your time with your sisters.'

'Well—it's a fearful distance.' Why didn't you ask me all these things when I was staying with you. There's no time now. . . .

'Do you like living alone in London?'

'Well—I'm fearfully *busy*.'

'I expect you are. I think it's wonderful. But you must be awfully lonely sometimes.'

Miriam fidgeted and wondered how to go.

'Well—come down and see us again. I 'm glad I had this chance of talking to you about Hendie.'

'Perhaps she 'll be better in the winter. I think she 's really better in the cold weather.'

'Well—we 'll hope so,' said Mrs Green getting up. 'I can't think what 's the matter with her. There 's nothing to worry her, down here.'

'No,' said Miriam emphatically in a worldly tone of departure. 'Thank you so much for having me,' she said feebly as they passed through the flower-scented hall, the scent of the flowers hanging delicately within the stronger odour of the large wood-fire.

'I 'm glad you came. We thought it would be nice for both of you.'

'Yes it was very kind of you. I 'm sure she wants a complete rest.' Away from us, away from you, in some new place. . . .

In the open light of the garden, Mrs Green's eyes were almost invisible points. She ought to do her hair smaller. The fashionable bundle of little sausages did not suit a large head. The eyes looked more sunken and dead than Eve's with her many headaches. But she was strong—a strong hard thunder-cloud at breakfast. Perhaps very unhappy. But wealthy. Strong, cruel wealth, eating up lives it did not understand. How did Eve manage to read *Music and Morals* and Olive Schreiner here?

CHAPTER XXVIII

'Miss Dear to see you, Miss.'

'Is there any one else in the waiting-room?'

'No, miss—nobody.'

Miriam went in briskly. . . . 'Well? How is the decayed gentlewoman?' she said briskly from the doorway. She hardly looked. She had taken in the close-fitting bonnet and chin-bow, and the height-giving look of the long blue uniform cloak together with the general aspect of the heavily shaded afternoon room. . . .

'Oh, she's very well.'

Miss Dear had stood quite still in her place half-way down the room between the sofa and the littered waiting-room table. She made a small controlled movement with her right hand as Miriam approached. Miriam paused with her hand on a *Navy League,* absorbed in the low sweet even tone. She found herself standing reverently, pulled up a few inches from the dark figure. Suddenly she was alight with the radiance of an uncontrollable smile. Her downcast eyes were fixed upon a tall slender figure in a skimpy black dress, tendrils of fine gold hair dancing in the rough wind under a cornflower-blue toque, a clear living rose-flush. . . . Something making one delicate figure more than the open width of the afternoon, the blue afternoon sea and sky. She looked up. The shy sweet flower-pink face glowed more intensely under the cap of gold hair clasped flatly down by the blue velvet rim of the bonnet. The eyes, now like Weymouth Bay, now like Julia Doyle's, now a clear expressionless blue, were fixed on hers; the hesitating face was breaking again into watchful speech. But there was no speech in the well-remembered outlines moulding the ominous cloak. Miriam flung out to stem the voice, rushing into phrases to open the way to the hall and the front door.

Miss Dear stood smiling, and laughing her little smothered obsequious laugh, just as she had done at Bognor, making one feel like a man.

'Well—I 'm most frightfully busy,' wound up Miriam cheerfully, turning to the door. 'That 's London—isn't it? One never has a minute.'

Miss Dear did not move. 'I came to thank you for the concert tickets,' she said in the even thoughtful voice that dispersed one's thoughts.

'Oh yes. Was it any good?'

'I enjoyed it immensely,' said Miss Dear gravely. 'So did Sister North,' she added, shaking out the words in delicate laughter.

. . . *I* don't know 'Sister *North*.' . . . 'Oh, good,' said Miriam opening the door.

'It was most kind of you to send them. I 'm going to a case to-morrow, but I shall hope to see you when I come back.'

'Sister North sported a swell new blouse,' said Miss Dear in clear intimate tones as she paused in the hall to take up her umbrella.

'I hope it won't rain,' said Miriam formally, opening the front door.

'She was no *end* of a swell,' pursued Miss Dear, hitching her cloak and skirt from her heels with a neat cuffed gloved hand, quirked compactly against her person just under her waist, and turned so that her elbow and forearm made a small compact angle against her person. She spoke over her shoulder, her form slenderly poised forward to descend the steps: 'I told her she would knock them.' She was aglow with the afternoon sunlight streaming down the street.

Miriam spoke as she stepped down with delicate plunges. She did not hear and paused, turning, on the last step.

'It was too *bad* of you,' shouted Miriam smiling, 'to leave my sister alone at the Decayed Gentlewomen's.'

'I couldn't help myself,' gleamed Miss Dear. 'My time was up.'

'Did you *hate* being there?'

Miss Dear hung, poised and swaying to some inner breeze.

Miriam gazed, waiting for her words, watching the in-turned eyes control the sweet lips flowering for speech.

'It was rather comical '—the eyes came round, clear pure blue—'until your sister came.' The tall slender figure faced the length of the street; the long thin blue cloak, flickering all over, gave Miriam a foresight of the coming swift hesitating conversational progress of the figure along the pavement, the poise of the delicate surmounting head, slightly bent, the pure brow foremost, shading the lowered thoughtful eyes, the clear little rounded dip of the indrawn chin.

'I 'm glad she gave me your address,' finished Miss Dear, a little furrow running along her brow in control of the dimpling flushed oval below it. 'I 'll say au revoir and not good-bye, for the present.'

'Good-bye,' flung Miriam stiffly at the departing face. Shutting the neglected door, she hurried back through the hall and resumed her consciousness of Wimpole Street with angry eager swiftness. . . . Eve, getting mixed up with people . . . it is right . . . *she* would not have been angry if I had asked her to be nice to somebody. . . . I did not mean to do anything . . . I was proud of having the tickets to send . . . if I had not sent them, I should have had the thought of all those nurses, longing for something to do between cases. They are just the people for the Students' Concerts . . . if she comes again . . . 'I can't have social life, unfortunately,' how furious I shall feel saying that, 'you see I 'm so fearfully full up—lectures every night and I 'm away every week-end . . . and I 'm not supposed to see people here——'

CHAPTER XXIX

MIRIAM had no choice but to settle herself on the cane-seated chair. When Miss Dear had drawn the four drab-coloured curtains into place, the small cubicle was in semi-darkness.

'I hope the next time you come to tea with me it will be under rather more comfortable circumstances.'

'This is all right,' said Miriam, in abstracted impatient continuation of her abounding manner. Miss Dear was arranging herself on the bed as if for a long sitting. The small matter of business would come now. Having had tea, it would be impossible to depart the moment the discussion was over. How much did the tea cost here? That basement tea-room, those excited young women and middle-aged women, watchful and stealthy and ugly with poverty and shifts, those teapots and shabby trays and thick bread and butter were like the Y.W.C.A. public restaurant at the other end of the street—fourpence at the outside; but Miss Dear would have to pay it. She felt trapped . . . 'a few moments of your time to advise me,' and now half the summer twilight had gone and she was pinned in this prison face to face with anything Miss Dear might choose to present; forced by the presences audible in the other cubicles to a continuation of her triumphant tea-room manner.

'You must excuse my dolly.' She arranged her skirt neatly about the ankle of the slippered bandaged foot.

Any one else would say, 'What is the matter with your foot?' . . . It stuck out, a dreadfully padded mass, dark in the darkness of the dreadful little enclosure in the dreadful dark hive of women, collected together only by poverty.

'Have you *left* your association?'

'Oh *no*, dear; not *permanently* of course,' said Miss Dear, pausing in her tweakings and adjustments of draperies to glance watchfully through the gloom.

'I 'm still a member there.'

'Oh yes.'

'But I 've got to look *after* myself. They don't give you a chance.'

'No——'

'It 's rush in and rush out and rush in and rush out.'

'What are you going to do?' . . . what do you want with me? . . .

'What do you mean, de-er?'

'Well, I mean, are you going on nursing?'

'Of *course*, de-er. I was going to tell you.'

Miriam's restive anger would not allow her to attend fully to the long story. She wandered off with the dreadful idea of nursing a 'semi-mental' sitting in a deck-chair in a country garden, the hopeless patient, the nurse half intent on a healthy life and fees for herself, and recalled the sprinkling of uniformed figures amongst the women crowded at the table, all in this dilemma, all eagerly intent; all overworked by associations claiming part of their fees or taking the risks of private nursing, all getting older; all, anyhow as long as they went on nursing, bound to live on illness; to live with illness knowing that they were living on it. Yet Mr Leyton had said that no hospital run by a religious sisterhood was any good . . . these women were run by doctors. . . .

'You see, de-er, it 's the best thing any sensible nurse can do as soon as she knows a sufficient number of influenchoo peopoo—physicians and others.'

'Yes, I see.' . . . But what has all this to do with me. . . .

'I shall keep in correspondence with my doctors and friends and look *after* myself a bit.'

'Yes, I see,' said Miriam eagerly. 'It 's a *splendid* plan. What did you want to consult me about?'

'Well, you see it 's like this. I must tell you my little difficulty. The folks at thirty-three don't know I 'm here, and I don't want to go back there, just at present. I was wondering if, when I leave here, you 'd mind my having my box sent to your lodgings. I shan't want my reserve things down there.'

'Well—there isn't much *room* in my room.'

'It 's a flat box. I got it to go to the colonies with a patient.'

'*Oh*, did you go?' . . . Nurses did see life; though they were never free to see it in their own way. Perhaps some of them . . . but then they would not be good nurses.

'Well, I didn't *go*. It was a chance of a lifetime. Such a de-er old gentleman—one of the Fitz-Duff family. It would have been nurse-companion. He didn't want me in uniform. My word. He gave me a complete outfit, *took* me round, coats and skirts at Peters, gloves at Penberthy's, a *lovely* gold-mounted umbrella, everything the heart could desire. He treated me just like a daughter.' During the whole of this speech she redeemed her words by little delicate bridling movements and adjustments, her averted eyes resting in indulgent approval on the old gentleman.

'Why didn't you go?'

'He *died*, dear.'

'Oh, I see.'

'It could go under your bed, out of the way.'

'I 've got hat-boxes and things. My room is full of things, I 'm afraid.'

'P'raps your landlady would let it stand somewhere.'

'I might ask her—won't they let you leave things here?'

'They *would*, I dare say,' frowned Miss Dear, 'but I have special reasons. I don't wish to be beholden to the people here.' She patted the tendrils of her hair, looking about the cubicle with cold disapproval.

'I dare say Mrs Bailey wouldn't mind. But I hardly like to ask her, you know. There seems to be luggage piled up everywhere.'

'Of course I should be prepared to pay a fee.'

. . . What a wonderful way of living . . . dropping a trunk full of things and going off with a portmanteau; starting life afresh in a new strange place. Miriam regarded the limber capable form outstretched on the narrow bed. This dark little enclosure, the forced companionship of the crowd of competing adventuresses, the sounds of them in the near cubicles, the perpetual sound, filling the house like a sea, of their busy

calculations . . . all this was only a single passing incident
. . . beyond it were the wide well-placed lives of wealthy
patients.

'Miss Younger is a sweet woman.'

Miriam's eyes awoke to affronted surprise.

'You know, de-er; the wan yow was sitting by at tea-time.
I told you just now.'

'Oh,' said Miriam guiltily.

Miss Dear dropped her voice: 'She's told me her whole
story. She's a dear sweet Christian woman. She's working
in a settlement. She's privately engaged, to the bishop. It's
not to be published yet. She's a sweet woman.'

Miriam rose. 'I've got to get back, I'm afraid.'

'Don't hurry away, dear. I hoped you would stay and
have some supper.'

'I really can't,' said Miriam wearily.

'Well, perhaps we shall meet again before Thursday. You'll
ask Mrs Bailey about my box,' said Miss Dear getting to her
feet.

'Fancy you remembering her name,' said Miriam with loud
cheerfulness, fumbling with the curtains.

Miss Dear stood beaming indulgently.

All the way down the unlit stone staircase they rallied each
other about the country garden with the deck chairs.

'Well,' said Miriam from the street, 'I'll let you know about
Mrs Bailey.'

'All right, dear, I shall expect to hear from you; au revoir!'
cried Miss Dear from the door. In the joy of her escape into
the twilight Miriam waved her hand towards the indulgently
smiling form and flung away, singing.

CHAPTER XXX

'Regular field-day, eh, Miss Hens'n? Look here——' Mr Orly turned towards the light coming in above the front door to exhibit his torn waistcoat and broken watch-chain. 'Came for me like a fury. They 've got double strength y' know, when they 're under. Ever seen anything like it?'

Miriam glanced incredulously at the portly frontage.

'Fancy breaking the *chain*,' she said, sickened by the vision of small white desperately fighting hands. He gathered up the hanging strings of bright links, his powerful padded musicianly hands finding the edges of the broken links and holding them adjusted with the discoloured ravaged fingers of a mechanic. 'A good tug would do it,' he said kindly. 'A chain 's no stronger than the weakest link,' he added with a note of dreamy sadness, drawing a sharp sigh.

'Did you get the tooth out?' clutched Miriam, automatically making a mental note of the remark that flashed through the world with a sad light, a lamp brought into a hopeless sick-room . . . keeping up her attitude of response to show that she was accepting the apology for his extremities of rage over the getting of the anaesthetist. Mrs Orly appearing in the hall at the moment, still flushed from the storm, joined the group and outdid Miriam's admiring amazement, brilliant smiles of relief garlanding her gentle outcry. 'Hancock busy?' said Mr Orly, in farewell, as he turned and swung away to the den followed by Mrs Orly, her unseen face busy with an interrupted errand. He would not hear that her voice was divided. . . . No one seemed to be aware of the divided voices . . . no men. Life went on and on, a great oblivious awfulness, sliding over everything. Every moment things went that could never be recovered . . . on and on, and it was always too late, there was always some new thing obliterating everything, something that looked new, but always turned out to be the same as everything else, grinning with its sameness in an awful blank where one tried to remember the killed things. . . . If only every one would stop for a moment and let the thing that was always hovering be there, let it settle and intensify. But the whole of life was a conspiracy to prevent it. Was there something wrong in it? It could not be a coincidence the way life *always* did that . . . she had reached the little conservatory on the half landing, darkened with a small forest of aspidistra. The dull dust-laden leaves identified themselves with her life. What had become of her autumn of hard work that was to lift her out of her personal affairs and lead somewhere? Already the holiday freshness and vigour had left her; and nothing had been done. Nothing was so strong as the desire that everything would stop for a moment, and allow her to remember. . . . Wearily she mounted the remaining stairs to Mr Hancock's room. 'I think,' said a clear high confident voice from the chair and stopped. Miriam waited with painful eagerness while the patient rinsed her mouth; 'that that gentleman thinks himself a good deal cleverer than he is,' she resumed, sitting back in the chair.

'I am afraid I'm not as familiar with his work as I ought to be, but I can't say I've been very greatly impressed as far as I have gone.'

'Don't go any further. There's nothing there to go for.'

Who are you speaking of? How do you know? What have *you* got that makes you think he has nothing?—Miriam almost cried aloud. Could she not see, could not both of them see that the quiet sheen of the green-painted window-frame cast off their complacent speech? Did they not hear it tinkle emptily back from the twined leaves and tendrils, the flowers and butterflies painted on the window in front of them? The patient had turned briskly to the spittoon again, after her little speech. She would have a remark ready when the brisk rinsing was over. There could be no peace in her presence. Even when she was gagged, there would be the sense of her sending out little teasing thoughts and comments. They could never leave anything alone . . . oh, it was *that* woman . . . the little gold knot at the back of the cheerful little gold head; hair that curled tightly about her head when she was a baby and that had grown long and been pinned up, as the clever daughter of that man; getting to know all he had said about women. If she believed it she must loathe her married state and her children . . . how *could* she let life continue through her? Perhaps it was the sense of her treachery that *gave* her that bright brisk amused manner. It was a way of carrying things off, that maddening way of speaking of everything as if life were a jest at everybody's expense. . . . All 'clever' women seemed to have that, *never* speaking what they thought or felt, but always things that sounded like quotations from men; so that they always seemed to flatter or criticize the men they were with, according as they were as clever as some man they knew, or less clever. *What* was she like when she was alone and dropped that bright *manner*. . . . 'Have you made any New Year resolutions? I don't make any. My friends think me godless, *I* think *them* lacking in common sense' . . . exactly like a man; taking up a fixed attitude . . . having a sort of prepared way of taking everything . . . like the Wilsons . . . anything else was 'unintelligent' or 'absurd' . . . their impatience meant something. Somehow all the other people were a reproach. If, some day, every one lived in the clear light of science, 'waiting for the pronouncements of science in all the affairs of life,' waiting for the pronouncements of those sensual dyspeptic men with families, who thought of women as existing only to produce more men . . . admirably fitted by nature's inexorable laws for her biological role . . . perhaps she agreed or pretended to think it all a great lark . . . the last vilest flattery . . . she had only two children . . . si la femme avait plus de sensibilité, elle ne retomberait pas si facilement dans la grossesse. . . . La femme, c'est peu galant de le dire, est la femelle de l'homme. The Frenchman at any rate *wanted* to say something else. But why want to be gallant . . . and why not say: man, it is not very graceful to say it, is the male of woman? If women had been the recorders of things from the beginning it would all have been the other way round . . . Mary. Mary, the Jewess, write something about Mary the Jewess; the Frenchman's Queen of Heaven.

Englishmen; the English were 'the leading race.' 'England

and America together — the Anglo-Saxon peoples — could govern the destinies of the world.' *What* world? . . . millions and millions of child-births . . . colonial women would keep it all going . . . and religious people . . . and if religion went on there would always be all the people who took the Bible literally . . . and if religion were not true, then there was only science. Either way was equally abominable . . . for women.

The far end of the ward was bright sunlight . . . there she was, enthroned, commanding the whole length of the ward, sitting upright, her head and shoulders already conversational, her hands busy with objects on the bed towards which her welcoming head was momentarily bent; like a hostess moving chairs in a small drawing-room . . . chrysanthemums all down the ward—massed on little tables . . . a *parrot* sidling and bobbing along its perch, great big funny solemn French grey, fresh clean living French grey, pure in the sunlight, a pure canary-coloured beak . . . clean grey and yellow . . . in the sun . . . a curious silent noise in the stillness of the ward.

'I couldn't hear; I wasn't near enough.'

'Better late than never, I *said*.'

'D' you *know*, I thought you'd only been here a few days, and to-day when I looked at your letter I was simply *astounded*. You're sitting up.'

'I should hope I am. They kept me on my back, half starving, for three weeks.'

'You look very pink and well now.'

'That's what Dr Ashley-Densley said. You ought to have seen me when I came in. You see I'm on chicken now.'

'And you feel better.'

'Well—you can't really tell how you are till you're up.'

'When are you going to get up?'

'To-morrow, I hope, dear. So you see you're just in time.'

'Do you mean you are going away?'

'They turn you out as soon as you're strong enough to stand.'

'But—*how* can you get about?'

'Dr Ashley-Densley has arranged all that. I'm going to a convalescent home.'

'*Oh*, that's very nice.'

'Poor Dr Ashley-Densley, he was dreadfully upset.'

'You've had some letters to cheer you up.' Miriam spoke impatiently, her eyes rooted on the pale leisurely hands, mechanically adjusting some neatly arranged papers.

'*No*, de-er. My friends have all left me to look after my*self* this time, but since I've been sitting up, I've been trying to get my affairs in order.'

'I thought of bringing you some flowers, but there was not a single shop between here and Wimpole Street.'

'There's generally women selling them outside. But I'm glad you didn't; I've too much sympathy with the poor nurses.'

Miriam glanced fearfully about. There were so many beds with forms seated and lying upon them . . . but there seemed no illness or pain. Quiet eyes met hers; everything seemed serene; there was no sound but the strange silent noise of the sunlight and the flowers. Half-way down the ward stood a large threefold screen covered with dark American cloth.

'She's unconscious to-day,' said Miss Dear; 'she won't last through the night.'

'Do you mean to say there is someone *dying* there?'

'*Yes*, *de*-er.'

'Do you mean to say they don't put them into a separate room to *die*?'

'They can't, dear. They haven't got the *space*,' flashed Miss Dear.

Death, shut in with one lonely person. Brisk nurses putting up the screen. Dying eyes cut off from all but those three dark surrounding walls, with death waiting inside them. Miriam's eyes filled with tears. There, just across the room, was the end. It had to come, somewhere; just that; on any summer's afternoon . . . people did things; hands placed a screen, people cleared you away. . . . It was a relief to realize that there were hospitals to die in; worry and torture of mind could end here. Perhaps it might be easier with people all round you than in a little room. There were hospitals to be ill in and somewhere to die neatly, however poor you were. It was a relief . . . 'she 's always the last to get up; still snoring when everybody 's fussing and washing.' That would be me . . . it lit up the hostel. Miss Dear liked that time of fussing and washing, in company with all the other cubicles fussing and washing. To be very poor meant getting more and more social life, with no appearances to keep up, getting up each day with a holiday feeling of one more day and the surprise of seeing everybody again; and the certainty that if you died some-body would do something. Certainly it was this knowledge that gave Miss Dear her peculiar strength. She was a nurse and knew how everything was done. She knew that people, all kinds of people, were *people* and would do things. When one was quite alone one could not believe this. Besides no one *would* do anything, for me. I don't want any one to. I should hate the face of a nurse who put a screen round my bed. I shall not die like that. I shall die in some other way, out in the sun, with—yes—oh, yes—Tah-dee, t'*dee*, t'dee—t'dee.

'It must be funny, for a nurse, to be in a hospital.'

'It 's a little too funny sometimes, dear—you know too much about what you 're in for.'

'Ilikeyourredjacket. Good *heavens*!'

'That 's nothing, dear. He does that all the afternoon.'

'How can you stand it ?'

'It 's Hobson's choice, madam.'

The parrot uttered three successive squawks, fuller and harsher and even more shrill than the first.

'He 's just tuning up; he always does in the afternoon, just as everybody is trying to get a little sleep.'

'But I never *heard* of such a thing! It 's monstrous, in a hospital. Why don't you all complain.'

''Sh, dear; he belongs to matron.'

'Why doesn't she have him in her room ? Shut *up*, Polly.'

'He 'd be rather a roomful in a little room.'

'Well—what is he *here* ? It 's the wickedest thing of its kind I 've ever heard of; some great fat healthy woman . . . why don't the *doctors* stop it ?'

'Perhaps they hardly notice it, dear.   There's such a bustle going on in the morning when they all come round.'

'But hang it all, she's here to look after you, not to leave her luggage all over the ward.'

The ripe afternoon light . . . even outside a hospital . . . the strange indistinguishable friend, mighty welcome, unutterable happiness.   O death, where is thy sting?   O grave, where is thy victory?   The light has no end.   I know it and it knows me, no misunderstanding, no barrier.   I love you—people say things.   But nothing that anybody says has any meaning.   Nothing that anybody says has any meaning. There is something more than anything that anybody says, that comes first, before they speak . . . vehicles travelling along through heaven; everybody in heaven without knowing it; the sound the vehicles made all together, sounding out through the universe . . . life touches your heart like dew; that is *true* . . . the edge of his greasy knowing selfish hair touches the light; he brushes it; there is something in him that remembers.   It is in everybody; but they won't stop.   Maddening.   But they know.   When people die, they must stop. Then they remember.   Remorse may be complete; until it is complete you cannot live.   When it is complete something is burned away . . . ou-agh, flows out of you, burning, inky, acid, flows right out . . . purged . . . though thy sins are as *scarlet*, they shall be white as snow.   *Then* the light is there, nothing but the light, and new memory, sweet and bright; but only when you have been killed by remorse.

This is what is meant by a purple twilight.   Lamps alight, small round lights, each in place, shedding no radiance, white day lingering on the stone pillars of the great crescent, the park railings distinct, the trees shrouded but looming very large and permanent, the air wide and high and purple, darkness alight and warm.   Far, far away beyond the length of two endless months, is Christmas.   This kind of day lived for ever.   It stood still. The whole year, funny little distant fussy thing, stood still in this sort of day. You could take it in your hand and look at it. Nobody could touch this. People and books and all those things that men had done, in the British Museum, were a crackling noise, outside. . . . Les yeux gris, vont au paradis. That was the two poplars, standing one each side of the little break in the railings, shooting up; the space between them shaped by their shapes, leading somewhere. I *must* have been through there; it's the park. I don't remember. It isn't. It's waiting. One day I will go through. Les yeux gris, vont au paradis. Going along, along, the twilight hides your shabby clothes. They are not shabby. They are clothes you go along in, funny; jolly. Everything's here, any bit of anything, clear in your brain; you can look at it. What a terrific thing a person is; bigger than anything. How *funny* it is to be a person. You can never not have been a person. Bouleversement. It's a fait bouleversant. *Christ*-how-rummy. It's enough. Du, Heilige, rufe dein Kind zurück, ich habe genossen das irdische Glück; ich habe geliebt und gelebt. . . . Oh let the solid ground not fail beneath my feet, until I am quite quite sure. . . . Hallo, old Euston Road, beloved of my soul, my own country, my native heath. There'll still be a glimmer on the table when I light the lamp . . . how shall I write it down, the *sound* the little boy made as he carefully carried the milk jug ? . . . going along, trusted, *trusted*, you could see it, you could see his mother. His legs came along, little loose feet, looking after themselves, pottering, behind him. All his body was in the hand carrying the milk jug. When he had done carrying the milk jug he would run; running along the pavement amongst people, with cool round eyes, not looking at anything. Where the crowd prevented his running, he would jog up and down as he walked, until he could run again, bumping solemnly up and down amongst the people; boy.

The turning of the key in the latch was lively with the vision of the jumping boy. The flare of the match in the unlit hall lit up eternity. The front door was open, eternity poured in and on up the stairs. At one of those great staircase windows, where the last of the twilight stood, a sudden light of morning would not be surprising. Of course a letter; curly curious statements on the hall-stand.

That is mother-of-pearl, nacre; twilight nacre; crépuscule nacre; I must wait until it is gone. It is a visitor; pearly freshness pouring in; but, if I wait, I may feel different. With the blind up, the lamp will be a lamp in it; twilight outside, the lamp on the edge of it, making the room gold, edged with twilight.

I *can't* go to-night. It's all *here*; I *must* stay here. Botheration. It's Eve fault. Eve would rather go out and see Nurse Dear than stay here. Eve *likes* getting tied up with people. I *won't* get tied up; it drives everything away. Now I've read the letter, I must go. There'll be afterwards when I get back. No one has any power over me. I shall be coming back. I shall always be coming back.

Perhaps it had been Madame Tussaud's that had made this row of houses generally invisible; perhaps their own awfulness. When she found herself opposite them, Miriam recognized them at once. By day, they were one high long lifeless smoke-grimed façade fronted by gardens colourless with grime, showing at its thickest on the leaves of an occasional laurel. It had never occurred to her that the houses could be occupied. She had seen them now and again as reflectors of the grime of the Metropolitan Railway. Its smoke poured up over their faces as the smoke from a kitchen fire pours over the back of a range. The sight of them brought nothing to her mind but the inside of the Metropolitan Railway; the feeling of one's skin prickling with grime, the sense of one's smoke-grimed clothes. There was nothing in that strip between Madame Tussaud's and the turning into Baker Street but the sense of exposure to grime . . . a little low grimed wall surmounted by paintless sooty iron railings.   On the other side of the road, a high brown wall, protecting whatever was behind, took the grime in one thick covering, here it spread over the exposed gardens and façades turning her eyes away.   To-night they looked almost as untenanted as she had been accustomed to think them.   Here and there on the black expanse, a window showed a blurred light.   The house she sought appeared to be in total darkness. The iron gate crumbled harshly against her gloves as she set her weight against the rusty hinges.   Gritty dust sounded under her feet along the pathway and up the shallow steps leading to the unlit doorway.

Her flight up through the sickly, sweet-smelling murk of the long staircase ended in a little top back room brilliant with unglobed gaslight.   Miss Dear got her quickly into the room and stood smiling and waiting for a moment for her to speak. Miriam stood nonplussed, catching at the feelings that rushed through her and the thoughts that spoke in her mind.   Distracted by the picture of the calm tall gold-topped figure in the long grey skirt and the pale pink flannel dressing-jacket. Miss Dear was smiling the smile of one who has a great secret to impart.   There was a saucepan or frying-pan or something —with a handle—sticking out. . . .   'I 'm glad you 've brought a book,' said Miss Dear.   The room was closing up and up . . . the door was shut.   Miriam's exasperation flew out.   She felt it fly out.   What would Miss Dear do or say?   'I 'oped you 'd come,' she said, in her softest, most thoughtful tones. 'I 've been rushing about and rushing about.'   She turned with her swift limber silent-footed movement to the thing on the gas-ring.   'Sit down dear,' she said, as one giving permission, and began rustling a paper packet.   A haddock came forth and the slender thoughtful fingers plucked and picked at it and lifted it gingerly into the shallow steaming pan.   Miriam's thoughts whirled to her room, to the dark sky-domed streets, to the coming morrow.   They flew about all over her life. The cane-seated chair thrilled her with a fresh sense of anger.
    'I 've been shopping and rushing about,' said Miss Dear,

disengaging a small crusty loaf from its paper bag. Miriam stared gloomily about and waited.

'Do you like haddock, dear?'

'Oh—well—I don't know—yes, I think I do.'

The fish smelled very savoury. It was wonderful and astonishing to know how to cook a real meal, in a tiny room; cheap . . . the lovely little loaf and the wholesome solid fish would cost less than a small egg and roll and butter at an A.B.C. How did people find out how to do these things?

'You know how to cook?'

'Haddock doesn't hardly need any cooking,' said Miss Dear, shifting the fish about by its tail.

'What is your book, dear?'

'Oh—*Villette*.'

'Is it a pretty book?'

She didn't want to know. She was saying something else. . . . How to mention it? Why say anything about it? But no one had ever asked. No one had known. This woman was the first. She, of all people, was causing the first time of speaking of it.

'I bought it when I was fifteen,' said Miriam vaguely, 'and a Byron—with some money I had; seven and six.'

'Oh yes.'

'I didn't care for the Byron; but it was a jolly edition; padded leather with rounded corners and gilt-edged leaves.'

'*Oh!*'

'I 've been reading this thing ever since I came back from my holidays.'

'It doesn't look very big.'

Miriam's voice trembled. 'I don't mean that. When I 've finished it, I begin again.'

'I wish you would read it to me.'

Miriam recoiled. Anything would have done; *Donovan* or anything. . . . But something had sprung into the room. She gazed at the calm profile, the long slender figure, the clear grey and pink, the pink frill of the jacket falling back from the soft

fair hair turned cleanly up, the clean fluffy curve of the skull,
the serene line of the brow bent in abstracted contemplation
of the steaming pan. 'I believe you 'd like it,' she said brightly.

'I should love you to read to me when we 've 'ad our supper.'

'Oh—I 've had my supper.'

'A bit of haddock won't hurt you, dear. . . . I 'm afraid
we shall have to be very knockabout; I 've got a knife and a
fork but no plates at present. It comes of living in a *box*,'
said Miss Dear pouring off the steaming water into the slop-pail.

'I 've had my supper—really. I 'll read while you have
yours.'

'Well, don't sit out in the middle of the room, dear.'

'I 'm all right,' said Miriam impatiently, finding the beginning of the first chapter. Her hands clung to the book. She
had not made herself at home as Eve would have done, and
talked. Now, these words would sound aloud, in a room.
Someone would hear and see. Miss Dear would not know
what it was. But she would hear and see something.

'It 's by a woman called Charlotte Brontë,' she said, and
began, headlong, with the gaslight in her eyes.

The familiar words sounded chilly and poor. Everything
in the room grew very distinct. Before she had finished the
chapter, Miriam knew the position of each piece of furniture.
Miss Dear sat very still. Was she listening patiently like a
mother, or wife, thinking of the reader as well as of what was
read, and with her own thoughts running along independently,
interested now and again in some single thing in the narrative,
something that reminded her of some experience of her own,
or some person she knew? No, there was something different.
However little she saw and heard, something was happening.
They were looking and hearing together . . . did she feel
anything of the grey . . . grey . . . grey made up of all the
colours there are; all the colours, seething into an even grey
. . . she wondered as she read on almost by heart, at the rare
freedom of her thoughts, ranging about. The book was cold
and unreal compared with what it was when she read it alone.
But something was happening. Something was passing to and
fro between them, behind the text; a conversation between

them that the text, the calm quiet grey that was the outer layer of the tumult, brought into being. If they should read on, the conversation would deepen. A glow ran through her at the thought. She felt that in some way she was like a man reading to a woman, but the reading did not separate them like a man's reading did. She paused for a moment on the thought. A man's reading was not reading; not a looking and a listening so that things came into the room. It was always an assertion of himself. Men read in loud harsh unnatural voices, in sentences, or with voices that were a commentary on the text, as if they were telling you what to think . . . they preferred reading to being read to; they read as if they were the authors of the text. Nothing could get through them but what they saw. They were like showmen. . . .

'Go on, dear.'

'My voice is getting tired. It must be all hours. I ought to have gone; ages ago,' said Miriam settling herself in the little chair with the book standing opened on the floor at her side.

'The time does pass quickly, when it is pleasantly occupied.'

A cigarette, now, would not be staying on. It would be like putting on one's hat. Then the visit would be over; without having taken place. The incident would have made no break in freedom. They had been both absent from the room nearly all the time. Perhaps that was why husbands so often took to reading to their wives, when they stayed at home at all; to avoid being in the room listening to their condemning silences or to their speech, speech with all the saucepan and comfort thoughts simmering behind it.

'I haven't had much time to attend to study. When you 've got to get your living, there 's too much else to do.'

Miriam glanced sharply. Had she wanted other things in the years of her strange occupation? She had gone in for nursing sentimentally, and now she knew the other side; doing everything to time, careful carrying out of the changing experiments of doctors. Her reputation and living depended on that; their reputation and living depended on her. And she had to go on, because it was her living. . . . Miss Dear was dispensing little gestures with bent head held high and in-turned eyes. She was holding up the worth and dignity of her career. It had meant sacrifices that left her mind enslaved. But, all the same, she thought excuses were necessary. She resented being illiterate. She had a brain somewhere, groping and starved. What could she do? It was too late. What a *shame* . . . serene golden comeliness, slender feet and hands, strange ability and knowledge of the world, and she knew, *knew* there was something that ought to be hers. Miriam thrilled with pity. The in-turned eyes sent out a challenging blue flash that expanded to a smile. Miriam recoiled, battling in the grip of the smile.

'I wish you 'd come round earlier to-morrow, dear, and have supper here.'

'How long are you going to stay here?' . . . to come again and read further and find that strange concentration that made one see into things. Did she really like it?

'Well, dear, you see, I don't know. I must settle up my affairs a little. I don't know where I am with one thing and another. I must leave it in the hands of an 'igher power.' She folded her hands and sat motionless with in-turned eyes, making the little movements with her lips that would lead to further speech, a flashing forth of something. . . .

'Well, I 'll see,' said Miriam getting up.

'I shall be looking for you.'

CHAPTER XXXI

It was . . . jolly; to have something one was obliged to do every evening—but it could not go on. Next week-end, the Brooms, that would be an excuse for making a break. She must have other friends she could turn to . . . she must *know* one could not go on. But bustling off every evening regularly to the same place with things to get for somebody was evidently good in some way . . . health-giving and strength-giving. . . .

She found Miss Dear in bed; sitting up, more pink and gold than ever. There was a deep lace frill on the pink jacket. She smiled deeply, a curious deep smile that looked like 'a smile of perfect love and confidence' . . . it *was* partly that. She was grateful, and admiring. That was all right. But it could not go on; and now illness. Miriam was aghast. Miss Dear seemed more herself than ever, sitting up in bed, just as she had been at the hospital.

'Are you ill?'

'Not really ill, de-er. I 've had a touch of my epileptiform neuralgia.' Miriam sat staring angrily at the floor.

'It 's enough to *make* any one ill.'

'*What* is?'

'To be sitoowated as I am.'

'You haven't been able to hear of a case?'

'How can I take a case, dear, when I haven't got my uniforms?'

'Did you sell them?'

'*No*, de-er. They 're with all the rest of my things at the hostel. Just because there 's a small balance owing, they refuse to give up my box. I 've told them I 'll settle it as soon as my pecooniary affairs are in order.'

'I see. That was why you didn't send your box on to me? You know I could pay that off if you like, if it isn't too much.'

'No, dear, I couldn't hear of such a thing.'

263

'But you *must* get work, or something. Do your friends know how things are?'

'There is no one I should care to turn to at the moment.'

'But the people at the Nursing Association?'

Miss Dear flushed and frowned. 'Don't think of *them*, dear. I've told you my opinion of the superintendent, and the nurses are in pretty much the same box as I am. More than one of them owes me money.'

'But surely if they knew——'

'I tell you I don't *wish* to apply to Baker Street at the present time.'

'But you *must* apply to *someone*. *Something* must be done. You see I can't, I shan't be able to go on indefinitely.'

Miss Dear's face broke into weeping. Miriam sat smarting under her own brutality . . . poverty is brutalizing, she reflected miserably, excusing herself. It makes you helpless and makes sick people fearful and hateful. It ought not to be like that. One can't even give way to one's natural feelings. What ought she to have done? To have spoken gently . . . you see, dear . . . she could hear women's voices saying it . . . my resources are not unlimited, we must try and think what is the best thing to be done . . . humbug . . . they would be feeling just as frightened, just as self-protecting, inside. There were people in books who shouldered things and got into debt, just for any casual, helpless person. But it would have to come on somebody, in the end. What then? Bustling people with plans . . . 'it's no good sitting still waiting for Providence,' . . . but that was just what one wanted to avoid . . . it had been wonderful, sometimes in the little room. It was *that* that had been outraged. It was as if she had struck a blow.

'I *have* done something, dear.'

'What?'

'I've sent for Dr Ashley-Densley.'

'There is our gentleman,' said Miss Dear tranquilly, just before midnight. Miriam moved away and stood by the window as the door split wide and a tall grey-clad figure plunged lightly into the room. Miriam missed his first questions in her observation of his well-controlled fatigue and annoyance, his astonishing height and slenderness and the curious wise softness of his voice. Suddenly she realized that he was going. He was not going to take anything in hand or do anything. He had got up from the chair by the bedside and was scribbling something on an envelope . . . no sleep for two nights he said, evenly, in the soft musical girlish tones. A prescription . . . then he 'd be off.

'Do you know Thomas's?' he said colourlessly.

'Do you know Thomas's—the chemist—in Baker Street?' he said, casting a half-glance in her direction as he wrote on.

'I do,' said Miriam coldly.

'Would you be afraid to go round there now?'

'What is it you want?' said Miriam acidly.

'Well, if you 're not afraid, go to Thomas's, get this made up, give Miss Dear a dose and, if it does not take effect, another in two hours' time.'

'You may leave it with me.'

'All right. I 'll be off. I 'll try to look in some time to-morrow,' he said turning to Miss Dear. 'Bye-bye,' and he was gone.

When the grey of morning began to show behind the blind, Miriam's thoughts came back to the figure on the bed. Miss Dear was peacefully asleep, lying on her back with her head thrown back upon the pillow. Her face looked stonily pure and stern; and colourless in the grey light. There was a sheen on her forehead, like the sheen on the foreheads of old people. She had probably been asleep ever since the beginning of the stillness. Everybody was getting up. 'London was getting up.' That man in the *Referee* knew what it was, that feeling when you live right *in* London, of being a Londoner, the thing that made it *enough* to be a Londoner, getting up, in London; the thing that made real Londoners different from every one

else, going about with a sense that made them *alive*. The very
idea of living anywhere but in London, when one thought about
it, produced a blank sensation in the heart. What was it I said
the other day? 'London's got me. It's taking my health,
and eating up my youth. It may as well have what remains.
. . .' Something stirred powerfully, unable to get to her
through her torpid body. Her weary brain spent its last strength
on the words, she had only half meant them when they were
spoken. *Now*, once she was free again, to be just a Londoner,
who would ask nothing more of life? It would be the answer
to all questions; the perfect unfailing thing, guiding all one's
decisions. And an ill-paid clerkship was its best possible
protection; keeping one at a quiet centre, alone in a little
room, untouched by human relationships, undisturbed by the
necessity of being anything. Nurses and teachers and doctors,
and all the people who were doing special things surrounded
by people and talk, were not Londoners. Clerks were, unless
they lived in suburbs. The people who lived in St Pancras
and Bloomsbury and in Seven Dials and all round Soho and
in all the slums and back streets everywhere were. She would
be again, soon . . . not a woman . . . a Londoner.

She rose from her chair feeling hardly able to stand. The
long endurance in the cold room had led to nothing but the
beginning of a day without strength—no one knowing what she
had gone through. Three days and nights of nursing Eve had
produced only a feverish gaiety. It *was* London that killed you.

'I will come in at lunch-time,' she scribbled on the back of
an envelope, and left it near one of the hands outstretched on
the coverlet.

Outdoors it was quite light, a soft grey morning, about
eight o'clock. People were moving about the streets. The
day would be got through somehow. To-morrow she would
be herself again.

'Has she applied to the Association to which she belongs?'
'I think she wishes for some reason to keep away from them

just now. She suggested that I should come to you, when I asked her if there was any one to whom she could turn. She told me you had helped her to have a holiday in a convalescent home.' These were the right people. The quiet grey house, the high-church room, the delicate outlines of the woman, clear and fine in spite of all the comfort. . . . The All Souls Nursing Sisters. . . . They *were* different . . . emotional and un-hygienic . . . cushions and hot-water bottles . . . good food . . . early service—Lent—stuffy churches—fasting. But they would not pass by on the other side. . . . She sat waiting . . . the atmosphere of the room made much of her weeks of charity and her long night of watching, the quiet presence in it knew of these things without being told. The weariness of her voice had poured out its burden, meeting and flowing into the patient weariness of the other woman and changing. There was no longer any anger or impatience. Together, consulting as accomplices, they would see what was the best thing to do—whatever it was would be something done on a long long road going on for ever; nobody outside, nobody left behind. When they had decided, they would leave it, happy and serene, and glance at the invisible sun and make little confident jests together. She was like Mrs Bailey — and someone farther back—mother. This was the secret life of women. They smiled at God. But they all flattered men. All these women. . . .

'They ought to be informed. Will you call on them—to-day? Or would you prefer that I should do so?'

'I will go—at lunch-time,' said Miriam promptly.

'Meanwhile I shall inform the clergy. It is a case for the parish. You must not bear the responsibility a moment longer.'

Miriam relaxed in her capacious chair, a dimness before her eyes. The voice was going on, unnoticing, the figure had turned towards a bureau. There were little straggles about the fine hair—Miss Jenny Perne—the Pernes. She was a lonely old maid. . . . One must listen . . . but London had sprung back . . . in full open midday roar; brilliant and fresh; dim, intimate, vast, from the darkness. This woman preferred

some provincial town . . . Wolverhampton . . . Wolverhampton
. . . in the little room in Marylebone Road Miss Dear was
unconsciously sleeping—a pauper.

There was a large bunch of black grapes on the little table
by the bedside, and a book.

'Hullo, you literary female,' said Miriam, seizing it . . . *Red
Pottage* . . . a curious novelish name, difficult to understand.
Miss Dear sat up, straight and brisk, blooming smiles. What
an easy life. The light changing in the room and people
bringing novels and grapes, smart new novels that people
were reading.

'What did you do at lunch time, dear?'

'Oh I had to go and see a female unexpectedly.'

'I found your note and thought perhaps you had called in
at Baker Street.'

'At your Association, d'you mean? Oh, my dear lady!'
Miriam shook her thoughts about, pushing back 'She owes
money to almost every nurse in this house and seems to have
given in in every way,' and bringing forward 'one of our very
best nurses for five years.'

'Oh, I went to see the woman in Queen Square this morning.'

'I know you did, dear.' Miss Dear bridled in her secret way,
averted, and preparing to speak. It was over. She did not
seem to mind. 'I liked her,' said Miriam hastily, leaping
across the gap, longing to know what had been done, beating
out anywhere to rid her face of the lines of shame. She was
sitting before a judge . . . being looked through and through.
. . . Noo, Tonalt, suggest a tow-pic. . . .

'She's a sweet woman,' said Miss Dear patronizingly.

'She's brought you some nice things' . . . poverty was
worse if you were not poor enough. . . .

'Oh, *no*, dear. The curate brought these. He called twice
this morning. You did me a good turn. He's a real friend.'

'Oh—oh, I'm so glad.'

'Yes—he's a nice little man. He was most dreadfully upset.'

'What can he do?'

'How do you mean, dear?'

'Well, in general?'

'He's going to do everything, dear. I'm not to worry.'

'How splendid!'

'He came in first thing and saw how things stood, and came in again at the end of the morning with these things. He's sending me some wine, from his own cellar.'

Miriam gazed, her thoughts tumbling incoherently.

'He was most dreadfully upset. He could not write his sermon. He kept thinking it might be one of his own *sisters* in the same sitawation. He couldn't rest till he came back.'

Standing back . . . all the time . . . delicately preparing to speak . . . presiding over them all . . . over herself too . . .

'He's a real friend.'

'Have you looked at the book?' There was nothing more to do.

'No, dear. He said it had interested him very much. He reads them for his sermons, you see' . . . she put out her hand and touched the volume . . . John's books . . . Henry is so interested in photography . . . unknowing patronizing respectful gestures. . . . 'Poor little man. He was dreadfully upset.'

'We'd better read it.'

'What time are you coming, dear?'

'Oh—well.'

'I'm to have my meals regular. Mr Taunton has seen the landlady. I wish I could ask you to join me. But he's been so generous. I mustn't run expenses up, you see, dear.'

'Of course not. I'll come in after supper. I'm not quite sure about to-night.'

'Well—I hope I shall see you on Saturday. I can give you tea.'

'I'm going away for the week-end. I've put it off and off. I must go this week.'

Miss Dear frowned. 'Well dear, come in and see me on your way.'

Miss Dear sat down with an indrawn breath.

Miriam drew her Gladstone bag a little closer. 'I have only a second.'

'All *right*, dear. You 've only just *come*.'

It was as if nothing had happened the whole week. She was not going to say anything. She was ill again, just in time for the week-end. She looked fearfully ill. Was she ill? The room was horrible—desolate and angry. . . .

Miriam sat listening to the indrawn breathings.

'What is the matter?'

'It 's my epileptiform neuralgia again. I thought Dr Ashley-Densley would have been in. I suppose he 's off for the week-end.'

She lay back pale and lifeless-looking with her eyes closed.

'All right, I won't go, that 's about it,' said Miriam angrily.

'Have another cup, dear. He said the picture was like me and like my name. He thinks it 's the right name for me—"You 'll always be able to inspire affection," he said.'

'Yes, that 's true.'

'He wants me to change my first name. He thought Eleanor would be pretty.'

'I *say*; look here.'

'Of course I can't make any decision until I know certain things.'

'*D*' you mean to say . . . *good*ness!'

Miss Dear chuckled indulgently, making little brisk movements about the tea-tray.

'So I 'm to be called Eleanor Dear. He 's a dear little man. I 'm very fond of him. But there is an earlier friend.'

'Oh——'

'I thought you 'd help me out.'

'*I*?'

'Well, dear, I thought you wouldn't mind calling and finding out for me how the land lies.'

Miriam's eyes fixed the inexorable shapely outlines of the tall figure. That dignity would never go; but there was something that would never come . . . there would be nothing but fuss and mystification for the man. She would have a house and a dignified life. He, at home, would have death. But these were the women. But she had liked the book. There was something in it she had felt. But a man reading, seeing only bits and points of view, would never find that far-away something. She would hold the man by being everlastingly mysteriously up to something or other behind a smile. He would grow sick to death of mysterious nothings; of things always centring in her, leaving everything else outside her dignity. Appalling. What *was* she doing all the time, bringing one's eyes back and back each time after one had angrily given in, to question the ruffles of her hair and the way she stood and walked and prepared to speak?

'*Oh* . . . ! of *course* I will—you wicked woman.'

'It's very puzzling. You see, he's the earlier friend.'

'You think if he knew he had a rival—— Of course. Quite right.'

'Well, dear, I think he ought to *know*.'

'So I'm to be your mamma. What a *lark*.'

Miss Dear shed a fond look. 'I want you to meet my little man. He's longing to meet you.'

'Have you mentioned me to him?'

'Well, dear, who should I mention if not you?'

'So I thought the best thing to do would be to come and ask you what would be the best thing to do for her.'

'There's nothing to be done for her.' He turned away and moved things about on the mantelpiece. Miriam's heart beat rebelliously in the silence of the consulting-room. She sat waiting stifled with apprehension, her thoughts on Miss Dear's familiar mysterious figure. In an unendurable impatience she waited for more, her eye smiting the tall averted figure on the hearthrug, following his movements . . . small framed coloured pictures — very brilliant — photographs? — of dark and fair women, all the same, their shoulders draped like 'The Soul's

Awakening,' their chests bare, all of them with horrible masses
of combed out waving hair like the woman in the Harlene shop,
only waving naturally.   The most awful minxes . . . his ideals.
What a man.   What a ghastly world.   'If she were to go to the
south of France, at once, she might live for years' . . . this is
hearing about death, in a consulting-room . . . no escape . . .
everything in the room holding you in.   The Death Sentence.
. . . People would not die if they did not go to consulting-
rooms . . . doctors make you die . . . they watch and threaten.

'What is the matter with her?'   Out with it, don't be so
important and mysterious.

'Don't you know, my dear girl?'   Dr Densley wheeled
round with searching observant eyes.

'Hasn't she told you?' he added quietly, with his eyes on his
nails.   'She's phthisical.   She's in the first stages of pul-
monary tuberculosis.'

The things in the dark room darkled with a curious dull
flash along all their edges and settled in a stifling dusky gloom.
Everything in the room dingy and dirty and decaying, but the
long lean upright figure.   In time, too, he would die of something.   Phthisis . . . that curious terrible damp mouldering
smell, damp warm faint human fungus . . . in Aunt Henderson's
bedroom. . . . But she had got better. . . . But the curate ought
to know.   But perhaps he, too, perhaps she had *imagined*
that. . . .

'It seems strange she has not told such an old friend.'

'I'm not an old friend.   I've only known her about two
months.   I'm hardly a friend at all.'

Dr Densley was roaming about the room.   'You've been
a friend in need to that poor girl,' he murmured contemplating
the window curtains.   'I recognized that when I saw you in
her room last week.'   How superficial. . . .

'Where did you meet her?' he said, a curious gentle high
tone on the where and a low one on the meet, as if he were
questioning a very delicate patient.

'My sister picked her up at a convalescent home.'

He turned very sharply and came and sat down in a low chair
opposite Miriam's low chair.

'Tell me all about it, my dear girl,' he said sitting forward so that his clasped hands almost touched Miriam's knees.

'And she told you I was her oldest friend,' he said, getting up and going back to the mantelpiece.

'I first met Miss Dear,' he resumed after a pause, speaking like a witness, 'last Christmas.   I called in at Baker Street and found the superintendent had four of her disengaged nurses down with influenza.   At her request, I ran up to see them. Miss Dear was one of the number.   Since that date she has summoned me at all hours on any and every pretext.   What I can, I have done for her.   She knows perfectly well her condition.   She has her back against the wall.   She's making a splendid fight.   But the one thing that would give her a chance, she obstinately refuses to do.   Last summer I found for her employment in a nursing home in the south of France.   She refused to go, though I told her plainly what would be the result of another winter in England.'

'Ought she to marry?' said Miriam suddenly, closely watching him.

'Is she thinking of marrying, my dear girl?' he answered, looking at his nails.

'Well of course she *might*——'

'Is there a sweetheart on the horizon?'

'Well, she inspires a great deal of affection.   I think she is inspiring affection *now*.'

Dr Densley threw back his head with a laugh that caught his breath and gasped in and out on a high tone, leaving his silent mouth wide open, when he again faced Miriam with the laughter still in his eyes.

'Tell me, my dear girl,' he said, smiting her knee with gentle affection, 'is there someone who would like to marry her?'

'What I want to *know*,' said Miriam very briskly 'is whether such a person ought to know about the state of her health.' She found herself cold and trembling as she asked.   Miss Dear's eyes seemed fixed upon her.

'The chance of a tuberculous woman in marriage,' recited Dr Densley, 'is a holding up of the disease with the first child; after the second, she usually fails.'

Why children? A doctor could see nothing in marriage but children. This man saw women with a sort of admiring pity. He probably estimated all those women on the mantelpiece according to their child-bearing capacity.

'Personally, I do not believe in forbidding the marriage of consumptives; provided both parties know what they are doing; and if they are quite sure they cannot do without each other. We know so little about heredity and disease, we do not know always what life is about. Personally, I would not divide two people who are thoroughly devoted to each other.'

'No?' said Miriam coldly.

'Is the young man in a position to take her abroad?'

'I can't tell you more than I know,' said Miriam impatiently getting up.

Dr Densley laughed again and rose.

'I'm very glad you came, my dear girl. Come again soon and report progress. You're so near you can run in any time when you're free.'

'Thank you,' said Miriam politely, scrutinizing him calmly as he waved and patted her out into the hall.

Impelled by an uncontrollable urgency, she made her way along the Marylebone Road. Miss Dear was not expecting her till late. But the responsibility, the urgency. She must go abroad. About Dr Densley. That was easy enough. There was a phrase ready about that somewhere. Three things. But she could not go abroad to-night. Why not go to the Lyons at Portland Road station, and have a meal and get calm and think out a plan? But there was no time to lose. There was not a moment to lose. She arrived at the dark gate breathless and incoherent. A man was opening the gate from the inside. He stood short and compact in the gloom, holding it open for her.

'Is it Miss Henderson?' he said nervously as she passed.

'Yes,' said Miriam stopping dead, flooded with sadness.

'I have been hoping to see you for the last ten days,' he said hurriedly and as if afraid of being overheard. In the impenetrable gloom, darker than the darkness, his voice was a thread of comfort.

'Oh, yes.'

'Could you come and see me?'

'Oh, yes, of course.'

'If you will give me your number in Wimpole Street, I will send you a note.'

'My *dear*!'

The tall figure, radiant, lit from head to foot, 'as the light on a falling wave' . . . 'as the light on a falling wave.' . . .

Everything stood still as they gazed at each other. Her own self gazed at her out of Miss Dear's eyes.

'Well, I 'm *bothered*,' said Miriam at last, sinking into a chair.

'No need to be bothered any more, dear,' laughed Miss Dear.

'It 's extraordinary.' She tried to recover the glory of the first moment in speechless contemplation of the radiant figure now moving chairs near to the lamp. The disappearance of the gas, the shaded lamp, the rector's wife's manner, the rector's wife's quiet stylish costume; it was like a prepared scene. How funny it would be to know a rector's wife.

'He 's longing to meet you. I shall have a second room to-morrow. We will have a tea-party.'

'It was to-day, of course.'

'Just before you came,' said Miss Dear, her glowing face bent, her hands brushing at the new costume. 'You 'll be our greatest friend.'

'But how grand you are.'

'He made my future his care some days ago, dear. "As long as I live, you shall want for nothing," he said.'

'And to-day it all came out.'

'Of course he 'll have to get a *living*, dear. But we 've decided to ignore the world.'

What did she mean by that? . . .

'You won't have to.'

'Well, dear, I mean let the world go by.'

'I see. He's a jewel. I think you've made a very good choice. You can make your mind easy about that. I saw the great medicine-man to-day.'

'It was all settled without that, dear. I never even thought about him.'

'You needn't. No woman need. He's a man who doesn't know his own mind and never will. I doubt very much whether he has a mind to know. If he ever marries he will marry a *wife*, not any particular woman; a smart worldly woman for his profession, or a thoroughly healthy female who'll keep a home in the country for him and have children and pour out his tea and grow things in the garden, while he flirts with patients in town. He's most *awfully* susceptible.'

'I expect we shan't live in London.'

'Well, that'll be better for you, won't it?'

'How do you mean, de-er?'

'Well, I ought to tell you Dr Densley told me you ought to go abroad.'

'There's no need for me to go abroad, dear, I shall be all right if I can look *after* myself and get into the air.'

'I expect you will. Everything's happened just right, hasn't it?'

'It's all been in the hands of an 'igher power, dear.'

Miriam found herself chafing again. It had all rushed on, in a few minutes. It was out of her hands completely now. She did not want to know Mr and Mrs Taunton. There was nothing to hold her any longer. She had seen Miss Dear in the new part. To watch the working out of it, to hear about the parish, sudden details about people she did not know— intolerable.

CHAPTER XXXII

THE short figure looked taller in the cassock, funny and hounded, like all curates; pounding about and arranging a place for her and trying to collect his thoughts while he repeated how good it was of her to have come. He sat down at last to the poached eggs and tea, laid on one end of the small, book-crowded table.

'I have a service at four-thirty,' he said, busily eating and glaring in front of him with unseeing eyes, a little like Mr Grove only less desperate because his dark head was round and his eyes were blue—'so you must excuse my meal. I have a volume of Plato here.'

'Oh, yes,' said Miriam doubtfully.

'Are you familiar with Plato?'

She pondered intensely and rushed in just in time to prevent his speaking again.

'I *should* like him, I know—I've come across extracts in other books.'

'He is a great man; my favourite companion. I spend most of my leisure up here, with Plato.'

'What a delightful life,' said Miriam enviously, looking about the small crowded room.

'As much time as I can spare from my work at the Institute and the Mission chapel; they fill my *active* hours.'

Where would a woman, a wife-woman, be, in a life like this? He poured himself out a cup of tea; the eyes turned towards the tea-pot were worried and hurried; his whole compact rounded form was a little worried and anxious. There was something—bunnyish about him. Reading Plato, the expression of his person would still have something of the worried rabbit about it. His face would be calm and intent. Then he would look up from the page, taking in a thought, and

277

something in his room would bring him back again to worry. But he was too stout to belong to a religious order.

'You must have a very busy life,' said Miriam, her attention wandering rapidly off hither and thither.

'Of course,' he said turning away from the table to the fire beside which she sat, 'I think the clergy should keep in touch to some extent with modern thought—in so far as it helps them with their own particular work.'

Miriam wondered why she felt no desire to open the subject of religion and science; or any other subject. It was so extraordinary to find herself sitting tête-à-tête with a clergyman, and still more strange to find him communicatively trying to show her his life from the inside. He went on talking, not looking at her, but gazing into the fire. She tried in vain to tether her attention. It was straining away to work upon something, upon some curious evidence it had collected since she came into the room; and even with her eyes fixed upon his person and her mind noting the strange contradiction between the thin, rippling many-buttoned cassock and the stout square-toed boots protruding beneath it, she could not completely convince herself that he was there.

'. . . novels; I ask my friends to recommend any that might be helpful.'

He had looked up towards her with this phrase.

'Oh yes, *Red Pottage*,' she said grasping hurriedly and looking attentive.

'Have you read that novel?'

'No. I imagined that *you* had, because you lent it to Miss Dear.'

'Miss Dear has spoken to you of me?'

'Oh yes.'

'Of you, she has spoken a great deal. You know her very well. It is because of your long friendship with her that I have taken courage to ask you to come here and discuss with me about her affairs.'

'I have known Miss Dear only a very short time,' said Miriam, sternly, gazing into the fire. Nothing should persuade her to become the caretaker of the future Mrs Taunton.

'That surprises me very much indeed,' he said propping his head upon his hand by one finger held against a tooth. He sat brooding.

'She is very much in need of friends just now,' he said suddenly and evenly towards the fire, without removing his finger from his tooth.

'Yes,' said Miriam gravely.

'You are, nevertheless, the only intimate woman friend to whom just now she has access.'

'I've done little things for her. I couldn't do much.'

'You were sorry for her.' Mr Taunton was studying her face and waiting.

'Well—I don't know; she'—she consulted the fire intensely, looking for the truth—'she seems to me too strong for that.' Light! Women have no pity on women . . . they *know* how *strong* women are; a sick man *is* more helpless and pitiful than a sick woman; almost as helpless as a child. People in order of strength . . . women, men, children. This man without his worldly props, his money and his job and his health, had not a hundredth part of the strength of a woman . . . nor had Dr Densley. . . .

'I think she *fascinated* me.'

Mr Taunton gathered himself together in his chair and sat very upright.

'She has an exceptional power of inspiring affection— affection and the desire to give her the help she so sorely needs.'

'Perhaps that is it,' said Miriam judicially. But you are very much mistaken in calling on me for help . . . 'domestic work and the care of the aged and the sick'—very convenient —all the stuffy nerve-racking never-ending things to be dumped on to women—who are to be openly praised and secretly despised for their unselfishness—I've got twice the brain-power you have. You are something of a scholar; but there is a way in which my time is more valuable than yours. There is a way in which it is more right for you to be tied to this woman than for me. Your reading is a habit, like most men's reading, not a quest. You don't want it disturbed.

But you are kinder than I am. You are splendid. It will be awful—you don't know how awful yet—poor little man.

'I think it has been so, in my case, if you will allow me to tell you.'

'Oh, yes, *do*,' said Miriam a little archly—'of course—I know—I mean to say Miss Dear has told me.'

'Yes,' he said eagerly.

'How things are,' she finished, looking shyly into the fire.

'Nevertheless, if you will allow me, I should like to tell you exactly what has occurred and to ask your advice as to the future. My mother and sisters are in the midlands.'

'Yes,' said Miriam in a carefully sombre non-committal tone; waiting for the revelation of some of the things men expect from mothers and sisters and wondering whether he was beginning to see her unsuitability for the role of convenient sister.

'When my rector sent me to look up Miss Dear,' he began heavily, 'I thought it was an ordinary parish case, and I was shocked beyond measure to find a delicately nurtured, ladylike girl in such a situation. I came back here to my rooms and found myself unable to enter into my usual employments. I was haunted by the thought of what that lonely girl, who might have been one of my own sisters, must be suffering and enduring and I returned to give what relief I could, without waiting to report the case to my rector for ordinary parish relief. I am not dependent on my stipend and I felt that I could not withhold the help she ought to have. I saw her landlady and made arrangements as to her feeding, and called each day myself to take little things to cheer her—as a rule when my day's work was done. I have never come in contact with a more pathetic case. It did not occur to me for . . . a moment, that she viewed my visits and the help I was so glad to be able to give . . . in . . . in any other light . . . that she viewed me as other than her parish priest.'

'Of *course* not,' said Miriam violently.

'She is a singularly attractive and lovable nature. That, to my mind, makes her helplessness and resourcelessness all the more painfully pathetic. Her very name——' He paused, gazing

into the fire. 'I told her lately in one of her moments of deep
depression that she would never want for friends, that she
would always inspire affection wherever she went, and that as
long as I lived she should never know want. Last week—the
day I met you at the gate—finding her up and apparently very
much better, I suggested that it would be well to discontinue
my visits for the present, pointing out the social reasons and
so forth . . . I had with me a letter from a very pleasant Home
in Bournemouth. She had hinted, much earlier, that a long
rest in some place such as Bournemouth was what she wanted,
to set her up in health. I am bound to tell you what followed.
She broke down completely, told me that, socially speaking, it
was too late to discontinue my visits; that people in the house
were already talking.'

'People in *that* house!'—you little simpleton—'Who? It
is the most monstrous thing I ever heard.'

'Well—there you have the whole story. The poor girl's
distress and dependence were most moving. I have a very
great respect for her character and esteem for her personality
—and of course I am pledged.'

'I see,' said Miriam narrowly regarding him. Do you want
to be saved?—ought I to save you?—why should I save you?—it
is a solution of the whole thing, and a use for your money—
you won't marry her when you know how ill she is.

'It is of course the immediate future that causes me anxiety
and disquietude. It is there I need your advice and help.'

'I see. Is Miss Dear going to Bournemouth?'

'Well; that is just it. Now that the opportunity is there, she
seems disinclined to avail herself of it. I hope that you will
support me in trying to persuade her.'

'Of course. She *must* go.'

'I am glad you think so. It is obvious that definite plans
must be postponed until she is well and strong.'

'You would be able to go down and see her.'

'Occasionally, as my duties permit, oh, yes. It is a very
pleasant place, and I have friends in Bournemouth who would
visit her.'

'She ought to be longing to go,' said Miriam on her strange

sudden smile. It had come from somewhere; the atmosphere was easier; suddenly in the room with her was the sense of bluebells, a wood blue with bluebells, and dim roofs, roofs in a town . . . sur les toits . . . and books; people reading books under them.

Mr Taunton smiled too.

'Unfortunately that is not so,' he said leaning back in his chair and crossing his legs comfortably.

'You know,' he said turning his blue gaze from the fire to Miriam's face, 'I have never been so worried in my life as I have during the last ten days. It's upsetting my winter's work. It is altogether too difficult and impossible. I cannot see any possible adjustment. You see, I cannot possibly be continually interrupted and in such—strange ways. She came here yesterday afternoon with a list of complaints about her landlady. I *really* cannot attend to these things. She sends me *telegrams*. Only this morning there was a telegram. "Come at once. Difficulty with chemist." Of course it was impossible for me to leave my work at a moment's notice. This afternoon, I called. It seems that she was under the impression that there had been some insolence . . . it absorbs so much *time* to enter into long explanations with regard to all these people. I cannot do it. That is what it comes to. I cannot do it.'

Ah! You've lost your temper; like any one else. You want to shelve it. Any one would. But, being a man, you want to shelve it on to a woman. You don't care who hears the long tales as long as you don't. . . .

'Have you seen her doctor?'

'No. I think, just now, he is out of town.'

'*Really?* Are you sure?'

'You think I should see him.'

'Certainly.'

'I will do so on the first opportunity. That is the next step. Meantime I will write, provisionally, to Bournemouth.'

'Oh, she must go to Bournemouth anyhow; that's settled.'
'Perhaps her medical man may help there.'
'He won't make her do anything she doesn't mean to do.'
'I see you are a reader of character.'
'I don't think I am. I always begin by idealizing people.'
'Do you indeed?'
'Yes, always; and then they grow smaller and smaller.'
'Is that your invariable experience of humanity?'
'I don't think I'm an altruist.'
'I think one must have one's heroes.'
'In life or in books?'
'In both perhaps—one has them certainly in books—in records. Do you know this book?'

Miriam sceptically accepted the bulky volume he took down from the book-crowded mantelshelf.

'Oh, how interesting,' she said insincerely when she had read *Great Thoughts from Great Lives* on the cover. . . . I ought to have said I don't like extracts. 'Lives of great men all remind us We can make our lives sublime,' she read aloud under her breath from the first page. . . . I ought to go. I can't enter into this. . . . I hate 'great men,' I think. . . .

'That book has been a treasure-house to me—for many years. I know it now almost by heart. If it interests you, you will allow me, I hope, to present it to you.'

'Oh, you must not let me deprive you of it—oh *no*. It is very kind of you; but you really mustn't.' She looked up and returned quickly to the fascinating pages. Sentences shone out striking at her heart and brain . . . names in italics; Marcus Aurelius . . . Lao-Tse. Confucius . . . Clement of Alexandria . . . Jacob Boehme. 'It's full of the most fascinating things. Oh no; I couldn't think of taking it. You must keep it. Who is Jacob Boehme? That name always *fascinates* me. I must have read something, somewhere, a long time ago. I can't remember. But it is such a *wonderful* name.'

'Jacob Boehme was a German visionary. You will find, of course, all shades of opinion there.'

'All contradicting each other; that's the worst of it. Still, I suppose all roads lead to Rome.'

'I see you have thought a great deal.'

'Well,' said Miriam feverishly, 'there's always *science*, always all that awful business of science, and no getting rid of it.'

'I think—in that matter—one must not allow one's mind to be led away.'

'But one must keep an *open* mind.'

'Are you familiar with Professor Tyndall?'

'Only by meeting him in books about Huxley.'

'Ah—he was very different; very different.'

'Huxley,' said Miriam with intense bitterness, 'was an egoistic *adolescent*—all his life. I *never* came across *anything* like his conceited complacency in my life. The very look of his side-whiskers—well, there you have the whole man.' Her heart burned and ached, beating out the words. She rose to go, holding the volume in hands that shook to the beating of her heart. Far away in the bitter mist of the darkening room was the strange little figure.

'Let me just write your name in the book.'

'Oh, well, really, it is too bad—thank you very much.'

He carried the book to the window-sill and stood writing, his bent head very dark and round in the feeble grey light. Happy monk, alone up under the roof with his Plato. It was a *shame*.

CHAPTER XXXIII

'WHAT a *huge* room!'

'Isn't it a big room? Come in, young lady.'

Miriam crossed to the fireplace through a warm, faintly sweet atmosphere. A small fire was smoking and the gas was partly turned down, but the room was warm with a friendly brown warmth. Something had made her linger in the hall until Mrs Bailey had come to the dining-room door and stood there, with the door wide open and something to communicate waiting behind her friendly greetings. As a rule, there was nothing behind her friendly greetings but friendly approval and assurance. Miriam had never seen the dining-room door open before, and sought distraction from the communicativeness by drifting towards it and peering in. Once in, and sitting in the chair between the fireplace and Mrs Bailey's tumbled work-basket standing on the edge of the long table, bound to stay taking in the room until Mrs Bailey returned, she regretted looking in. The hall and the stairs and her own room would be changed now she knew what this room was like. In her fatigue she looked about, half taking in, half recoiling from the contents of the room. 'He stopped and got off his bicycle, and I said you don't seem very pleased to *see* me.' Already he knew that they were tiresome strangers to each other. 'I can't go dancing off to Bournemouth at a moment's notice, dear.' 'Well, I strongly advise you to go as soon as you can.' 'Of *course* I'm going, but I can't just dance off.' 'Don't let him get into the habit of associating you with the idea of worry.' If she didn't *worry* him, and was always a little ill, and pretty. . . . 'He says he can't do without her. I've told him, without reserve, what the chances are, and given them my blessing.' Did he really feel that, suddenly sitting there in the consulting-room? If only she wouldn't be so mysterious and important about nothing. . . .

There was a hugeness in the room, radiating from the three-armed dim-globed chandelier, going up and up; to the high heavily-moulded smoke-grimed ceiling, spreading out right and left along the length of the room, a large enclosed quietness, flowing up to the two great windows, hovering up and down the dingy rep and dingy lace curtains and the drab-coloured Venetian blinds, through whose chinks the street came in. Tansley Street was there, pressing its secret peace against the closed windows. Between the windows a long strip of mirror, framed in tarnished gilt, reflected the peace of the room. Miriam glanced about, peering for its secret; her eye running over the length of the faded, patterned, deep-fringed table cover, the large cracked pink bowl in the centre, holding an aspidistra . . . brown cracked leaves sticking out; the faded upholstery of the arm-chair opposite her, the rows of dining-room chairs across the way, in line with the horsehair sofa; the piano in the space between the sofa and the window; the huge mirror in the battered tarnished gilt frame sweeping half-way up the wall above the mantelpiece, reflecting the pictures and engravings hung rather high on the opposite wall, bought and liked long ago, the faded hearthrug under her feet, the more faded carpet disappearing under the long table, the dark stare of the fireplace, the heavy marble mantelpiece, the marble-cased clock, the opaque pink glass fat-bodied jugs scrolled with a dingy pattern, dusty lustres, curious objects in dull metal. . . .

'It 'll give my chicks a better chance. It isn't fair on them—living in the kitchen and seeing nobody.'

'And you mean to risk sending the lodgers away?'

'I 've been thinking about it some time. When the dining-room left, I thought I wouldn't fill up again. Miss Campbell 's going too.'

'Miss Campbell?'

'The drawn-room and drawn-room bedroom . . . my word . . . had her rooms turned out every week, carpets up and all.'

'Every *week*!'

'Always talking about microbes. My *word*.'

'How awful.   And all the other people?'

'I 've written them,' smiled Mrs Bailey at her busily inter-
lacing fingers.

'Oh!'

'For the 14th prox.; they 're all weekly.'

'Then, if they don't stay as boarders, they 'll have to trot
out at once.'

'Well, I thought if I was going to begin I 'd better take the
bull by the horns.   I 've heard of two.   Norwegian young
gentlemen.   They 're coming next week, and they both want
large bedrooms.'

'I think it 's awfully plucky, if you 've had no experience.'

'Well, young lady, I see it like this.   What *others* have done,
I can.   I feel I must do something for the children.   Mrs
Reynolds has married three of her daughters to boarders.
She 's giving up.   Elsie is going into the typing.'

'You haven't written to *me*.'

'You stay where you are, young lady.'

'Well—I think it 's awfully sweet of you, Mrs Bailey.'

'Don't you think about that.   It needn't make any difference
to you.'

'Well—of course—if you heard of a boarder——'

Mrs Bailey made a little dab at Miriam's knee.   'You stay
where you *are*, my dear.'

'I do hope it will be a success.   The house will be completely
changed.'

'I know it 's a risk.   But if you get on it pays better.   There 's
less work in it and you 've got a house to live in.   Nothing
venture, nothing *have*.   It 's no good to be backward in coming
forward, nowadays.   We 've got to march with the times.'

Miriam tried to see Mrs Bailey presiding, the huge table
lined with guests.   She doubted.   Those boarding-houses in
Woburn Place, the open windows in the summer, the strange
smart people, in evening dress, the shaded lamps; Mrs Bailey
would be lost.   She could never hold her own.   The quiet
house would be utterly changed.   There would be people
going about, in possession, all over the front steps and at the
dining-room windows and along the drawing-room balcony.

INTERIM

CHAPTER I

MIRIAM thumped her Gladstone bag down on to the doorstep. Stout boots hurried along the tiled passage and the door opened on Florrie in her outdoor clothes smiling brilliantly from under the wide brim of a heavily trimmed hat. Grace, in a large straight green dress, appeared beside her from the open dining-room door. Miriam finished her cadenza with the door knocker while Florrie bent to secure her bag, saying on a choke of laughter, '*Come* in.'

'You've just been out,' said Miriam listening to Grace's soothing reproaches for her lateness. 'Shall I come in or shall I burst into tears and sit down on the doorstep?'

Florrie laughed aloud, standing with the bag.

'Bring her in,' scolded Mrs Philps from the dining-room door.

Grace took her by the arm and drew her along the passage.

'I'm one mass of mud.'

'Never mind the mud, come in out of the rain,' scolded Mrs Philps backing towards the fire, 'you must be worn out.'

'No, I don't feel tired now I'm here; oh, what a heavenly fire.'

Miriam heard the front door shut with a shallow suburban slam and got herself round the supper table to stand with Mrs Philps on the hearthrug and smile into the fire. Mrs Philps patted her arm and cheek.

'Is the door really shut, O'Hara?' said Miriam, turning to Florrie coming into the room.

'Of course it is,' choked Florrie, coming to the hearthrug to pat her; 'I'll put the chain up if you like.'

'Sit down and rest before you go upstairs,' said Mrs Philps, propelling her gently backwards into the largest of the velvet arm-chairs. Its back sloped away from her; the large square cushion bulging out the lower half of the long woollen anti-macassar prevented her from getting comfortably into the chair. She sat on the summit of the spring and said it was not cold.

'Wouldn't you like to come up before supper?' suggested Grace in answer to her uneasy gazing into the fire.

'Well, I feel rather grubby.'

'Give her some hot water,' murmured Mrs Philps, taking up the *Daily Telegraph*.

Grace preceded her up the little staircase, carrying her bag.

'Will you have your milk hot or cold, Miriam?' called Florrie from below.

'Oh, hot, I think, please, I shan't be a *second*,' said Miriam into the spare room, hoping to be left.

Grace turned up the gas. 'M-m, darling,' she murmured with timid gentle kisses, 'I'm so glad you have come.'

'So am *I*. It's glorious to be safely here. . . . I shan't be a second. I'll come down as I am and appear radiant to-morrow.'

'You're *always* radiant.'

'I'm simply grubby; I've worn this blouse all the week; oh, *bliss*, hot water. Sit on the rocking-chair while I ablute and unpack my bag.'

'D'you mind if I don't, Miriam darling? Aunt and I called on the Unwins to-day and I haven't put my hat by yet. We've got three clear days.'

'All right; oh, my dear, you don't know how glad I am I'm here.'

Grace came back murmuring from the door to repeat the gentle kisses.

When the door was shut, the freshness and quietude of the room enfolded Miriam, smoothing away grubbiness and fatigue. Opening her Gladstone bag she threw on to the bed her new cream nun's veiling blouse and lace tie, her brush-bag and sponge-bag and shoes and a volume of Schiller and a bundle of note-paper and envelopes. A night-gown was put ready for her on the bed, frilled in an old-fashioned way with hand-made embroidery. Her bag went under the bed for nearly four days. Nothing grubby anywhere. No grubbiness for four days. In the large square mirror her dingy blouse and tie looked quite bright under the gas-light screened by the frosted globe. Her hair had been flattened by her hat becomingly over the broad top of her head, and its mass pushed down in a loose careless bundle with good chance curves reaching low on to her neck. She poured the hot water into one of the large cream-coloured basins, her eye running round the broad gilt-edged band ornamenting its rim, over the gleaming marble cover of the washstand, the gleaming tiles facing her beyond the rim of the basin, the highly polished woodwork above the tiles. She snuffed freshness everywhere. While the fresh unscented curdiness of the familiar Broom soap went over her face and wrists and hands she began to hunger for the clean supper, for the fresh night in the freshness of the large square bed, for the clean, solid, leisurely breakfast. Pushing back her hair she sponged the day from her face, sousing luxuriously in the large basin and listening to Grace moving slowly about upstairs. Seizing a towel, she ran up the little single flight and stood towelling inside Grace's door.

'Hallo, pink-face,' laughed Grace tenderly, smoothing tissue paper into a large hat-box.

'I say, it must be an *enormous* one.'

'It is; it's huge,' smiled Grace.

'You must show it to me to-morrow.'

Miriam ran downstairs and back to the mirror in her room to look at her clean untroubled face.

'Don't run about the house, come down to supper,' called Florrie from below.

'Have they brought the sausages?' asked Mrs Philps, acidly.

'Yes,' scowled Florrie.

'Don't forget to tell Christine how we like them done,' said Grace frowning anxiously.

Miriam took her eyes from the protruding eyes of the Shakespeare on the wall opposite, and shut away within her her sharp sense of the many things ranged below him on the mantelpiece behind Florrie, the landscape on one side of him, the picture of Queen Victoria leaning on a walking-stick between two Hindu servants, receiving an address, on the other side, the Satsuma vases and bowls on the sideboard behind Mrs Philps, the little sharp bow of narrow curtain-screened windows behind Grace, the clean gleam on everything.

'Chris*tine*?'

'Oh, yes, didn't you know? She's been with us a month——'

'What became of Amelia?'

'Oh, we had to let her go. She got fat and lazy.'

'They all do! they're all the same.'

'Go on, Miriam.'

'Well,' said Miriam from the midst of her second helping, 'they both listened, and the steps came shambling up their stairs—and they heard the man collapse with a groan against their door. They waited and, well, all at once the man, well, they heard him being violently *ill*.'

'Oh, *Miriam*!'

'Yes; wasn't it awful? and then a feeble voice like a chant—"a-a-a-ah-oo—oo-oo-oo, kom and hailpemee. *Oh*, Meester Bell, kom, oh, I am *freezing* to death, *what* a pity, what a pity"—and then silence.' She fed rapidly, holding them all silently eager for her voice again to fill out the spaces of their room.

'For about half an hour they heard him break out, every few minutes, "*Oh*, Meester Bell, dear pretty Mr Bell, kom. I am freezing to death, whatta pity—whattapity."' The Brooms sat breaking one against the other into fresh laughter. Miriam ate rapidly, glancing from face to face. '"What-eh-pitie—what-eh-pitie,"' she moaned. 'Can't you hear him?'

Grace choked and sneezed and drank a little milk. They were all still slowly and carefully eating their first helping.

'You do come across some funny people,' said Mrs Philps, mopping her eyes and dimpling and sighing upon the end of her laughter.

'*I* didn't come across him. It was at Mag's and Jan's boarding-house.'

Mrs Philps had not begun to listen at the beginning. But Grace and Florrie saw the whole thing clearly. Mrs Philps did not remember who Mag and Jan were. She would not unless one told her all about their circumstances and their parents. Florrie's face was preparing a question.

'Then they must have——' went on Miriam.

There was a subdued ring at the front door bell.

'There's Christine; shall we have her in to change the plates, aunt?' frowned Florrie.

'No, let 'er changer dress. We can put the plates on the sideboard.'

'Then they must both have gone to sleep again,' said Miriam when Florrie returned from letting Christine in, 'because they did not hear him go downstairs and he wasn't there in the morning.'

'A good thing, I should think,' observed Mrs Philps.

'He wasn't there,' said Miriam cheerfully, 'er—not in *person*.'

'Oh, *Miriam*!' protested Grace hysterically.

'*Oh—oh !*' cried the others.

Miriam watched the second course appearing from the sideboard—she greeted the blancmange and jam with a soft shout, feeling as hungry as when supper had begun.

'Isn't she *rude*!' chuckled Florrie, putting down a plate of bananas and a small dish of chocolates.

'Ooo-*ooo*!' squealed Miriam.

'Be quiet and behave yourself and begin on that,' said Grace, giving her a plate of blancmange.

'Oh, yes, and *then*,' said Miriam, inspired to remember more of her story, 'it all came out. He must have got down somehow to his room in the morning. But he lay on the floor—he told them at dinner: "all of mee could not find thee bed at once"!'

'Oh—oh—oh!'

'He had been,' she cried, raising her voice above the tumult, 'to a birthday party; "twenty-seex wheeskies and sodahs. . . ."'

'Why did he talk like that? Was he an Irishman?'

'Oh, can't you hear? He was a Hindu. They all talk like that. "I will kindly shut the door." When they write letters they begin, "Honoured and spanking sir,"' wept Miriam; 'they find spanking in the dictionary and their letters are like that all the way through, masses of the most amazing adjectives.'

'Why did Mag and Jan leave that boarding-house?' asked
Florrie into the midst of Miriam's absorption with the solid
tears on Mrs Philps's cheekbones. She was longing for Mrs
Philps to see the second thing, not only the funniness of spanking addressed to a civil servant, but exactly how spanking
would look to a Hindu. If only they could see those things as
well as produce their heavenly laughs.

'Oh, *I* don't know,' she said wearily; 'you see they never
meant to go there. They wanted a place of their own.' If
only they could realize Mag and Jan. There was never enough
time and strength to make everything clear. At every turn
there was something they saw differently. 'They *are* a pair,'
she breathed sleepily. '*No*, thanks,' she answered formally to
an offer of more blancmange. She was beginning to feel strong
and sleepy. 'No, thanks,' she repeated formally as the heavy
dish of bananas came her way.

'She wants a chocolate,' said Florrie from across the table.
Miriam revived a little.

'Take *two*,' begged Mrs Philps.

'They're so huge,' said Miriam, obeying and leaving the
chocolates on her plate while her mind moved about seeking
a topic. They were all beginning on bananas. It would be
endless. By the time it came to sitting over the fire she would
be almost asleep. She stirred uneasily. Someone must be
seeing her longing and impatience.

Miriam lost threads while Christine cleared away supper,
pondering the thick expressionless figure and hands and the
heavy sallow sullen face. She was very short. The Brooms
watched her undisturbed, from their places by the fire, now and
again addressing instructions in low frowning voices from the
midst of conversation.

'*Do* sit down,' said Mrs Philps at intervals.

'I've been sitting down all day,' said Miriam, swaying on
her toes. 'I think we *did* half believe it,' she pursued with bit-
ing heartiness, aching with the onset of questions, speaking to

make warmth and distraction for Christine.   She had never
thought about it.   *Had* they half believed it?   Had any one
ever put it to them in so many words?   Giving an opinion
opened so many things.   It was impossible to show everything,
the more opinions you expressed the more you misled people
and the further you got away from them.   'Because,' she
continued with a singing animation—Christine glanced—'we
never heard any one come in—although'—the room enclosed
her even more happily with Christine there, everything looked
even more itself—'we stayed awake till what seemed almost
morning, always till long after the ser—m—our domestic staff
had gone to bed.   Their rooms were on the same floor as the
night nursery.'

Christine was padding out with a tray, her back to the room;
she had a holiday every year and regular off times and plenty
of money to buy clothes and presents; probably she had some
sort of home.   When she had taken away the last of the supper
things and closed the door, Grace patted the arm of the vacant
arm-chair.

'I like this best, said Miriam, drawing up a little carved
wooden stool.

'Oh, *don't* sit on that,' cried Mrs Philps.

'I 'm all right,' said Miriam hurriedly, looking at no one and
drawing herself briskly upright with her eyes on the clear blaze.
Grace and Florrie were close on either side of her in straight
chairs, leaning forward towards the fire.   Mrs Philps sat back
in the smaller of the arm-chairs, its unyielding cushion sending her body forward, her small chest crouched, her head
bent and propped on her hand, half facing their close row and
gazing into the fire.   There was a silence; Florrie cleared her
throat and glanced at Miriam.   Miriam half turned with weary
resentment.

'Did you used to hang up stockings, Miriam?' said Florrie
quickly.

Miriam assented hastily, staring at the fire.   Florrie patiently
cleared her throat.   With weary animation Miriam dropped
phrases about the parcels that were too big for the stocking, the
feeling of them against one's feet when one moved in the

morning. Shy watchful glances came to her from Florrie.
Grace took her hand and made encouraging sympathetic
sounds. How secure they were, sitting, with all the holiday
ahead, over the fire which would be lit again for them in the
morning. This was only the fag-end of the first evening and
it was beginning to be like the beginning of a new day. Things
were coming to her out of the fire, fresh and new, seen for the
first time; a flood of images. She watched them with eyes
suddenly cool and sleepless, relaxing her stiff attitude and
smiling vaguely at the fire-irons.

'She's tired; she wants to go to bed,' said Mrs Philps, turning her head.

The two heads came round.

'Do you, my sweet?' asked Grace, pressing her hand. 'You
shall have breakfast in bed if you like.'

Miriam grimaced briskly in her direction.

'Did you have a Noah's *ark*,' she asked, smiling at the fire.

'Yes; Florrie had one. Uncle George gave it to her.'

They began describing.

'Didn't you love it?' broke in Miriam presently. 'Do you
remember—' and she recalled the Noah's ark as it had looked
on the nursery floor, the offended stiffness of the rescued family,
the look of the elephants and giraffes and the green and yellow
grasshoppers and the red lady-bird, all standing about alive
amongst the little stiff bright green trees. 'We had a farm-
yard too, pigs; and ducks and geese and hens with feathers.
We used to stand them all out together on the floor, and the
grocer's shop and all our dolls sitting round against the nursery
wall. It used to make me *perfectly* happy. It would still.'
Every one laughed. 'It would. It *does* only to think of it.
And there was a doll's house with a door that opened and a
staircase and furniture in the rooms. I can smell the smell of
the inside at this moment. But the thing I liked best and
never got accustomed to was a little alabaster church with
coloured glass windows and a place inside for a candle. We
used to put that out on the floor too. I wish I had it now. . . .
The kaleidoscope. Do you *remember* looking at the kaleidoscope? I used to cry about it sometimes at night; thinking

of the patterns I had not seen.   I thought there was a new
pattern every time you shook it, for ever.   We had a huge one
with very small bits of glass.   They clicked smoothly when the
pattern changed and were very beautifully coloured. . . . Oh,
and do you remember those things—did you have a little paper
theatre ?'

They were all looking at her, not at the little theatre.   She
wished she had not mentioned it.   It was so sacred and so
secret that she had never thought of it or even mentioned it to
herself all these years.   She rushed on to the stereoscope, her
eyes still on the little cardboard stage, hearing the sound of the
paper scraping over the little wooden roller as the printed
scenes came round backwards or forwards, and plunged into
descriptions of deep views of the insides of cathedrals in sharp
relief in a clear silver light, mountains, lakes, statuary in clear
light out of doors, and came back to the dolls, pressing alone
wearily on through the dying interest of the hearers, to discover with sleepy enthusiasm the wisdom and indifference and
independence of Dutch dolls, the charm of their wooden
bodies, the reasons why one never wanted to put any clothes
on them, the dear kind friendliness of dolls with composition
heads—'I don't believe I've ever loved any one in the world as
I loved Daisy.   Yes, I know—we had one too; it belonged to
Eve, it was enormous and had real hair and a leather trunk for
its clothes and felt huge and solid when you carried it; but it
was as far away from you as a human being—yes, the rag dolls
were simply funny—I never understood all that talk about the
affection for rag dolls.   We used to scream at ours and hold
them by the skirts and see which could bang their heads hardest
against the wall.   They were always like a Punch and Judy
show.   The composition dolls I mean were painted a soft
colour, very roundly moulded heads, with a shape, just a little
hair, put on in soft brown colour, and not staring eyes but soft
bluey grey with an *expression*; looking at something, looking at
the same thing you looked at yourself.'

Mrs Philps yawned and Florrie began making a move.

'I suppose it's bed-time,' said Miriam.   They were all
looking sleepy.

'Have a glass of claret, Miriam, before you go,' said Mrs Philps.

'No, thank you,' said Miriam, springing up and dancing about the room.

'Giddy girl,' chuckled Mrs Philps affectionately.

Grace and Florrie fetched dust sheets from the hall cupboard and began spreading them over the furniture. Miriam pulled up in front of a large oil-painting over the sofa; its distances, where a meadow stream that was wide in the foreground with a stone bridge and a mill-wheel and a cottage half hidden under huge trees, grew narrow and wound on and on through tiny distant fields until the scene melted in a soft-toned mist, held all her early visits to the Brooms in the Banbury Park days before they had discovered that she did not like sitting with her back to the fire. She listened eagerly to the busy sounds of the Brooms. Someone had bolted the hall door and was scrooping a chair over the tiles to get up and put out the gas. Dust sheets were still being flountered in the room behind her. Grace's arm came round her waist. 'I'm so glad you've come, sweet,' she said in her low steady shaken tones.

'So 'm I,' said Miriam. 'Isn't that a jolly picture?'

'Yes. It's an awfully good one, you know. It was one of papa's.'

'What's O'Hara doing in the kitchen?'

Taking Grace by the waist, Miriam drew into the passage, trying to prance with her down the hall. The little kitchen was obscured by an enormous clothes-horse draped with airing linen.

'She's left a miserable fire,' said Mrs Philps from behind the clothes-horse.

'She hasn't done the saucepans, aunt,' scolded Florrie from the scullery. 'Never mind, we can't have 'er down now. It's neely midnight.'

Miriam emerged smoothly into the darkness and lay radiant. There was nothing but the cool sense of life pouring from some inner source and the deep fresh spaces of the darkness all round her. Perhaps she had awakened because of her happiness. . . . Clear, gentle, and soft in a melancholy minor key, a little thread of melody sounded from far away in the night straight into her heart. There was nothing between her and the sound that had called her so gently up from her deep sleep. She held in her joy to listen. There was no sadness in the curious sorrowful little air. It drew her out into the quiet neighbourhood . . . misty darkness along empty roads, plaques of lamplight here and there on pavements and across house fronts . . . blackness in large gardens and over the bridge and in the gardens at the backs of the rows of little silent dark houses, a pale lambency over the canal and reservoirs. Somewhere amongst the little roads a group of players gently and carefully hooting slow sweet notes as if to wake no one, playing to no one, out into the darkness. Back out of the fresh darkness came the sweet clear music . . . the waits; of course. She rushed up and out heart foremost, listening, following the claim of the music into the secret happy interior of the life of each sleeping form, flowing swiftly on across a tide of remembered and forgotten incidents in and out amongst the seasons of the years. It sent her forward to to-morrow, sitting her upright in morning light, telling her with shouts that the day was there and she had only to get up into it. . . . The little air had paused on a tuneful chord and ceased. . . . It was beginning again nearer and clearer. She heard it carefully through. It was so *strange*. It came from far back amongst the generations where everything was different; telling you that they were the same. . . . In the way those people were playing, in the way they made the tune sound in the air, neither instrument louder than the others, there was something that *knew*. Something that everybody knows. . . . They show it by the way they do things, no matter what they say. . . . Her heart glowed and she stirred. How rested she was. How fresh the air was. What freshness came from everything in the room. She stared into the velvety blackness, trying to see the furniture. It was the thick close-drawn curtains that made the perfect velvety darkness. . . . Behind the curtains and the Venetian blinds the windows were open at the top letting in the garden air.   The little square of summer showed brilliantly in this darkest winter blackness.   It was more than worth while to be wakened in the middle of the night at the Brooms'.   The truth about life was in them.   She imagined herself suddenly shouting in the night.   After the first fright they would understand and would laugh.   She yawned sleepily towards an oncoming tangle of thoughts, pushing them off and slipping back into unconsciousness.

Miriam picked up the blouse by its shoulders and danced it up and down in time to the girls' volleys of affectionate raillery.   'Did you sleep well?' broke in Mrs Philps, sitting briskly up and superciliously grasping the handle of the large coffee-pot with her small shrivelled hand.   Christmas Day had begun.   The time for trying to say suitable things about the presents was over.   All the six small hands were labouring amongst the large things on the table.   The blouse hung real, a blouse, a glorious superfluity in her only just sufficient wardrobe. 'Yes, thank you, I *did*,' she said ardently, lowering it to her knees.   The rich strong coffee was flowing into the cups.   In a moment Grace would be handing plates of rashers and Florrie would have finished extracting the eggs from the boiler. She laid the blouse carefully on the sofa and heard in among the table sounds the greetings that had followed her arrival downstairs.   The brown and green landscape caught her eye, old and still, holding all her knowledge of the Brooms back and back, fresh with another visit to them.   She turned back to the table with a sigh.   Someone chuckled.   Perhaps at something that was happening on the table.   She glanced about.   The fragrant breakfast had arrived in front of her.   '*Don't* let it get cold,' laughed Florrie, drawing the mustard-pot from the cruet-stand and rapping it down before her.

There was something that she had forgotten, some point that was being missed, something that must be said at this moment to pin down the happiness of everything.   She looked up at Shakespeare and Queen Victoria.   It was going away.

'*Mustard*,' said Florrie tapping the table with the mustard-pot.

'Did you hear the waits?' asked Mrs Philps with dreary acidity.

That was it. She turned eagerly. Mrs Philps was sipping her coffee. Miriam waited politely with the mustard-pot in her hand until she had put down her cup and then said anxiously, offering it to Mrs Philps: 'They played——'

'Help yourself,' laughed Mrs Philps.

'—a most lovely curious old-fashioned thing,' she went on anxiously. Florrie was watching her narrowly.

'That was *The Mistletoe Bough*,' bridled Mrs Philps, accepting the mustard.

'Oh, that's *The Mistletoe Bough*,' mused Miriam, thrilling. Then Mrs Philps had heard, and felt the same in the night. Nothing was missing. Everything that had happened since she had arrived on the doorstep came freshly back and on into to-day, flowing over the embarrassment of the parcels. There was nothing to say; no words that could express it; a tune. . . . '*That's The Mistletoe Bough* . . .' she said reflectively.

Florrie was sitting very upright exactly opposite, quietly munching, her knife and fork quiet on her plate. Grace's small hands and mouth were gravely labouring. She began swiftly on her own meal, listening for the tune with an intelligent face. If Florrie would take off her attention she could let her face become a blank and recover the tune. Impossible to go on until she had recalled it. She sought for some distracting remark. Grace spoke. Florrie turned towards her. Miriam radiated agreement and sipped her hot coffee. Its strong aroma flowed through her senses. She laughed sociably. Someone else laughed.

'Of *course* they don't,' said Florrie in her most grinding voice and laughed.

Two voices broke out together. Miriam listened to the tones, glancing intelligence accordingly, umpiring the contest, her mind wandering blissfully about. Presently there was a silence. Mrs Philps had bridled and said something decisive. Miriam guiltily reread the remark. She could not think of anything that could be made to follow it with any show of sincerity, and sat feeling large and conspicuous. Mrs Philps's face had grown dark and old. Miriam glanced restively at her meaning. . . . Large terrible illnesses, the doctor coming, trouble amongst families, someone sitting paralysed; poverty, everything being different. . . .

'D' you like a snowy Christmas, Miriam?' asked Florrie shyly.

Miriam looked across. Florrie looked very young, a child speaking on sufferance, saying the first thing that occurs lest someone should remark that it was time to go to bed. Hilarious replies rushed to Miriam's mind. They would have re-awakened the laughter and talk, but there would have been resentment in the widowed figure at the head of the table, the figure that had walked with arch dignity into the big north London shop and chosen the blouse. The weight in the air was dreadful.

'There don't seem to be snowy Christmases nowadays,' she said, turning deferentially to her hostess with her eyes on Florrie's child's eyes.

'Christmas is a *very* different thing to what it was,' breathed Mrs Philps, sitting back with folded hands from her finished meal.

'Oh, I don't know, aunt,' corrected Grace anxiously. 'Aren't you going to have your toast and marmalade? You lived in the north all your young Christmases. It's always colder there. Take some toast, aunt.'

'We used to burn Yule logs,' flickered Mrs Philps, plaintively refusing the toast.

Miriam waited, imagining the snow on the garden where the frilled shirts used to hang out to bleach in the dew . . . the great flood, the anxiety in the big houses.

'Yule logs would look funny in this grate,' laughed Florrie.

'Oh, I don't know,' pressed Grace. 'We had some last year. Haven't we got any this year, aunt?'

'I ordered some wood; I don't know if it's come.'

Miriam could not imagine the Brooms with burning logs. Yes, she could. They were nearer to burning logs than any one she knew. It would be more real here; more like the burning logs in the Christmas numbers. The glow would shine on to their faces and they would see into the past. But it was all in the past. Yule logs and then, no yule logs. Every one, even the Brooms, were being pushed forward into a new cold world. There was no time to remember.

'They don't build grates for wood nowadays,' ruled Mrs Philps.

Who could stop all this coming and crowding of mean little things? But the wide untroubled leisure of the Brooms' breakfast-table was shut away from the mean little things. . . .

'Are you coming to church, Miriam?'

Miriam looked across the doomed breakfast-table and met the watchful eyes. Behind Florrie, very upright in her good, once best stuff dress, two years old in its features and methodically arrived at morning wear, the fire still blazed its extravagant welcome, the first of Christmas morning was still in the room. When they had all busied themselves and gone, it would be gone. She glanced about to see that every one had finished and put her elbows on the table.

'*Well*,' she said abundantly—there was an expectant relaxing of attitudes—'I should *like* to go very much. *But*'—Grace, fidgeting her brooch, had flung her unrestrained burning affectionate glance—'when I saw Mr La Trobe climbing into the pulpit'—Florrie's eyes were downcast and Mrs Philps was blowing her nose, her eyes gazing wanly out above her handkerchief toward the little curtained bow-window—Miriam dimpled and glanced sideways at Grace, catching her shy waiting eyes—'I should stand up on my seat . . . give one loud shriek'—the three laughters broke forth together—'and fall gasping to the ground.'

'Then you'd certainly better not go,' chuckled Florrie amidst the general wiping away of tears. 'I saw the Miss Pernes at Strudwick's on Friday; Miss Perne and Miss Jenny.'

'Oh, did you?' responded Miriam hurriedly. The room lost something of its completeness. There was a coming and a going, the pressing grey of an outside world. 'How are they?'

'They seemed very well. They don't seem to change.'

'Oh; I'm so glad.'

'They asked for you.'

'*Oh !*'

'I didn't say we were expecting you.'

'*Oh*, it 's such an age——'

'We always say you 're very busy and hard-worked,' smiled Grace.

'Yes, that 's it. . . .'

'You didn't go often even when Miss Haddie was alive.'

'No; she was awfully good; she used to come down and see me in the West End when I first came to town.'

'How they *like* the West End!'

'Aunt, I don't blame them.'

'She used to write to you a lot, didn't she, Miriam?'

'She used to come and talk to me in a tea-shop at six-fifteen . . . yes, she wrote regularly,' said Miriam irritably.

'You were awfully fond of Miss Haddie, weren't you?'

Miriam peered into space, struggling with a tangle of statements. Her mind leapt from incident to incident, weaving all into a general impression—so strong and clear that it gave a sort of desperation to her painful consciousness that nothing she saw and felt was visible to the three pairs of differently watchful eyes. Poured chaotically out it would sound to them like the ravings of insanity. All contradictory, up and down, backwards and forwards, all true. The things they would grasp, here and there, would misrepresent herself and the whole picture. Why would people insist upon talking about things —when nothing can ever be communicated? . . . She felt angrily about in the expectant stillness. She could see their minds so clearly; why wouldn't they just look and see hers instead of waiting for some impossible pronouncement? Yes would be a lie. No would be a lie. Any statement would be a lie. All statements are lies. I like the Pernes better than I like you. I like all of you better than the Pernes. I hate you. I hate the Pernes. I, of course you must know it, hate *everybody*. I adore the Pernes so much that I can't go and see them. But you come and see us. Yes; but you insist. Then you like us only as well as you like the Pernes; you like all sorts of people as well perhaps better than you like us. I have nothing to do with any one. You shall not group me anywhere. I am everywhere. Let the day go on. Don't sit there worrying me to death. . . .

'They always send you their love and say you are to go and see them.'

'Oh, yes, I *must* go; some time.'

'They are wonderfully fond of their girls. . . . It's one of the greatest pleasures of their lives keeping up with the old girls.'

Fatigue was returning upon Miriam; her face flushed and her hands were large and cold. She drew them down on to her unowned knees. A mild yes would bring the sitting to an end.

'But you see I'm *not* an old girl,' she said impatiently.

No one spoke. Florrie's mind was darkly moving towards the things of the day. Perhaps Mrs Philps and Florrie had been thinking of them for some minutes.

'You know it does make a difference,' she pursued, obsequiously collecting attention, 'when people are your employers. You can never feel the same.'

Every one hovered, and Mrs Philps smiled in triumphant curiosity.

'I shouldn't have thought it made any difference to you, Miriam,' said Florrie, flushing heavily.

'I think I know what Miriam means,' said Grace, gently radiating; 'I always feel a pupil with them, much as I like them.'

'Grace, d'you know you're my pupil?' said Miriam, leaping out into laughter. 'I can *see* Grace,' she drove on, carrying them all with her, ignoring the swift eyes upon the dim things settling heavily down upon her heart, '*gazing* out of the window in the little room where I was supposed to be holding a German class.'

'Yes, I know, Miriam darling, but now you know me you know I could never be any good at languages.'

'You're my pupil.'

'It seems absurd to think of you as a teacher now we know you,' chuckled Florrie. 'Aren't you glad it's over, Miriam?'

'I *loved* the teaching. I've never left off longing to go back to school myself,' yawned Miriam absently.

'You won't get much sympathy out of Florrie.'

'I was a perfect *fool*,' beamed Florrie.

Every one laughed.

'I often think now, chuckled Florrie, rosy and tearful, 'when I open the front door to go out, how glad I am there's no more *school*.'

Miriam looked across, laughing affectionately.

'Why did you like your school so much, Miriam?'

'I didn't like it except now and again terrifically in flashes. I didn't know what it was. I hadn't seen other schools. I didn't know what we were doing. It wasn't—a—genteel school for young ladies, there was nothing of that in it.'

'You never know when you're happy,' reproved Mrs Philps.

'Oh, I don't *know*, aunt, I think you *do*,' appealed Grace, her eyes full of shy championship.

'I'm very happy, thank you; aren't we all happy, dear brethren?' chirped Miriam towards the cruet-stand.

'Silly children!'

'Now, aunt, you *know* you are. You know you enjoy life tremendously.'

'Of course I do,' cried Mrs Philps, beaming and bridling. In a devout low tone she added: 'It's the little simple things that make you happy; the things that happen every day.'

For a moment there was nothing but the sound of the fire flickering in the beamy air.

'Hadn't we better have her *in*, aunt?' muttered Grace.

Florrie got up briskly and rang the bell.

They all went busily upstairs. Even Grace did not linger.

'Let me come and help make my bed,' said Miriam, going with her to the door.

'No, you're to rest.'

'I don't want to rest.'

'Then you can run round the room.'

She turned back towards the silent disarray. Busy sounds came from upstairs. A hurried low reproving voice emerged on to the landing: '—and light the drawing-room fire as soon as you've finished clearing and when the postman comes leave the letters in the *box*.'

Christine came downstairs without answering. In a moment she would be coming in. Moving away from the attraction of the blouse, Miriam wandered to the fireside. Her eyes turned towards the chair in the corner half-hidden by the large arm-chair. There they were, on the top of the pile of newspapers and magazines. *Dare's Annual* lay uppermost, its cover bright with holly. Her hands went out . . . to look at them now would be to anticipate the afternoon. But there would be at least two *Windsors* that she had not seen. She drew one out and stood turning over the leaves. It would be impossible to look round and say 'A happy Christmas' and then go on reading, and just as bad to stop reading and not say anything more. She planted herself in the middle of the hearthrug with her face to the room. Why should she stand advantageously there while Christine unwillingly laboured? Why should Christine be pleased to be spoken to? She thought 'A happy Christmas' in several different voices. They all sounded insulting. Christine was still making noises in the kitchen. There was time to escape. The drawing-room door would be bolted and that meant getting one of the hall chairs and telling the whole house of an extraordinary impulse. Upstairs her bed would still be being made or her room dusted. She drew up the little stool and sat dejectedly, close over the fire as if with a heavy cold in her head and anxiously deep in the pages of the magazine. Perhaps Christine would think she did not hear her come in. . . . She guessed the story from the illustrations and dropped into the text half-way through the narrative. No woman who did typewriting from morning till night and lived in a poor lodging could look like that . . . perhaps some did . . . perhaps that was how clerks *ought* to look . . . she skimmed on; moving automatically to make room for boots that were being put down in the fender; ready to speak in a moment if whoever it was did not say anything; the figure turned to the table. It was Christine. If she blew her nose and coughed Christine would know she knew she was there. She turned a page swiftly and wrapped herself deeply in the next. When Christine had gone away with a trayful she resumed her place on the hearthrug ready to see her for the first time when she came in again and catch her eye and say, 'Good *morning*, I wish you a happy Christmas.' Christine came shapelessly in and began collecting the remaining things with sullen hands. Her face was closed and expressionless and her eyes downcast. Miriam's eyes followed it, waiting for the eyes to lift, her lips powerless. It was too late to say good morning. Sadness came growing in the room. Her thoughts went homelessly to and fro between her various world and the lumpy figure moving sullenly along the edge of an unknown life. Stepping observantly in through the half-open door with with a duster bunched carefully in her hand came Florrie. Miriam flung out a greeting that swept round Christine and out into a shining world. It brought Florrie to her side, shy and eager. Christine, taking her final departure, looked up. Miriam flushed through her laughter, steadily meeting the expressionless brown glitter of Christine's eyes.

'Hallo, Madam O'Hara,' she defended, collecting herself for the question that would follow Florrie's encirclement of her waist.

'Hallo, little Miriam; you *are* happy,' ground out Florrie shyly; 'are you rested?'

'Yes,' said Miriam formally, 'I think I am.'

They turned, Florrie withdrawing her arm, and stood looking into the fire.

'Oooch, isn't it cold?' said Grace from the doorway; 'have you done the hall chairs?'

'No, I came in here to get warm first.'

'It *is* cold,' said Grace, coming to the hearthrug; 'are you warm, Miriam darling?'

'I'm so warm that I think I ought to run upstairs for a constitutional and scrub my teeth,' said Miriam briskly, preparing to follow Florrie from the room.

Grace dropped her duster and put her arms upon her, raising an anxious pleading face. 'Stay here while I dust, sweetheart. You can scrub your teeth when we're gone. *Dear* pink-face.

How are you my sweet? Are you rested?' she asked between
gentle kisses dabbed here and there.

'Never berrer, old chap. I tell you, never *berrer*.'

Grace laughed gently into her face and stood holding her,
smiling her anxious pleading solicitous smile.

'I tell you, never *berrer*,' repeated Miriam.

'*Dear* sweet pink-face,' smiled Grace and turned carefully
away to her dusting. Miriam sank into an arm-chair, listening
to the soft smooth flurring of the duster over the highly polished
surfaces.

'Well,' she asked presently, 'how are things in general?'

Grace rose from her knees and carefully shut the door. She
came back with fear darkening the velvet lustre of her eyes.

'Oh, I don't know, Miriam dear,' she murmured, kneeling on
the hearthrug near Miriam's knees and holding her hands out
towards the fire. It's all over, thought Miriam, she's failed.
'I've got ever so many things to tell you. I want to ask your
advice.'

'Remember I've never even seen him,' argued Miriam
automatically, figuring the surroundedness, the sudden realization and fear, the recapturing of liberty, the hidden polite
determined retreat.

'Oh, but you always understand. Wait till we can talk,'
she sighed, rising from her knees and kissing Miriam's
forehead.

It was all over. Grace was clinging to some 'reasonable'
explanation of some final thing. She cast about in her mind
for something from her own scattered circumstances to feed
their talk when it should come. She would have to induce
Grace to turn away and go on . . . the end of the long history
of faithfully remembered details would be a relief . . . the
delicate depths of their intercourse would come back . . . its
reach backwards and forwards; and yet without anything
in the background . . . it seemed as if always something were
needed in the background to give the full glow to every day
. . . she must be made to see the real face of the circumstance
and then to know and to feel that she was not forlorn; that the
glow was there . . . first to brush away the delusion ruthlessly

. . . and then let the glow come back, begin to come back, from another source.

Left alone with silence all along the street, Christine inaudible in the kitchen, dead silence in the house, Miriam gathered up her blouse and ran upstairs. As she passed through the changing lights of the passage, up the little dark staircase past the turn that led to the little lavatory and the little bathroom and was bright in the light of a small uncurtained lattice, on up the four stairs that brought her to the landing where the opposing bedroom doors flooded their light along the strip of green carpet between the polished balustrade and the high polished glass-doored bookcase, scenes from the future, moving in boundless backgrounds, came streaming unsummoned into her mind, making her surroundings suddenly unfamiliar . . . the past would come again. . . . Inside her room—tidied until nothing was visible but the permanent shining gleaming furniture and ornaments; only the large box of matches on the corner of the mantelpiece betraying the movement of separate days, telling her of nights of arrival, the lighting of the gas, the sudden light in the frosted globe preluding freedom and rest, bringing the beginning of rest with the gleam of the fresh quiet room—she found the nearer past, her years of London work set in the air, framed and contemplable like the pictures on the wall, and beside them the early golden years in snatches, chosen pictures from here and there, communicated, and stored in the loyal memory of the Brooms. Leaping in among these live days came to-day. . . . The blouse belonged to the year that was waiting far off, invisible behind the high wall of Christmas. She dropped it on the bed and ran downstairs to the little drawing-room.

The fire had not yet conquered the mustiness of the air. The room was full of strange dim lights coming in through the stained-glass door of the little greenhouse. She pushed open the glass door, turning the light to a soft green, and sat sociably down in a low chair, her hands clasped upon her knees, topics racing through her mind in a voice thrilling with stored-up laughter. In her ears was the rush of spring rain on the garden foliage, and presently a voice saying, 'Where are we going this summer?' . . . By the time they came back she would be too happy to speak. Better perhaps to go out into the maze of little streets and, in wearying of them, be glad to come back. As she moved to the door she saw the garden in late summer fullness, the holidays over, their heights gleaming through long talks on the seat at the end of the garden, the answering glow of the great blossoms of purple clematis hiding the north London masonry of the little conservatory, the great spaces of autumn opening out and out, running down, rich with happenings, to where the high wall of Christmas again rose and shut out the future. She ran busily upstairs, casting away sight and hearing, and hurried thoughtlessly into her outdoor things and out into the street.

She wandered along the little roads, turning and turning until she came to a broad open thoroughfare lined with high grey houses standing back behind colourless railed-in gardens. Trams jingled up and down the centre of the road, bearing the names of unfamiliar parts of London. People were standing about on the terminal islands and getting in and out of the trams. She had come too far. Here was the wilderness, the undissembling soul of north London, its harsh unvarying all-embracing oblivion. . . . Innumerable impressions gathered on walks with the school-girls or in lonely wanderings; the unveiled motives and feelings of people she had passed in the streets, the expression of noses and shoulders, the indefinable uniformity, of bearing and purpose and vision, crowded in on her, oppressing and darkening the crisp light air. She fought against them, rallying to the sense of the day. It was Christmas Day for them all. They were keeping Christmas in their homes, carrying it out into the streets, going about with parcels, greeting each other in their harsh ironic voices. Long ago she had passed out of their world for ever, carrying it forward, a wound in her consciousness unhealed, but powerless to re-inflict itself, powerless to spread into her life. They and their world were still there, unchanged. But they could never touch her again, ensconced in her wealth. It did not matter now

that they went their way just in the way they went their way.
To hate them for past suffering, now that they were banished
and powerless, was to allow them to spoil her day. . . . They
were even a possession, a curious thing apart, unknown to any
one in her London life . . . *dear* north Londoners.

She paused a moment, looking boldly across at the figures
moving on the islands.   After all, they did not know that it was
cold and desolate and harsh and dreadful to be going about on
Christmas Day in a place that looked as this place looked, in
trams.   They did not know what was wrong with their clothes
and their bearing and their way of looking at things.   That
was what was so terrible, though.   What could teach them?
There were so many.   They lived and died in amongst each
other.   What could change them? . . . Her face felt drawn
and weariness was coming upon her limbs. . . . A group
was approaching her along the wide pavement, laughing and
talking, a blatter of animated voices; she turned briskly for
the relief of meeting and passing close to them . . . too near,
too near . . . prosperity and kindliness, prosperous fresh
laughing faces, easily bought clothes, the manner of the large
noisy house and large secure income, free movement in an
accessible world, all turned to dangerous weapons in wrong
hands by the unfinished, insensitive mouths, the ugly slur in
the speech, the shapelessness of bearing, the naïvely visible
thoughts, circumscribed by business, the illustrated monthly
magazines, the summer month at the seaside.   Their lives
were exactly like their way of walking down the street,.a confident blind trampling.   Speech was not needed to reveal their
certainties; they shed certainty from every angle of their unfinished persons.   Certainty about everything.   Incredulous
contempt for all uncertainty.   Impatient contempt for all who
could not stand up for themselves.   Cheerful uncritical affection for each other.   And for all who were living or trying to
live just as they did. . . .

The little bushes of variegated laurel, grouped in railed-off
oblongs along the gravelled pathway between the two wide
strips of pavement, drew her gaze.   They shone crisply, their
yellow and green enamel washed clean by yesterday's rain.

She hurried along, feeling out towards them through downcast eyes. They glinted back at her unsunned by the sunlight, rootless sapless surfaces set in repellent clay, spread out in meaningless air. To and fro her eyes slid upon the varnished leaves. She saw them in a park set in amongst massed dark evergreens, gleaming out through afternoon mist, keeping the last of the light as the people drifted away, leaving the slopes and vistas clear . . . grey avenues and dewy slopes moved before her in the faint light of dawn, the grey growing pale and paler; the dew turned to a scatter of jewels and the sky soared up high above the growing shimmer of sunlit green and gold. Isolated morning figures hurried across the park, aware of its morning freshness, seeing it as their own secret garden, part of their secret day.

From the sunlit white façade of a large London house, the laurels looked down through a white stone-pillared balustrade. They appeared, coming suddenly with the light of a street lamp, clumped safely behind the railings of a Bloomsbury square. . . . The opening of a side street led her back into the maze of little roads. The protective presence of the little house was there, and she sauntered happily along through channels of sheltered sunlit silence.

What was she doing here? At Christmas time one should be where one belonged. Gathering and searching about her came the claims of the firesides that had lain open to her choice, drawing her back into the old life, the only life known to those who sat round them. They looked out from that life, seeing hers as hardship and gloom, pitying her, turning blind eyes unwillingly towards her attempts to unveil and make it known to them. She saw herself relinquishing efforts, putting on a desperate animation, professing interests and opinions and talking as people talk, while they watched her with eyes that saw nothing but a pitiful attempt to hide an awful fate, lonely poverty, the absence of any opening prospect, nothing ahead but a gloom deepening as the years wound themselves off. Those were the facts—as almost any one might see them. They made those facts live; they tugged at the jungle of feelings that had the power to lead one back through any small crushing maiming aperture. . . . In their midst lived the past and the thing that had ended it and plunged it into a darkness that still held that threat of destroying reason and life. Perhaps only thus could it be faced. Perhaps only in that way. What other way was there? Forgetfulness blotted it out and let one live on. But it was always there, impossible, when one looked back. . . . The little house brought forgetfulness and rest. It made no break in the new life. The new life flowed through it, sunlit. It was a flight down strange vistas, a superfluity of wild strangeness, with a clue in one's hand, the door of retreat always open; rest and forgetfulness piling up within one into strength.

The incidents Grace had described went in little disconnected scenes in and out of the caverns of the dying fire. She was waiting tremulously for a verdict. They seemed to Miriam so decisive that she found it difficult to keep within Grace's point of view. She stood in the picturesque suburb, saw the distant glimpse of Highgate Woods, the pretty corner house standing alone in its garden, the sisters in the dresses they had worn at the dance talking to their mother indoors, waited on by their polite admiring brother; their unconsciousness, their lives as they looked to themselves. Everything fitted in with the leghorn hats they had worn at the League garden party in the summer. She could have warned Grace, then, if she had heard about the hats. . . . Grace had not yet found out that people were arranged in groups. . . . The only honest thing to say now would be: 'Oh, well, of course with a mother and sisters like *that*; don't you see—what they are?' Her mind drew a little circle round the family group. It spun round them, on and on, as they went through life. She frowned her certainty into the fire, ranging herself with the unknown people she knew so well. If she did not speak, Grace would see in her something of the quality that was the passport into that smooth-voiced world. She imagined herself further and further into it, seeing everyday incidents, hearing conversations slide from the surfaces of minds that in all their differences made one even surface, unconscious, unbroken, and maddeningly unquestioning and unaware. . . . They were unaware of anything, though they had easy fluent words about everything. Underneath the surface that kept Grace off they were . . . amoebae, awful determined unconscious . . . octopuses . . . frightful things with one eye, tentacles, poison-sacs. . . . The surface made them, not they the surface; rules. They were civilization. But they knew the rules; they knew how to do the surface . . . they held to them and lived by them. It was a sort of game. They were martyrs, with empty lives, always awake, day and night, with unrelaxed wills. . . . She turned and met frank eyes still waiting for a verdict. All the strength of Grace's personality was quivering there; all the determined faith in reason and principle. Perhaps if she had a clear field she could disarm them . . . any one, every one. If she could get near enough, they would find out her reality and her strength. But they would not want to be like her. They would run in the end from their apprehension of her, back to the things she did not see. . . . They had done so. He had; it was clear. Or she could not have spoken of him. If you can speak of a thing, it is past. . . . Speaking makes it glow with a life that is not its own.

'There's a lot more to tell you,' said Grace, pressing her hand.

Miriam turned from the fire; Grace was looking as she had done when she began her story. Miriam sat back in her chair, searching her face and form, trying to find and express the secret of her indomitable conviction. Being what she was, why could she not be sufficient to herself? Entrenched in uncertainty, she seemed less than herself. Her careful good clothes, so exquisitely kept, the delicate old gold chain, the little pearled cross, the old fine delicate rings, the centuries of shadowy ecclesiasticism in her head and face, the look of waiting, gazing from grey stone-framed days upon a jewelled splendour, grew with her uncertainty small and limited. It was unbearable that they should have no meaning. . . . Grace was ready to take all she possessed into a world where it would have no meaning: ready to disappear and be changed. She was changed already. She could not get back and there was nothing to go forward to. Miriam dropped her eyes and sat back in her chair. The tide of her own life flowed fresh all about her; the room and the figure at her side made a sharply separated scene, a play watched from a distance, the end visible in the beginning, to be read in the shapes and tones and folds of the setting, the intentions and statements nothing but impotent irrelevance, only bearable for the opportunities they offered here and there, involuntarily, for sudden escape into the reality that nothing touched or changed. If only Grace could be forced to see the unchanging reality. . . .

'Oh, Miriam darling,' breathed Grace in an even, anxious tone. Miriam suppressed a desire to whistle.

'Oh, well, of course that may make a *difference*,' she said hurriedly, checking the thrill in her voice.

Far back in the caverns of the fire life moved sunlit. She dropped her eyes and drew away the hand that Grace had clasped. Life danced and sang within her; shreds of song; the sense of the singing of the wind; clear bright light streaming through large houses, quickening on walls and stairways and across wide rooms. Along clear avenues of light radiating from the future, pouring from behind her into the inner channels of her eyes and ears, came unknown forms moving in a brilliance, casting a brilliance across the visible past, warming its shadows, bathing its bright levels in sparkling gold. Her free hands lifted themselves until only the tips of her fingers rested on her knees and her hair strove from its roots as if the whole length would stand and wave upright.

'You see——' she said to gain a moment.

Suddenly her mind became a blank. Her body was heavy on her chair, ill-clothed, too warm, peevishly tingling with desires. She stirred, shrinking from her ugly, inexorable cheap clothes, her glasses, the mystery of her rigid, stupidly done hair; how and *how* did people get expression into their hair consciously and not by accident? Why did Grace like her in spite of all these things, in spite of the evil thoughts which must show. She did. She had felt nothing, seen nothing. She dissembled her face and turned towards Grace, gazing past her into the darkness beyond the range of the fire-light. Just outside the rim of her glasses Grace's firelit face gleamed on the edge of the darkness, half turned towards her.   Leaping into her mind came the realization that she was sitting there talking to someone . . . *marvellous* to speak and hear a voice answer.   Astounding; more marvellous and astounding than anything they could discuss.   Grace must know this, even if she were unconscious of it . . . some little sound they could both hear, a little mark upon the stillness, scattering light and relief.   She turned her eyes and met Grace's, velvety, deeply sparkling, shedding admiration and tyrannous love, patiently waiting.

'Well,' said Miriam, sleepily feeling for a thread of connected thought.

'D' you mean a difference about my taking aunt to call?' asked Grace with fear in her eyes.

'No, my dear,' said Miriam impatiently.   'Can't you see you can't do that anyhow?'

'They 've only been there five years,' said Grace in a low determined recitative.   'We 've lived in what 's almost the same neighbourhood, fifteen.   So it 's our place to call first.'

Miriam sighed harshly.   'That doesn't make a *scrap* of difference,' she retorted, flushing with anger.

'I wish I had your grasp of things, Miriam dear,' said Grace with gentle weariness.

'Well—we 've got to-morrow and Monday,' said Miriam, getting up with an appearance of briskness and striking random notes on the piano.

Grace laughed.   'I suppose we ought to light the gas,' she said, getting up.

'Why?'

'Oh, well—Florrie will be coming in and asking why we 're sitting in the dark.'

'What if she does?'

'Oh, I think I 'll light it, Miriam.'

Miriam sat down again and stared into the fire.   After supper they would all sit, harshly visible, round the hot fire, enduring the stifling unneeded gaslight.

CHAPTER II

MIRIAM rolled up the last pair of mended stockings. . . .

She looked at her watch again. It was too late now even to go round to Kenneth Street. She had spent New Year's Eve alone in a cold bedroom. Why could one not be sure whether it was right or wrong? It was only by sitting hour after hour letting one's fingers sew that the evening had come to an end. It could not be wrong to make up one's mind to begin the new year with a long night's rest in a tidy room with everything mended. But the feeling that the old year ought to be seen out with people had pricked all the time like conscience. It only stopped pricking now because it was too late. And there was a sadness left in the evening. . . . She lifted her coat from her knees and stood up. The room shone. In her throat and nostrils was the smell of dust coming from the floor and carpet and draperies. But the bright light of the gas and the soft light of the reading-lamp shone upon perfect order. Everything was mended and would presently be put away in tidy drawers. She was rested and strong, undisturbed by changes that would have come from social hours. No one had missed her. Many people scattered about in houses had thought of her. If they had, she had been there with them. She could not be everywhere, with all of them. That was certain. There was nothing to decide about that. The Brooms had missed her. They would have enjoyed their New Year's Eve better if she had been there. It would have been jolly to have gone again so soon, after the short half week, and sat down by the fire where Christmas lingered, and waited for the coming of the year with them. It would have been a loyalty to something. But it was too soon to be sitting about between comfortable meals talking, explaining things, making life stop, while reality went on far away. One still felt rested from Christmas and wanting to begin doing things. Perhaps it was not altogether through undecided waiting that the evening had come and gone by here in this room. Perhaps it was some kind of decision that could not be seen or expressed. Now that in solitude it had come to an end there was realization. Quiet realization of New Year's Eve; just quiet realization of New Year's Eve. One would pass on into the new year in an unbroken peace with the resolutions for the new life distinct in one's mind. She found an exercise book and wrote them down. There they stood, pitting the calm steady innermost part of her against all her other selves. Free desperate obedience to them would bring a revelation. No matter how the other selves felt as she kept them, if she kept them every moment of her life would go out from an inward calm.

The room was full of clear strength. There must always be a clear cold room to return to. There was no other way of keeping the inward peace. Outside one need do nothing but what was expected of one, asking nothing for oneself but freedom to return, to the centre. Life would be an endless inward singing until the end came. But not too much inward singing, spending one's strength in song; the song must be kept down and low so that it would last all the time and never fail. Then a song would answer back from outside, in everything. She stepped lightly and powerfully about the room putting away her mended things. . . . One would move like the wind always, a steady human south-west wind, alive, without personality or speech. No more books. Books all led to the same thing. They were like talking about things. All the things in books were unfulfilled duty. No more interest in men. They shut off the inside world. Women who had anything whatever to do with men were not themselves. They were in a noisy confusion, playing a part all the time. The only real misery in being alone was the fear of being left out of things. It was a wrong fear. It pushed you into things and then everything disappeared. Not to listen outside, where there was nothing to hear. In the end you came away empty with time gone and lost. To remember, whatever happened, not to be afraid of being alone.

She stood staring at the sheeny gaslit brown-yellow varnish of the wall-paper above the mantelpiece. There was no thought in the silence, no past or future, nothing but the strange thing for which there were no words, something that was always there as if by appointment, waiting for one to get through to it away from everything in life. It was the thing that was nothing. Yet it seemed the only thing that came near and meant anything at all. It was happiness and realization. It was being suspended, in nothing. It came out of oneself because it came only when one had been a long time alone. It was not oneself. It could not be God. It did not mind what you were or what you had done. It would be there if you had just murdered someone. It was only there when you had murdered everybody and everything and torn yourself away. Perhaps it was evil. One's own evil genius. But how could it make you so blissful? What was one, what had one done to bring the feeling of goodness and beauty and truth into the patch on the wall and presently make all the look of the distant world and everything in experience sound like music in a dream? She dropped her eyes. From the papered wall, radiance still seemed to flow over her as she stood, defining her brow and hair, shedding a warmth in the cold room. Looking again she found the wall less bright; but within the radius of her motionless eyes everything in the brightly lit corner glowed happily; not drawing her but standing complete and serene, like someone standing at a little distance, expressing agreement. Just in front of her a single neat warning tap sounded in the air, touching the quick of her mind. St Pancras clock—striking down the chimney. She ran across to the dark lattice and flung it open. In the air hung the echo of the first deep boom from Westminster. St Pancras and the nearer clocks were telling themselves off against it. They would have finished long before Big Ben came to an end. Which was midnight? Let it be St Pancras. She counted swiftly backwards; four strokes. Out in the darkness the dark world was turning away from darkness. Within the spaces of the night the surface of a daylit landscape gleamed for an instant tilted lengthways across the sky. . . . Little sounds came snapping faintly up through

the darkness from the street below, voices and the creaking
open of doors. Windows were being pushed open up and
down the street. The new year changed to a soft moonlit
breath stealing through the darkness, brimming over the faces
at the doors and windows, touching their brows with fingers of
dawn, sending fresh soothing healing fingers in amongst their
hair. Eleven . . . twelve. Across the rushing scale of St
Pancras bells came a fearful clangour. Bicycle bells, cab
whistles, dinner bells, the banging of tea-trays and gongs. Of
course. New Year. It must be a Bloomsbury custom. She
had had her share in a Bloomsbury New Year. Rather jolly
. . . rowdy; but jolly in that sort of way. She could hear the
Baileys laughing and talking on their doorstep. A smooth firm
foreign voice flung out a shapely little fragment of song.
Miriam watched its outline. It repeated itself in her mind
with the foreign voice and personality of the singer. She drew
back into her room.

Her resolutions kept her at work on Saturday afternoon.
A steady morning's work disposed of the correspondence and
the inrush of paid accounts. After lunch she worked in the
surgeries until they were ready for Monday morning, and made
an attack on the mass of clerical work that remained from the
old year. She sat working until she grew so cold that she
knew if she stayed on in the cold window-space she would
have the beginning of a cold. Better to go, and have late
evenings every day next week, cheered by the protests of the
Orlys and ending with warm hours in the den. As she got up
and felt the aching of her throat and the harsh hot chill running
through her nerves, she realized that anyhow she was in for a
cold. There was no room to go to get warm before going out.
There seemed to be no warmth anywhere in the world. Torpid
and stupid, miserably realizing the increasing glow of her nose
and the numb clumsiness of her feet, she put away the ledgers
and got into her outdoor things. She resented the sight of the
bound volume of *The Dental Cosmos* that she had put aside to

take home.   Her interest in it was useless; as useless as everything else in the freezing world.   Sounds of dancing and
chanting came up the basement stairs.   When their work was
done they could laugh and sing in a warm room.

Turning northwards towards the Marylebone Road, she met
a bleak wind and turned back and down Devonshire Street and
eastwards towards St Pancras through a maze of side streets.
The icy wind drove against her all the way.   When she crossed
a wide thoroughfare it was reinforced from the north.   Eddies
of colourless dust swirled about the pavements.   At every
crossing in the many little streets, there was some big vehicle
just upon her keeping her shrinking in the cold while it rumbled
over the cobbles, overwhelming her with a harsh grating roar
that filled the streets and the sky.   Darkness was beginning; a
hard black January darkness, utterly different from the friendly
exciting twilights of the old year standing far away with summer just behind them and Christmas ahead.

Inside the house a cold grey twilight was blotting out the
warm brownness.   A door opened as she turned the stairhead
on the second floor and a tall thin pale-faced young man in
dark clothes and a light waistcoat flashed past her and leaped
lightly downstairs.   Miriam carried her impression up to her
room, going hurriedly and stumbling on the stairs as she went.
Something hard, metallic, like a wire spring, cold and relentless.
Belonging to a cold dreadful darkness and not knowing it;
confident.   He had whistled going downstairs, or sung.   *Had*
he?   Perhaps he was the foreigner who had sung last night?
Perfectly and awfully dreadful.   The whole house and even
her own room had been changed in a twinkling.   Coming in,
it had had a warmth, even in the cold twilight.   Now it lay
open and bleak, all its rooms naked and visible, a house
'foreign young gentlemen' heard of and came to live in.   He
was one of the 'Norwegian young gentlemen' who had lived in
Mrs Reynolds's boarding-house in Woburn Place and this was
just another boarding-house to him.   Perhaps the house was
full of boarders.   She had grown accustomed to the Baileys
having come up from the basement to the ground floor and had
got into the habit of coming briskly through the hall with a

preoccupied manner, ignoring the invariable appearance of a peeping form at the partly opened door of the dining-room. It was strange now to reflect that the house had always been full of lodgers. What sort of people had they been? She could not remember ever having met a lodger face to face, or heard any sounds in the many downstairs rooms. Perhaps it had been partly through going out so early and coming back only when the A.B.C. closed, and being out or away so much at week-ends, but also she must have been oblivious. The house had been her own; waiting for her when she found it; the quiet road of large high grey mysterious houses, the two rows of calm balconied façades, the green squares at either end, the green door she waited for as she turned unseeing into the road from the quiet thoroughfare of Endsleigh Gardens, her triumphant faithful latchkey, the sheltered dimness of the hall, the great staircase, the many large closed doors, the lonely obscurity of her empty top floor. What had come now was the fulfilment of the apprehension she had had when Mrs Bailey had spoken the word boarders. Here they were. They would come and go and go up and downstairs from their bedrooms to that dining-room where the disturbing disclosure had been made, and the unknown drawing-room. Perhaps it would be a failure. She could not imagine Mrs Bailey and the two vague furtive children in skimpy blue serge dresses dealing with the young Norwegian gentleman. He would not stay. If boarders failed, Mrs Bailey might give up the house altogether. She found herself sitting in her outdoor things with the large volume heavy on her knees in the middle of the room. She felt too languid and miserable to get up and take the small chair and the large book to the table, and began wretchedly turning the pages with her gloved hands. Here it was. She glanced through the long article, reading passages here and there. There seemed to be nothing more; she had gathered the gist of it all in glancing through it at Wimpole Street. There was no need to have brought it home. It was quite clear that she belonged to the lymphatico-nervous class. It was the worst of the four classes of humanity. But all the symptoms were hers. She read once more the account of the nervo-bilious type. It was impossible to fit into that. Those people were dark and sanguine and energetic. It was very strange. Having bilious attacks and not having the advantages of the bilious temperament. It meant having the worst of everything. No energy, no initiative, no hopefulness, no resisting power; and sometimes bilious attacks. She was useless; an encumbrance; left out of life for ever, because it was better for life to leave her out. . . . She sat staring at the shabby panels of her wardrobe, hating them for their quiet merciless agreement with her thoughts. To stop now and come to an end would be a relief. But there was nothing anywhere that would come in and end her. Why did life produce people with lymphatico-nervous temperaments? Perhaps it was the explanation of all she had suffered in the past; of the things that had driven her again and again to go away and away, anywhere. She wrenched herself away from her thoughts and flung forward to the sense of sunshine, sudden beautiful things, unreasonable secret happiness, waiting somewhere beyond the blackness, to come again. But it would be mean to take them. She brought nothing to anybody. She had no right to anything. She ought to be branded and go about in a cloak. There was no one in the world who would care if she never appeared anywhere again. She sat shrinking before this thought. It was the plain and simple truth. Nothing that any kind and cheerful person might say could alter it. It would only make it worse. She wondered that she had never put it to herself before. It must always have been there since her mother's death. There were one or two people who thought they cared. But they only cared because they did not know. If they saw more of her, they would cease even to think they cared; and they had their own lives. She had gone on being happy exactly in the same way as she had forgotten there were people in the house; just going lymphatico-nervously about with her eyes shut. But any alternative was worse. Insincere. If one could not die, one must go dragging on, keeping oneself to oneself. That was why it was a relief to be in London; surrounded by people who did not know what one was really like. Social life, any sort of social life anywhere would not help. It only made it worse. Being like this was not a morbid state due to the lack of cheerful society. People who said that were wrong. The sign that they were wrong was the way they went about being deliberately cheerful and sociable. That was worse than anything; the refusal to face the truth. But at least they could endure people. If one could not endure any one, one ought to be dead, to sit staring in front of one until one was dead. The wardrobe did not disagree. She averted her eyes as from an observer. They fell upon her hopeless person dressed in the clothes in which she moved about in the world. She was bitterly cold. But she sat on, unable to summon courage to turn and face her room. Her eyes wandered vacantly back to the panels and down to the drawer below them and back again. The warm quiet booming of a gong came up through the house. She got to her feet and stood listening in amazement. Mrs Bailey had instituted a boarding-house gong!

She went out on to the landing; the gong ceased and rattled gently against its framework, released from hands that had stilled its reverberation. A voice sounded in the hall and then the dining-room door closed and there was silence. They were having tea. Of course; every day; life going on down there in the dining-room. Involuntarily her feet were on the stairs. She went down the narrow flight holding to the balustrade to steady the stumbling of her benumbed limbs. *What* was she doing? Going down to Mrs Bailey; going to stand for a moment close by Mrs Bailey's tea-tray. No; impossible to let the Baileys save her; having done nothing for herself. Impossible to be beholden to the *Baileys* for anything. Restoration by them would be restoration to shame. She had moved unconsciously. Her life was still her own. She was in the world, in a house, going down some stairs. For the present the pretence of living could go on. She could not go back to her room; nor forward to any other room. She pushed blindly on, bitter anger growing within her. She *had* moved towards the Baileys. It was irrevocable. She had departed from all her precedents. She would always know it. Wherever she found herself it would always be there, at the root of her consciousness, shaming her, showing in everything she did or said. Half-way downstairs she restrained her heavy movements and began to go swiftly and stealthily. Mean, mean, mean; utterly mean and damned, a sneaking evil spirit. She pulled herself upright and cleared her throat in a business-like way. The echo of Harriett's voice in her voice plumbed her for tears. But there were no tears. Only something close round her that moulded her face in lines of despair. The hall was in sight. She was going down to the hall to look for letters on the hall-table, and go back. She paused in the hall. If the dining-room door opened she would kill someone with a cold blind glance and go angrily on and out of the front door. If it did not open? It remained closed. It was not going to open. It came quietly wide as if someone had been waiting behind it with the handle turned. Mrs Bailey was in the hall with a firm little hand on her arm.

'*Well*, young lady?' Miriam turned full round, shrinking backwards towards the hall table. Mrs Bailey was clutching her hands. 'Won't you come in and have a cup of tea?'

'I can't,' whispered Miriam briskly, moving towards the dining-room door. 'I 've got to go out,' she murmured, standing just inside the open door.

'Going out?' asked Mrs Bailey in a refined little voice, throwing a proud fond shy glance towards Miriam from her recovered place behind the tea-tray. Her cheeks were flushed and her eyes sparkled brightly under the gaslight. Miriam's glance, elastic in the warmth coming from the room, swept from the flood of yellow hair on the back of the youngest Bailey girl sitting close at her mother's left hand, across to the far side of the table. The pale grey-blue eyes of the eldest Bailey girl were directed towards the bread and butter her hand was stretched out to take, with the unseeing look they must have had when she had turned her face towards the door. At her side, between her and her mother, sat the young Norwegian gentleman, a dark-blue upright form with a narrow gold bar set aslant in the soft mass of black silk tie bulging above the uncreased flatness of his length of grey waistcoat. He had reared his head smoothly upright and a smooth metallic glance had slid across her from large dark clear, easily opened eyes. He was very young, about twenty; the leanness of his dart-like, perfectly clad form led slenderly up to a lean distinguished head. Above the wide high pale brow where the bone stared squarely through the skin and was beaten in at the temples, the skull had a snakelike flatness, the polished hair was poor and worn.

'Yes,' murmured Miriam abstractedly, 'I 'm just going out.'

'Don't catch cold, young lady,' smiled Mrs Bailey.

'Oh, well, I 'll try not to,' said Miriam departing. They 'll never do it, she told herself as she made her way through the darkness towards her A.B.C. He 'll find out. He thinks he is learning English in an English family.

Mrs Bailey came up *herself* to do Miriam's room on Sunday morning. Miriam wondered, as she came archly in after a brisk tap on the door, how she knew that her visit caused dismay. The visit of the little maid did not break into anything. It only meant standing for a minute or so by the window, longing for the snuffling and shuffling to be over. But if Mrs Bailey were coming up every Sunday morning . . . She stood at Mrs Bailey's disposal, sheepishly smiling, in the middle of the room.

'You didn't expect to see *me*, young lady.' Miriam broadened her smile. 'I want to talk to you.'

They stood confronted in the room just as they had done the first time Mrs Bailey had been there with her and they had settled about the rent. Only that then the room had seemed large and real and at once inhabited, the crown of the large house and the reality of all the unknown rooms. Now it seemed to be at a disadvantage, one of Mrs Bailey's unconsidered attics, apart from the life that was beginning to flow all round her downstairs. Something in Mrs Bailey's face when she said, 'I was wondering if you would give Sissie a few French lessons,' spoke the energy of the new feeling and thought.

Miriam was astounded. She called up a vision of Sissie's pale steady grey-blue eyes, her characterless hair, her thickset swiftly ambling little figure. She was the kind of girl who after good schooling could spend a year in France and come back unable to speak French. But if Mrs Bailey wished it she would have to learn from somebody. So she conspired with an easy contemptuous conscience and they stood murmuring over the plan, Mrs Bailey producing one by one, fearfully, in a low motherly encouraging tone, the things she had arranged beforehand in her own mind.

Before she went, she bustled to the window and tweaked the ends of the little Madras muslin curtains.

'Why don't you go down to the drawn-room for a while?' she asked, tweaking and flicking. 'You'll have it all to yourself. Mr Elsing's gone out. I should go down if I was you and get a warm up.'

Miriam thanked her and promised to go and wondered whether the Norwegian's name was Helsing or Elsen. When Mrs Bailey had gone she walked busily about her affronted room. It must be Helsing. A man named Elsen would be shorter and stouter and kindly. Of course she would not go down to the drawing-room. She ransacked her Saratoga trunk and found a *Havet* and a phrase book. She would teach Sissie the rules of French pronunciation and two or three phrases every day and make some sort of beginning of syntax with *Havet*. There would be no difficulty in filling up the quarter of an hour. But it would be teaching in a bad cruel old-fashioned way. To begin at once with *Picciola* or *Le Roi des Montagnes* and talk to her in the character of a Frenchman wanting to become a boarder would be the best. . . . But Sissie would not grasp that slow way. It would be too long before she began to see that she was learning anything. But the smattering of phrases and rules from a book, handed out, without any trouble to herself, on her way to her room and before she wanted to go out, was too little to give in exchange for a proper breakfast ready for her in a warm room every day and the option of having single meals at any time for a very small sum. Because the Baileys were trying to turn themselves into

an English family prepared to receive foreigners who wanted
to learn English, she had promised the lessons as if she thought
the plan good.

She crept downstairs through the silent empty house, pausing
at the open drawing-room door to listen to the faint far-away
subterranean sounds coming from the kitchen. All the
furniture seemed to be waiting for someone or something.
That was a console table. She must have noticed the jar on it
as she came into the room, or somewhere else, it looked so
familiar. In the narrow strip of mirror that ran from the table
high up the wall between the two french windows, stood
the heavy self-conscious reflection of the elegant jug. It was
elegant and complete; the heavy, minutely moulded flowers and
leaves festooned about its tapering curves did not destroy its
elegance. It stood out alone and complete against the reflected
strip of shabby room. Extraordinary. Where had it come
from? It was an imitation of something. A reflection of
some other life. Had it ever been seen by anybody who knew
the kind of life it was meant to be surrounded by? She backed
into an obstacle and turned with her hand upon the low velvet
back of a little circular chair. Its narrow circular strip of
back was supported by little wooden pillars. She took possession of it. The coiled spring of the seat showed its humpy outline through the velvet and gave way crookedly under her when
she sat down. But she felt she was in her place in the room;
out amongst its strange spaces. In front of her about the
fireside, were two large arm-chairs upholstered in shabby
Utrecht velvet and a wicker chair with a woolwork cushion
on its seat and a dingy antimacassar worked in crewels thrown
over its high back. To her right stood a small battered three-
tiered lacquer and bamboo tea-table, and beyond it a large
circular table, polished and inlaid and strewn with dingy
books, occupied the end of the room between the fireplace and
the wall. On the other side of the fireplace stood a chiffonier
in black wood supporting and reflecting in its little mirror a
large square deeply carved dusty brown wooden box inlaid
with mother-of-pearl. Crowding against the chiffonier was a
large shabby bamboo tea-table and a scatter of velvet-seated

drawing-room chairs with carved, dusty, abruptly curving
backs and legs. Away to the left rose one of the high french
windows. The dingy cream lace curtains, almost meeting
across it, went up and up from the dusty floor and ended high
up, under a red woollen valence hanging from a heavy gilt
cornice. Between the curtains she could catch a glimpse of
the balcony railings and strips between them of the brown
brickwork of the opposite house. She stared at the vague
scatter of vases and bowls and small ornaments standing in
front of the large overmantel and dimly reflected in its dusty
mirror. Two tall vases on the mantelshelf, holding dried
grasses, carried her eyes up to two short vases holding dried
grasses standing on the wooden-pillared brackets of the overmantel, and back again to themselves. She rose and turned
away to shake off their influence and turned back again at once
to see what had attracted her attention. Satsuma; at either
end of the mantelpiece shutting in the scatter of vases and bowls
two large squat rounded Satsuma basins—with arched lids.
On the centre of each lid was a little gilded knob. Extraordinary. Unlike any Satsuma she had ever seen. Where
had they come from? She wandered about the room, eagerly
taking in battered chairs and more little tables and whatnots
and faded pictures on the faded walls. What was it that had
risen in her mind as she came into the room? She recalled
the moment of coming in. The *piano*. The quiet shock of it
standing there with the shut-in waiting look of a piano, confronting the large stillness of the room. Turning to face it,
she passed into the world of drawing-room pianos; the rosewood case, the faded rose silk pleating strained taut, its margin
hidden under a rosewood trellis; the little tarnished sconces,
for shaded candles, the small, leather-topped, easily twirling
stool with its single thick, deeply carved leg, a lady sitting,
tinkling and flourishing delicately through airs with variations; an English piano, perfectly wrought and finished, music
swathed and hidden in elegance. 'A little music.' But chiefly
the seated form, the small cooped body, the voluminous
draperies bulging over the stool and spreading in under the
keyboard and down about the floor, the elegantly straying

arms and mincing hands, the arch swaying of the head and
shoulders, the face bent delicately in the becoming play of
light. She opened the lid. It went back from the keys till it
lay flat, presenting a little music-stand folded into the sweep of
its upper edge. Mustiness rose from the keys. They were
loose and yellow with age. Softly struck notes shattered the
silence of the room. She stood listening with loudly beating
heart. The door would open and show a face with surprised
eyes staring into her betrayed consciousness. The house
remained silent. Her fingers strayed forward and ran up a
scale. The notes were all run down but they rang fairly true
to each other.

Moszkowski's *Serenade* sounded fearfully pathetic; as if the
piano were heart-broken. It could be made to do better.
Both the pedals worked, the soft one producing a woolly
sweetness, the loud a metallic shallow brilliance of tone.
She shut the heavy, softly closing, loose-handled door very
carefully. Its cold china knob told her callously that her
real place was in the little room upstairs with the bedroom
crockery cold in the mid-morning light. But she had already
shut the door. She came shyly back to the piano and sat down
and played carefully and obediently piece after piece remembered from her schooldays. They left the room triumphantly silent and heavy all round her. If she got up and went
away it would be as if she had not played at all. She could not
sit here playing Chopin. It would be like deliberately speaking
a foreign language suddenly, to assert yourself. Playing
pianissimo she slowly traced a few phrases of a nocturne. They
revealed all the flat dejection of the register. With the soft
pedal down she pressed out the notes in a vain attempt to key
them up. Through their mournful sagging the magic shape
came out. She could not stay her hands. Presently she no
longer heard the false tones. The notes sounded soft and
clear and true into her mind, weaving and interweaving the
sight of moonlit waters, the sound of summer leaves flickering
in the darkness, the trailing of dusk across misty meadows, the
stealing of dawn over grass, the faint vision of the Taj Mahal
set in dark trees, white Indian moonlight outlining the trees

and pouring over the pale façade; over all a hovering haunting consoling voice, pure and clear, in a shape, passing, as the pictures faintly came and cleared and melted and changed upon a vast soft darkness, like a silver thread through everything in the world. Closing in upon her from the schoolgirl pieces still echoing in the room, came sudden abrupt little scenes from all the levels of her life, deep-rooted moments still alive within her, challenging and promising as when she had left them, driven relentlessly on.

The last chord of the nocturne brought the room sharply back. It was unchanged; lifeless and unmoved; nothing had passed to it from the little circle where she sat enclosed. . . . Her heart swelled and tears rose in her eyes. The room was old and experienced, full like her inmost mind of the unchanging past. Nothing in her life had any meaning for it. It waited impassively for the passing to and fro of people who would leave no impression. She had exposed herself and it meant nothing in the room. Life had passed her by and her playing had become a sentimentai exhibition of unneeded life. . . . She was wretched and feeble and tired. . . . Life *has* passed me by; that is the truth. I am no longer a person. My playing would be the nauseating record of an uninteresting failure to people who have lived, or a pandering to the sentimental memories of people whom life has passed by. 'You played that like a snail crossed in love'; perhaps he was right. But something had gone wrong because I played with the intention of commenting on Alma's way of playing. That was not all. It did not end there. There was something in music when one played alone, without thoughts. Something present, and *new*. Not affected by life or by any kind of people. In Beethoven. *Beethoven* was the answer to the silence of the room. She imagined a sonata ringing out into it, and defiantly attacked a remembered fragment. It crashed into the silence. The uncaring room might rock and sway. Its rickety furniture shatter to bits. *Something* must happen under the outbreak of her best reality. She was on firm ground. The room was nowhere. She cast sidelong, half-fearful, exultant glances. The room woke into an affronted silence. She felt astonishment at the sudden loud outbreak of assertions turning to scornful disgust. Entrenched behind the disgust, something was declaring that she had no right to her understanding of music; no business to get away into it and hide her defects and get out of things and escape the proper exposure of her failure. In a man it would have been excusable. The room would have listened with respectful flattering indulgent tolerance till it was over and then have relapsed untouched. This dingy woman playing with the directness and decision of a man was like some strange beast in the room. It was too late to go back. She could only rush on, re-affirming her assertion, shouting in a din that must be reaching up and down the house and echoing out into the street the thing that was stronger than the feeling that had prompted her appeal for sympathy. It was the everlasting parting of the ways, the wrenching away that always came. The Baileys were going on downstairs with their planning, the Norwegian busy with his cold watchful grappling with England; all of them far away, flouted. The room became a background indistinguishable from any other indifferent background. All round her was height and depth, a sense of vastness and grandeur beyond anything to be seen or heard, yet stretching back like a sheltering wing over the past to her earliest memories and forward ahead out of sight. The piano had changed. It gave out a depth and fullness of tone. By careful management she could avoid the abrupt contrast between the action of the pedals. Presently the glowing and aching of the muscles of her forearms forced her to leave off. She swung round. The forgotten room was filled with friendly light. Triumphant echoes filled its wide spaces, pressed against the windows, filtered out into the quiet street, out and away into London. When the room was still there was an unbroken stillness in the house and the street. Striking thinly across it came the tones of the solitary unaccompanied violin.

CHAPTER III

MIRIAM let herself cautiously in. The whole house was hers; she was a *boarder*; but the right to linger freely in any part of it was bought by Sissie's French lessons, and being Sissie's teacher meant that the Baileys could approach familiarly at any moment. All her privileges were bought with a heavy price, here and at Wimpole Street. It 's us; our family; always masquerading. But the lessons made opportunities of being affable to the Baileys; removing the need for seeking them out purposely from time to time. Cut and dried. I 've *p*atriotic ballads cut and dried. I 'm cut and dried, everybody thinks. Moving and speaking stiffly, the stamp of my family, the minute anything is expected of me. Nobody knows me. I grow more and more unknown and more and more like what people think of me. But *I* know; and things go on coming; scraps of other people's things. No one in the world could imagine what it is to me to have this house; the fag-end of the Baileys' stock-in-trade. God couldn't know, completely. There 's something wrong about it; but damn, I can't help it. In my secret self I should love a prison. Walls. What *are* walls ?

If she scuffed her muddy shoes too cheerfully someone would appear at the dining-room door. Beyond the gaslight pouring down on to the smeary marble of the hall table and glimmering against the threatening dining-room door, the dim staircase beckoned her up into darkness. A few steps and she would be going upstairs. Where ? What for ?

'Hgh—HEE!' at the far end of the passage beyond the hall. . . . There was a line of bright light there, coming through the chink of the little door usually hidden in the darkness beyond where the Baileys disappeared down the basement stairs. Then there was a *room* there. The little door was

pushed open and a man's figure stood outlined against the
bright light and disappeared, shutting the door. There had
been a table and a lamp upon it. The sound of the laugh rang
in her head; a single lively deep-chested note followed by a
falsetto note that curved hysterically up. Men; gentlemen.
How long had they been there? They would not stay. How
had they come? Where had Mrs Bailey found them? Had
they already found out that it was not their sort of house?
Whom were they afraid of shocking with their refinement and
freedom? They were making a bright little world in there
by feeling themselves surrounded by people who would be
shocked. They did not know there was someone there they
could not shock. She imagined herself in the doorway.

'*Hullo!* Fancy you *here*.' . . . The dining-room door had
opened and Mrs Bailey was standing in the hall with the door
open behind her. Miriam was not prepared with a refusal of
the invitation to come in. She glanced over Mrs. Bailey's
shoulder and saw the two girls sitting at the fireside. Two
letters on the hall table addressed to the Norwegian told her
that the Baileys were alone. She yielded to Mrs Bailey's delighted manner and went in. She would stay, keeping on her
outdoor things, long enough to hear about the new people.
The close sickly sweet air of the room closed oppressively
round her heavy garments.

'Here you are, young lady, sit here,' said Mrs Bailey, piloting
her to a chair in front of the fire. There was a stranger sitting
at the fireside.

'Mr Mendizabble,' murmured Mrs Bailey as Miriam sat
down.

Miriam's affronted eyes took in the figure of a man sitting
on the wooden stool crowded in between the mantelpiece and
the easy chair occupied by Sissie; a man from a café. A foreign
waiter in his best clothes, sheeny, stripy, harsh pale grey, a
crimson waistcoat showing up the gleam of a gold watch-chain,
and crimson cloth slippers; an Italian, a Frenchman, a French-
Swiss. He was sitting bent conversationally forward with his
elbows on his knees and his hands clasped; quite at home.
They had evidently been sitting there all the evening. The
air was thick with their intercourse. Miriam received an

abrupt nod in answer to her murmur and her stiff bow and
followed with resentful curiosity the little foreign tune the
man began humming far away in his head.   He had not even
glanced her way and the tune was his response to Mrs Bailey's
introduction.   The remains of a derisive smile seemed to snort
from the firmly sweeping white nostrils above his tiny, trim,
bushily upward-curving black moustache.   It moulded the
strong closed lips and shone behind the whole of his curiously
square, evenly modelled face.   The Bailey girls were watching
him with shiny flushed cheeks and bright eyes.   His skin was
white and clean, matt; like felt.   Untouched and untried in
the exhausted air of the shabby room.   Certainly he was
some kind of strong 'outsider.'   An insolent waiter.   He had
turned away towards the fire after his nod.   From under a
firm black-lashed white lid a bright dark eye gazed derision into
the flames.

'Go on, Mr Mendizzable,' smiled Mrs Bailey, brushing at her
skirt with her handkerchief, 'we are most interested.'

'Hay, madame, that is all,' he laughed derisively in rich
singing, swaying tones towards the middle of the hearthrug.
'I skate from one end of their canal to another, faster than them
all.   I win their prize.   Je m'en fiche.'

'You skated all the way along the canal?'

'Ieeea skate their can*a*l.   That was Amsterdam.   I do many
things there.   I edit their newspaper.   I conduct a café.'

'Mts.   You *have* had some adventures.'

'That was not adventures in Amsterdam, mon Dieu!'   He
swayed drumming from foot to foot in time to his shouts.   Had
he really beaten those wonderful skaters?   Perhaps he had not.
She glanced at his brow, calm, firm, dead white under the soft,
crisply ridged black hair.   Perhaps he was Dutch; and that
was why he looked common and also refined.

At ten o'clock the youngest girl was sent to bed.   Miriam
scornfully watched herself miss her opportunity of getting
away.   She sat fascinated, resenting the interruption; enviously
filching the gay outbreaking kindness that robbed the departure

of humiliation and sent the girl away counting on to-morrow. He went out of his way to make *Polly Bailey* happy, and sat on by the dying fire unwearied, freshly humming to himself towards the dingy hearth scattered thinly with sparse dusty ash. Mrs Bailey returned, raked together the remains of the fire, and settled herself in her chair with a shiver. In a moment she would begin her questionings and the voice would sound again.

'You cold, mother darling? Come nearer the fire.'

Mrs Bailey pulled her chair a few inches forward, arching her neck and smiling her bright sweet smile. 'Oogh, it's parky upstairs.'

Miriam implored herself to go.

'Parky,' reiterated Mrs Bailey uncertainly, glancing daintily from side to side and smiling away a yawn behind her small rough reddened hand.

'Parky? What is parky?'

'*Parky*,' said Mrs Bailey, '*cold*; like a park.'

'Ah, I see. That is good. When I go upstairs I go to Hyde Park. I shall have in my bedroom a band and a mass meeting, and a policeman. Salvation Army band.'

Miriam sat stiffly through the laughter of the Baileys. Her refusal to join brought the discomforting realization of having laughed, several times during the past hour. She had laughed in spite of herself, flinging her laughter out across the hearth-rug towards the dying fire, leading the laughter of the Baileys, holding them off and herself apart. Now suddenly by refusing to share their laughter when they led the way she had openly separated herself from them. Then they knew she stayed on under a charm. They had witnessed her theft from the wealth *they* had provided, her gratitude to him for the store of memories she had gathered. It was the price. It stung and tried to humiliate her. She sat steadily on, flouting it. The grouping would not recur. Why did not Mrs Bailey make him go on talking? A cold gloom spread sideways from the polished arch of the grate, encroaching on the corner where he sat drumming and humming. She drew her eyes with an air of absorption towards the dying fire. Its aspect was unendurably bleak. Her mind shrank from it, only to meet the sense of the cold darkness waiting upstairs. Mrs Bailey's voice bridged the emptiness. Some inner link was restored. Somewhere in her voice was something that rang restoringly round the world. The disconnected narrative was flowing again. The chilly hearth glowed with a small dull brilliance. The foreign voice went on and on, narrative dialogue commentary, running flowing leaping, in the voice that rang whatever it said in bright sunshine. She listened openly, apologizing in swift affectionate glances for her stiff middle-class resentment of his vulgar appearance. Was he vulgar? She tried in vain to recall her first impression. That curious blending of sturdy strength and polished refinement in the handsome head was something well known in the head of a friend. She forced her friends to apologize and submit to the charm.

It was nearly midnight. The grey of to-morrow morning kept pressing on her attention. She gathered herself together to go, and rose reluctantly. The outer chill came down to meet her rising form. The glow of life was left there at the heart of the circle by the fire. The little man leapt up—'Hah, *good* night all'—and pushed past her and out of the room. Mrs Bailey had made some remark towards her as she neared the door. She professed not to hear and went slowly on in the wake of the footsteps leaping up the dark flights. They crossed the landing next below hers and ceased. When she rounded the stairs, light blazed from a wide-open door and a little melody sounded for an instant in a smooth swaying falsetto. As soon as she had passed, the door was violently slammed. All those stories were *true*. And the first one about the skating. She imagined the white brow under a fur cap and the square, short, strong, well-knit form swaying strongly from side to side, on and on, ironically winning.

Sissie read her set of phrases in heavy docility. Her will and the shapeless colourless voice murmuring from the back of her throat were given to the lesson; but the kindly sullen profile smouldered in slumber. Miriam pondered at ease, contrasting the two voices as they placed one after the other the little trite sentences upon the empty air. That Sissie should speak her French in the worst kind of English way did not really matter. But why was it? What did it mean? They all had something in common—all the people who spoke French like this?

A slender young man darted noiselessly into the room and began busily dusting the sideboard. He was wearing a striped cotton jacket. Mrs Bailey had acquired a manservant. It was impossible. He would not be able to be kept. It was like a play. He was like a character in a farce, rushing on and whisking things about. It was a play; amateur theatricals, Mrs Bailey rushing radiantly about, stage-managing. It was pretending things were different when they were not; breaking up the atmosphere of the house. Where did she get her ideas? Coming back to her surveillance, she listened intently.

'Wait a minute,' she said, 'we will begin all over again. I see exactly what it is. There's no difficulty. You can learn all about pronunciation in a few minutes.'

Sissie had started. Controlling herself she took her attention from the book long enough to give Miriam a sympathetic glancing smile.

'Let the words *ring* in your head, *into* your nose and against your forehead.' Sissie sat back smiling, and sat watching Miriam's face. 'It's *we* who speak *through* the nose. And mouth. In gusts, whoof, whoof, from the chest; all sound and no enunciation.' Sissie's eyes were roving intently about Miriam's face. 'They *stop* the breath at the lips and in the nose. Bong. That's through the nose. *Bon!* D' you hear; like a little explosion. Hold the lips tight before the *b* and explode the word up into the nose, partly closing the back of the throat and mouth. It's all like that and the pronunciation does not vary. When you know the few rules and get the vowels pure and explode the consonants, that's all there is.'

Sissie waited, controlling an apologetic smile. She had realized nothing but the violent outburst and was secretly laughing over the idea of explosions.

'Say matin,' suggested Miriam patiently.

'Mattong,' murmured Sissie.

'Say mattah,' persisted Miriam. The youth came flourish-in with the coal box. 'That's right. Now try forcing the *ah* up into your nose and shutting your nose on it.'

'It's time to lay the table, Emyou,' stated Sissie reprovingly towards the hearthrug.

'Pliz?' The young man reared a mild fair crested head above the rim of the table.

'Lay the table, tarb, paw dinnay,' snapped Sissie. 'I shall have to go, Miss Henderson,' she added, getting gently up and ambling to the door. The young man shot murmuring from the room. They appeared to collide in the hall.

Miriam found herself in the midst of a train of thought that had distracted her during her morning's work. *Cosmopolis*, she scribbled in her note-book. The world of science and art is the true cosmopolis. Those were not the words in *Cosmopolis* but it was the idea. Perhaps no one had thought of it before the man who thought of having a magazine in three languages. It would be one of the new ideas. Tearing off the page, she laid it on the sofa-head and sat contemplating an imagined map of Europe, with London, Paris, and Berlin joined by a triangle, the globe rounding vaguely off on either side. All over the globe, dotted here and there, were people who read and thought, making a network of unanimous culture. It was a tiring re-flection; but it brought a comfortable assurance that somewhere beyond the hurrying confusion of everyday life something was being done quietly in a removed real world that led the other world. People arrived independently at the same conclusions in different languages, and in the world of science they com-municated with each other. That made cosmopolis. Yet it was an awful thought that the world might gradually become all one piece; perhaps with one language; perhaps English if those people were right who talked about Anglo-Saxon supremacy. 'England and America together could rule the world.' It sounded secure and comforting, like a police station; it would be wonderful to belong to the race whose language was spoken all over the world. All the foreigners would simply have to become English. But that brought a dreadful sense of loss. Foreign languages had a beauty that could not be found in English, and the world would be *ruled* by the kind of English people who could never get the sound of a foreign word and who therefore had all sorts of appalling obliviousness.

'You write that, miss?'

'Yes,' said Miriam leaping through surprise and indignation to delight. Sissie and Émile were back again in the room hurrying and angry. The little man bid them a loud good-evening; a table-cloth was floundering out across the large table. Miriam returned to her note-book. He was *writing*, with a scrap of pencil taken from his pocket, on her piece of paper, held against the wall. 'There, miss,' he shouted gruffly, handing it to her. 'Lies,' she read, scribbled in a rounded hand across her words, and underneath: 'There is NO cosmopolis. Bernard Mendizabal.'

'Oh, yes, there *is* a cosmopolis,' argued Miriam, looking up and out from a whirl of convincing images. He was walking about in the window space in his extraordinary clothes, short and somehow too square for his clothes, making his clothes look square. His square, roundly modelled head was changeably sculptured by the gaslight as he paced up and down. His distinction seemed to be sharpened by her words as she said, 'Vous avez tort, monsieur.' She had a sense of Émile and Sissie glancing and affronted while she slid down her sentence to leap, flouting them, forsaking her crowding thoughts, and catch at any cost, the joy of saying and hearing no matter what in foreign speech. She would pay for the moment any price to make it sound and keep it sounding in the room. The spaces of her separate life in the house became a background for this familiar forgotten joy so unexpectedly renewed.

'*No*, miss!' shouted Mr Mendizabal. She cast a fierce general scowl towards his promenading figure. He was another of those foreigners who care for nothing in England but practising English. Then she would fight her theory.

'Je n'ai pas tort,' he thundered, standing before her with his hands in his pockets. He was taking her French for granted. In her thankfulness she sat docile before a torrent of words, taking in nothing of their meaning, throwing out provisional phrases according to his tone of question or assertion. The Baileys coming in and out of the room would see 'an animated French conversation' and Sissie and Émile would forget her desperate onslaught in their admiration of the spectacle. The more she kept it glowing and emphatic and alive the further she was redeemed. She gave no glance their way. Dinner must be almost ready. Soon she would have to go. The gong would tell her. Till then she could remain immersed in the tide of words. The little man was earnest and enraged. He used his French easily and fluently. It was not wonderful to him suddenly to become French, to feel the things he expressed change, become clear neat patterns, lose some of their meaning, fall open to attack; the pain of the failure of words so set out, was made bearable by the wonder of the journey from speech to speech. He remained himself, apparently unaware of the change of environment, or indifferent to it. *En dèche*. What did that mean? 'Vous devez me voir en *dèche*. That seemed to be his summing up, the basis of his denial of a cosmopolis. She attended. The only way he declared, as if recalling an earlier assertion, of proving the indifference of every one to every one else is to be *en dèche*. Smiling comprehensively just before he turned on his heel and swung round, she drifted out of the room amidst the clangour of the gong . . . *en dèche* . . . *déchéance*? . . . somehow at a disadvantage. She thought of her written phrases in French. They sounded a little grandiloquent. Someone seemed to be declaiming them from a platform. He probably had not realized what she was trying to say. But he was a cosmopolitan, and he denied that there was any cosmopolis, any sympathy between races, even between individuals. He was a pessimist. With all his charm and zest he believed in nothing and nobody. And he spoke from experience. Perhaps it was only in thoughts, not in life, that these things existed. People talked about cosmopolis because they wanted to believe it. Had he said that?

CHAPTER IV

SITTING down almost the moment Mr Mendizabal brought him into the room and playing *Wagner*. With many wrong notes and stumbling phrases, but self-forgetfully, in the foreign way. Keeping bravely on, making the shape come even in the most difficult parts. He was hearing the Queen's Hall orchestra all the time, and he knew that any one who knew it could hear it too. He was one of those people who stand in the arena and talk about the music and know that there are piano scores and get them and play them. It was amazing that there should be piano scores of Wagner. Did he play because he wanted to remember the orchestra; without thinking of the people who were listening? He did not know the Baileys and their boarders. He could not imagine how extraordinary it was to hear Wagner in the room, suddenly offered to the *Baileys*. They knew something important was going on; sitting close round the piano surprised and attentive, busily speculating, in scraps, hampered by the need to appear to be listening. Afterwards they would talk to him, arching and laughing, Mr Mendizabal's friend. Perhaps he would come and play Wagner again; there would be music in the room undisturbed by their forced attention. This was only a beginning.

At the end of the overture he sat quite still, making no movement of turning towards the room. The group about the piano were taken by surprise, waiting for him to turn. When they began making exclamations his hands were on the piano again. The room was silenced by strange little sentences of music. He played short fragments, unfamiliar things with strange phrasing, difficult to trace, unmelodious, but haunted by suggested melody; a curious flattened wandering abrupt intimate message in their phrases; perhaps Russian or Brahms. Not

345

Wagner writing down the world in sound nor Beethoven speaking to one person. Other foreign musicians, set apart, glancing, and listening to strange single things, speaking in pain, just out of clear hearing, their speech unfinished. Russian or Hungarian. Dvor-tchak. I will ask him. Perhaps he plays Chopin.

The Baileys were growing weary of listening. They ·were becoming strangers in their own dining-room, with a wonderful important evening going on all round them. Miriam consulted Sissie, probing enviously for the dark busy, sulkily hidden thoughts going to and fro behind her attitude of listening. Her eyes were drawing pictures of Mr Bowdoin's back view and noting his movements. Mrs Bailey was still smiling her pride. Her tired eyes were strained brightly towards the performance with the proper expression of delighted appreciation. But now and again they moved observantly across the slender shabby form and revealed her circling thoughts. When she looked at the back of the thatch of soft fine fair hair she was seeing that officeful of men painting posters, the first arrival of Mr Mendizabal, their resentment of his quick work, the poster he thought of in the night, here, and worked out at the office in an hour, the musician playing so gravely, not knowing that he was being seen as the man who was forced by Mr Mendizabal to play a Beethoven sonata on the typewriter with his hair in curl-papers. If Mrs Bailey went too deeply into her speculations, she would be too confused to ask him to come again. Perhaps Mr Mendizabal would bring him anyhow. He was lounging back in his chair with his hands in his pockets. His face seemed to be laughing ironically behind a proud smile. He respected music. He admired Bowdoin for his talent. He was showing him off. It was charming. Like Trilby. Men laughing at each other and admiring each other . . . She had left off listening. Mr. Bowdoin was sitting there at her side, separate from his music, sitting there, English, a little altered by going out into foreign music. A sort of foreigner with an English expression. Her glance had shown her an English profile, a blunted irregular aquiline, a little defaced about the mouth and chin by the influence on the muscles of a common way of speaking. But the back of his head was foreign, the outline of his skull fine and delicate, a delicate arch at the top and the back flattened a little under the soft fall of hair. He was stopping. He sat still, facing the piano. There were stirrings and murmurs and uncertain attempts at applause. Mr Mendizabal rose and stood over him, as if to smite him on the shoulder.

'What do you think about when you play *Beethoven*?' said Miriam hastily. His face came round and Mr Mendizabal turned hilariously away to the room.

'By-toven himself, I think,' said Mr Bowdoin quietly.

'If I get a *Beethoven's Sonatas*, would you play one?'

'I *will* play one for you. But not this evening, I think.' He turned back to the piano and Miriam gazed at his undrawn profile. He was quite English and had all the English thoughts and feelings about the little group gathered behind him in the room. But there was something besides. He was a musician and that made him understand. He knew the room was impervious to music and was ill at ease after the first joy of playing, and could not convince his hearers by vitality and exuberance as a foreigner would do, even with quite fragile, subdued, delicately controlled music.

'If you care about music,' he said towards the piano, 'will you come one evening and let me play to you on my own piano?'

'I should like it more than anything,' said Miriam.

'It will be an honour and a great pleasure to me if you will come,' he said in his quiet weary voice. 'I will take the liberty of writing to suggest an evening.'

Miriam's abrupt rising and blind movement left her standing opposite the lady-help, who was standing with a foot on the fender and an elbow on the mantelpiece, on the other side of the hearthrug. After only two days in the house she seemed already more at home than the Baileys; talking derisively across at Mr Mendizabal who was marching up and down the far side of the room with his hands in pockets shouting raillery and snorting.

'D'you like London, Miss Scott?' said Miriam uncontrollably to her averted talking face. Miss Scott completed her sally; the Baileys were talking to Mr Bowdoin, just behind

at the piano. Perhaps no one had witnessed her wild attack.
But she could not take her eyes off Miss Scott's face. It
turned towards her still wearing its derisive smile.

'What was that you said, Miss Henderson? I beg your
pardon,' she stated encouragingly. She was not in the least
impressed by being spoken to. Her swift amused glance was
all she could manage without breaking into shouts of laughter.
Her laughter-shaken person was the front of a barricade of
derision. Miriam repeated her question, fearfully consulting
the small sheeny satin dress, with the lace collar, the neat slipper
on the fender, the heavy little fringe stopping abruptly at the
hollow temples above high cheekbones and slightly hollow
cheeks and leading back to a tiny knot at the top of the head.
Perhaps she was a lady.

'Ye see so little of it unless yerra wealthy,' she said in curious
tonguey tones, standing upright on the hearthrug and flinging
back her head with every other word; backing away with a
balancing movement from foot to foot. She laughed on her
last word and stood shaking with laughter, her elbow on the
far corner of the mantelshelf and her foot once more on the
fender. Perhaps she was still laughing at some jest of Mr
Mendizabal's.

'Arrya fond of London, Miss Henderson?' she chuckled
and went on without waiting for an answer, with rhythmically
flinging head: 'It 's ahl very well if ya can go out to theeaturras
and consurruts and out and about; but when the season comes
and the people are in the parruk and in thayre grand houses
having parrties and gaities and yew 've just got to do nothing
I think its draydefle.' She laughed consumedly, throwing back
her head.

Miriam got herself across the room and outside the door.
On the hall table lay a letter; from Eve; witnessing her discomfort; soothing, and reproaching. Eve would have stayed
and talked to the musician.

Up in her cold room everything vanished into the picture
of Eve, deciding, away down in green Wiltshire, to leave off
teaching; smiling, stretching out her firm small hands and
taking hold of *London*. London changed as she read. She sat

stupefied. It seemed impossible, terrifying, that Eve, penniless, and with her uncertain health, should leave the wealthy comfort of the Greens after all these years. Too excited to read word by word, she scanned the pages and learned that Madame Leroy, a friend of Mrs Green who had a flower shop in Bruton Street, had engaged her. . . . *I decorated the table for dinner each night when she was here at Christmas . . . the Greens have been charming, quite excited about the plans . . . coming up next week* . . . Miriam leapt to her feet and began hastily putting on her things. 'Eve is coming to London for a six months' course in floral decorations. She is putting up at a hostel.' She pulled on her cold sodden shoes. 'Eve is going to be an assistant in a flower shop at fifteen shillings a week. She has taken a cubicle at a branch of the Young Women's Bible Association.' By the time she was ready she felt she must have dreamed the news. Eve, not a governess, free, in London, just as she was herself. Another self, in London. Eve being led about and taught London, going about under the same skies, in the streets, feeling exactly as she felt. Nothing would have changed before she came. The rain gently thudding on the roof and rattling against the landing skylight was Eve's rain. She was listening to it and hearing it in exactly the same way.

The girls did not realize the news at all. They kept going off into questions about details until the fact of Eve's coming disappeared altogether and only Eve's point of view and Eve's courage and her difficulties remained. . . . One had told it the wrong way. Better not to have given any facts at all but just to have said, 'Eve's coming to London; isn't it weird?' But then they would have said, 'Is she coming to London to see the queen?' The queen. That would have been true. She was coming to London partly to see the queen. Perhaps the trouble was that they had been cheated by not being told exactly how Eve was only just managing to come at all and how scraped everything would be. But at least they realized that one had people belonging to one who made up their minds and did definite things. It was amazing to decide to come to London and be a florist. They realized that and nothing else.

She would be able to tell Mr Hancock on Monday; first him, first thing in the morning and the Orlys during the day.

Mr Hancock understood at once, making no response at all at first and then standing quietly about near her as she busied herself with her dusting, really giving himself to taking in the simple stupendous fact; and really realizing it before asking any questions and asking them in a tone that showed he knew what it meant and going on showing all day in his manner that he knew what it was that kept her so brisk about her work. He was divine; he was a divine person. She would never forget being able to say just anyhow, 'H'm, I've got a *sister* coming to London'; and his immediate silent approach across the room, drying his hands. Of *course* the Orlys immediately said, 'Oh, how nice for you, you won't be so lonely.' *What* did people mean about loneliness? It was always the people arranged in groups and seeming so lost and isolated and lonely who said that. To-night she would begin turning out her room for Eve's reception. No. It was the Dante lecture. The day Eve came she would buy some flowers. She understood now why people wanted to put flowers in their rooms when people were coming. She would be a hostess. Some people bought flowers and carried them home when they were alone. It must be like inviting a guest to keep you company. Like saying you were alone and not liking being alone and putting flowers about to tell you all the time that you did not want to be alone, but were. People *talked* about these things. 'I always buy flowers when I am alone.' Like suddenly taking off all their things and showing that they had a crooked body. If they were really miserable about being alone they would be too miserable to buy flowers. If they really wanted the flowers enough to buy them they were already not alone. If they bought the flowers in that fussy excited thoughtless way people seemed to do things, they were neither really ever alone or ever really with people. They were in that sort of state that made social life a talkative nothingness sliding about on nothing.

At the end of the afternoon she wandered forgetfully into the warmth of the empty waiting-room. The house was silent. Her footsteps made no sound along the carpeted hall and were

lost in the thick Turkey carpeting of the waiting-room floor.
The room was lit only by the firelight. From its wide clear
core, striped by black bars, a broad rose-gold shaft glowed out
across the room, reaching the copper vessels on the black oak
sideboard and the lower part of the long mirror between the
windows where the midmost piece of copper gleamed in reflection. She stood still, holding the warm air in her nostrils.
Everything was blotted out and then restored to its place. What
place? Why was it good? What was she trying to remember? In the familiar firelit winter darkness was a faint dry
warm scent . . . mimosa. It was a repetition. It had been
there last year, suddenly; dryly fragrant in the winter darkness
of the warm room preparing for the light and warmth of the
evening. It had seemed then like some wealthy extravagance,
bringing a sense of the freedom of wealth to have things out of
season, and a keen sudden memory in the dark London room
of the unspoken inexpressible beauty of Newlands. Its soft-
toned, softly carpeted and curtained effect, fragrant with clusters
of winter flowers, standing complete somewhere in the secret
black spaces of her mind. But now here it was again, just at
the same moment, just before the winter darkness began to give
way. Perhaps mimosa came at this time of year suddenly in
the shops, before the spring flowers, and careful people like
Mrs Orly could buy it. Then in London mimosa was the
sign of *spring*. It was like the powdery fragrance of a clear
warm midsummer evening, like petal-dust; pollen-dust; the
whole summer circling in the glow of firelight. Then Eve
would not come this winter. The darkest secret winter-time
of London was over again. It would come again in single
moments and groups of days, but its time was gone. The
moment of realization of spring had come by surprise; here
lay all the spring days ahead leading on to summer spread out
for any one to see, calling to Eve or to any one who might have
come into the room, to whom one could have said, 'Doesn't
the smell of mimosa make you realize the winter is over?' and
here within, lit up as if by a suddenly switched on electric light,
was one's own real realization going back and back; in pictures
that grew clearer, each time something happened that switched

on a light within the black spaces of your mind. Things that
no one could share, coming again and again just as some outside thing was beginning to interest you, as if to *remind* you
that the inmost reality comes to you when you are alone.

The prospect of Eve's coming was changed. The pang of the
mimosa came nearer than anything she could bring. Perhaps it
would be possible to tell her about this moment? Perhaps
her coming had made it more real. Yet now it did not seem
to matter so much whether she came or not. In a way it seemed
as though the fact of her coming threatened something.

'Antoine Bowdoin.' If she had had a solemn letter from
him first, she would never have undertaken to go and hear him
play. The formal courtly old-fashioned phrases had nothing
to do with the hours of music. She had thought of nothing
but the music on the good piano and now when she had forgotten all about it there was this awful result: the 'few friends'
gathered together in his room on a fixed date so that she might
go and hear him play. She would have to sit, with a party,
and afterwards find something to say. An Englishman, solemn
and polite, playing foreign music, with English friends politely
and solemnly sitting round. There was no word of Mr Mendizabal. He was not going. If he had been, Mr Bowdoin would
not have said, 'I will call at six-thirty for the purpose of escorting you to my rooms.' He was like a jailer. Perhaps the
walk would be an opportunity of getting over nervousness.
There would be music at once, no meal to get through. She
would thank him very much for the great treat and when it
was over there would only be Eve and the accomplishment of
having heard a good piano played by a musician. He could
be dropped. He could be asked to come just once and play
for Eve. That would be a great London evening for Eve.
The sense of a complex London life crowded with engagements made her pace in spite of her weariness up and down the
platform at Gower Street. Its familiar sulphurous gloom, the
platform lights shining murkily from the midst of slowly

rolling clouds of grey smoke, the dark forms and phantom white faces of waiting passengers emerging suddenly as she threaded the darkness, revived her. By the time the train rolled slowly in behind its beloved black dumpy high-shouldered engine with its large unshrieking mushroom bell-whistle, the journey had changed from being an expedition to a spot within five minutes' walk of Sarah's, unconfessed to Sarah, and had become a journey on the Metropolitan; going indeed outside the radius into blackness, but going so far only because the Dante lecture, wandered out of London, was waiting there; and to be repeated at the end of the evening safely returning through increasing gloom until the climax of Gower Street was reached again. Miss Scott was *Scotch*.

She reached the little hall in the suburban road in good time and sat in a forward row, gazing at the little platform where presently the educative voice would be standing. She was conscious of a stirring and buzzing all about her that had been absent in the London hall. The first series of lectures had not brought any sense of an audience. Here the many audible centres of culture, the eager discussions and sudden incisive remarks, the triumphant intensity on the faces of some of the women caught as she glanced now and then apprehensively about, the curious happy briskness of the men, made her feel that the lecturer was superfluous. All these people were the cultured refined kind who did not trouble much about their clothes. There were no furs to be seen; the women wore large, rather ugly coats or ulsters or capes and bashed muddly-looking hats and had mufflers or long scarves. In the London audience herself and her clothes had been invisible, here they were just right, a sort of hall-mark. In her black dress with her clumsy golf-cape thrown back from her shoulders, her weather-worn felt hat softened perhaps to harmony with her head in the soft light, she could perhaps pass for a cultured person. '*Bianchi* and *Neri*,' whispered her neighbour eagerly in the midst of a long sentence addressed to a girl at her side. She was an Englishwoman. But her mind was so at home in the Middle Ages that she spoke the names and used the Italian pronunciation without a touch of pedantry, and as eagerly and

interestedly as any one else might say 'They're engaged!' The
clergyman in the row in front would drawl out the words with
an unctuous suggestion of superior knowledge. He would use
them to crush someone. Most of the men present were a little
like that, using their knowledge like a code or a weapon. But
the women were really interested in it, they were like people
who had climbed a hill and were eagerly intent on what they
could see on the other side. It was refreshing and also in some
way comforting to be with them. They represented something in life that was going to increase. Perhaps it would increase too much; they seemed so headlong and unaware of
anything else. Did she want a world made up of women like
this? If she spoke to them they would assume she was one of
themselves and look busily at her with unseeing eyes, fixed
only on all the things they thought about, until they perceived
that she was a fraud. Long intercourse with them might
make her able to talk like they did, but never to think in the
way they did. Never to have the extraordinary busy assured
appearance presented by their persons when you could not see
their eager faces; a look that made them seem to be going very
fast in some direction that completely satisfied them, so that if
a fire broke out behind them suddenly they would regard it
not as an adventure that might have been expected, but as an
annoying interruption, like tripping over a stone.

She could see that when he read the sonnets he forgot how
learned he was. The little lecture had had its own fascination.
But it was a lecture; something told by a specialist to an audience. This was Dante's voice, and they all listened as they
could; the lecturer as well. All his knowledge was put aside
and he listened as he read. She sat listening, her shocked mind
still condemning her for not having discovered for herself that
it was wrong to have a post-office savings account and that
betting and gambling and lotteries were wrong because they
produced nothing. For a time she flashed about with the
searchlight of this new definition of vice. Money can't produce money. Then all trade was wrong in some way. Dissipation of value without production . . . there was some
principle that all civilization was breaking. How did this

man know that it was wrong to imagine affection if there was
no affection in your life, that dreaming and brooding was a
sort of beastliness. Love was actual and practical, moving
all the spheres and informing the mind. That was true.
That was the truth about everything. But who could attain
to it? Dante knew it because he loved Beatrice. How could
humanity become more loving? How could social life come to
be founded on love? How can I become more loving? I do
not know or love any one but myself. It did not mean being
loved. It was not anything to do with marriage. Dante only
saw Beatrice. But this is the awful truth; however one may
sit as if one were not condemned, and forget again. This is
the difficult thing that *every one* has to do. Not dogmas. This
man believes that there is a God who loves and demands that
man shall be loving. That is what will be asked. That is the
judgment. It is true because it breaks into you and con-
demns you. Everything else is distraction and sham. The
humble yearning devotion in the voice reading the lines made
it a prayer, the very voice a prayer to a spirit waiting all round,
present in himself, in every one listening, in the very atmosphere. It was there, to be had. It was like something left
far behind one on a dark road and still there; to be had for the
asking, to be had by merely turning towards it. She looked
into the eyes of Dante across the centuries as into the eyes of
a friend. But then these people were the same. It was the
truth about everybody, 'the goodwill in all of us.'

She travelled back towards London in a dream. Her compartment was empty. All the people in the world, full of
goodwill without troubling or even thinking about it, were
away somewhere else. Just as she had learned what people
were, there was nobody. There was no love in her nature.
If there were, she would not have been sitting here alone. If a
man love not his brother whom he hath seen, how shall he
love God whom he hath not seen? There was a catch in that
like a riddle. Heads I win, tails you lose. If you keep quite
quiet and gentle, asking for nothing, not being anything, not
holding on to anything in your life, nor thinking about anything in your life, there is something there . . . behind you.

That must be God, the way to Christ; the edge of the way to Christ. Keeping quiet and coming to that, you feel what you are and that you have never begun being anything but your evil natural self. You feel thick with evil.

That was prayer. One could become more loving. It is answered at once. Just turning towards something, in a desire to be different, begins to change you!

At Praed Street the carriage began to fill with seated forms. This was the beginning of new life. Keeping perfectly still and looking at no one, she realized the presence of her fellow-travellers, all just like herself, living from within by the contact with the edge of Christ. All *knowing* the thing that to her was only a little flicker just dawning in a long life of evil. It made them kindly in the world and able to understand each other. Perhaps it was the explanation of all the fussing. Every one in the world was bathed in the light of love except herself. It was not certain that a whole lifetime of prayer and gentleness and self-control would destroy enough of the thick roots of evil in her to bring her through into the Paradiso. But if prayer, just the turning away from all who knew, begging to be destroyed and made loving, brought such an immediate sense of the evil in oneself and the good in every one else, there was no end to what it might do. Prayer was the work to do in life, nothing else. But the turning to the unseen God of love and giving up one's self-will meant being changed in a way one could not control or foresee; dropping everything one had and cherished secretly and having things only in common with other people. It would mean going forward with nothing into an unknown world; *always* being agreeable, and agreeing. I *love* all these people, she murmured in her mind, and felt a glow that seemed to radiate out to all the corners of the compartment. It 's *true*. This is life. This is the only way in. It may be that I am so bad that I can only sit, with all my evil visible, silent amongst humanity for the rest of my life, learning to love them, and then die out completely because I am too bad to be quite new-born.

Her eyes were drawn towards the face of the woman sitting opposite to her; a shapeless body, a thin ravaged face strained and sheeny with fatigue and wearing an expression of undaunted sweetness and patience. Children and housework and a selfish husband and nothing in life of her own. She was at the disposal of every one for kind actions. She would be *really* sympathetic and shocked about an earthquake in China. Was that it? Was that being *inside*? Was that all there was? The woman did not see the wonderful gold-brown light in the carriage; nor the beauty of the blackness outside. In her brain was the pain and pressure of everything she had to do. She was good and sweet; perfectly good and sweet. But there was something irritating about her. Her obliviousness of everything but 'troubles,' other people's as much as her own. Yet she would love a day in the country. The fields and the flowers would make her cry. It was her obliviousness that made one afraid of associating with her. Being in conversation with her or in any way associated with her life, there would always be the dreadful imprisoned feeling of knowing she did not *think*. . . . Her glance slid over the other seated forms and fell, leaving her struggling between her desire to feel in loving union with them and her inability to ignore the revelations pouring from their bearing and shapes, their clothes and the way they held their belongings. They were terrible and hateful because all their thoughts were visible. The terrible maddening thing about them was the thoughts they did not think. It made them worse than the woman, because to get on with them one would have to pretend to see life as they saw it. It would be so easy and deceitful with each one alone, knowing exactly what line to take.

She wrenched herself back to her prayer. Instantly the thought came that all these people far away in themselves wanted to be more loving. She drew herself together and sat up staring out towards the darkness. That was an answer again! A state of mind that came from the state of prayer. But then one would need always to be in a state of prayer. It would be very difficult. It would be almost impossible even to remember it in the rush of life. It would mean being a sort of fool, without judgments or opinions. It would *spoil* everything. There would be no time for anything. Nothing beyond one's daily work and all the rest of the time being all things to all men. It meant that now at this moment one must give up the sense of the train going along in the darkness and the sense of the dark streets waiting lamplit under the dark sky and go out to the people in the carriage and then on to the people at Tansley Street. She thought of people she knew who did this, appearing to see nothing in life but people, and recoiled. *Places* to them were nothing but people; there was something they missed out that could not be given up. Something goes if you lose yourself in humanity. You cannot find humanity by looking for God only there. Making up your mind that God is to be found only in humanity is humanism. It was Comte's idea. Perhaps Unitarians are all Comtists. That is why they dress without style. They are more interested in social reform than the astoundingness of there being people *anywhere*. But to see God everywhere is pantheism. What *is* Christianity? Where are Christians? Evangelicals are humanitarians; rushing about in ulsters. Anglicans know all about the beauty of life and like comfort. But they are snobs and afraid of new ideas. Convents and monasteries stop your mind. But there is a God or a Christ, there is something always there to answer when you turn away to it from everything. Perhaps one would have to remain silent, for years, for a lifetime, and in the end begin to understand.

At Gower Street it was eleven o'clock. She was faint with hunger. She had had no dinner and there was nothing in her room. She wandered along the Euston Road hoping to meet a potato-man. The shop-fronts were black. There was nothing to meet her need but the empty stretch of lamplit pavement leading on and on. Rapid walking in the rain-freshened air relieved her faintness, but she dreaded waking in the night with gnawing hunger to keep her awake and drag her up exhausted in the morning. A faint square of brighter light on the pavement ahead came like an accusation. Passing swiftly across it she glanced bitterly at the frosted door through which

it came. Restaurant. Donizetti Brothers. The whole world
had conspired to leave her alone with that mystery, shut in and
hidden every day the whole of her London time behind its
closed frosted doors and forcing her now to admit that there
was food there and that she must go in or have the knowledge
of being starved through fear.   Her thoughts flashed painfully
across a frosted door long ago in Baker Street, and she saw the
angry handsome face of the waiter who had shouted 'Roll and
butter' and whisked away from the table the twisted cone of
serviette and the knives and forks.   That was in the middle of
the day. It would be worse at night. Perhaps they would
even refuse to serve her. Perhaps it was impossible to go into
a restaurant late at night alone. She was coming back.   There
was nothing to be seen behind the steamy panes on either side
of the door but plants standing on oil-cloth mats. Behind them
was again frosted glass. It was not so grand as Baker Street.
There was no menu in a large brass frame with 'Schweppe's'
at the top. She pushed open the glass door and was confronted by another glass door blankly frosted all over. Why
were they so secret ? Inside the second door, she found herself
at the beginning of a long aisle of linoleum. On either side
people were dotted here and there on short velvet sofa seats
behind marble-topped tables. In the close air there was a
strong smell made up of all kinds of meat dishes. A waiter
flicking the crumbs from a table glanced sharply round at her
and went off down the room. He had seen the shifts and
miseries that haunted all her doings. They were apparent in
the very hang of her cloak. She could not first swing down the
restaurant making it wave for joy, as it did when she walked
across Trafalgar Square in the dark, and then order a roll and
butter. After this it would never wave for joy again. A short
compact bald man in a white apron was hurrying down the
aisle, towards *her*. He stopped just in front of her and stood
bowing and indicating a near empty table with his short arm,
and stood silently hovering while she dragged herself into place
on the velvet sofa. The waiter rushing up with a menu was
gently waved away and the little man stood over the side of
the table, blocking out the fuller end of the restaurant. Hardly

able to speak for the beating of her heart, she looked up into a little firm round pallid face with a small snub nose and curious pale waxy blue eyes and said furiously, 'Oh, please, just a roll and butter and a cup of cocoa.'

The little man bowed low with a beaming face and went gently away. Miriam watched him go down the aisle, bowing here and there right and left. The hovering waiter came forward questioningly to meet him and was again waved aside and she presently saw the little man at a speaking-tube and heard him sing in a soft smooth high monotone, 'Un-sho-co-lat.' He brought her things and arranged them carefully about her and brought her an *Illustrated London News* from another table. She sipped and munched and looked at all the pictures. The people in the pictures were real people. She imagined them moving and talking in all manner of circumstances and suffered their characteristics gently, feeling as if someone were there, gently, half-reproachfully holding her hands tied behind her back. The waiter roamed up and down the aisle. People came in, sometimes two or three at a time. The little man was sitting writing with a stern bent face at a little table at the far end of the restaurant in front of a marble counter holding huge urns and glass dishes piled with buns and slices of cake. He did not move again until she rose to go, when he came once more hurrying down the aisle. Her bill was sixpence and he took the coin with a bow and waited while she extricated herself from the clinging velvet, and held the door wide for her to pass out.

'Good evening, thank you very much,' she murmured, hoping that he heard, in response to his polite farewell. She wandered slowly home through the drizzling rain warmed and fed and with a glow at her heart. Inside those frightful frosted doors was a home, a bit of her own London home.

The hall gas was out. The dining-room door stood ajar showing a faint light, and light was coming from the little room at the end of the passage. Miriam cautiously pushed open the dining-room door. Mrs Bailey was sitting alone poised socially in a low arm-chair by the fire with the gas turned low. Miriam came dutifully forward in response to the entrancement of her smile and stood on the hearthrug enwrapped in her evening, invaded by the sense of beginning it anew with Mrs Bailey. When had she seen Mrs Bailey last? She could tell her now about Eve in great confidential detail and explain that she could not *at present* afford to come to Tansley Street. That would be a great sociable conversation and the engagement with Mr Bowdoin would remain untouched. She stood in a glow of eloquence. Mrs Bailey preened and bridled and made little cheerful affectionate remarks and waited silent a moment before asking if it rained. Miriam forgot Eve and gathered herself together for some tremendous communication. Was it raining? She glanced at the outside London world and was lost in inter-changing scenes, her mind split up, pressing several ways at once. Mrs Bailey saw all these scenes and felt and understood them exactly as she did. There was no need to answer the question. She glanced stonily towards her and saw the down-cast held-in embarrassment of her waiting form. In a dry professional official voice she said, gazing at the hearthrug with an air of judicial profundity, '*No*, at least, oh yes, I *think* it is raining,' and drifted helplessly towards the window. The challenge was behind her. She would have to face it again. A borrowed voice said briskly within her, Yes, it's pouring, I *hope* it will be fine to-morrow, what *weather* we have had; well, *good* night, Mrs Bailey. I have been to a lecture, she said in imagination, standing by the window. It was what any other boarder would have said and then, 'So fine, such a splendid lecturer,' and told the subject and his name and one idea out of the lecture, and they would have agreed and gone cheerfully to bed, with no thoughts. To try and really tell anything about the lecture would be to plunge down into misrepresenta-tions and misunderstandings and end with the lecture vanished. To say anything real about it would lead to living the rest of her life with the Baileys helping them with their plans. She turned and came busily back.

'It's very late,' she murmured. Mrs Bailey smiled and

yawned. 'At least not so very late, not quite to-morrow,' she
pursued, turning round to the clock and back again to consult
the pictures and the wall paper. Just staying there was answering Mrs Bailey's question. Suddenly she laughed out and
turned, laughing, as if she were about to communicate some
mirthful memory. 'It 's too *absurd*,' she said, distracted
between the joy of her lingering laughter and the need for
instantly inventing an explanation. Mrs Bailey was laughing
delightedly. 'There was a most absurd thing,' chanted Miriam
above her laughter; a gentle tap took Mrs Bailey scurrying to
the door.

'May I have a *candle*, Mrs Bailey?' murmured a low voice
in a curious solidly curving intonation.

'Certainly, doctor,' answered Mrs Bailey's voice in the hall.
She scurried away downstairs.

Miriam turned towards the window and stood listening to
St Pancras clock striking midnight. Then those men in the
little back sitting-room were *doctors*. How pleased and proud
Mrs Bailey must be. How wonderful of her to say nothing
about them. Can I have a *candle*, missuz Bailey? Wrapped
away in the suave strong courteous voice were the knowledge
and the fineness of a world no one in the house knew anything
about. Mrs Bailey dimly knew, and screened it, fearing to lose
it. She had the wonderful voice all to herself.

'Good evening.' The voice was in the *room*. Miriam
turned instantly; a square strong-looking man a little over
middle height with flat pale fair hair smooth on a squarish
head above grave, bluntly moulded features was moving easily
forward from the door. They met at the end of the table,
standing one each side the angle of the fireside corner, smiling
as if her murmured response to his greeting had been a speech
in a play ready-made to bring them together. Miriam felt
that if she had said, 'Oh I 'm so glad,' he would have responded,
'Yes, so am I.'

'My name 's von Heber,' he announced quietly, his restrained, uncontrollably deepening smile sending out a radiance
all round her. It was as if they had met before without the
opportunity of speaking, and here, at last, was the opportunity

and they had first to smile out their recognition of its perfection.
They stood in a radiant silence, his even tones making no break
in their interchange. She felt a quality in him she had not
met before. In the ease of his manner there was no trace of
the complacent assumption of the man of the world. His
deference was no mask worn to decorate himself. It was
deliberate and yet genuine. It was the shape in which he
presented to her, personally, set above and away from her
ugly clothes and her weariness, the beam of delight which had
been his inward greeting. The completeness and confidence
of his delight, his own completeness and security, revealed to
her an unknown reading of life that she longed to hold and
fathom. She offered in return, as a measure of her qualifi-
cation, the laughter she had laughed to Mrs Bailey, hoping he
had heard it.

'I find this custom of putting down the light at eleven very
inconvenient,' he was saying. Miriam smiled and listened
eagerly for more of the low, even, curiously curving intonations.
'I propose to take the London medical examination in July,
and I've a good deal of hard work to get through prior to
that date.'

He had not been going to stop speaking, but Miriam found
an immense welcoming space for the word she summoned in
vain desperately from far-away Wimpole Street.

'The *con*joint,' she declared at last eagerly, almost before
the word reached her consciousness.

'The conjoint,' he repeated and, as his voice went on, Miriam
contemplated the accumulation they had gathered. She stood
smiling, growing familiar with the quality of his voice, gathering the sense of a word here and there. Through his talk, he
smiled a quizzical pleased appreciation of this way of listening.
She felt as if they were talking backwards, towards something
already said and, when she took in 'I'm taking the post-
graduate *course* at your great hospital near here,' she tried in
vain to resist the temptation of leading his talk down into detail.
The way to preserve the charm unbroken would be to let him
go on talking. She might even listen carefully, and learn the
meaning of the post-graduate course and its place in the

London medical world; the whole of the London medical world was being transformed by this man into something simple and joyful. But the eager words had escaped her. 'Oh; that's the one with the glorious yarn.'

'Tell me the yarn,' he chuckled gently, showing a row of strong squarish flawless teeth.

'Well,' she said, 'the big surgeons were operating and the patient was collapsing and one said, "I think it is time we called in Divine aid." "Nonsense," said the other, "I don't believe in unqualified assistants."'

'That's great,' he declared; 'that's one of the greatest yarns I've heard. I shan't forget it.'

He was not shocked and she had told the story as evenly and as much without emphasis as he would have done himself. She suddenly realized that this was the way to say things. It made no pause and did not disturb anything. She was learning from him every moment. He was *utterly* different from the men she knew. He did not resent her possession of the story nor attempt to cap it.

'You've got some very great men over here,' he said; 'some of the very greatest'; and he began outlining the Canadian reputation of names that were amongst the pinnacles of Wimpole Street conversation. She learned exactly why Victor Horsley was great in the world, and what it was that Dr Barker did to fractured knee-caps. When Mrs Bailey came up it was half-past twelve. He accepted his candle and thanked her gravely and gravely took his leave. Miriam and Mrs Bailey were left confronted. Miriam laughed a social laugh, unintentionally, and listened happily to Mrs Bailey's kind brisk echo of it as she stood turning out the gas. They turned to each other in the hall and laughed good night. Mrs Bailey was like a happy excited girl. She trotted busily and socially downstairs humming a tune towards a sociable waiting world, flouting difficulties with the sweep of the laughter in her voice.

Your Barker and your Horsley, mused Miriam slackening her speed on the stairs; the sound of the low quiet glad confident voice steadying the aspect of the world, and a strange new sense of the London medical world dotted by men who were world-famous, approached from afar, reverently, for specialist training, by already qualified medical men, competed together within her as she prepared for bed, going serenely through all the tiresome little processes. Something in the centre of life had steadied and clarified.   It sent a radiance like sunlight through the endless processes of things; even a ragged tooth-brush was a part of the sunlit scene; not unnoticed, or just dismal, but a part of the sunlit scene.

CHAPTER V

STILL talking, Mr Bowdoin went up the rubbish-strewn steps and opened the dusty blistered door with his latchkey. Miriam followed him into a dark bare passage and down carpetless stairs into a large chilly twilit basement room. Nothing was visible but a long kitchen table lit by a low barred window at the far end of the room.

'I will light a lamp for you in a moment,' he murmured, in his formal cockney monotone; 'my friends will be arriving soon and before they come I should like to show you my sketches.'

Miriam sat down silently. The feeling of the neighbourhood was in the room. A heavy blankness lay over everything. She felt nowhere. It had been difficult to take part in conversation walking along the Farringdon Road. It was strange enough to know that any one lived in a road almost in the City; and paying a visit there was like stepping out of the world.

With his slow even speech Mr Bowdoin rebuked her here even more strongly for her outbreak of excited talk and loud laughter about Devonshire. He had not felt that they were walking along, outside London, in blank space, free, and exactly alike in their thoughts. He had not had that moment when they turned into the strange dead road *east* of Bloomsbury, nowhere, and he had seemed like herself at her side and he ought to have laughed and laughed. His sudden searching look—are you mad or intoxicated, with your sudden Billingsgate manners?—had said that Farringdon Road was in the world and that he intended to conduct himself in the usual manner of a gentleman escorting a lady. As he lit a little lamp on the corner of the table she glanced at the back of his hair and imagined him sitting at a typewriter with it in curl-papers, and determined to be at ease.

'What a jolly room!' she exclaimed as the lamplight wavered up, and then sat looking at her hands. It would be cruel to look about the room. She had seen kitchen chairs standing sparsely about in the spaces unoccupied by the table, a cottage piano standing at right angles to the low window and one picture over the piano. There was nothing else in the room. The floor was covered with strips of coarse worn oilcloth and there was nothing above the empty mantelpiece. 'It is quite Bohemian,' said Mr Bowdoin, lighting the piano candles. 'Let me take your cloak.' Miriam slipped off her golf-cape and he disappeared between curtains at the end of the room opposite the window.

This was Bohemia! She glanced about. It was the explanation of the room. But it was impossible to imagine Trilby's milk-call sounding at the door. It was Bohemia; the table and chairs were *Bohemian*. Perhaps a big room like this would be even cheaper than a garret in St Pancras. The neighbourhood did not matter. A Bohemian room could hold its own anywhere. No furniture but chairs and a table, saying, when you brought people in, 'I am a Bohemian,' and having no one but Bohemians for friends. There must be a special way of behaving in English Bohemia. Perhaps when the friends came she would find it out.

'I have the sketches in a drawer here,' said Mr Bowdoin, coming back through the curtains and turning up an end of the tablecloth. . . .

Ah! C'est le pied de Trilby. Wee. D'après nature? Nong. De mémoire, alors? . . . où rien ne troublera Trilby, qui dorrr-mira, thought Miriam. She took the little water-colour sketches one by one and listened carefully to Mr Bowdoin's descriptions of the subjects, trying to think of something to say. It was wonderful that he should take so much trouble on a holiday. The words in his descriptions brought Devonshire scenes alive into her mind, and she could imagine how he felt as he looked at them. *Plats d'épinards*. It was like the difference between the French and English Bohemia. But the true thing in it was that he had wanted to do them. That gave him his right to call himself a Bohemian. He would have tried to write if he wanted to and have gone to live in a garret in Fleet Street.

'Why don't you put them about the room?' she asked insincerely. It was false and cruel; a criticism of the room which was beginning to show its real character; not interfering; plain and clear for things to happen and shine out in their full strength. And it was a flattery of the pictures, which were nothing.

'Well, they 're just beginnings. Hardly worthy of exhibition. I hope to attain to something better in the future.'

Where did he find all his calm words and self-confidence. Perhaps it was the result of having a room to invite friends to and talk about things in. But how could anybody do anything with people coming and going, confusing everything by perpetually *saying* things? She stared obediently at sketch after sketch until her eyes ached. It was going on too long. Her strength was ebbing out and the evening was still to come. He liked showing his sketches and thought she was entertained. Even in Bohemia people thought it was necessary always to be doing some definite thing.

There was a knocking at the front door upstairs. Mr Bowdoin went quickly up and came down with a tall lady. He introduced her and she bowed and at once took off her outdoor things. While he was putting them away behind the curtains she sat briskly down on a chair at the far end of the room in a line with Miriam and arranged her hair and her dress with easy unconcerned movements. She did not look in the least Bohemian. She sat drawn up in her chair very tall and thin in a clumsy dress with a high stiff collar-band. Her head and hair above her thin dingy neck were — common. Undoubtedly. She looked like a post-office young lady. She was quite old, twenty-seven or twenty-eight. While the other people came in she sat very still and self-possessed, as if nothing were happening. Was that dignity? Not attempting to hide your peculiarities and defects, but just keeping perfectly still and calm whatever happened? There were two men and another woman. They stood about in the gloom near the door while Mr Bowdoin carried away their things and came back and murmured 'Miss Rogers' and 'Miss Henderson,' and then sat down in a row on the kitchen chairs in line near the piano. Their faces were above the reach of the lamplight. Their bodies had the subdued manner of the less important sitters in a parish church. Mr Bowdoin was putting the little lamp on the top of the piano. The light ran up the wall. The picture was a large portrait of Paderewski. It was amongst Miriam's records of Queen's Hall posters, coming and going amongst other posters of musicians, passed by with a hurried glance, soon obliterated by the oncoming of the blazing flower-baskets as she hurried down Langham Place, sore with her effort to forget the reminders of music beyond her reach. Looking at it now, she felt as if all she had missed were suddenly brought to her; her sense of thwarting and loss was swept away. She sat up relieved, bathed in sunshine. The room was full of life and warmth and golden light. She eagerly searched the features until Mr Bowdoin took the lamp off the piano and sat down, murmuring, 'I will give you a sonata of Bytoven.' The outline of the face shone down through the gloom. She could recall each feature in perfect distinctness. All the soft weakness of the musical temperament was there, the thing that made people call musicians a soft weak lot. But there was something else; perhaps it was in all musicians who were such great executants as to be almost composers. The curious conscious half-pleading sensitive weakness of the mouth and chin were dreadful; a sort of nakedness, as if a whole weak nature were escaping there for every one to see; and then suddenly reined in; held in and back by the pose of the reined-in head. The great aureole of fluffily hair was shaped and held in shape by the same power. The whole head, soft and weak in all its details, was resolute and strong. If the face were raised to look outwards it would be weak, pained and suffering and almost querulously sorrowful; but in its own right pose it was happy and strong. The pose of the head gave it its grip on the features and the hair and made *beauty*. The pose of *listening*. The eyes saw nothing. The reined-in face was listening, intently, from a burning bush. There was some reason not yet understood why musicians and artists wore long hair.

The long sonata came to an end while Miriam was still revolving amongst her thoughts. When Mr Bowdoin sat back from the piano she returned to the point where she had begun and determined to stop her halting circular progress from group to group of interesting reflections, and to listen to the next thing he might play. She was aware he was playing on his own piano better than he had done at Tansley Street, but also more carefully and less self-forgetfully. Perhaps that was why she had not listened. She could not remember ever before having definite thoughts, while music was going on, and felt afraid lest she were ceasing to care for music. She found it would be quite easy to speak coolly, with an assumption of great appreciation and ask him to play some definite thing. Just as she was about to break into the silence with a remark, one of the big curtains was suddenly drawn aside by a little old lady bearing a tray of steaming cups. She stood just inside the curtains, her delicate white-haired lace-capped head bowing from side to side of the room graciously, a gentle keen smile on her delicately shrivelled face. 'My mother,' murmured Mr Bowdoin as he went down the room for the tray. Slender and short as he was, she was invisible behind him as he bent for the tray and when he turned with it to the room she had disappeared.

Miriam gazed at the dark curtains hoping for her return and dreading it. Nothing suitable to an enthusiastic Bohemian evening could be said in a courtly manner. . . . She accepted a cup of coffee without a word as if Mr Bowdoin had been a waiter, and sat flaring over it. She felt as if nothing could be said until there had been some reference to the vision. She hoped every one had bowed and remembered with shame that she had only stared. Every one seemed to be stirring; but the beginnings of speech went forward as if the little old lady had never appeared. Mr Bowdoin had sat down with the men on the other side of the room and the woman had crossed over to a chair near Miss Rogers and was in eager conversation with her. Miss Rogers has only lately joined musical circles, she heard Mr Bowdoin say in an affectionate indulgent tone. That accounted for the way she deferred to him and sat in a sort of complacent exclusive rapture, keeping her manner unchanged before the onslaught of the eagerly talking woman. The woman was in the circle and did not seem to think it strange that Miss Rogers should be a candidate. She was talking about some orchestra somewhere, of something she wanted to play; '*he* conducting,' she finished in a tone of worship. Her voice was refined and she talked easily, but she also had the common uneducated look, and she was talking about Camberwell. Mr Bowdoin was a conductor of an orchestra. Those people played in orchestras, or wanted to. The three men were talking in eager happy sentences and laughing happily and not noisily. There was something here that was lacking in Miss Szigmondy's prosperous musical people, something that kept them apart from the world where they made their living. They worked hard in two worlds.

When Mr Bowdoin was at the piano again they all sat easy and at home, in easy attitudes, affectionately listening. The room seemed somehow less dark and their forms much more visible and bigger. The empty white coffee cups standing about on the table caught the light. Miriam's stood alone at the end of the table. Mr Bowdoin had taken it from her but without entering into conversation, and she was left with her prepared remark about the piano and her plea for a performance of the *Tannhäuser* overture going unsaid round and round in her mind. She sat ashamed before the restrained impersonal enthusiasm that filled the room. Even Miss Rogers was sitting less stiffly. Her own stiffness must make it obvious that she was not in a musical circle. Musical circles had a worldly *savoir-faire* of their own, the thing that was to be found everywhere in the world. To be in one would mean having to talk like that eager worshipping woman or to be calm and easily supercilious and secret like Miss Rogers. Even here, the men were apart from the women; to join the men would be easy enough, to say exactly what one thought and talk about all sorts of things and laugh. But the women would hate that and one would have to be intimate with the women, and rave about music and musicians. Mr Bowdoin had probably thought she would talk to those women. But after talking to them how could one listen to music? Their very presence made it almost impossible. She was unable to lose herself in the Wagner overture. It sounded out thinly into the room. Paderewski was looking away to where there was nothing but music sounding in a wooden room just inside an immense forest somewhere in Europe. She began thinking secretly of the world waiting for her outside and felt that she was affronting every one in the room; treacherously and not visibly as before. She had got away from them but they did not know it. Mr Bowdoin passed from the overture, which was vociferously applauded, and went on and on till she ceased altogether to try to listen and he became a stranger, sitting there playing seriously and laboriously alone at his piano. She wished he would play a waltz, and suddenly blushed to find herself sitting there at all.

They all seemed to get up to go at the same moment and when they drifted out into the street seemed all to be going the same way. Miriam found herself walking along the Farringdon Road between Mr Bowdoin and the shorter of the two other men, longing for solitude and to be free to wander slowly along the new addition to her map of London at night. Even with Bohemians evenings did not end when they ended, but led to the forced companionship of walking home. The tall man and the two women were marching along ahead at a tremendous pace and she was obliged to hasten her steps to keep up with her companions' evident intention of keeping them in view. Perhaps at the top of the road they would all separate.

'We will escort Miss Henderson to her home and then I'll come on with you to Highgate.'

'To *Highgate*!' exclaimed Miriam, almost stopping. 'Are you going to walk to Highgate *to-night*?'

They both laughed.

'Oh, yes,' said Mr Bowdoin,' that's nothing.'

Highgate. The mere thought of its northern remoteness seemed to be an insult to London. No wonder she had found herself a stranger with these people. Walking out to Highgate at night and getting up as usual the next morning. Magnificent trong hard thing to do. Horrible. Walking out to Highgate, talking all the time' . . . they could never have a moment to realize anything at all; rushing along saying things that covered everything and never stopping to realize. Talking *about* people and things and never being or knowing anything, and perpetually coming to the blank emptiness of *Highgate*. Their unconsciousness of everything made them the right sort of people to have the trouble of living in Highgate. They probably walked about with knapsacks on Sunday. But to them even the real country could not be country. All 'circles' must be like that in some way; doing things by agreement. The men talking confidently about them, *completely* ignorant of any sort of reality. She came out of her musings when they turned into the Euston Road and ironically watched the men keeping up their talk across the continual breaking up of the group by passing pedestrians.

'*You*'ll have to walk *back*,' she interrupted, suddenly turning to Mr Bowdoin; 'the buses will have stopped.'

'I never ride in omnibuses,' frowned Mr Bowdoin. 'I shall be back by two.'

Miriam waited a moment inside the door at Tansley Street listening for silence. The evening fell away from her with the departing footsteps of the two men. She opened the door upon the high quiet empty blue-lit street and moved out into a tranquil immensity. It was everywhere. Into her consciousness of the unpredictable incidents of to-morrow's Wimpole Street day, over the sure excitement of Eve's arrival in the evening, flowed the light-footed leaping sense of a day new begun, an inexhaustible blissfulness, everything melted away into it. It seemed to smite her, calling for some spoken acknowledgment of its presence, alive and real in the heart of the London darkness. It was not her fault that Eve was not coming to stay at Tansley Street. It came out of the way life arranged itself as long as you did not try to interfere. Roaming along in the twilight she lost consciousness of everything but the passage of dark silent buildings, the drawing away under her feet of the varying flags of the pavement, the waxing and waning along the pavement of the streams of lamp-light, the distant murmuring tide of sound passing through her from wide thoroughfares, the gradual approach of a thoroughfare, the rising of the murmuring tide to a happy symphony of recognizable noises, the sudden glare of yellow shop-light under her feet, the wide black road, the joy of the need for the understanding sweeping glance from right to left as she moved across it, the sense of being swept across in an easy curve drawn by the kindly calculable swing of the traffic, of being a permitted co-operating part of the traffic, the coming of the friendly kerb and the strip of yellow pavement, carrying her on again.

CHAPTER VI

MIRIAM came forward seeing nothing but the golden gaslight pouring over the white table-cloth. She sat down near Mrs Bailey within the edge of its radiance. The depths of the light still held unchanged the welcome that had been there when she had come in and found Émile laying the table. There was no change and no disappointment. The smeary mirrors and unpolished furniture were bright in the gaslight, showing distances of interior and gleaming passages of light. In the spaces between the pictures the walls sent back sheeny reflections of the glow on the table. People coming in one by one saying good evening in different intonations and sitting down sending out waves of inquiry, left her undisturbed. There were five or six forms about the table, besides Sissie sitting at the far end opposite her mother. They made sudden statements about the weather one after the other. They were waiting to have their daily experience of the meal changed by something she might do or say. Émile was handing round plates of soup. Presently they would all be talking and would have forgotten her. Then she could see them all one by one and get away unseen, having had dinner only with Mrs Bailey. Mrs Bailey was standing up carving the joint. When the sounds she made were all that was to be heard, she responded to the last remark about the weather or asked some fresh question about it as if no one had spoken at all. When she was not speaking, every movement of her battle with the joint expressed her triumphant affectionate sense of Miriam's presence. She had made no introductions. She was saying secretly, There you are, young lady. I told you so. Now you 're in your right place. It 's quite easy, you see. The joint was already partly distributed. Émile was handing *three* piled dishes of vegetables. A generous plateful of well-browned meat and gravy appeared before

Miriam with Mrs Bailey's strong small toil-disfigured hand firmly grasping its edge.   She took it to pass it on.

'That's yorce, my child,' said Mrs Bailey.   The low murmur was audible round the silent table.

Asserting her independence with a sullen formality, Miriam thanked her and looked about for condiments without raising her eyes to the range of those other eyes, all taking photographs now that she was forced into movement.   Mrs Bailey placed a cruet near her plate.   'Yorce,' she pondered, getting angrily away into thought.   Mrs Bailey *could* not know that it might be said to be more correct than 'yourz.'   It was an affectation. She had picked it up somewhere from one of those people who carefully say 'off-ten' instead of 'awfen' and it gave her satisfaction to use it, linked rebukingly up with the complacent motherly patronage of which she had boasted to the whole table.   The first of Émile's dishes appeared over her left shoulder and she saw, as she turned unprepared, raised heads turned towards her end of the table.   She scooped her vegetables quickly out of the dishes.   In her awkward movements and her unprotected raised face she felt, and felt all the observers seeing, the marks of her disgrace.   They saw her looking like Eve nervously helping herself to vegetables in the horrible stony cold dark restaurant of the hostel.   They saw that she resented Mrs Bailey's public familiarity and could do nothing. She tried to look bored and murmured 'Thank you' when she had taken her third vegetable.   It sounded out like a proclamation in the intense silence and she turned angrily to her plate trying to remember whether she had heard any one else thank Émile for vegetables.

After all, she was paying for the meal and her politeness to Émile was her own affair.   Abroad people bowed or raised their hats going in and out of shops and said 'Monsieur' to policemen.   Her efforts to eat abstractedly and to appear plunged in thought made her feel more and more like a poor relation.   The details of her meeting with Eve kept appearing in and out of her attempt to get back her sense of Mrs Bailey's house as a secret warmth and brightness added to the many resources of her life.   Mrs Bailey knew that her house had been

transformed by the meeting with Eve, and was trying to tell
her that she was not as independent as she thought.

What were the exact things she had told Mrs Bailey? She
had talked excitedly and scrappily and all the time Mrs Bailey
had been gathering information and drawing her own conclusions
about the Hendersons. Mrs Bailey saw Eve's arrival at the
station and her weary resentment of having everything done for
her in the London manner, her revenge in the cab, sitting back
and making the little abstracted patronizing sounds in response
to everything that was said to her, taking no interest, and at last
saying, '*How* you run on.'   She saw something of the hostel.

'Where's Mr Mendizzable?' demanded Sissie.

The Girls' Friendly; that was the name of that other thing.
But that was for servants. The Young Women's Bible Association was the worst disgrace that could happen to a gentlewoman. Eve had liked it. She had suddenly begun going
about with an interested revived face eagerly doing what she
was told. She was there now, it was her only home, and she
must have all her meals there for cheapness; there would be no
outside life for her. Her life was imprisoned by those women,
consciously goody conscientious servants with flat caps, domi-
nating everything, revelling in the goody atmosphere; the
young women in the sitting-room all looking *raw*, as if they
washed very early in the morning in cold water and did their
shabby hair with cold hands; the superintendent, the watchful
official expression on her large well-fed elderly high-school-girl
face, the *way* she sat on a footstool with her arms round her
knees pretending to be easy and jolly, while she recited that
it was a privilege and a joy for sisters to be so near to each other,
as if she were daring us to deny it. I shan't see very much of
Eve. She won't want me to. She will strike up a friendship
with one of those young women.

Miriam found herself glancing up the table towards the
centre of a conflict. They were all joined in conflict over some
common theme. No one was outside it; the whole table was
in an uproar of voices and laughter. It was nothing but
Miss Scott saying things about Mr Mendizabal and every one
watching and throwing in remarks. Miss Scott was neighing

across the table at something that had been said and was preparing to speak again without breaking into her laughter. All faces were turned her way.

'What's that Mr Joe-anzen says?' laughed Mrs Bailey towards the last speaker. The invisible man opposite Miss Scott was not even Mr Helsing; only the younger fainter Norwegian, and this side of him an *extraordinary* person . . . an abruptly bulging coarse fringe, a coarse-grained cheek bulging from under an almost invisible deep-sunken eye, and abruptly shelving bust under a coarse serge bodice.

'Mr Yo-hanson says Mr Mendy-zahble likes n-gaiety.' Miriam glanced across the table. That was *all*. That little man with an adenoid voice and a narrow sniggering laugh that brought a flush and red spots all over his face, and shiny straight Sunday-school hair watered and brushed flat, made up the party. Next to him was only Polly. Then came Miss Scott on Sissie's left; then Sissie and round the corner the Norwegian. Every one looked dreadful in the harsh light, secret and secretly hostile to every one else, unwilling to be there; and even here, though there was nothing and no one, there was that everlasting conversational fussing and competition.

'Quite right,' hooted the bulky woman in a high pure girlish voice, 'I doan blame 'im.'

Miriam turned towards the unexpectedness of her voice and sat helplessly observing. The serge sleeves were too short to cover her heavy red wrists; her pudgy hands held her knife and fork broadside, like salad servers. Her hair was combed flatly up over her large skull and twisted into a tiny screw at the top just behind the bulge of her fringe. Could she possibly be a boarder? She looked of far less consequence even than the Baileys. Her whole person was unconsciously ill at ease, making one feel ashamed.

'Mrs m-Barrow is another of 'em,' said the little man with his eyebrows raised as he sniggered out the words.

'I *am*, Mr Gunna, I doan believe in goan abate with a face like a fiddle.'

Mr Gunner's laughter flung back his head and sat him upright and brought him back to lean over his plate shaking noiselessly with his head sunk sideways between his raised shoulders as if he were dodging a blow. The eyes he turned maliciously towards Mrs Barrow were a hard opaque pale blue. His lips turned outwards as he ate and his knife and fork had an upward tilt when at rest. Some of his spots were along the margin of his lips, altering their shape and making them look angry and sore. The eating part of his face was sullen and angry, not touched by the laughter that drew his eyebrows up and wrinkled his bent forehead and sounded only as a little click in his throat at each breath.

'There's plenty of glum folks abate,' scolded Mrs Barrow.

Miriam was aware that she was recoiling visibly, and tried to fix her attention on her meal. Mrs Bailey was carving large second helpings and Émile's vegetable dishes had been refilled. None of these people thought it extraordinary that there should be all this good meal and a waiter, every day.

It would be shameful to come again for the sake of the meal, feeling hostile. Besides, it would soon be unendurable; they would be aware of criticisms and would resent them. The only way to be able to come would be to pretend to laugh at remarks about people and join in discussions on opinions about cheerfulness and seriousness and winter and summer. They would not know that one was not sincere. They were perfectly sincere in their laughter and talk. They all had some sort of common understanding, even when they disagreed. It was the same everlasting problem again, the way people took every-thing for granted. They would be pleased, would turn and like one if one could say heartily, '*Isn't* he a funny little man, mts, my *word*,' or 'Well, I don't see anything particularly funny about him,' or '*Oh*, give me the *summer*.' But if one did that one would presently be worn and strained with lying, left with an empty excitement, while they went serenely on their way, and the reality that was there when one first sat down with them would have gone. Always and always in the end there was nothing but to be alone. And yet it needed people in the world to make the reality when one was alone. Perhaps just these uninterfering people, when one had forgotten their personal peculiarities and had only the consciousness of them in the distance. One might perhaps then wonder sometimes

longingly what they were saying about the weather. But to
be *obliged* to meet them daily—— She chided herself for the
scathing glance she threw at the unconscious guests. Gunner
was smiling sideways down the table again, prepared to execute
his laugh when he should have caught an eye and sent his grin
home. Miriam almost prayed that nothing should provoke
him again to speech. During a short silence she cleared her
throat elaborately to cover the sound of his eating. Several
voices broke out together, but Mrs Bailey was suddenly saying
something privately to her. She raised her head towards the
bright promise and was aware of Mr Gunner thoughtful and
serene. There was a pleasant intelligence somewhere about
his forehead. If only she could think his head clear and cool
and not have to hear again the hot dull hollow resonance of his
voice, how joyfully she would be listening to Mrs Bailey. 'I 've
got a very special message for you, young lady,' she had said
and now went on with her eye on the conflict at the end of
the table into which Mr Gunner was throwing comments and
exclamations from afar. The room beamed softly in its golden
light. From the heart of the golden light Mrs Bailey was
hurrying towards her with good tidings.

'*Hah !*' . . .

Mrs Bailey looked round, cloaking her vexation in a bridling
smile as Mr Mendizabal came in sturdily beaming. He sat
down amidst the general outcry and Émile busied himself to lay
him a place. He shouted answers to every one, sitting with his
elbows on the table. Putting her elbows on the table, Mrs Bailey
applauded with little outbursts of laughter. She had dropped
the idea of delivering her message. Miriam finished her pudding hurriedly. The din was increasing. No one was aware of
her. Cautiously rising she asked Mrs Bailey to excuse her.

'You go, miss ?' shouted Mr Mendizabal suddenly looking
her way. He looked extraordinary, not himself.

Eve's shop was a West End blaze of flowers. The window
was blocked with flowers in green jars, tied up in large bundles.

In front were gilt baskets of hothouse flowers. Propped in the middle were a large flower anchor and a flower horseshoe, both trimmed with large bows of white satin ribbon—women in white satin evening dresses with trains, bowing from platforms; on either side were tight dance-buttonholes pinned on to heart-shaped velvet mounts.

It was strange to be able to go in. . . . Going in to see an employee was not the right way to go into a West End shop. . . . There *was* Eve; standing badly in a droopy black dress on a bare wet wooden floor. Cut flowers in stone jam-pots, masses of greenery lying on a wet table.

'Hallo, aren't your *feet* wet?' demanded Miriam irritably.

Eve started and turned, looking. She was exhausted and excited, grappling dreamily with abrupt instructions, with a conservatory smell competing with them; trying to become part of a clever arrangement to collect the conservatory smell for sale. She stepped slenderly forward; all her old Eve manner, but determined to guard against disturbance; making sounds without speaking, and the faint shape of a tired smile. She was worn out with the fatigue of trying to make herself into something else, but liking it and determined not to be reminded of other things. Even her hair seemed to be changed. Full of pictures of Eve, gracefully dressed and with piled brown hair, Miriam's eyes passed in fury over the skimpy untidy sham shop-assistant, beginning a failure defensively, *imagining* behind it that she was taking hold of London.

'Won't you catch *cold*?'

'You get used to it,' mouthed Eve nervously, turning her head away and waiting, fumbling a scattered spray of smilax. Eve had always loved smilax. Did it seem the same to her now?

'Fancy *you*,' said Miriam, 'in all this damp.'

They were both miserable, and Eve was not going to put it right. All her strength and interest was for this new thing.

'Do you like it?' said Miriam beginning again.

'Yes, awfully,' flushed Eve, looking as if she were going to cry. It was too late.

'I suppose it's awfully interesting?' asked Miriam formally, opening a conversation with a stranger.

'Mps,' said Eve warmly, 'I simply love it. It makes you frightfully tired at first, but I find I can do things I never dreamed I could. I don't *mind* standing in the wet a bit now. You have to if you 're obliged to.'

Eve was *liking* hardness imposed by other people. *Liking* the prices of her new life. Accepting them without resentment. People would despise and like her for that. Perhaps she would succeed in staying on if her strength did not give way. Her graceful dresses and leisurely brown hair going further and further away.

'Do you *serve*?'

'Ssh. I 'm learning to.' Eve would not look, and wanted her to be gone.

'I 'm free for lunch,' said Miriam snappily, holding to the disappearing glory of her first coming out into London in the middle of a week-day. Eve should have guessed and stopped being anything but Eve being taken out to lunch. 'We could go to an A.B.C.'

'Oh, I can't come *out*,' murmured Eve ignoringly.

Miriam ordered another cup of coffee and went on reading. There was plenty of time. Eve would not appear at Tansley Street until half-past. In looking up at the clock she had become aware of detailed people grouped at tables. She plunged back into Norway, reading on and on. Each line was wonderful; but all in a darkness. Presently on some turned page something would shine out and make a meaning. It went on and on. It seemed to be going towards something. But there was nothing that *any one* could imagine, nothing in life or in the world that could make it clear from the beginning, or bring it to an end. If the man died the author might stop. Finis. But it would not make any difference to anything. She turned the pages backwards, rc-reading passages here and there. She could not remember having read them. Looking forward to portions of the dialogue towards the end of the book she found them familiar; as if she had read them before.

She read them intently. They had more meaning read like that, without knowing to what they were supposed to refer. They were the *same*, read alone in scraps, as the early parts. It was all one book in some way, not through the thoughts, or the story, but something in the author. People who talked about the book probably understood the strange thoughts and the puzzling hinting story that began and came to an end and left everything as it was before. The author did not seem to suggest that you should be sorry. He seemed to know that at the end everything was as before, with the mountains all round. . . . The electric lights flashed out all over the A.B.C. at once. Miriam remained bent low over her book. Only you had been in Norway, in a cottage up amongst the mountains and out in the open. She read a scene at random and another and began again and read the first scene through and then the last. It was all the *same*. You might as well begin at the end. In *Norway*, up among the misty mountains, in farms and cottages looking down on fiords with glorious scenery about them all the time, are people, sitting in the winter by fires and worrying about right and wrong. They *wonder*, but more gravely and clearly than we do. Torrents thunder in their ears and they can see mountains all the time even when they are indoors. Ibsen's *Brand* is about all those worrying things, in magnificent scenery. You are *in* Norway while you read. That is why people read books by geniuses and look far-away when they talk about them. They know they have been somewhere you cannot go without reading the book. *Brand*. You are in the strangeness of Norway—and then there are people saying things that might be said anywhere. But with something going in and out of the words all the time. Ibsen's genius. You can't understand it or see where it is. Each sentence looks so ordinary, making you wonder what it is all about. But taking you somewhere, to stay, forgetting everything, until it is finished. An hour ago Ibsen was just a name people said in a particular way, a difficult wonderful mystery, and *improper*. Why do people say he is improper? He is exactly like every one else, thinking and worrying about the same things. But putting them down in a background that is more real than people or thoughts.

The life in the background is in the people. He does not know this. Why did he write it? A book by a genius is alive. That is why Ibsen is superior to novels; because it is not quite about the people or the thoughts. There is something else; a sort of lively freshness all over even the saddest parts, preventing your feeling sorry for the people. Every one ought to know. It ought to be on the omnibuses and in the menu. All these people fussing about not knowing of Ibsen's *Brand*. A volume, bound in a cover. Alive. Precious. What *is* genius? Something that can take you into Norway in an A.B.C.

She wandered out into Oxford Street. There was a vast fresh gold-lit sky somewhere behind the twilight. Why did Ibsen sit down in Norway and write plays? Why did people say 'Ibsen' as if it were the answer to something? Walking along Oxford Street with a read volume of Ibsen held against you is walking along with something precious between two covers which makes you know you are rich and free. She wandered on and on in an expansion of everything that passed into her mind out and out towards a centre in Norway. She wondered whether Ibsen were still alive. A vast beautiful Norway and a man writing his thoughts in a made-up play. Genius. People go about saying 'Ibsen's *Brand*' as if it were the *answer* to *something*, and Ibsen knows no more than any one else. . . .

She arrived at Tansley Street as from a great distance, suddenly wondering about her relationship with the sound of carts and near footfalls. Mrs Bailey was standing in the doorway seeing someone off. *Eve*. Forgotten.

'I couldn't get here before; I'm *so* sorry.'

Mrs Bailey had disappeared. Eve stepped back into the hall and stood serenely glowing in the half-light.

'Are you going?'

'I must, in a minute.'

Eve was looking sweet; slenderly beautiful and with her crimson-rose bloom; shy and indulgent and unenviously admiring as she had been at home; and Mrs Bailey had been having it all.

'Can't you come upstayers?'

'Not this time; I'll come again some time.'

'Well; you must just tell me; wot you been doing? Talking to Mrs Bailey?'

'Yes.' Eve had been flirting with Mrs Bailey; perhaps talking about religion.

'Isn't she funny?'

'I *like* her, she's perfectly *genuine*, she means what she says and really *likes* people.'

'Yes; I know. Isn't it funny?'

'I don't think it's funny; it's very beautiful and rare.'

'Would you like to be here always?'

'Yes; I could be always with Mrs Bailey.'

'Every day of your life for ever and ever?'

'*Rather*.'

'Yes; I know. And y'know there are all *sorts* of interesting people. I wish you lived here, Eve.' Eve glanced down wisely smiling and moved slenderly towards the door. 'What about Sunday? Couldn't you come round for a long time?'

'No,' breathed Eve restrainingly, 'I'm going to *Sallie's*.' All Eve's plans were people. She moved, painfully, through things, from person to person.

Dr Hurd held the door wide for Miriam to pass out and again his fresh closely-knit worn brick-red face was deeply curved by the ironically chuckling hilarious smile with which he had met the incidents of the 'awful German language.' 'That of the *fatherland*, the happy *fatherland*, nearly *dislocates* my *jaw*,' she could imagine him heartily and badly singing with a group of Canadian students. She smiled back at him without saying anything, rapidly piercing together the world that provoked his inclusive, deeply carved smiles; himself, the marvellous little old country he found himself in as an incident of the business of forcing himself to be a doctor, his luck in securing an accomplished young English lady to prepare him for the struggle with the great medical world of Germany; his triumphant chuckling satisfaction in getting in first before the other fellows with an engagement to take her out. . . . The grandeur of this best bedroom of Mrs Bailey's was nothing to him. The room was just a tent in his wanderings. For the moment he was going to take a young lady to a concert. That was how he saw it. He was a simple boyish red-haired open extension of Dr von Heber. When she found herself out in the large grime and gloom of the twilit landing she realized that he had lifted her far further than Dr von Heber into Canada; he was probably more Canadian. The ancient gloom of the house was nothing to him, he would get nothing of the quality of England in his personal life there, only passing glimpses from statements in books and in the conversation of other people. He did not see her as part of it all in the way Dr von Heber had done, talking at the table that night and wanting to talk to her because she was part of it. He saw her as an accomplished young lady, but a young lady like a Canadian young lady, and a fellow was a fool if he did not arrange to take her out quick before the other fellows. But there was nothing in it but just that triumph. 'I'll get a silk hat before Sunday.' He would prepare for her to go all the way down to the Albert Hall as a young lady being taken to a concert; the Albert Hall on Sunday was brass bands; he thought they were a concert. His world was thin and open; but the swift sunlit decision and freedom of his innocent reception of her in his bedroom lifted the dingy brown house of her long memories into a new background. She was to be fêted, in an assumed character and whether she like it or no. The four strange men in the little back sitting-room were her competing friends, the friends of all nice young ladies. He was the one who had laughed the laugh she had heard in the hall, of course. They never appeared, but somehow they had got to know of her and had their curious baseless set ways of thinking and talking about her. Being doctors and still students they ought to be the most hateful and awful kind of men in relation to women, thinking and believing all the horrors of medical science; the hundred golden rules of gynaecology; if they had been Englishmen they would have gone about making one want to murder them; but they did not; Dr Hurd was studying gyn'kahl'jy, but he did not apply its ugly lies to life; to Canadians, women were people . . . but they were all the *same* people to Dr Hurd.

That evening both Dr Heber and Dr Hurd appeared at dinner. Mrs Bailey tumultuously arranged them opposite each other to her right and left. Miriam could not believe they were going to stay until they sat down. She retreated to the far end of the table, taking her place on Sissie's right hand, separated from Dr von Heber by the thin Norwegian and the protruding bulk of Mrs Barrow. Mr Mendizabal with a pencil and paper at the side of his plate was squarely opposite to her. His *méfiant* sallies to the accompaniment of Sissie's giggles and Miss Strong's rapid sarcastic remarks, made a tumult hiding her silence. She heard nothing of the various conversations sprouting easily all round the table. The doctors were far-off strongholds of serenity, unconscious of their serenity, unconscious of her and of their extraordinary taking of the Baileys and Mr Gunner for granted. . . . Dr von Heber was a silence, broken by small courteously curving remarks. Dr Hurd laughed his leaping delighted laugh in and out of an unmeditated interchange with Mr Gunner and Mrs Bailey. If she had been at their end of the table they would not have perceived her thoughts, but they would have felt her general awareness and got up at last disliking her. They changed the atmosphere, but could not make her forget the underlying unchanged elements nor rid her of her resentment of their unconsciousness of them. There was a long interval before the puddings appeared. Mrs Bailey was trying to answer questions about books. Dr Hurd did not care for reading, but liked to be read to, by his sisters, in the evening, and had come away, at the most exciting part of a book. 'A wonderful authoress, what's her name now? Rosie . . . Newchet.' . . . He was just longing to know how it ended. Was it sweet and wonderful, or too dreadful for anything, to contemplate a student, a fully qualified doctor, having Rosa Nouchette Carey read to him by his sisters? Dr von Heber was not joining in. Did he read novels and like them? No one had anything to say. No one here knew even of Rosa Nouchette Carey. And that man Hunter . . . he's great. He's father's favourite. What's this, *Mr Barnes of New York*?

'Archibald Clavering Gunter,' said Miriam suddenly, longing to be at the other end of the table.

'Beg pardon?' said Sissie, turning aside for a moment from watching Mr Mendizabal's busy pencil.

'There he is,' shouted Mr Mendizabal, flinging out his piece of paper; 'gastric ulcer—there he is.' There was a drawing of a sort of crab with huge claws. 'My beautiful gastric ulcer.'

'Have you been to the ospital to-day, Mr Mendizzable?' asked Mrs Bailey through the general laughter.

'I have been, madame, and I come away. They say they welcome me inside again soon. Je m'en fiche.'

The faces of both doctors were turned inquiringly. Dr Hurd's look of quizzical sympathy passed on towards Miriam and became a mask of suppressed hysterical laughter. Perhaps he and Dr Heber would scream and yell together afterwards and make a great story of a man in a London pension. Dr Hurd would call him a *cure*. 'My word, isn't that chap a *cure*?' Brave little man. Caring for nothing. How could he possibly have a gastric ulcer and look so hard and happy and strong. *What* was Dr von Heber silently thinking?

The doctors disappeared as soon as dinner was over, Dr von Heber gravely rounding the door with some quiet formal phrases of politeness, and the group about the table broke up.

'He's a bit pompous,' Mr Gunner was saying presently to someone from the hearthrug. Was he daring to speak of Dr von Heber?

Presently there were only the women left in the room. Miriam felt unable to depart and hung about until the table was cleared and sat down under the gas protected by her notebook. The room was very quiet. Sissie and Mrs Bailey were mending near a lamp at the far end of the table. Miriam's thoughts left her suddenly. The tide of life had swept away, leaving an undisturbed stillness, a space swept clear. She was empty and nothing. In all the clamour that had passed she had no part. In all the noise that lay ahead, no part. Strong people came and went and never ceased, coming and going and acting ceaselessly, coming and going, and here, at her centre, was nothing, lifeless thoughtless nothingness. The four men studied apart in the little room, away from the empty lifeless nothingness.

The door opened quietly. Mrs Bailey and Sissie looked expectantly up and were silent. Something had come into the room. Something real, clearing away the tumult and compelling peaceful silence. She exerted all her force to remain still and apparently engrossed, as Dr von Heber placed an open notebook and a large volume on the table exactly opposite to where she sat and sat down. He did not see that she was astonished at his coming, nor her still deeper astonishment in the discovery of her unconscious certainty that he would come. A haunting familiar sense of unreality possessed her. Once more she was part of a novel; it was right, true like a book, for Dr Heber to come in in defiance of every one, bringing his studies into the public room in order to sit down quietly opposite this fair young English girl. He saw her apparently gravely studious, and felt he could 'pursue his own studies' all the better for her presence. She began writing at random, assuming as far as possible the characteristics he was reading into her appearance. If only it were true; but there was not in the whole world the thing he thought he saw. Perhaps if he remained steadily like that in her life she could grow into some semblance of his steady reverent observation. He did not miss any movement or change of expression. Perhaps you need to be treated as an object of romantic veneration before you can become one? Perhaps in Canada there were old-fashioned women who *were* objects of romantic veneration all their lives, living all the time as if they were Maud or some other woman from Tennyson. It *was* glorious to have a real, simple homage coming from a man who was no simpleton, coming simple, strong, and kindly from Canada to put you in a shrine. I have

always liked those old-fashioned stories because I have always
known they were *true*.   They have lived on in Canada.   Canadian men have kept something that Englishmen are losing.
She turned the pages of her note-book and came upon the scrap
crossed through by Mr Mendizabal.   She read the words
through, forcing them to accept a superficial meaning.   Disturbance about ideas would destroy the perfect serenity that
was demanded of her.   Be good, sweet maid, and let who will
be clever.   Easy enough if one were perpetually sustained by a
strong and adoring hand.   Perhaps more difficult really to be
good than to be clever.   Perhaps there were things in this
strong man that were not perfectly good and serene.   He
exacted his own serenity by sheer force; that was why he worshipped and looked for natural serenity.

Presently she stirred from her engrossment and looked across
at him as if only just aware of his presence.   He did not meet
her look but a light came on his face and he raised his head and
turned towards the light to aid her observation.   The things
that are beginning to be called silly futile romances are true.
Here *is* the strong silent man who does not want to talk and
grin.   He would love laughter.   Freed from worries and sustained by him, one could laugh all one's laughter out and dance
and sing through life to a happy sunsetting.   Was he *religious*?
She found she had risen to her feet with decision and began
collecting her papers in confusion as if she had suddenly made a
great clamour.   Dr von Heber rose at once and, with some quiet
murmuring remark, went away from the room.   Miriam felt
she must get into the open and go far on and on and on.   Going
upstairs through the house and into her room for her outdoor
things, she found her own secret belongings more her own.   In
the life she shyly glanced at, out away somewhere in the bright
blaze of Canadian sunshine, her own secret belongings would
be more her own.   That was one of the secrets of the sheltered
life, one of the things behind the smiles of the sheltered women;
their own secret certainties intensified because they were surrounded; perhaps in Canada men respected the secret certainties of women which they could never share.   With your
feet on that firm ground what would it matter how life went on

and on? There was someone in the hall. Mr Mendizabal in a funny little short overcoat.

'You go out, miss?' he said cheerfully.

'I'm going for a walk,' she said eagerly, her eyes on the clear grey and black of the hat he was taking from the hall stand.

'I too go for a walk,' he murmured cramming the soft hat on to his resisting hair and opening the door for her.

This was one of those *mild* February days; it is a mistake to imagine that the winter is gone; but it is gone in your mind; you can see ahead two summers and only one winter. 'I go with you' was meant as a question. It was on the tip of her tongue to turn and say, 'You should have said, "Shall I go with you?"' She was rebuked by a glimpse of Mr Mendizabal swinging sturdily unconsciously along on the gutter side of the narrow width of pavement, swinging his stick, the strong modelling of his white face unconscious under his strong black hair and the jaunty sweep of his black-banded grey hat. 'Jaunty and debonair'; but without a touch of weakness. What a lovely *mild* evening; extraordinary for the time of year; he would be furious at being interrupted for that, thinking of her as a stiff formal *institutrice* and shouting something ironic that would bring the world about their ears. Quel beau temps; that was it.

'Quel *beau* temps.' They had reached the Gower Street kerb and stood waiting to plunge through the passing traffic.

'Une soirée superbe, mademoiselle,' shouted Mr Mendizabal in a smooth flattened squeal as they crossed side by side; 'hah-*eh*!' he squealed, pushing her off to dart clear of a hansom and away to the opposite kerb. Miriam pulled back just in time, receiving the angry yell of the driver full in her upturned face. Mr Mendizabal was waiting unconcernedly outside the chemist's, singing, with French words. She disposed hastily of the incident, eager to be walking on through the darkness towards the mingled darkness and gold of the coming streets. They went along past the grey heights of University College

Hospital, separate creatures of mysteriously different races—
she expected that when they reached the light she would find
herself alone—and swung with one accord round into the
brilliance of the Tottenham Court Road; the tide of light and
sound raising them into a companionship that needed no bending into shapes of conversation. It was something to him and
it was something to her, and they threaded their way together,
meeting and separating and rejoining, unanimous and apart.
We are both *batteurs de pavé*, she thought; both people who
must be free to be nothing; saying to everything, 'Je m'en
fiche.' The hushed happiness that had begun in the dining-
room half an hour ago seized her again suddenly, sending her
forward almost on tiptoe. It was securely there; the vista it
opened growing in beauty as she walked. There was some
source of light within her, something that was ready to spread
out all round her and ahead and flow over the past. It con-
firmed scenes she had read and wondered at and cherished,
seeking in vain in the world for women who were like the
women described in them. She understood what women in
books meant by *sacred*: 'It is all too sacred for *words*.' There
was no choice in all that; only secret and sacred beauty; unity
with all women who had felt in the same way; the freedom of
following certainties. Outside it, was this other self untouched
and always new, her old free companion attending to no one.
She tossed Mr Mendizabal shreds of German or French whenever the increasing throng of passing pedestrians allowed them
to walk for a moment side by side.

His apparent oblivion of her incoherence gave full freedom
to her delight in her collection of idioms and proverbs. Each
one flung out with its appropriate emphasis and the right foreign
intonation gave her a momentary change of personality. He
caught the shreds and returned them woven into phrases increasing her store of convincing foreignness, comfortably, from
the innocence of his polyglot experience, requiring no instruc-
tive contribution from her, reassuringly assuming her equal
knowledge, his conscious response being only to her joyousness,
his eyes wide ahead, his features moulded to gaiety. The
burden of her personal dinginess and resourcelessness in a

strong resourceful world was hidden by him because he was
not aware of dinginess and resourcelessness anywhere. Dingy
and resourceless, she wandered along, keeping, as long as her
scraps of convincing impersonation should hold out, to her
equal companionship with his varied experience; bearing within her in secret unfathomable abundance the gift of ideal
old-English rose and white gracious adorable womanhood given
her by Dr Heber. At the turning into Oxford Street they lost
each other. Miriam wandered in solitude amidst jostling
bodies. The exhausted air rang with lifeless strident voices in
shoutings and heavy thick flattened unconcerned speech; even
from above a weight seemed to press. Clearer space lay
ahead; but it was the clear space of Oxford Street and pressed
upon her without ray or break. Once it had seemed part of the
golden West End; but Oxford Street was not the West End.
It was more lifeless and hopeless than even the north of London; more endurable because life was near at hand. Oxford
Street was like a prison. The embarrassment of her enterprise
came upon her suddenly; the gay going off was at an end;
perhaps she might get away and back home alone up a side
street. Amidst the shouting of women and the interwoven
dark thick growlings of conversations, she heard Mr Mendizabal's ironic snorting laugh not far behind her. Glancing
round from the free space of darkness she had reached she saw
him emerge shouldering from a group of women, short and
square and upright and gleaming brilliantly with the remains
of his laughter. A furious wrath flickered over her. He came
forward with his eyes ahead unseeing, nearer, near, safe at her
side, *her* little foreign Mr Mendizabal, mild and homely.

'Here is Ruscino's, mademoiselle, *all*ons, we will go to
Ruscino, *all*ons!' 'Ruscino,' in electric lights round the top
of the little square portico, like the name of a play round the
portico of a theatre, the sentry figure of the commissionaire, the
passing glimpse of palm ferns standing in semi-darkness just
inside the portico, the darkness beyond, suddenly became a
place, separate and distinct from the vague confusion of it in
her mind with the Oxford Music Hall; offering itself, open
before her, claiming to range itself in her experience; open,

with her inside and the mysteries of the portico behind. Continental London ahead of her, streaming towards her in mingled odours of continental food and wine, rich intoxicating odours in an air heavy and parched with the flavour of cigars, throbbing with the solid, filmy, thrilling swing of music. It was a café! Mr Mendizabal was evidently a *habitué*. She could be, by right of her happiness abroad. She was here as a foreigner, all her English friends calling her back from a spectacle she could not witness without contamination. Only Gerald knew the spectacle of Ruscino's. 'Lord, Ruscino's! *Lord !*' . . . In a vast open space of light, set in a circle of balconied gloom, innumerable little tables held groups of people wreathed in a brilliancy of screened light, veiled in mist, clear in sharp spaces of light, clouded by drifting spirals of smoke. They sat down at right angles to each other at a little table under the central height. The confines of the room were invisible. All about them were worldly wicked happy people.

She could understand a life that spent all its leisure in a café; every day ending in warm brilliance, forgetfulness amongst strangers near and intimate, sharing the freedom and forgetfulness of the everlasting unchanging café, all together in a common life. It was like a sort of dance, every one coming and going poised and buoyant, separate and free, united in freedom. It was a heaven, a man's heaven, most of the women were there with men, somehow watchful and dependent, but even they were forced to be free from troublings and fussings whilst they were there . . . the wicked cease from troubling and the weary are at rest. . . . She was there as a man, a free man of the world, a continental, a cosmopolitan, a connoisseur of women. That old man sitting alone with a grey face and an extinguished eye was the end of it, but even now the café held him up; he would come till death came too near to allow him movement. He was horrible, but less horrible than he would be alone in a room. He had to keep the rules and manage to behave. As long as he could come he was still in life. . . .

White muslin wings on a black straw hat, a well-cut check costume and a carriage, bust forward, an elegant carriage imposing secrets and manners. Miriam turned to watch her proceeding with a vague group of people through the central light towards the outer gloom.

'Voilà une petite qui est jolie,' she remarked judicially.

'Une jeune fille avec ses parents,' rebuked Mr Mendizabal. Even he, wicked fast little foreigner, did not know how utterly meaningless his words were. He was here, in Ruscino's, quite simply. He sat at home, at the height of his happy foreign expansiveness. He had no sense of desperate wickedness. He gave no help to the sense of desperate wickedness; pouring like an inacceptable nimbus from his brilliant strong head, was a tiresome homeliness. She flung forth to the music, the shining fronds of distant palm ferns; sipped her liqueur with downcast eyes and thought of an evening along the *digue* at Ostend, the balmy air, the telescoping brilliant interiors of the villas, the wild arm-linked masquerading stroll, Elsie had really looked like an unprincipled Bruxelloise. Foreigners were all innocent in their depravity. To taste the joy of depravity one must be English.

'Hah; Strelinsky! Ça va bien, hein?' A figure had risen out of the earth at Mr Mendizabal's elbow and stood looking down at him; another foreigner. She glanced with an air of proprietorship; a slender man in a thin faded grey overcoat, a sharp greyish yellow profile and small thin head under a dingy grey felt hat. Strelinsky. Mr Mendizabal stood sturdily up, bowing, with square outstretched hand, wrapped in the radiating beam of his smile.

'I present you Mr Strelinsky. A musician. A composer of music.' His social manner was upon him again; fatherliness, strong responsible hard-working kindliness. The face under the grey hat turned slowly towards her. She bowed and looked into eyes set far back in the thin mask of the face. Her eyes passed in question from the expressionless eyes to the motionless expressionless face. How could he be a composer; looking so . . . vanishing? Strelinsky . . . *Morceau pour piano* . . . that must be *he* standing here.

'Did you write this?' she said abruptly and hummed the beginning. It sounded shapeless and toneless, but there was a little tune just ahead. She broke off short of it, not sure that he was attending. The world burst into laughter. His face turned slowly and stopped looking downwards across her, his eyes fixed in a dead repetition of the laughter in which she was drowning. He stood in space in a faded coat and hat, a colourless figure clothed by her feebleness in lively dignity and wisdom. Grouped inaccessibly beyond the vast space were solid tables filled with judges; dim figures sat in judgment in the amber light under the gallery where palms stood; she was drowning alone, surrounded by a distant circle of palms.

Eleven. 'We must go, miss,' stated Mr Mendizabal cordially. Miriam rose. The tide of café life flowed all round her. She wandered blissfully out through the misty smoke-wreathed golden light, threading her way amongst the tables towards the black and gold of the streets. Far away behind her, staying in the evening, Strelinsky blocked the view, moving, fixed avertedly, with eyes in his shoulders along an endless narrowing distance of café.

CHAPTER VII

PERHAPS Dr von Heber had really suddenly thought downstairs that it would be nice to go to church, not knowing that that was one of the real effects of falling in love . . . just thinking in the course of his worldly studies that there was church and he was in himself a church-goer and ought to go more often, and coming up to borrow a prayer book from the *Baileys*. No. Suddenly in the room, standing in the unknown drawing-room for the first time, in his steady urbane confident way, waiting, a little turned towards the piano. The Baileys had neither spoken nor moved; they were afraid of him; but Mrs Bailey would have made herself say, 'Well, doctor,' to the amazing apparition. They simply waited, held off by his waiting manner. '*I think this is a good evening to go to church.*' What have you been doing all this time? Where do you go, going out so often? What are you doing sitting here playing? We ought to be going to church; we two. Here I am professing church-going and idiotically confessing myself come all the way from Canada without a prayer book, and making a pretence of borrowing your prayer book because we *must* be in church together. Dr Hurd's impressions had had no effect upon him. But now he had gone back into his own life not only thinking that she was not a church-goer, but feeling sure that her own private life of coming and going had no thoughts of him in it.

Dr Hurd sitting on the omnibus with *amusement* carving deep lines on his brick-red face and splintering out of his eyes into the hot afternoon glare; the neat new bowler with the red hair coming down underneath it, the well-cut Montreal clothes on his tough neat figure; immovable, there for the afternoon. Forced to go on and on, isolated with the brick-red grin and the splintering green eyes, through the afternoon heat, in the midst of a glare of omnibus people, on their way to a brass band in the Albert Hall, thinking they were going to a *concert*. He did not know what made a concert. Sitting with the remains of his grin, waiting for the things he had been taught to admire, unable to find anything without his mother and sisters; missing Canadian ladies with opinions about everything; waiting all the time to be managed in the Canadian women's way. He must have told the others about it afterwards, his face crinkling at them and they listening and agreeing.

It had begun the moment after he had suggested the concert. 'I'll get a new top hat before then.' The awful demand for a jest. His way of waiting as if one were some queer being he was waiting to see say or do something any one could understand, was the same as the English way, only more open. But English people like that did not care for music and did not have books read to them. Perhaps his parents belonged to the other sort of English and he had the stamp of it, promising seriousness and a love of beautiful things, and forced by life into the jesting way of worldly people who seemed to have no sacred patches at all. Quick words, bathed in laughter heaped up into a questioning of what the *matter* was. Men, demanding jests and amusement; women succeeding only by jesting satirically about everything.

'Von Heber's a man who'll *carve* his way. My! He's *great*.' Carve his way; one of those phrases that satisfy and worry you; short, and leaving out nearly everything; Dr von Heber going through life with a chisel, intent on carving; everybody envying him; the von Heber not seen or realized. His way is carved. He *is* his way. Going ahead further and further away as one listened. His poverty and drudgery behind him, at Winnipeg, amongst the ice. Hoisting himself out of it, *making* himself into a doctor; a graduate of McGill. Standing out among the graduates with even the very manner of success more marked in him than in them with their money and ease; sailing to England steady-minded in the awful risk of borrowed money. It's wrong, insulting, to him to think of it while he is still in the midst of the effort. A sort of treachery to know the details at all. Thinking disperses his general effect. In the strength and sunshine of him there is power. The things he has done are the power in him; no need to know the gossipy details; that was why the facts sounded so familiar; reproachful, as Dr Hurd brought them out.

I knew *all* about him when I met his sunshine. I ought to have rushed away garlanded with hawthorn, with some woman, and waited till he came again. Dr Hurd looks like an old woman; an old gossip. Old men are worse gossips than old women. They can't keep their hands off. They make phrases. Dr Hurd is a dead, dead old woman. Handling things like an old man. It was so natural to listen. 'Natural' things get you lost and astray . . . kiss-in-the-ring 'just a little harmless nonsense . . . there's no harm in a little gay nonsense, chickie.' There's no such thing as harmless nonsense. Dissipation makes you forget everything. Secret sacred places. George and John, faithful and steady, can't make those. They smile *personally* and the room or the landscape is immediately silly and tame.

'I never met a chap who could make so much of what he knows . . . pick up . . . and bring them out better than the chap could himself.' The four figures sitting in the little room round the lamp. Dr Hurd talking his gynaecology simply; a relief, a clear clean place in the world of women's doctors. Dr Winchester talking for Dr von Heber, his brown beard and his frock-coat, just for the time he was talking before Dr von Heber had grasped it all, looking like a part of the professional world. Dr Wayneflete's white criminal face, his little white mouth controlledly mouthing. Wayneflete's brilliant; but he's not got von Heber's strength nor his manner. He's quiet though, that chap. He'd do well over here. That spreads your thoughts about, painfully and wholesomely. Dr Hurd spreads his thoughts about quite simply.

The moment was so surprising that I forgot it. I always forget the things that surprise me. She was hating me and hating everything. I must have told her I was going away. When I said 'You can have Bunnikin back' she suddenly grew older than I. 'Oh, *Bunn*ikin!' Their beloved Bunnikin, as smartly dressed as Mrs Corrie, in the smart country house way and knowing how to gush and behave. . . . 'Bunnikin's too *simple.*' Sybil in her blue cotton overall in the amber light in the Louis Quinze drawing-room, one with me, wanting me because I was not simple. I thought she hated me all the time because I was not worldly. I should not have known I was not simple unless she had told me; that child.

. . . Dear Mr Bowdoin . . . and I think I can promise you an audience. . . . I regret that I cannot come on Thursday and I am sincerely sorry that you should think I desired an audience. The extraordinary pompous touchiness of men. Why didn't he see I did not dream of suggesting he should come again just to see me? I've forgotten Mr Bowdoin. And the Museum. Everything. . . . I sit here . . . playing to hide myself from the Baileys and he is away somewhere making people happy. 'They do not care . . . they see me, they shout, "Ah! *Don Clement!*" I amuse them, I laugh, they think I am happy. Voilà tout, mademoiselle. . . . Il n'y a qu'une chose qui m'amuse.'

CHAPTER VIII

A DAY of blazing heat changed the season suddenly. Flat
threatening sunlight travelled round the house. The shadowy
sun - blinded flower - scented waiting - room held street - baked
patients in its deep arm-chairs. Some of them were languid.
But none of them suffered. They kept their freshness and
freedom from exhaustion by living away from toil and grimy
heat; in cool clothes, moving swiftly through moving air in
carriages and holland-blinded hansoms; having ices in expensive shade; being waited on in the cool depths of West End
houses; their lives disturbed only by occasional dentistry. The
lean dark patients were like lizards, lively and darting and
active even in the sweltering heat.

Miriam's sunless room was cool all day. Through her grey
window she could see the sunlight pouring over the jutting
windows of Mr Leyton's small room and reflected in the grimy
sheen of the frosted windows of the den. Her day's work was
unreal, as easy as a dream. All about her were open sunlit
days that her summer could not bring, and that yet were hers
as she moved amongst them; a leaf dropped in the hall, the
sight of a summer dress, summer light coming through wide
open windows took her out into them. Summer would never
come again in the old way, but it set her free from cold, and let
her move about unhampered in the summers of the past.
Summer was happiness. . . . Individual things were straws
on the stream of summer happiness.

At tea time in the den there was a darkening hush. It was
like a guest, turning every one's attention to itself, abolishing
differences, setting free unexpected sympathies. Every one

spoke of the coming storm and looked beautiful in speaking. The day's work was discussed as if in the presence of an unseen guest.

She set out from the house of friends to meet the darkened daylight . . . perhaps the sudden tapping of thunder-drops upon her thin blouse. The street was a livid grey, brilliant with hidden sunlight.

The present can be judged by the part of the past it brings up. If the present brings up the happiness of the past, the present is happy.

Purgatory. The waters of Lethe and Eunoe, 'forgetfulness and sweet memory'; and then heaven. The Catholics are right about expiation. If you are happy in the present something is being expiated. If life contains moments of paradise you must be in purgatory looking across the vale of asphodel. You can't be in hell. . . . Yet hell would not be hell without a knowledge of heaven. If once you 've been in heaven you can never escape. Yet Dante believed in everlasting punishment.

Bathing in the waters of Lethe and Eunoe unworthily is drinking one's own damnation. But happiness crops up before one can prevent it. Perhaps happiness is one long sin, piling up a bill. It is my secret companion. Waiting at the end of every dark passage. I did not make myself. I *can't* help it.

Brilliant . . . *brilliant*; and someone was seeing it. There was no thunderstorm, no clouds or pink edges on the brilliant copper grey. She wandered on down the road hemmed by flaring green. The invisible sun was everywhere. There was no air, nothing to hold her body separate from the scene. The grey brilliance of the sky was upon the pavement and in the green of the park, making mauve shadows between the trees and a mist of mauve amongst the further green. The high housefronts stood out against the grey, eastern-white, frilled below with new-made green, sprouting motionlessly as you looked . . . white plaster houses against the blue of the Mediterranean, grey mimosa trees, green-feathered lilac of wistaria. Between the houses and the park the road glared wooden grey, dark, baked grey, edged with the shadowless stone grey of the pavement. Summer. Eternity *showing*. . . .

The Euston Road was a narrow hot channel of noise and un-breathable odours, the dusty exhausting cruelty of the London summer, leading on to the feathery green-floored woods of Endsleigh Gardens edged by grey house-fronts, and ending in the cool stone of St Pancras Church.

In the twilit dining-room one's body was like a hot sun throbbing in cool dark air, ringed by cool walls holding darkness in far corners; coolness poured out through the wide-open windows towards the rain-cool grey façades of the opposite houses, cool and cool until the throbbing ceased.

All the forms seated round the table were beautiful; far-away and secret and separate, each oneself set in the coming of summer, unconscious. One soul. Summer is the soul of man. Through all the past months they had been the waiting guests of summer.

The pain of trying to get back into the moment of the first vision of spring, the perfect moment before the thought came that spring was going on in the country unseen, was over. The moment came back of itself . . . the green flush in the squares, the ripples of emerald-fringed pink geraniums along the balconies of white houses.

After dinner Miriam left the dining-room, driven joyfully forth, remaining behind, floating and drifting happily about, united with every one in the room as her feet carried her step by step without destination, going everywhere, up through the staircase twilight.

The drawing-room was filled with saffron light, filtering in through the curtains hanging motionless before the high french windows. Within the air of the room, just inside the faint smell of dusty upholstery was the peace of the new-found

summer. Mrs Bailey's gift. There had been no peace of
summer last year in her stifling garret. This year the summer
was with her, in the house where she was. Far away within
the peace of the room was the evening of a hot summer day at
Waldstrasse, the girls sitting about, beautiful featureless forms
together for ever in the blissful twilight of the cool *Saal* and
sitting in its little summer-house. *Ulrica*, everybody, her dark
delicate profile lifted towards the garden, her unconscious
pearly beauty grouped against the undisturbing presence of
Fräulein Pfaff. Miriam turned to the near window and peered
through the thick mesh of the smoke-yellowed lace curtain.
Behind it the french window stood ajar. Drawing aside the
thick, dust-smelling lace she stepped out and drew the door to
behind her. There were shabby drawing-room chairs standing
in an irregular row on the dirty grey stone, railed by a balustrade of dark maroon-painted iron railings almost colourless
with black grime. But the elastic outer air was there and, away
at the end of the street, a great gold-pink glow stood above and
showed through the feathery upper branches of the trees in
Endsleigh Gardens. A number of people must have been
sitting out before dinner. That was part of their dinner-time
happiness. Presently some of them would come back. She
scanned the disposition of the chairs. The little comfortable
circular velvet chair stood in the middle of the row, conversationally facing the high-backed wicker chair. The other
chairs were the small stiff velvet-seated ones. The one at the
north end of the balcony could be turned towards the glowing
sky with its back to the rest of the balcony. She reached and
turned it and sat down. The opposite houses with their balconies on which groups were already forming stood sideways,
lost beyond the rim of her glasses. The balcony of the next
house was empty; there was nothing between her and the vista
of green feathering up into the intense gold-rose glow. . . .
She could come here every night, filling her life with green
peace; preparing for the stifling heat of the nights in her garret.
This year, with dinner in the cool dining-room and the balcony
for the evening, the summer would not be so unbearable. She
sat still, lifted out into garden freshness. . . . Benediction.

People were stepping out on to the balcony behind her, remarking on the beauty of the evening, their voices new and small in the outer air. If she never came out again this summer would be different. It had begun differently. She knew what lay ahead and could be prepared for it.

She would find coolness at the heart of the swelter of London if she could keep a tranquil mind. The coolness at the heart of the central swelter was wonderful life, from moment to moment, pure *life*. To go forward now, from this moment, alive, keeping alive, through the London summer. Even to go away for holidays would be to break up the wonder, to snap the secret clue and lose the secret life.

The rosy gold was deepening and spreading.

Miriam found herself rested as if by sleep. It seemed as if she had been sitting in the stillness for a time that was longer than the whole of the working day. To recover like this every day, to have at the end of every day a cool *solid* clear head and rested limbs and the feeling that the strain of work was so far away that it could never return. The tireless sense of morning and new day that came in moving from part to part of her London evenings, and strongest of all at the end of a long evening, going on from a lecture or a theatre to endless leisure, reading, the happy gaslight over her book under the sloping roof, always left her in the morning unwilling to get up, and made the beginning of the day horrible with languor and breakfast a scramble, taken to the accompaniment of guilty listening for the striking of nine o'clock from St Pancras church, and the angry sense of Mr Hancock already arriving cool and grey-clad at the morning door of Wimpole Street. To-night, going strong and steady to her hot room, sleep would be silvery cool. She would wake early and fresh, and surprise them all at Wimpole Street, arriving early and serene after a leisurely breakfast.

The rosy light shone into far-away scenes with distant friends. They came into her mind rapidly one by one, and stayed grouped in a radiance, sharper and clearer than in experience. She recalled scenes that had left a sting, something still to be answered. She saw where she had failed; her friends saw what she had meant, in some secret unconscious part of them that was turned away from the world; in their thoughts with themselves when they were alone. Her own judgments, sharply poised in memory upon the end of some small incident, reversed themselves, dropped meaningless, returned reinforced, went forward, towards some clearer understanding. Her friends drifted forward, coming too near, as if in competition for some central place. To every claim, she offered her evening sky as a full answer. The many forms remained, grouped, like an audience, confronted by the evening.

The gold was fading, a soft mistiness spreading through the deepening rose, making the leafage darker and more opaque. Presently the sky would be mother-of-pearl above a soft dark mass and then pure evening grey outlining the dark feathery tree-tops of a London square turning to green below in the lamplight, sinking to sleep, deeply breathing out its freshness to meet the freshness pouring through the streets from the neighbouring squares. Freshness would steal over the outside walls of the houses already cool within. Only in the garrets would the sultry day remain under the slowly cooling roofs.

There was still a pale light flowing into the dusk of the garret. It must be only about nine o'clock. . . . The gas flared out making a winter brilliance. . . . *Dante, Six Sermons*. . . . Kuenen's *Life of Dante* . . . Gemma Donati, *Gemma*, busily making puddings in the world lit by the light of the Mystic Rose; swept away by the rush of words . . . a stout Italian woman . . . *Gem*ma; Bayatrichay . . . they were bound to reach music . . . a silent Italian woman in a hot kitchen scolding, left out of the mystic rose . . . *Lourdes* . . . *Le Nabab* . . . 'atroce comédie de bonheur conjugale sans relâche' . . . the Frenchman *expressing* what the Englishman only thinks . . . 'the wife' . . . I met my WIFE! . . . red nose and check trousers, smoky self-indulgent married man, all the self-indulgent

married men in the audience guffawing. . . . 'You must be
ready to face being taken for granted, you must hide your
troubles, learn to say nothing of your unnoticed exhausting
toil, wear a smile above the heart that you believe is breaking;
stand steady in face of the shipwreck of all your dreams. Remember that although he does not know it, in spite of all his
apparent oblivion and neglect, if you *fail*, his universe *crumbles*.'
. . . Men live their childish ignorant lives on a foundation of
pain and exhaustion. Down in the fevered life of pain and
exhaustion there is a deep certainty. There is no deep certainty in the lives of men. If there were they would not be
for ever talking with conceited guilty lips as if something were
waiting if they stopped, to spring on them from behind. . . .
The Evolution of the Idea of God. . . . I have forgotten what that
is about . . . a picture of a sort of Madonna . . . *corn* goddess,
with a child and sheaves of corn. . . . *The Mechanism of Thought.*
. . . *Thirty Sane Criticisms.* . . . *Critique de la Pensée moderne*;
traduit par H. Navray, Mercure de France. . . . How did he
begin? Where was he when he came out and began saying
everybody was wrong? How did he get to know about it all?
She took down a volume unwillingly . . . there was something
being lost, something waiting within the quiet air of the room
that would be gone if she read. It was not too late. Why did
men write books? Modern men? The book was open. Her
eyes scanned unwillingly. Fabric. How did he find his
words? No one had ever said *fabric* about anything. It
made the page alive . . . a woven carpet, on one side a beautiful
glowing pattern, on the other dull stringy harshness . . .
'there is a dangerous *looseness*' . . . her heart began beating
apprehensively. The room was dead about her. She sat
down tense, and read the sentence through. 'There is a dangerous looseness in the fabric of our minds.' She imagined
the words spoken, 'looseness' was ugly, making the mouth ugly
in speech. There is a looseness in the fabric of our minds.
That is what he would have said in conversation, looking nowhere and waiting to floor an objection. 'There is a *dangerous*,'
he had written. That introduced another idea. You were not
supposed to notice that there were two statements, but to read

smoothly on, accepting. It was deliberate. Put in deliberately to frighten you into reading more. Dangerous. The adjective is the sentence, personal, a matter of opinion. People who read the books do not think about *adjectives*. They like them. Conversation is *adjectives*! . . . All the worry of conversation is because people use adjectives and rush on. . . . But you can't describe . . . but 'dangerous' is not a descriptive adjective. . . . 'There is a twisted looseness,' that describes . . . that is Saxon . . . *Abendmahl* . . . dangerous, French . . . the Prince of Wales uses the elegant Norman idiom. . . . 'Dangerous' is an idea, the language of ideas. It expresses nothing but an opinion about life . . . a threat daring you to disagree. Dangerous to what? . . . Man is a badly made machine . . . an oculist could improve upon the human eye . . . and the mind wrong in some way too . . . logic is a cheap arithmetic. *Imagination.* What *is* imagination? Is it his imagination that has found out that mind is loose? Is not imagination mind? It is his imaginative mind. A special kind of mind. But if mind discovers that mind is unreliable, its conclusion is also unreliable. That's logic. . . . Barbara. All mind is unreliable. Man is mind, therefore man is unreliable. . . . Then it is useless to try and know anything . . . books go on . . . he has invented imagination. Images. Fabric. But he did not invent 'dangerous.' That is cheek. By this sin fell the angels. Perhaps he is a fallen angel. I was right when I told Eve I had sold my soul to the devil. . . . 'Quite a good afterglow,' and then wheeling alertly about to capture and restate some thread . . . and then later, finding you still looking. 'M'yes; a fine . . . fuliginous . . . *pink*. . . . God's had a strawberry ice for supper' . . . endless inexhaustible objections . . . a cold grim scientific world . . . Alma knew it. In that clear bright house with the satisfying furniture . . . now let's all make Buddhas. Let's see who can make the best Buddha. . . . Away from them you could forget; but it was going on all the time . . . somehow ahead of everything else that was going on. . . . She got up and replaced the book. It was on her shelf; a signed copy; extraordinary. It was an extraordinary privilege. No one else could write books like that; no one else knew so much about everything. Right or wrong, it was impossible to give up hearing all he had to say . . . and they were kind, alive to one's life in a way other people were not. . . .

She strolled to the window, finding renewal in the familiar creaking of her floor in the house, here. . . . She went back across the happy creaking and turned out the gas and came again to the window. The sky was dark enough to show a brilliant star; here and there in the darkness of the opposite housefronts was an oblong of golden light. The faint blue light coming up from the street lit up the outer edges of the grey stone window-sills. The air under the wooden roof of the window space was almost as close as it was under the immense height of upper coolness. . . . Down at the end of the road were the lamplit green trees; plane-tree shadows on the narrow pavement. She put on her hat in the dark.

Crossing the roadway to reach the narrow strip of pavement running along under the trees she saw single dark figures standing at intervals against the brilliant lamplit green and swerved back to the wide pavement. She had forgotten they would be there. They stood like sentinels. . . . Behind them the lamplit green flared feverishly. . . . In the shadow of St Pancras Church there were others, small and black in a desert . . . lost quickly in the great shadow where the passers-by moved swiftly through from light to light. Out in the Euston Road along the pavements shadowed by trees and left in darkness by the high spindling shaded candles of the lamps along the centre of the roadway, they came walking, a foreign walk, steadily slow and wavy and expressive, here and there amongst the shapeless expressionless forms of the London wayfarers. The high stone entrance of Euston Station shone white across the way. Any one can go into a station. Within the entrance gravelled darkness opened out on either side. Silence all round and ahead, where silent buildings had here and there a lit window. Where was the station? Immense London darkness and stillness alone and deserted like a country place at night, just beyond the noises of the Euston Road. A murder might happen here. The cry of an engine sounded, muffled and far away. Just ahead in the centre of the approaching wide mass of building was a wide dimly lit stone archway. The rattle of a hansom sounded from an open space beyond. Its light appeared swaying swiftly forward and lit the archway. The hansom bowled through in startling silence, nothing but the jingle and dumb leathery rattle of the harness, and passed, the plonking of the horse's hoofs and the swift slur of the wheels sounding out again in the open space. The archway had little side pathways for passengers roofed by small arching extensions of the central arch . . . *indiarubber* . . . pavement to muffle . . . the building was an hotel; Edwards's daylight Family Hotel . . . expensive people lodging just above the arch, travelling, coming to London, going away from London, with no thought of the dark secret neighbourhood. A courtyard opened out beyond the arch. It was not even yet the station. There was a road just ahead going right and left, with lamps; just in front to the left across the road a lit building with a frosted lower window and a clock . . . a post office. Miriam went through the swing door into warm yellow gaslight. At the long counter people stood busily occupied or waiting their turn, with their backs to the dusty floor space, not noticing the grey space of dusty floor and the curious warm gleam of the light falling upon it from behind the iron grille along the counter. The clerks were fresh and serene and unhurried, making a steady quiet workaday feeling; late at night. It swung the day round, morning and evening together in the gaslit enclosure. She stood at the counter sharing the sense of affairs. She could be a customer for a penny stamp. Waiting outside was the walk back through the various darkness, the indiarubber pathway . . . knowing her way.

She let herself into the hall with an air of returning from a hurried necessary errand. Beyond the mysterious Bailey curtains partly screening the passage to the front door she saw Dr Hurd standing at the dining-room door; 'Good night,' he

laughed back into the room and turned, meeting her as she
emerged into the light.   He paused smiling.

'Here's Miss Henderson,' he said into the room.   Miriam was
passing the door.   'Aren't you coming in?' he urged smiling.

'Ho, I've just been to the post office,' said Miriam, passing
into the room.   'Ho, isn't it a perfect evening?' she announced,
taking in Dr Wayneflete standing tall with small bent pale face
at the end of the table and the other two rising from their places
by the fireside.   Dr Hurd closed the door and came and flopped
down in the easy-chair in front of the piano.

'I know you won't sit here, Miss Henderson.'

'No, Miss Henderson doesn't care for cushions,' murmured
Dr von Heber at her side.   'Take this chair,' he pursued and
sat near as she sat down in a little stiff chair facing the fireplace,
Dr Winchester subsiding a little behind her on the other side.

'It's a purfect evening,' murmured Dr Waynflete.   Miriam
turned and searched his white bent face.   She had never seen
him speaking in a room.   The thought behind the white,
slightly bulging forehead was his own, Waynflete, brilliant,
keeping him apart; the little narrowing peak of livid white face,
the green shadows about the small pale mouthing lips, the fact of
his heart-disease and his Irish parentage were things that dared
to approach and attach themselves to him; that people knew.

'A purfect evening,' he repeated, plucking gently at the
threads of the table-cloth.   He would never originate a remark
or ask a question except of patients or an engineer standing
near some difficult machinery.   He knew everything by just
being about.   He was head and shoulders above the other three.
Delicate, of gentle blood and narrow fragile body; a strong
spirit; impossible of approach by speech; everything she said
would carry her away from him; perhaps he was already planning his escape.   One day he would suddenly fall down, dead;
young and unknown to any one in the world, carrying away
his mystery.

'Eleven o'clock.'   She had shattered the silence he had built.

'You don't call that late,' said Dr von Heber, released and
rushing to rescue her.   He sat bland and square and simple
beneath the coming long procession of years and days; but his

firmly dimpled swift Canadian smile, brilliant with the flash of
the flawless perfect arch of his strong even teeth, brought past
and future into the moment, giving them to the sudden charm
of this meeting, referring back to that first evening by the table.

'Oh, no; it's frightfully early.'

'That's a most delightful hyperbole.'

'I shall summons you for calling me an isosceles triangle.'

Dr Waynflete laughed too . . . a small sound drowned by
Dr Hurd's thwack on the arm of his chair as he flung back his
head for his laugh.

'It *has* been wonderful to-day, don't you *think*? Did you
see the extraordinary light this afternoon?'

'Well, no; we were all of us immured, but we were out this
evening; we thought it the best specimen of London weather
we'd struck so far.'

'There's nothing whatever the matter with London weather.
It's *perfect*; the most perfect in the world.' Dr Hurd resumed
his shakings of laughter, restrained to listen. Dr Winchester
was sitting bent forward smiling dreamily.

'I know you won't like me to call that a hyperbole, but you
won't quite expect me to say I unreservedly agree.'

'It isn't a question of agreement or disagreement. It's a
simple fact.' Dr Hurd again struck his chair and sat forward
feeling for a handkerchief in a side pocket, his face a tearful
grin turned upon Dr von Heber.

'You are a loyal champion.'

'English weather does not want a champion. It's so wonderful. Perhaps you are thinking of Italian skies and that sort of
thing; in countries where the weather does not change or not
suddenly; only at fixed seasons. That's very nice in a way.
You can make plans. But I know I should long for grey days
and changes in the sky. A grey day is not melancholy; it's
exciting. You can see everything. The sun makes everything pale and blinds you.'

'There I think you mistaken. Nothing beautifies like sunlight, and if you've the sun behind you, you get the ahead
prospect without being blinded.'

'I know what you mean; but I want both; for contrast

perhaps; no, that's silly; the grey days for their own sake, the misty atmosphere. Fog. I think a real London fog is perfection; everything and the shapes and outlines of things looming up only as you pass them. Wonderful.'

'Well, there you leave us behind. I can't see anything either beautiful or in the least wonderful in your town fogs.'

'Quite so. A taste for town fog is an artificial taste. Town fog's not a natural phenomenon. It's just town dirt.'

'I don't care how it begins. It's perfect. It makes the whole day an adventure even if you're indoors. It's perfect to have the light on and nothing to be seen outside but a copper glare. Outside is a glorious adventure in a new unknown world. . . . In a way all our weathers are that. In a way the weather's enough, in itself, without anything else.'

'That seems to me a remarkable, a very extra-ordinary point of view. You can't in any circumstances make it a general defence of your climate. It's a purely personal notion.'

'It isn't. Even people who say they don't like fogs are different; interested in the effect while it is on.'

'Uneasy, no doubt, like animals in a trap.'

'I refer to Miss Henderson's extra-ordinairy valuation of weather as enough in itself. I consider that is one of *the* most *extra-ordinairy* points of view I ever heard stated.'

'No one can deny the quahl-ty of interest to the vagaries of your western European climut; from our point of view it's all interest and no climut; ye can't tell from day to day what season ye'll be in and they all seem—stormy.'

'The seasons crop up all the year round, sometimes three in one day. That's just the fascinating thing.'

'Quite so, we find that varry disturbing.'

'Our sudden changes of temperature keep us hardy.'

'That's true; you're a hardy people. Your weather suits you, beyond a doubt.'

'In *Ireland*, the weather changes every few minutes.'

'Hah, Wayneflete.'

'Granted. No doubt that assisted my parents to decide to leave; I don't wonder at it.'

'You're temperate. You've got the sea at a stone's throw

all round. You don't have notable extremes. But there's
our trouble. Your extremes, when they come, ain't arranged
for. There's no heat like your English heat, and, my word,
your English houses in the winter'd take some beating.'

'You mean boarding-houses.'

'Not entirely. Though I admit your English hoames are
unique in the matter of comfort. There's nothing in the
world like a real good *English hoame*. And not only in the
matter of comfort.'

'Yes but look here, von Heber. I know your fine English
parlours with fine great fires to sit around, what they call 'cosy'
over here, but, my life, why don't they warm their corridors
and sleeping rooms?'

'We don't be*cause* it's unhealthy. A cold bedroom keeps
you hardy and you *sleep* better.'

'And not only warm them but light them. My word, when
they take you out of their warm parlours into cold corridors
and land you in an ice-house with a little bit of a flickering
candle.'

'You're not tempted to read in bed and you go to sleep in
healthy bracing air; it keeps you *hardy*.'

'Do you never read after you retire?'

'I do; and have the gas and a lamp to keep warm. I like
warm rooms and I think in many ways it must be lovely to be
able to wear muslin dresses indoors in snowy weather and put
on a fur coat to go out; but I should be sorry to see the American
warm house idea introduced into England.'

'You're willing to be inconsistent then.'

'Consistency is the something of something minds.'

'I guess our central-heated residences would appeal to you.'

'I know they would. But I should freeze in the winter;
because I shouldn't be able to wear a fur coat.'

'How so?'

'I'm an anti-vivisectionist.'

'Then you'd best stay where they're not needed. Your
winters don't call for them. It's the funniest thing in *life* the
way your wimmun go around in furs.'

'Furs are frightfully becoming; like lace and violets.'

'Then you exonerate them although you 're against the slaying evidently, as well as the use of beasts for experiment.'

'They don't think.'

'My word, that 's true; but all the thinking in creation won't keep an Eskimo warm without furs.'

'There 's no need for any one to live up there. The Hudson's Bay Commissioners are tradespeople.'

'That 's a big proposition.'

'Well?'

'You 'd advocate every one living in temperate climes to spare the beasts?'

'There 's no reason except trade for any one to live in snow.'

'There 's a mighty except.'

'Well?'

'What about phthisical subjects who need dry cold climes?'

'Wool and astrakhan.'

'Well I guess furs 'll be worn for a bit yet.'

'That doesn't affect the question.'

'I gather you reckon the beasts oughtn't help advance science.'

'They don't. Doctors are as ill as anybody.'

'True enough. You consider that invalidates medical science?'

'Of course they are overworked and many of them splendid. But illness doesn't decrease. If one disease goes down another goes up.'

'Great *Caesar*, where did you come across that?'

'Even so; but suppose they *all* went up?'

'Besides, you talk about animals advancing science. Even if there wasn't that great French physiologist or chemist or something who looked at the result of experiments on animals and said, "Hélas, nous avons les mains vides." He declared that there 's nothing to be learned about *human* bodies from animals, and even if there were, the thing is that the animals have no choice. We 've no right to force them to suffer.'

'An animal 's constituted differently to a man. You can't compare them in the matter of sensitiveness to pain.'

'I knew you 'd say that. If people really want to advance

science by experiments on bodies they should offer their own bodies.'

'Someone's been working on your mind if you believe animals suffer more than men.'

'I'd rather see a woman suffer than a man and a man rather than a child and a child rather than an animal. Animals are bewildered and don't understand. They have nothing to help them. They don't understand their sufferings.'

'You rate men lower than women in power to endure pain.'

'They get more practice.'

'You're right there.'

'They're less sensitive.'

'That's debatable, Wayneflete.'

'Women appear to be callous over the sufferings of other women and to make a fuss over men. It's because sick men are more helpless and pitiful. Women *appear* to be. But the sun *appears* to go round the earth.'

'I doubt if ever there'll come a time when we'll have live humanity in our experimental laboratories.'

'Science has got to go ahead anyway.'

'But if it goes ahead by forcing sensitive creatures with . . . sensitive nervous systems, to bear fear and pain . . . we shall lose more morally than we shall gain scientifically even if we gain scientifically, and we don't, because nearly every one is *ill*.'

'You consider knahludg can be bought at too high a price.'

'Well; look at the continental luminaries; where there are no restrictions; they don't even care about their patients, only diseases interest them, and in general, not only in science, they don't really know anything, the Germans and the French, you have only to look at them. They are brutal.'

'That's a large statement. If you'll pardon me I should say there's a certain amount of insular prejudice in that.'

'I have not a scrap of insular prejudice. I like foreigners. They are more intelligent than Englishmen. But there's something they don't know that makes them all alike. I once heard a wealthy old Jew say that he'd go to Germany for diagnosis and to England for treatment, and he'd had operations and illnesses all over the world. That expresses it.'

'You infer that the English have more humanity.'

'They don't regard the patient as a case in the way continentals do.'

'Well I guess when we 're sick we all like to go home.'

'You mean the Jew had no home. But he chose the English to go home to when he was ill.'

'That 's true in more senses than one. This country 's been a home for the Jews right away back.'

'It 's a great country. That 's sure.'

'Science has got to go away ahead. If you 're going to be humanitarians over here you must leave continental science out of your scheme. So long as you carry out their results you can't honestly cry down their methods.'

'You must cry down their methods if you don't approve of them.'

'You can't put back. You can't prevent association between the different lands; especially in matters of science.'

'What I 'm saying. You 've got to accept the goods, even supposing your particular constitution of mind inclines you to bulleave them ill-gotten.'

'It 's a case of good coming out of evil.'

'That 's Jesuitical, the end justifying the means. I don't believe that. Why should science go ahead so fast? Where 's the hurry, as you say in Canada?'

'Well, you 've only to look around to see that.'

'I *don't* see it. Do you mean that people who make scientific experiments do it because they want to improve the world? They don't. It 's their curiosity.'

'Divine curiosity I 've heard it called.'

'The divine curiosity of Eve . . . that 's the answer to the Mosaic fable about woman. She was interested in the serpent, and polite to him and gossiped with him. Science is scandal-mongering; gossip about the universe. Men talk about women gossiping. My word!'

'Stars! I 'd like some of our chaps to hear you say that.'

'It is. Darwin gossiped about monkeys and in his old age he looked exactly like one, and regretted that he had neglected music.'

'You can't have it both ways.   Each man must pursue one line or another.'

'Poor dears, yes.'

'You're inclined to pity us all.'

'That's English humanitarianism, maybe.'

'I'm not a humanitarian.   I can't bear humanity, in the mass.   I think it's a frightful idea.'

'A fairly solid idea.'

'I prefer . . . the equator, and the moon, and the plane of the ecliptic; I think the plane of the ecliptic is a perfectly lovely thing.'

'It's a scientific discovery.'

'Yes but not on the body of an animal.'

'The body of the chap who began all that had some pretty hard sufferings.'

'Do you know the schoolboy's definition of the equator?'

'No, but I guess it's a good one.'

'A menagerie lion running round the world once in every twenty-four hours.   I think it's an absolutely perfect idea.'

'I guess that's good enough to stop on.'

'You off, Winchester?'

In the breaking of the group, Dr von Heber came near with his smile.   Dr Hurd was noisily stretching himself, laughing and coughing.   No one was listening.   They were quite alone among their friends, his friends, Canada.

'This has been a charming ending to a very lovely day,' he said quietly.   Miriam beamed and was silent.

'Did you see the afterglow?' she asked humbly.   His smile reappeared.   He took in what she said, but beamed because they were talking.   She tried to beat back her words, but they were on her lips and she was already moving away when she spoke.

'A fine . . . fuliginous . . . *pink*, wasn't it?'

'Where is the *harm*, child, in your sitting up at a piano, even behind a curtain; in a large room in Gower Street, I can't imagine why you say *Gower* Street; playing, with the soft pedal either down or *up*, the kind of music that you play so beautifully? Can you see her difficulty, Jan?'

'Not even with the most powerful of microscopes.'

Lolling on the windowsill of their lives to glance at a passing show. The blessed damozel looked out. Leaning, heavy on the golden balcony. *She* knew why not. Heavy blossoming weight, weighed down with her heavy hair, the sky blossoming in it, facing, just able to face without sinking, the rose-gold world, blossoming under her eyes.

Thin hard fingers of women chattering and tweaking. They go up sideways, witches on broomsticks, and chatter angrily in the distance. They cannot stop the sound of the silent crimson blossoming roses.

'I don't approve of séances.'

'Have you ever been to one?'

'No; but I know I don't. It was something about the woman when she asked me.'

'That is a personal prejudice.'

'It is not a prejudice; how can it be *pre* after I have seen her?'

'Séances are wrong; because you have taken a dislike to Madame Devine.'

'It can't be right to make half a guinea an hour so easily. And she said a guinea for occasional public performances.' That's all; they know now. I had made up my mind. I wanted them to *see* me tempted and refusing for conscience sake.'

'Good Lord; you'd be a millionaire in no time; why not take it until you are a millionaire and then if you don't like it, chuck it?'

'I should like it all right, my part.'

'Well, surely that is all that concerns you. You have nothing whatever to do with what goes on on the other side of the curtain. I think if you would like the job you are a fool to hesitate, don't you, Jan?'

'A fool there was and he made his prayer; yes, I think it is foolish to refuse such an admirable offer.'

'A rag and a bone and a hank of hair; that just describes Madame Devine.' That's not true; smooth fat thinness with dark filmy cruel clothes that last; having supper afterwards; but it would be true in a magazine; a weird medium; the grocer's wife with second sight was fat and ordinary; a simple woman. Peter, the rough fisherman.

'Now you are being unchristian.'

'I'm not. I love the rag and bone and hank of hair type. Sallow. Like Mrs Pat. . . . The *ingénue*. Sitting in a corner dressed in white, reading a book. A fat pink face. You can imagine her at forty.'

'Now you are being both morbid and improper.'

'I'm not morbid. Am I, Jan?'

'No, I do not call you morbid. I call Gracie Harter-Jones morbid.'

'Who is she?'

'We met her at Mrs Mackinley's. She says she is perfectly miserable unless she is in a morbid state. She's written a book called *The Purple Shawl of Ceremony*.'

'She must be awfully clever.'

'She's mad. She revels in being mad. Like "The Sun shivered. Earth from its darkest basements rocked and quivered."'

'Oh, go, I said, and see the swans harping upon the roof-tops in the corn. Where is the grey felt hat I saw go down, wrinkled and old, to meet the lily-leaf, where, where, my child, the little stick that crushed the wild infernal apple of the pit, where, where the pearl? Snarling he cried, I will not have you bless the tropics sitting in a sulky row, nor fling your banners o'er the stately wave; I heard shrill minstrelsies. . . . That's all awfully bad; but you can go on for ever.'

'*I* couldn't. I don't know how you do it. I think it's awfully clever. Jan and I roared over your Madeleine Francis Barry letter.'

'You can go on for days.'

'Barry-paroding.'

'You must not wait, nor think of words. If you are in the mood they come more quickly than you could speak or even think; you follow them and the whole effect entertains you. There's something in it. You never know what is coming and you swing about, as long as you keep the rhythm, all over the world. It refreshes you. Sometimes there are the most beautiful things. And you see all the things so vividly.'

'She's not morbid; she's mad.'

'I'm neither morbid nor mad. It's a splendid way of amusing yourself; better than imagining the chairs in front of you at a concert quietly collapsing.' They were scarcely listening. Both of them were depending on each other to listen and answer.

'Do you still go to Ruscino's every night, Miriam?'

'With the Spaniard? How is the Spaniard?'

'He's eaten up with dizizz.'

'With *what*?'

'That's what Miss Scott says.'

'How does she know?'

'All the doctors are prescribing for him.'

'Did they tell her?'

'I don't know. She just said it suddenly. Like she says things. The doctors are all awfully fond of him.'

'Why are they fond of him?'

'He is extraordinary. He has given up his poster work and does lightning silhouettes, outlines of heads, at five shillings each at some gardens somewhere. Sometimes he makes five pounds an evening at it.'

'So you *don't* go to Ruscino's every evening?'

'He had a few weeks of being awfully poor. One day he had only eightpence in the world. Of course he was having all his meals at Tansley Street. But that evening he found out that I had nothing at all. I had been telling him about my meal arrangements. I always pay Mrs Bailey at the time for my shilling dinners, and when I can't afford them I get a four-penny meal at a Y.W.C.A. He made me take his eightpence. The next day he *walked*, I found afterwards, all the way to South Kensington in the grilling heat to see a man about the silhouettes.'

'What a little brick.'

'He is like that to everybody.   And always so . . .'

'So what?'

'Oh, I can't express him.   But he's a Jew, you know, a Spanish Jew.   Isn't it extraordinary?'

'Well really Miriam I can't see that there is anything extraordinary about a man's being a Spanish Jew if he wants to.'

'I was most awfully surprised.   Mrs Bailey told me.   There is some Jewish girl he has been meeting in Kensington; he drew her portrait, a special one, for her father, for five guineas, and he has engaged himself to her because he thought she had money and now finds she has not, damn her, he said "damn her" to Mrs Bailey, and that he has been boring himself for nothing.   He is going into hospital for his gastric ulcer when the season is over and then going to disappear. He told me he never spoke to a woman more than twice; but that he is willing to marry any woman with enough money.'

'Wise man.'

'He has spoken more than twice to you.'

'Yes, but I know what he means.   Besides, we don't talk, in the society way.'

'How *do* you talk?'

'Oh, I don't know.   I air my theories sometimes.   He always disagrees.   Once he told me suddenly it was very bad for me to go about with him.'

'But you go.'

'Of course I do.'   The untold scenes were standing in the way.   There was no way of telling them. . . . Tansley Street life was more and more unreal to them the deeper it grew.   It was unreal to them because things were kept back.   They were still interested in stories of Wimpole Street, but even there now they only glanced in passing, their thoughts busy in the shared life they perpetually jested over.   They listened with reservations; not always believing; sitting in dressing-gowns believing or not as they chose; because one knew one had lost touch and tried to make things interesting to get back into the old glow.

'How did the dinner-party go off?'

'Beautifully.'

'Did you talk German?'

'There was no need; the man talked better English than anybody.'

'Why did it go off beautifully? Tell us about the beautiful things.'

The strange silent twilight, the reassuring shyness of all the guests; no attempt to talk about anything in particular; cool hard face and upright coldly jewelled body; the sense of success with each simple remark. The evening of music. Life-marked people; their marks showing without pain, covered, half-healed by the hours of kindness.

'It's something in the Orlys.'

'What do you think it is?'

'It's something frightfully beautiful.'

'They are very nice people.'

'That doesn't mean anything at all.'

'The secret of beauty is colour and texture. The ointment will preserve the colour and the texture of your skin—in any climate. Read her the piece about the movement of the hands over a tea-tray.' '"In pouring out tea never allow the hands to fall slack, or below the level of the tray. Keep them well in view, moving deftly among the articles on the tray; sitting well back on the seat of the chair, the body upright and a little inclined forward from the hips—see Chap. III, 'How to Sit'—so that the movements of the wrist and hands are in easy harmony with the whole body. Restrain the hands. Do not let the fingers splay out. Do not cramp them or allow any effort to appear in the movement of any part of the hand."'

'Good heavens! Can't you *see* those women? But that must be by an American.'

'Why an American?'

'Oh, I don't know. You can tell. Are you going to try all these things?'

'Rather. We're going in heavily for beauty culture.'

'We are going to skip, and have Turkish baths, and steam our faces.'

'I suppose one ought.'

'I think so. I don't see why one should look old before one's time. One's life is ageing and ravaging. After a Turkish bath one feels like a new-born babe.'

'But it would take all one's time and money.'

'Even so. It restores your self-respect to feel perfectly groomed and therefore perfectly self-possessed. It makes the office respect you.'

'I know. I hate the grubbiness of snipe-life—sometimes.'

'Only sometimes?'

'Well, I forget about it. If I didn't I should go mad of grit and dust.'

'We *are* mad of grit and dust. That's why we think it's time to do something.'

'H'm.'

'You really like the Orlys, don't you?'

'You can't like everybody at once. You have to choose. That's the trouble. If you are liking one set of people very much you get out of touch with the others.'

'You have so many sets of people.'

'I haven't. I hardly know anybody.'

'You have hosts of friends.'

'I haven't. In the way you mean. I expect I give you wrong impressions.'

'Well, I think you've capacity.—Don't you think she has a capacity, von Bohlen?'

'She has some very nice friends and some extraordinary ones.'

'Like the Flat.'

'How is the Flat?'

'Is she still living on a hard-boiled egg and a bottle of stout?'

'And sending notes?'

'"Come round at once my state of mind is awful"?'

'She's moved. I forgot to tell you. She came to tell me. She stood on the landing and said she had taken up journalism. Writing articles, for *The Taper*. Isn't it wonderful?'

'Isn't *what* wonderful?'

'Suddenly being able to write articles. She's met some people called occultists and says she has never been so happy

in her life.'   Are you going to say anything?   Why do you
not think it wonderful?

Miriam flung down Tansley Street telling her news.   Her
conflict with the June dust and heat of the Euston Road had
made her forget it.   Back in her own world it leapt at her from
every sunlit paving-stone; drawing her on almost at a run.
There was enough to carry her leaping steps right down
through London, to the edge of some unfamiliar part and back
again, but her room called her; she would go in and up to it
and come out again.

Hopeless impossibility . . . good *reliable* Budge-Whitlock at
fifteen.   You won't get a Primus under twenty-five.   Those
other makes are not made to last; giving way inside somewhere
where you could not see, suddenly; in the midst of the traffic;
the man's new bicycle, coming in *two*, in Cheapside.   Mr
Leyton smiling, 'I 've got a message for you from Winthrop;
well, that 's not strictly true.   The fact is he wants to advance
the money without your knowing it; commissioned me to see
what I can do.   You needn't hesitate; he 's got plenty of spare
cash.   I 'll buy the machine and you 'll owe the price to me.'
Kind kind Winthrop, talking in the workshop.   'It 's a ph-pity
she shouldn't av a ph-ph-machine if she wants one without
waiting t-ph save up frit.' . . . 'I say, Miss Henderson, here 's
a chance for you; new machine going half-price.   No bunkum.
It 's Lady Slater's.   She 's off to India.   I 'll overhaul it for
you.   Pay as you like, through her steward.   My advice is,
you close.   You won't get a better chance' . . . reaping the
benefit of Mr Leyton's eternal talk about bicycling . . . no
trouble; overhauled and reliable; coming out of space.

Lifted off the earth, sitting at rest in the moving air, the
London air turning into fresh moving air flowing through your
head, the green squares and high houses moving, sheering
smoothly along, sailing towards you changed, upright, and
alive, moving by, speaking, telescoping away behind unfor-
gotten, still visible, staying in your forward-looking eyes, being

added to in unbroken movement, a whole, moving silently to the sound of firm white tyres circling on smooth wood, echoing through the endless future to the riding ring of the little bell, ground easily out by firm new cogs. . . . *Country* roads flowing by in sun and shadow; the ring of the bell making the hedges brilliant at empty turnings . . . all there in your mind with dew and freshness as you threaded round and round and in and out of the maze of squares in evening light; consuming the evening time by leaving you careless and strong; even with the bad loose hired machine.

She let herself in and swept into the dining-room, taking in —while she said eagerly, crossing the room, 'I 've bought a machine. A Wolverhampton Humber. With Beeston tyres. B.S.A. fittings. Ball bearings'—the doctors grouped about the mantelpiece. They gathered round her. She was going backwards; through a scene she recognized; in a dream. Dr von Heber's welcoming smile stood at the end of it. They could not be there idle at that time of day, she assured herself as she talked. She knew they were there before she came in, without even thinking of them. She sat down in their midst, confidently saying the phrases of the scenes as they came towards her, backwards unfolding. The doctors went back with her, brothers, supporting and following. Her bicycle led the way. Their bright world had made it for her.

They had seen the English country with her. It was more alive to them. They would remember. Dr von Heber was taking it in, with his best ruminating smile, as a personal possession; seeing it with English eyes. Her last year's ride through the counties was shared now. It would go to Canada.

'It 's coming all the way from *Bakewell*.'

'Where will that place be?'

'Oh, I don't know; somewhere; in the north I think. Yorkshire. No, the Peak. The Peak district. Peek, Freen. They bake splendidly. The further north you get the better they bake.' The scene was swaying forward into newness. Dr Winchester suddenly began talking about the historical interest of the neighbourhood. They had all been down to look at the

Old Curiosity Shop . . . there was something about it . . . and there was a better local story of their kind. She told Mr Leyton's story of the passage in Little Gower Place, body snatchers carrying newly buried bodies through it by night from St Pancras churchyard to the hospital.

'You don't say so! To think we 've gone along there this while and not known!'

'That shop in Lincoln's Inn isn't the shop Dickens meant. It 's been pulled down. It 's only the site. Some people think Dickens is sentimental.'

'Those who think so are hypercritical. Besides, being sentimental don't prevent him being one of your very greatest men.'

'*You* should appreciate him highly. If ever there was any man revealed abuses. . . . You ought to read our Holmes's *Elsie Venner*. We call it his medicated novel over at home,' smiled Dr von Heber. He was speaking low, making a separate conversation. The others were talking together.

'Yes,' murmured Miriam. 'I must.' They both smiled a wide agreement. 'I 've got it over at home,' murmured Dr von Heber, his smile deepening forwards. You shall read it when you come. *We 'll* read it, he sat smiling to himself. She tried to stay where he was, not to be distracted by her thoughts. It must be Holmes's worst book. A book written on purpose, to prove something.

'Didactic,' she said with helpless suddenness, 'but I like Holmes's breakfast books.'

'You 've read those?'

'Yes,' said Miriam wearily. He had caught something from her thoughts. She saw him looking smaller, confined to the passing English present, a passing moment in his determined Canadian life. His strong unconsidered opinions held him through it and would receive and engulf him for ever when he went back. Perhaps he had not noticed her thoughts.

'Well, I must bid you a welcome adoo,' she said, getting up to go.

'Now *where*,' he smiled, rising, and surrounding her with his smile, 'where did you discover Artemus *Ward*?'

CHAPTER IX

IT was Mrs Bailey coming up the top flight clearing her throat. Tapping at the door.

'Ah! I thought the young lady was in. I *thought* so.' Mrs Bailey stood approving inside the door. The sunlight streamed on to her shabby skirt. The large dusty house, the many downstair rooms, the mysterious dark-roomed vault of the basement, all upright in her upright form; hurried smeary cleansings, swift straightening of grey-sheeted beds, the strange unfailing water-system, gurgling cisterns, gushing taps and lavatory flushes, the wonder of gaslight and bedroom candles, the daily meals magically appearing and disappearing; her knowledge of the various mysteriously arriving and vanishing people, all beginning and ending in her triumphant, reassuring smile that went forward outside beyond these things, with everybody.

Now that she was there, bearing and banishing all these heavy things, the squat green teapot on the table in the blaze of window-light, the Chinese lantern hanging from the hook in the ceiling, the little Madras muslin curtains at either end of the endmost lattices, made a picture and set the room free from the challenge of the house accumulating as Miriam had come up through it and preventing the effect she had sought when she put out the green teapot on the sunlit table. She was receiving Mrs Bailey as a guest, backed up by the summery little window-room. She stood back in the gloom, dropping back into the green lamplit stillness of the farm-house garden. *The Song of Hiawatha* sounded on and on amongst the trees, the trunk of the huge sheltering oak lit brightly by the shaded lamp on the little garden table, the forms in the long chairs scarcely visible. She offered Mrs Bailey the joy of her journey down, her bicycle in the van, Miss Szigmondy's London guests, the sixteenth-century ingle, the pine-scented bedrooms with sloping floors, the sandy high-banked lanes and pine-clad hills, the strange talk with the connoisseur, the kind stupid boyish mind of the London doctor who had *seen* myopic astigmatism across the lunch table and admitted being beaten in argument without resentment; the long dewy morning ride to Guildford; the happy thorns in her hands keeping the week-end still going on at Wimpole Street; her renewed sense of the simplicity of imposing-looking people, their personal helplessness on the surface of wealthy social life; the glow of wealthy social life lighting the little wooden window-room, gleaming from the sheeny flecks of light on the well-shaped green teapot.

Mrs Bailey advanced to the middle of the floor and stood looking towards the window. 'My word, aren't we *smart*?' she breathed.

'I like the teapot and the lantern, don't you?' said Miriam.

'Very pretty, mts, very pretty, young lady.'

'It reminds me of week-ends. It *is* a week-end. That is my drawing-room.'

'That's it. It's a week-end,' beamed Mrs Bailey. But she had come for something. The effect was not spoiled by giving a wrong, *social* impression of it, because Mrs Bailey was busily thinking behind her voice. When she had gone the silent effect would be there, more strongly. Perhaps she had some new suggestion to make about Sissie.

'Well, young lady, I want to talk to you.' Mrs Bailey propped one elbow on the mantelpiece and brushed at her skirt. Miriam waited, watching her impatiently. The Tansley Street life was fading into the glow of the oncoming holiday season. Rain was cooling the July weather, skirmishy sunlit April rain and wind, drawing her forward. There was leisure in cool uncrowded streets and restaurants and in the two cool houses, no pressure of work, the gay easy August that was almost as good as a holiday, and the certainty, beyond the rain, of September brilliance.

'Well, you know I've a great regard for you, young lady.'

Miriam stared back at the long row of interviews with Mrs Bailey and sought her face for her invisible thoughts.

'Well, to come straight to the point without beating about the bush, it 's about him, that little man, you know who I mean.'

'Who?'

'Mendizzable.'

Miriam's interest awoke and flared. That past patch of happy life had been somehow or other visible to Mrs Bailey. She felt decorated and smiled into the room.

'Well; you know I don't believe in talk going about from one to another. In *my* opinion people should mind their own business and not listen to tittle-tattle, or if they do, keep it to themselves without passing it on and making mischief.'

'Has someone been trying to make mischief about poor little Mr Mendizabal?'

'Well, if it was about him I wouldn't mind so much. Little villain. That 's my name for him.'

'Fascinating little villain, if he must be called a villain.'

'Well; that 's what I 've got to ask you, my chahld; are you under a fascination about him? You 'll excuse me asking such a question.'

Solicitude! *what* for?

'Well. I *did* think him fascinating; he fascinated me, he would anybody. He would fascinate Miss *Scott* if he chose.'

''Er? 'Er be fascinated by anybody? She thinks too much of number one for that.'

. . . Miss Scott. Dressing so carefully, so full of independent talk and laughter and not able to be fascinated . . . too far-seeing to be fascinated.

'But why do you ask? I 'm not responsible for Mr Mendizabal's being a fascinating little man.'

'Fascinating little *devil*. You should have heard Dr Winchester.'

Something hidden; all the time; behind the politeness of the house.

'Dr *Win*chester?'

'Dr Winchester. Do you remember him coming out into the hall one evening when you were brushing your coat?'

'And brushing it for me. Yes.'

'He didn't know how to let you go.' There was a trembling

in Mrs Bailey's voice. 'He said,' she pursued breathlessly, 'he was in two minds to come with you himself.'

'*Where ?   Why ?*'

'Why?   He *knew* that fella was waiting for you round the corner.'

Suddenly appearing, brushing so carefully.   Why not have spoken and come?

'Well, now we're coming to it.   I can't tell you how it all happened, that's between Mr Gunner and Miss S.   They got to know you was going out with Mendizzable and where you went.   It's contemptible, I know, if you like, but there's many such people about.'

Miriam checked her astonishment, making a mental note for future contemplation of the spectacle of Mr Gunner, or Miss Scott, following her to Ruscino's.   They had told Mrs Bailey and talked to the doctors. . . . Spies talking; idle; maliciously picking over her secret life.

'Dr Winchester said he was worried half out of his senses about you.'

'Why not have said so?'

'You may be wondering,' Mrs Bailey flushed a girlish pink, 'why I come up to-day telling you all this.   That's just what *I* say.   That's just the worst of it.   He never breathed a word to me till he went.'

Dr Winchester *gone* . . . the others gone . . . of *course*. Next week would be August.   They had all vanished away; out of the house, back to Canada.   Dr von Heber gone without a word.   Perhaps *he* had been worried.   They *all* had.   That was why they had all been so nice and surrounding.   That was the explanation of everything.   They were brothers.   Jealous brothers.   The first she had had.   This was the sort of things girls had who had brothers.   Cheek.   If only she had known and shown them how silly they were.

'Lawk!   I wish to goodness he'd come straight to me at once.'

'Well!   It's awfully sweet of them from their point of view. They were such *awfully* nice little men in their way.   *Why* didn't they come to me, instead of all this talk?   They knew me well enough.   All those long talks at night.   And all the time they were seeing a foolish girl fascinated by a disreputable foreigner. How dare they?'

'That's what I say. I can't forgive him for that. They're all alike. Selfish.'

'All old men like Dr Winchester are selfish. Selfish and weak. They get to think of nothing but their comforts. And keep out of everything by talk.'

'It's not him I mean. It's the other one.'

'Which?' What was Mrs Bailey going to say? What? Miriam gazed angrily.

'That's what I must tell you. That's why I asked you if you was under a fascination.'

'Oh, well, they've gone. What does it matter?'

'I feel I ought to tell you. He, von Heber, had made up his mind to *speak*. He was one in a thousand, Winchester said. "She's lost von Heber," he said. He thought the *world* of her, 'e sez,' gasped Mrs Bailey. 'My *word*, I wish I'd known what was going on.'

Miriam flinched. Mrs Bailey must be made to go now.

'Oh, really,' she said in trembling tones. 'He was an awfully nice man.'

'My word. Isn't it a pity?' said Mrs Bailey with tears in her eyes. 'It worries me something shocking.'

'Oh, well, if he was so stupid.'

'Well, you can't blame him after what Mendizzable *said*.'

'You haven't told me.'

'He said he'd only to raise his finger. Oh, lawk! Well there you are, now you've got it all.'

Mrs Bailey *must* go. Mr Mendizabal's mind was a French novel. He's said French thoughts in English to the doctors. They had believed. Even Canadian men can have French minds.

'Yes. Well, I see it all now. Mr Mendizabal's vanity is his own affair. . . . I'm sure I hope they've all had an interesting summer. I'm awfully glad you've told me. It's most interesting.'

'Well, I felt it was my duty to come up and tell you. I felt you ought to know.'

'Yes. I'm awfully glad you've told me. It's like, er, a storm in a teacup.'

'It's not them I'm thinking of. Lot of low-minded gossips. That's my opinion. It's the harm they do I'm thinking of.'

'They can't do any harm. As for the doctors, they're quite able to take care of themselves.' Miriam moved impatiently about the room. But she could not let herself look at her thoughts with Mrs Bailey there.

'Well, young lady,' murmured Mrs Bailey dolorously at last, 'I felt I couldn't do less than come up, for my *own* satisfaction.'

She thinks I have made a scandal, without consulting her. Her mind flew, flaming, over the gossiping household, over Mrs Bailey's thoughts as she pondered the evidence. Wrenching away from the spectacle, she entrenched herself far off; clutching out towards the oblivion of the coming holidays; a clamour came up from the street, the swaying tumult of a fire-engine, the thunder of galloping horses, the hoarse shouts of the firemen; the outside life to which she went indifferent to any grouped faces either of approval or of condemnation.

'I'm awfully sorry you've had all this, Mrs Bailey.'

'Oh, that's nothing. It's not that I think of.'

'Don't think about anything. It doesn't matter.'

'Well, I've got it off my mind now I've spoken.'

'It *is* abominable, isn't it? Never mind. I don't care. People are perfectly welcome to talk about me, if it gives them any satisfaction.'

'That is so. It's von Heber I'm so mad about.'

'They're all alike as you say.'

'He might have given you a chance.'

Dr von *Heber*; suddenly nearer than any one. Her own man. By his own conviction. Found away here, at Mrs Bailey's; Mrs Bailey's regret measuring his absolute genuineness. Gone away.

She steadied herself to say, 'Oh, if he's selfish.'

'They're all that, every one of them. But we've all got to settle in life, sooner or later.'

That was all, for Mrs Bailey. She rallied woefully in the

thought that Mrs Bailey knew she could have settled in life if she had chosen.

Flickering faintly far away was something to be found behind all this, some silent thing she would find by herself if only Mrs Bailey would go.

Fascinated. How did they find the word? It was true; and false. This was the way people talked. These were the true-false phrases used to sum up things for which there were no words.

They had no time. They were too busy. That was in the scheme. They were somehow prevented from doing anything. Dr von Heber had been saved. The fascinating eyes and snorting smile had saved him; coming out of space to tell him she was a flirt. He had boasted. 'She adore me; hah! I tell you she adore me,' he would say. It was history repeating itself. Max and Ted. Again after all these years. A *Jew*.

The unconscious, inexorable ship . . . gliding across the Atlantic. They would take up their bright Canadian life again. England, a silent picture, fading. Dear Dr von Heber, I owe it to myself just to inform you that the legend you heard about me was untrue. Wishing you a happy and prosperous career, yours truly. That would be saying I, fool, have discovered too late that I was not clever enough to let you imagine that you were the only kind of man in the world. Discreet women are sly. To get on in the world it is necessary to be sly. Von Heber is sly. Careful and prudent and sly. What did genius Waynflete think? Genius understands everything. Discreet proper clever women are open books to him. He will never marry. Whimsical old failure, Winchester, disappearing into British Columbia; failure; decorated in his evening conversations by having been to England. My dear von Heber, what the devil do you mean? When will you meet me? Choose your own weapons. That would be admitting not having the right to be as free and indiscreet as one chooses. 'A woman must march with her regiment; if she is wise she does'; something like that. If a woman is *sly* she marches with her regiment. All in agreement, being sly and discreet, helping each other. What for? What was the plot for? There's a *word* . . . *coercion*, that's the word. Better any sort of free life.

If he could have *seen*. But then he would have seen those other moments too. Von Heber. Power and success. Never any moments like that. Divided life all the time *always*. So much for his profession, so much for her, outside it with the regiment of women. Proper men can't bring the wild, gleaming, channel of flowers, pulling, dragging to fling yourself headlong down it and awake, dead. Dead if you do. Dead if you don't. Now Tomlinson gave up the ghost.

'You're just in time.' They had come back? He had come back for something?

'There's a surprise waiting for you upstairs'—*What* surprise, Mrs Bailey? How can you be happy and mysterious, cajoling to rush on into nothing, sweeping on, talking?—'a friend of yorce; Dr Winchester's room; she's longing to see you.'

'Good heavens!'

Miriam fled upstairs and tapped at the door of the room below her own. A smooth fluting thoughtful voice answered tranquilly from within the spaces of the room behind the closed door. There was no one with a voice like that to speak to intimately. It was a stranger, someone she had met somewhere and given the address to; a superior worldly person serenely answering the knock of a housemaid. She went in. Tall figure, tall skirt and blouse standing at the dressing-table. The grime-screened saffron light fell on white hands pinning a skein of bright gold hair round the back of a small head.

'How do you do?' Miriam announced, coming forward with obedient reluctance. The figure turned; a bent flushed face laughed from tumbled hair.

''Ere I am, dear; turned up like a bad penny. I 'll shake
'ands in a minute.' With compressed lips and bent frowning
brow Miss Dear went on busily pinning. 'Bother my silly
hair,' she went on with deepening flush, 'I shall be able to talk
to you in a minute.'

Miriam clutched at the amazed resentment that flamed from
her up and down the sudden calm unconscious façade reared
between her and the demolished house, spread across the very
room that had held the key to its destruction. She fought
for annihilating words, but her voice had spoken ahead of
her.

'*El*eanor!'

With the word a soft beauty ran flickering, an edge of light
about the form searched by her gazing eyes. Their shared
past flowed in the room. The skirt was a shabby thin blue
serge, rubbed shiny, the skimpy cotton blouse had an ugly
greyish stripe and badly cut shoulders, one and eleven at an
awful shop, but she was just going to speak.

'There, that 's better,' she said lowering her hands to tweak
at the blouse, her blue eyes set judiciously on the face of the
important duchesse mirror, her passing servant. ''Ow *are*
you, dear?'

'*I* 'm all right,' thrilled Miriam, 'you 're just in time for
dinner.'

'I am 'fraid I don't look very *din*nery,' frowned Miss Dear,
fingering the loose unshapely collar of her blouse. 'I wonder
if you could let me have a tie, just for to-day, dear.'

'I 've got a lace one, but it 's crumply,' hazarded Miriam.

'I can manage it, I dare say, if you 'd let me avit.'

The gong sounded. 'I shan't be a second,' Miriam promised
and fled. The little stair-flight and her landing, the sunset
gilded spaces of her room flung her song out into the world.
The tie was worse than she had thought, its middle length
crushed and grubby. She hesitated over a card of small
pearl-headed lace pins, newly bought and forgotten. For
fourpence three-farthings the twelve smooth filmy pearl heads,
their bright sharp-pointed gilt shanks pinned in a perfect even
row through the neat oblong of the sheeny glazed card, lit up

her drawer, bringing back the lace-hung aisles of the West End shop, its counters spread with the fascinating details of the worldly life. The pins were the forefront of her armoury, still too blissfully new to be used. However Eleanor arranged the tie she could not use more than three.

'Thank you, dear,' she said indifferently, as if they were her own things obligingly brought in, and swiftly pinned one end of the unexamined tie to her blouse collar. With lifted chin she deftly bound the lace round and round close to her neck, each swathe firmly pinned, making a column wider than the width of the lace. Above her blouse, transformed by the disappearance of its ugly collar, her graceful neck went up, a column of filmy lace. Miriam watched, learning and amazed.

'That's better than nothing anyhow,' said Miss Dear from her sideways movements of contemplation. Three or four small pearly heads gleamed mistily from the shapely column of lace. The glazed card lay on the dressing-table crumpled and rent and empty of all its pins.

The dining-room was a buzz of conversation. The table was packed save for two chairs on Mrs Bailey's right hand. *Mrs Bailey* was wearing a *black satin blouse* cut in a V and a piece of black ribbon-velvet tied round her neck! She was in conversation, preening and arching as she ladled out the soup, with a little *lady* and a big old *gentleman* with a patriarch beard sitting on her right bowing and smiling, personally, towards Miriam and Miss Dear as they took their seats. Miriam bowed and gazed as they went on talking. The old gentleman had a large oblong head above a large expensive spread of smooth well-cut black coat; a huge figure, sitting tall, with easily moving head reared high, massy grey hair; unspectacled smiling glistening eyes and oblong fresh-cheeked face wreathed in smiles revealing gleaming squares of gold stopping in his front teeth. His voice was vast and silky, like the beard that moved as he spoke, shifting about on the serviette tucked by one corner into his neck. His little wife was like a kind bird,

soft curtains of greying black hair crimping down from a beautifully twisted topknot on either side of a clear gentle forehead.
Softly gleaming eyes shone through rimless pince-nez perched
delicately on her delicate nose, no ugly straight bar, a little
half-hoop to join them together and at the side a delicate gold
chain tucked over one ear.   She was about as old as mother
had been.   She was exactly like her, girlishly young, but
untroubled; the little white ringed left hand with strange un-
familiarly expressive finger-tips and curiously mobile turned-
back thumb-tip was herself in miniature.   It held a little piece
of bread, peaked, expressively, as she ate her soup.   She was
utterly familiar, no stranger; always known.   Miriam adored,
seeking her eyes till she looked, and meeting a gentle enveloping
welcome, making no break in her continuous soft animation.
The only strange thing was a curious *circular* sweep of her
delicate jaw as she spoke; a sort of wide mouthing on some of
her many quiet words, thrown in through and between and
together with the louder, easily audible, silky tones of her
husband.

Mrs Bailey sat unafraid, expanding in happiness.

'You *will* have a number of things to see,' she was saying.

'We are counting on this laddie to be our guide,' said the old
gentleman, turning hugely to his further neighbour.   Miriam's
eyes followed and met the face of Dr *Hurd* . . . *grinning*; his
intensest brick-red grin.   He had not gone!   These were
his *parents*.

'*He* needs a holiday too, the dear lad,' said the old gentleman
laying a hand on his shoulder.

Dr Hurd grinned a rueful disclaimer with his eyes still on
Miriam's and said, 'I shan't be sorry,' his face crinkling with
his unexploded hysterically leaping laugh.

Mrs Hurd's smiling little face flickered with quickly
smothered sadness.   They had come all the way from Canada
to share his triumph and were here smoothing his defeat . . .
Canadian old people.   A *Canadian* woman . . . that circular
jaw movement was made by the Canadian vowels.   They
disturbed a woman's small mouth more than a man's.   It
must affect her thoughts, the held-open mouth; *airing* them;

making them *circular*, sympathetically balanced, easier to go no
from than the more narrowly mouthed English speech. . . .

'Mr Gunner, sitting beside your son, is a violinist.'

'Ah! We shall hope to hear him.'

Mr Gunner, small and shyly smiling, next to him an *enormous*
woman with a large school-girl face, fair straight and school-
girl hair lifted in a flat wave from her broad forehead into an
angry peak, angrily eating with quickly moving brawny arms
coming out of elbow sleeves with cheap cream lace frilling,
reluctantly forced to flop against the brawny arms. Sallow
good-looking husband, olive, furious, cocksure, bilious type,
clubby and knowing, flat ignorance on the top of his unconscious shiny round black skull, both snatching at scraps of
Scott and Sissie and Gunner chaff, trying to smile their way
in, to hide their fury with each other. Too poor to get further
away from each other, accustomed to boarding-house life, eating
rapidly and looking for more. She had several brothers; a
short aristocratic upper lip and shapely scornful nostrils,
brothers in the diplomatic service or the army. There was
someone this side of the table they recognized as different, and
were watching; a tall man beyond Mrs Barrow, a strange *fine*
voice with wandering protesting inflections; speaking out into
the world, with practised polished wandering inflections, like
a tired pebble worn by the sea, going on and on, presenting
the same worn wandering curves wherever it was, always a
stranger everywhere, always anew presenting the strange wandering inflections; indiscriminately. That end of the table
was not aware of the Hurds. Its group was wandering outside
the warm glow of Canadian society. Eleanor Dear was feeling
at its doors, pathetic-looking with delicate appealing head and
thoughtful baby brow downcast. 'Us'll wander out this
evening, shall us?' murmured Miriam in a lover-like undertone. It was a grimace at the wide-open door of Canadian
life; an ironic kick *à la* Harriett. Her heart beat recklessly
round the certainty of writing and posting her letter. If he
cared he would understand. Mrs Hurd had come to show her
Canadian society, brushing away the tangles and stains of
accidental contacts; putting everything right. 'Of course we

will,' bridled Miss Dear, rebuking her vulgarity. Nothing mattered now but filling up the time.

The table was breaking up; the Hurds retiring in a backward-turning group talking to Mrs Bailey, towards the door. The others were standing about the room. The Hurds had gone. '*Oh*-no, *that*'s all right, Mrs Bailey; *I*'ll be all right.' It was the wandering voice. . . . It went on, up and down, the most curious different singing tones, the sentences beginning high and dropping low and ending on an even middle tone that sounded as if it were going on. It had a meaning without the meaning of the words. Mrs Bailey went on with some explanation and again the voice sent out its singing shape; up and down and ending on a waiting tone. Miriam looked at the speaker; a tall grey-clad man, a thin pale absent-minded face, standing towards Mrs Bailey, in a drooping lounge, giving her all his attention—several people were drifting out of the room—down-bent towards her small form; Eleanor Dear was waiting, sitting docile, making no suggestion, just right, like a sister; but his eyes never met Mrs Bailey's; they were fixed, burning, on something far away; his thoughts were far away, on something that never moved.

There was a loud rat-tat on the front door, more than a telegram and less than a caller; a claim, familiar and peremptory. Mrs Bailey looked sharply up. Sissie was ambling hurriedly out of the room.

'Oh, *dear*,' chirruped Eleanor softly, '*some*one wants to come in.'

'Well; I'll say good night,' said the grey figure and turned easily with a curious waiting halting lounge, exactly like the voice, towards the door. It could stop easily, if any one were coming in, and wander on again in an unbroken movement. The grey shoulders passing out through the door with the gaslight on them had no look of going out of the room, desolate, they looked *desolate*.

The room was almost empty. Mrs Bailey was listening undisguisedly towards the hall. Sissie came in looking watchfully about.

'It's Mr Rodkin, mother dear,' she said sullenly.

'*Rod*kin? '*Im*?' gasped Mrs Bailey, transfigured.

'Can I come in?' asked a deep hollow insinuating voice at the door. 'How do you do, Mrs Bailey?'

Mrs Bailey had flung the door wide and was laughing and shaking hands heartily up and down with a small swarthy black-moustached little man with an armful of newspapers and a top hat pushed back on his head.

'*Well*,' he said, uncovering a small bony sleek black head and sliding into a chair, his hat sticking out from the hand of the arm clasping the great bundle of newspapers. 'How *grand* you are. Moy wort. What's the meaning of it?' His teeth gleamed brilliantly. He had small high prominent cheek-bones, yellow beaten-in temples and a yellow hollow face; yet something almost dimpling about his smile.

'Aren't we?' chuckled Mrs Bailey taking his hat.

Mr Rodkin drew his hand over his face, yawning. 'Well, I've been *every*where since I left; *Mos*cow, *Pe*tersburg, Ba*toom*, Harr-*bin*, *every*where. Moy *wort*. Miss Sissie, you are a grown-up grand foine young lady. What is it all about? No joke; *tell* me, I say.'

Mrs Bailey sat at ease smiling triumphantly. 'A grand foine dinner. . . . Well, you wouldn't have me *starve* my boarduz.'

'*Boarders*,' murmured Mr Rodkin, '*My* God!' He jerked his head back with a laugh and jerked it down again. 'Well, it's good business anyhow. *Bless* my heart!'

They talked familiarly on, two tired worn people in a little blaze of mutual congratulation. Mr Rodkin had come to stay, at once, without going away. He noticed no one but the Baileys and questioned on and on, yawning and laughing with sudden jerks of his head.

Coming back from sitting flirting with Eleanor at Donizetti's, Miriam wandered impatiently into the dark dining-room. Eleanor was not her guest. Why didn't she go up to her room and leave her to the dim street-lit dining-room and the nightly journey up through the darkness to her garret, in freedom?

'Bed-time,' she hinted irritably, tugging at the tether.

'Bed-time,' echoed Eleanor, her smooth humouring nurse's

voice bringing in her world of watchful diplomatic manœuvring, scattering the waiting population of the familiar dim room.

'I'm going to bed,' stated Miriam, advancing towards the windows.

On the table under the window that was the most brightly lit by the street-lamps was a paper, a pamphlet, coloured; blue. She took it up. It hung limply in her hand, the paper felt pitted and poor, like very thin blotting paper. *Young Ireland* she read printed in thick heavy black lettering across the top of the page. The words stirred her profoundly, calling to something far away within her, long ago. Underneath the thick words, two short columns side by side began immediately. They went on for several pages and were followed by short paragraphs with headings; she pressed close to the lit window, peering; there were blotchy, badly printed asterisks between small groups of lines. Heavy black headings further on, like the title, but smaller, and followed by thick exclamation signs. It was a sort of little newspaper, the angry print too heavy for the thin paper. Green. It was green all through. *Ireland;* Home Rule.

'I *say*,' she exclaimed eagerly. 'That was the grey man. *Irish*. That's all going on still,' she said solicitously to a large audience.

'*What*, dear?' asked Eleanor's figure close to her side.

'Ireland,' breathed Miriam. 'We've got a Home Ruler in the house. Look at this; green all through. It.'s some propaganda, in London, very angry.'

'I 'ope the Home Ruler isn't green all through,' chuckled Eleanor smoothly.

'It's the wearin' o' the green,' scolded Miriam. 'The Emerald Isle. We're so stupid. An Irish girl I knew told me she "just couldn't bear to face thinking" of the way we treat our children.'

Leaving Eleanor abruptly in darkness in her bedroom, she shut the door and stepped into freedom. The cistern gurgled from the upper dark freshness. Her world was uninvaded. Klah-rah *Buck*, in reverent unctuousness, waiting for responsive awe from those sitting round. He meant Clara Butt. Then she had been to Canada. Little Mrs Hurd had sat birdlike

at a Morning Musical hearing the sweep of the tremendous
voice. I have never heard it, but I know how it rolls tremendously out and sweeps. I can hear it by its effect on them.
They would not believe that. Rounding the bend of the little
staircase, she was surprised by a light under the box-room door.
Mrs Bailey, at midnight, busy in the little box-room? How
could she find room to have the door shut? Her garret felt
fresh and free. Summer rain pattering on the roof in the darkness. *The Colonization of Ulster.* Her mind turned the pages
of a school essay, page after page, no red-ink corrections, the
last page galloping along one long sentence; 'until England
shall have recognized her cruel folly.' '10; *excellent*, E.B.R.'
A fraud and yet not a fraud. Never having thought of Ireland
before reading it up in Green, and then some strange indignation and certainty, coming suddenly while writing; there for
always. I had forgotten about it. A man's throat was cleared
in the box-room. The tone of the wandering voice. Mrs
Bailey had screwed him into that tiny hole. '*I* 'll be all *right.*'
What a shame. He must not know any one knew he was there.
He did not know he was the first to disturb the top landing.
He did not disturb it. There were no English thoughts in
there, nothing of the downstairs house. Julia Doyle, Dublin
Bay, *Clontarf*; fury underneath, despairing of understanding,
showing how the English understood nothing, themselves nor
any one else. But the Irish did not care for *anything*. Mere-
dith was partly Celtic. *That* was why his writing always felt
to be pointing in some invisible direction. He wrote so much
because he did not care about anything. Novelists were angry
men lost in a fog. But how did they find out how to do it?
Brain. Frontal development. But it was not certain that
that was not just the extra piece wanted to control the bigger
muscular system. Sacrificed to muscle. Going about with
more muscles and a bit more brain, if *size* means *more*, doing
all kinds of different *set* pieces of work in the world, each in a
space full of problems none of them could agree about.

'*Gracious!* You 'll 'ave to be up early in the morning to say
all those names, de-er.'

CHAPTER X

ELEANOR'S cab rumbled away round the corner. Mrs Bailey
was still standing at the top of the steps. Miriam ran up the
steps looking busily ahead. 'It 's going to be a lovely evening,'
she said as she passed Mrs Bailey. She was safely in the hall.
But the front door was closed and Mrs Bailey was in the hall
just behind her. She turned abruptly, almost colliding with
her, into the dining-room. Mrs Bailey's presence was there,
waiting for her in the empty room. Behind her just inside the
door was Mrs Bailey, blocking the way to the untrammelled
house. 'There 's quite a lot of August left,' she quoted from
the thoughts that had poured down to meet her as she stood
facing the stairs. The clock on the mantelpiece was telling
the time of Mrs Bailey's day. The empty room was waiting
for the next event, a spread meal, voices sounding towards
a centre, distracting attention from its increasing shabbiness.
There was never *long* for it to remain sounding its shabbiness,
the sound of dust, into the empty space. Events going on and
on, giving no time to get in, behind the dusty shabbiness, to
the sweet dreams and health and quiet breathing.

'What a jolly big room this *is*, isn't it?' she demanded,
turning towards Mrs Bailey's shapely skimpy form. Mrs
Bailey knew she was chafing in the airless shabby room. The
windows closed to keep the dust *out* made the dust *smell*.

'Isn't it?' agreed Mrs Bailey cordially.

'You *must* have been glad to get rid of the lodgers and have
possession of the whole house.'

'Yes,' said Mrs Bailey straightening the sideboard cloth.

Hearty agreement about the advantages and disadvantages
of boarders and then, I think it 's very *plucky* of you, and away
upstairs. A few words about the interest of having boarders
to begin getting to the door with.

'The Irishman's an interesting specimen of humanity.'

'Isn't he interesting?' laughed Mrs Bailey, moving further
into the room.

'It's much more interesting to have boarders than lodgers,'
said Miriam, moving along the pathway of freedom towards
the open door. Mrs Bailey stood silent, watching politely.
There was no way out. Mrs Bailey's presence would be waiting
in the hall, and upstairs, unappeased. Miriam glanced towards her without meeting her eyes and sat limply down on
the nearest chair.

'Phoo—it's rather a relief,' she murmured.

Mrs Bailey went briskly to the door and closed it and came
freely back into the room, a little exacting figure who had seen
all her selfish rejoicing. She would get up now and walk about
the room, talking easily and eloquently about Eleanor's charm
and go away leaving Mrs Bailey mystified and disposed of.

'My *word*,' declared Mrs Bailey, tweaking the window curtains. Then Mrs Bailey *was* ready and anxious to talk her over
and impart her opinion. After seeming to like her so much
and being so attentive and sending her off so gaily and kindly,
she had some grievance. It was not the bill. It was a matter
of opinion. Mrs Bailey had been charmed and had yet seen
through her. Seen what? What was the everlasting secret
of Eleanor? She imagined them standing talking together,
politely, and joking and laughing. Mrs Bailey would like
Eleanor's jokes; they would be in agreement with her own
opinions about things. But she had formed some idea of her
and was ready to express it. If it explained anything one would
have to accept it, from Mrs Bailey. To make nice general
remarks about her and inquire insincerely about the bill, would
be never to get Mrs Bailey's uninfluenced opinion. She would
not give it unless she were asked.

'I'm awfully sorry for her,' she said in Eve's voice. That
would mean just her poverty and her few clothes and delicate
health. There could be an insincere discussion. It might
end in nothing and the mean selfish joy would still be waiting
upstairs as soon as one had forgotten that it was mean and
selfish.

'So am *I*,' said Mrs Bailey heartily. There was anger in her face. There really *was* something, some really bad opinion about Eleanor. Mrs Bailey thought these things more important than joyful freedom. She was one of those people who would do things; then there were other people too; then one need not trouble about what it was, or warn people against Eleanor. The world would find out and protect itself, passing her on. If Mrs Bailey felt there was something wrong, no one need feel blamed for thinking so. There was. *What* was it?

'I'm the last to be down on any one in difficulties,' said Mrs Bailey.

'Oh, yes.' It was coming.

'It's the *way* of people *I* look to.' She stopped. If she were not pressed she would say no more.

'Oh, by the way, Mrs Bailey, has her bill been settled?' The voice of Mrs Lionel. . . . 'She's unsquashable, my dear, absolutely unsquashable. You never saw *anything* like it in your *life*. But she's done frrerself in Weston.' It might finish the talk.

'That's all in order, young lady. It's not that at all.'

'Oh, I know. I'm glad though.'

'I had my own suspicions before you told me you'd be responsible. I never thought about that.'

'No, I see.'

'It's the *way* of people.'

'Well, you know I told you at once that you must have her here at your own risk after the first week, and that I hardly knew anything about her.' If she had paid the two weeks so easily, perhaps Mr Taunton was still looking after her needs. No. She would have mentioned him. He had dropped her entirely; after all he had said.

'I'm not blaming you, young lady.' Perhaps Mrs Bailey had offered advice and been rebuffed in some way. There would be some mysterious description of character; like the Norwegian. . . . 'Selfish in a way I couldn't describe to you.' . . .

'If I'd known what it was going to be, I'd not have had her in the house two days.'

. . . some man . . . who? . . . but they were out all day

and Eleanor had been with her every evening. Besides, Mrs Bailey would sympathize with that. . . . She was furiously angry; 'not two days.' But she *had* been charmed. Charmed and admiring.

'Did she flirt with someone?'

'That,' said Mrs Bailey gravely, 'I can't tell you. She may have; that's her own affair. I wouldn't necessary blame her. Every one's free to do as they like provided they behave theirselves.' Mrs Bailey was brushing at her skirt with downcast eyes.

This woman had opened Dr von Heber's letter; knew he was coming next year; knew that he 'would not have permitted' any talk at all, and that all her interference was meaningless. *He* was coming, carrying his suitcase out of the hospital, no need for the smart educated Canadian nurses to think about him. Taking ship. . . . Coming back. Perhaps she resented having been in the wrong.

'It was funny how she found a case so suddenly,' said Miriam drawing herself upright, careless, like a tree in the wind. She had already forgotten she would always feel like that, her bearing altered for ever, held up by him, like a tree in the wind, every one powerless to embarrass her. Poor Mrs Bailey.

'You see I feel I drove her to it, in a way.'

Mrs Bailey listened smiling keenly.

'Yes, you *see*,' pursued Miriam cheerfully, 'I told her she would be all right for a week. I blamed *you* for that, said you were flourishing and she could pay when her ship came home.'

'That's what you told her, eh?'

'Well and then when she admitted she had no money and I knew I couldn't manage more than a week, I advised her to apply to the C.O.S. She said she would and seemed delighted, and when I asked her about it later she cried and said she hadn't been. I said she must do *something* and then suddenly this case appeared. *Where* I don't know.'

'I don't blame her for not wanting to go *there*.'

'Why?'

'My word. I'd as soon go straight to the parish.'

'Wilberforce believes in them. He says if you really want to help the helpless you will not flaunt your name in subscription lists but hand your money over to the C.O.S. They are the only charitable organization that does not pauperize.'

'Him? Wilberforce? He has a right to his own opinions, I don't deny. But if he'd ever been in difficulties he might change them. *Insulting*, that's my opinion. My word, the *questions* they ask. You can't call your soul your own.'

'I didn't know that. That friend my sister brought here was being helped by them.'

'How is Miss Henderson?'

'Perfectly happy. Being with the Greens again seems *paradise*, she says, after London. She's satisfied now.'

'Mts. She's a sweet young lady; them's fortunate as have her.'

'Well, now she's tried something else, she appreciates the beautiful home. I don't think she wants to be free.'

'Quite so. Persons differ. But she's her own mistress; free to leave.'

'Of course it's nicer now. The children are at school. She's confidential companion. They all like her so much. They invented it for her.'

'Quite right. That's as it should be.'

'And she is absolutely in Mrs Green's confidence now. I don't know what poor Mrs Green would do without her. She went back just in time for a most *fearful* tragedy.'

'Tss; dear—*dear*,' murmured Mrs Bailey waiting with frowning, calm eagerness. Miriam hesitated. It would be a long, difficult story to make Mrs Bailey see stupid commercial wealth. She would see wealthy 'people,' a 'gentleman' living in a large country house, and not understand Mr Green at all; but *Eve*, getting the bunch of keys from the ironmonger's and writing to Bennett to find out about Rupert Street . . . and the *detective*. She would have it in her mind like a novel and never let it go. It would be a breach of confidence. . . . She paused, not knowing what to do with her sudden animation. It was too late to get back into being an impartial listener, on the verge of going away. She had told everything, without the interesting details. Mrs Bailey was waiting for them. They were still safe. She might think it was an illness or something about a relative. The only thing to do now was to stay and work off the unexplained animation on anything Mrs Bailey might choose to say.

'Well,' said Mrs Bailey presently, 'to return to our friend. What I say is, why doesn't she go to the clergy, in her own parish?'

'Go on the parish, m'm.'

'Not necessarily on the parish. The clergy's most helpful and sympathetic. They might tell her of those who would help her.'

'They might. But it's most awfully difficult. *Nobody* knows what ought to be done about these things.'

'That is so. But there's a right and a wrong in everything. There's plenty of people willing to help those that will help theirselves. But that's very different to coming into a person's house to try and get money out of strangers.'

'I *say*!'

'It is I *say*. I never felt so ashamed in my life.'

'I *say*! . . . Did they tell you?'

'Mrs Hurd came to me herself.'

'Mrs Hurd. Of course, it would be.'

'My word! I *was* wild. And them only just come into my house.'

'Yes, of course; I *say*!'

'Tellin' them she was *ill*.'

'She is ill, you know.'

'There's some imagines theirselves ill. If she was anything like as ill as I am, she might have something to complain about.'

'I think she's rather plucky. She doesn't want to give in. It's a kind of illness that doesn't show much. I know her doctor. He's a Harley Street man. *He* says that her kind of disorder makes it absolutely impossible for the patient to tell the truth. I don't believe that. It's just one of those doctory things they all repeat.' . . . What is truth? said jesting Pilate and did not wait for an answer. *Their* idea of truth——

'Well, if she is ill why doesn't she act according?'

'Look *after* herself a bit. Yes. That's what she wants to do. But not give in.'

'Quite so. That's a thing a person can understand. But that doesn't make it right to come to private people and behave in the way she has done. Strangers. I never met such conduct, nor heard of it.'

'No.'

'She's got relatives, I suppose; or friends.'

'Well, that's just it. I don't think she has. I suppose the truth is all her friends are tired of helping her.'

'Well, I'm not judging her there. There's none can be so cruel as relatives, as *I* know, my word.'

'Yes.'

'They'll turn from you when you're struggling to the utmost to help yourself, going on ill, left with four young children, your husband cut off and not a *penny*.'

'Yes.'

'I agree with her there. I owe all I have, under Providence, to my own hands and the help coming from strangers I had no claim on. But why doesn't she act open? That's what *I* say and I know it. There's always those ready to help you if you'll do your part. It's all take and no give with some.'

'Vampires. People *are* extraordinary.'

'You'd say so if you had this house to manage.'

'I suppose so.'

'You get your eyes open. With one and another.'

'I'd no idea she'd even been talking to the Hurds.'

'Talk? Well I don't mind telling you now she's gone.'

'Well, she won't come back again. If she ever does, Mrs Bailey, I hereby refuse all responsibility. On your head be it if you take her in. *I* can't keep her.'

'Well, as I say, I'm free to tell you. They used to go upstairs into the drawn-room, mornings, after breakfast. I could hear that woman's voice going on and on. I was up and down the stairs. What's more, she used to stop dead the minute I came in.'

'Well, I am sorry you've had all this.'

'I 'm not blaming you, young lady.'

'What about all the others?'

'Rodkin and Helsing and Gunner 's out all day.'

'Yes, but the others? The Manns and the Irish journalist.'

'She 'd be clever to get anything out of any of *them*.'

'I wonder she didn't try Mrs Barrow. She 's kind, I 'm sure, and gullible.'

'She 's very kind, no doubt, in her way. Anyway she 's not one of those who live on a widow woman and pay nothing.'

The old sense of the house was crumbling. To Mrs Bailey it was *worry* and things she could not talk about to any one, and a few nice people here and there. And all the time she was *polite*; as if she liked them all, equally. And they were polite. Every one was polite. And behind it was all this. Shifts and secrets and strange characters. When they were all together at Mrs Bailey's dinner, they were all carrying things off, politely. Perhaps already she regretted having sent away the lodgers.

'The doctors were nice people to have in the house.'

'Wasn't they dear boys? *Very* nice gentlemen. Canadians are the ones to my mind, though I believe as much as any in standing by your own. But you 've got to consider your interests.'

'Of course.'

'That 's why I mean to ad*vert*iss. My word, those Hurds are good friends if you like. I couldn't tell you. The old man 's put an advert for me in the Canadian place in the city.'

'Then you 'll have a houseful of Canadians.'

'That 's what I *hope*. The more the better of their kind.'

'We shall all be speaking Canadian.'

'Well, since we 're on the subject, Mrs Hurd advises me to *go* to Canada. Says it 's all work and no pay over here. Everybody expects too much for too little.'

How *could* she rejoice in the idea of a house full of Canadians? All the same. Canadian. It would change the house more and more. Mrs Bailey would not mind that. The house meant nothing to her just as it was, with its effect. She had to make it pay. If another house would pay better she would just as soon have another house. 'You wouldn't like to leave London; there's no place like London.' The Hurds thought every one in the house *selfish*, living on Mrs Bailey's work, enjoying the house for nothing, forgetting her. It was true. They were all uneasy in her presence. . . .

CHAPTER XI

MIRIAM got up early the next morning and went to her window in her nightgown. There was a thick August haze in the square. The air smelt moist. She leaned out into the chill of it. Her body was full of sleep and strength; all one strength from head to feet. She heard life in the silence, and went through her getting up as quickly as possible, listening all the time to the fresh silence.

She went downstairs feeling like a balloon on a string; her feet touching the stairs lightly as if there were no weight in her body. At the end of the long journey, came the smiling familiar surprise of the hall. The hall-table was clear, a stretch of grey marble in the morning light. The letters had been taken into the dining-room. There was something, a package, on the far corner, a book package, with a note, Silurian blue, *Eleanor*. Small straggly round handwriting, yes, Eleanor's, *R. Rodkin, Esq. Ah!* Mr *Rodkin.* How had she done it? When? Carrying off a book. Pretending she had forgotten, and writing. Sly cleverness. What a blessing she had gone. Booming through her uneasiness came a great voice from the dining-room. 'Through the misty corridors of the *Dawn*' it bellowed. She went gladly in towards poetry. Mrs Bailey was presiding over an early breakfast. The Irishman, sitting back mirthfully in his chair on the far side of the table and, at his side, a big stout man with a bushy black beard, brilliant laughing eyes staring at nothing from a flushed face. Mrs Bailey was watching him with a polite smile; he looked as though he were at supper; making the room seem hot, obliterating the time of day.

'I expect you had a rough crossing,' she said politely.

'I *saw* her,' he bellowed, flinging back his head and roaring out words and laughter together. 'She walks in *Beauty*. I saw her sandalled feet; upon the *Hills*.'